# NEVER ASK
# THE DEAD

*By Gary Donnelly*

a&b

# NEVER ASK
# THE DEAD

## GARY DONNELLY

Allison & Busby Limited
11 Wardour Mews
London W1F 8AN
*allisonandbusby.com*

First published in Great Britain by Allison & Busby in 2021.

A CIP catalogue record for this book is available from
the British Library.

First Edition

ISBN 978-0-7490-2547-2

Typeset in 11/16 pt Sabon LT Pro by
Allison & Busby Ltd.

The paper used for this Allison & Busby publication
has been produced from trees that have been legally sourced
from well-managed and credibly certified forests.

Printed and bound by
CPI Group (UK) Ltd, Croydon, CR0 4YY

*For my parents*
*Christine and Paddy Donnelly*
*All you had you gave us*

'. . . be a great feigner and dissembler . . . a skilful deceiver always finds plenty of people who will let themselves be deceived.'

Machiavelli, *The Prince*

Why is it we never ask the dead,
Who form a scabbard for a blade,
Their flesh a bullet's bed?
'Why you were lost
From breath and put to clay?
Why were you taken and not saved?'
Go on, and dig in the cold ground
Linger not on orders obeyed
Or fates misaligned.

Speak the name that's chiselled
On the wind-weathered marker.
Ask the price of their blood,
Weigh their hearts on Anubis' scale,
Know why them and not you, or I.
We never ask the dead, we fear
Not their silence, but their reply.

They say: 'My name mattered only
Because it mattered less.
You were late, but I was on time.
Ready in the wrong place, lesser than,
And the next in line.'

Fragment of a poem by Roddy Grant, originally part of
his scrapbook, TOPBRASS: A SECRET HISTORY

# PROLOGUE

Strabane, a border town. County Tyrone,
North-west Northern Ireland. Late December 1979

The rusty glow of a street lamp rippled in puddles outside
the fortified police station, and the cold and unforgiving
rain fell. He splashed straight through them, his feet
already soaked, and approached the armoured hatch where
he would be seen and there waited. He didn't need to rap
or call for attention. They had already spotted him and
would be watching him right now, assessing the solitary,
dark figure who stood, soaked to the skin, as 1979 ticked
slowly down to detonate a new decade. The Christmas
cessation of violence observed by the IRA – annual alms
to overworked volunteers, their assorted enemies and the
long-suffering people who lived day and night under the
cloud of the Long War – still held, but only just. They'd
promised two days of peace, and the clock was ticking.
At midnight, the war was back on, and the witching hour
approached. The peelers and Brits who eyed him through
peepholes and on the green, fuzzy output of a concealed

camera probably did so with both trepidation of what he might be, and annoyance that he was bringing them any kind of work at all during this lull. After a time, he heard the unbolting of the hatch and it opened, wide enough to show a pair of eyes and the muzzle of a gun.

'Yeah?'

'I need to speak to the Branch,' he said. Special Branch. The secretive army within the Royal Ulster Constabulary, RUC. The Branch had its origins in the Metropolitan Police's Special Irish Branch, to give it its original and correct title. They had been tasked to deal with the Fenian dynamite campaign against English targets in the 1880s that was organised by Jeremiah O'Donovan Rossa. Almost a hundred years later and another war was on, and there were more bombs exploding than Rossa would have ever dared hope. A pause from the cop who appraised him from behind the hatch. His eyes narrowed.

'Who are you?'

He glanced away, not wanting his face to be seen. 'A friend,' he said.

Which could mean many things. The peeler kept the gun pointed on him, waited for more but got only the hiss of the unrelenting rain. The cop told him to hold on and quickly snapped the armoured hatch shut. As expected, he wanted to call it in. The man who stood in the rain could be anyone. A plain-clothed soldier, coming in from the cold, his cover compromised; a Branch man who needed help and would trust only one of his own in the secret police; or a mad dog Provo that had a gun in his waistband and wanted them to open the gates before he started shooting, happy to go down fighting so long as he took more of the enemy with him. But he was none of the above. Here, in the cold and rain, nearly eighty miles from his Belfast home, he was undergoing a metamorphosis. There was dark magic at work this devil's hour, and in truth, he did not know what he was in this moment, nor what he would be transformed into. The sound of a bolt snapping, and another hatch opened, above him this time, and then a voice. English, barking as only a Brit soldier knew how.

'Hands on your fucking head. Now!' He didn't bother to look up, he knew that the proboscis of a standard long rifle was trained on him. He did as asked, and the door that was set into the large armoured gates was unbolted and quickly opened. Two RUC officers, flanked by two soldiers, emerged and fanned around him, guns pointed. One of the peelers let go of the semi-automatic rifle he was holding and swung it on his back, then frisked him.

'He's clean!' he shouted.

The two Brits seized him and marched him through the gate. He was half carried, half dragged across a rutted and waterlogged courtyard where armoured Land Rovers were parked. His bruised and battered body screamed out, but he gritted his teeth and did not give voice to his pain. He had screamed enough in the last two days. This night, he would speak his revenge. Through a door and along a corridor, the smell of frying eggs and the sour reek of sweat, talcum powder and the humidity of hot showers. A door opened by one of the peelers, and the Brits who had him by the arms stopped. He braced himself to be thrown into the room head first, but the hands released him and the young men marched away. A big hand pressed between his shoulder blades, firm but not aggressive, and he obeyed

11

the assertive suggestion that he enter the room. Inside was a table with two chairs. One peeler followed him in, invited him to take a seat which he did, but reluctantly. The cop pulled out a chair and sat opposite. Average height and build, dark hair in a middle parting that fell in curtains on his forehead. Maybe in his late twenties, older than he was. The cop wore a small moustache that suited him and had blue, intelligent eyes. They rested on his face and then creased into a concerned question.

'Do you need a doctor?'

He shook his head, though it still pained his neck to do so. His eyes were almost swollen closed, and black as the night he'd just emerged from. One of his lips was up like a tractor tyre, and that was what could be seen. His body was a cloudscape of bruises and broken skin. At some point, he would need a doctor and some antibiotics. But the medicine he needed first and foremost was not going to be dispensed at a pharmacy. The peeler asked him if he was sure and he said, quietly, that he was. In fact, it was sitting in the chair that he had a problem with, and part of him understood that perhaps he always would. They'd tied him to one in the isolated barn in South Armagh where they had set to work on him so systematically. It was a dark art to beat a man for three days, inflict the greatest possible hurt and yet manage to keep him breathing, not have him die from shock or blood loss, or rupture a vital organ, to have the temperance and clinical control to keep the blows to the head to a minimum.

'I want to speak to the Branch,' which he knew without being told this man was not. He expected him to ask his business.

Instead, he said: 'You any ID?'

'No.' He had a return bus ticket to Belfast and the clothes on his back. He'd left his wallet and anything that could identify him in a locked drawer in his home, and he hoped the state of his face would mean those who'd seen him here, so many miles from his locality, would barely recognise him in the light of an average day. The peeler tensed. He braced himself for the Brits to re-enter and lift him up by his sideburns, and drag him to another cell where two men would push his wrists back, bending them against the joint until his tendons screamed while a third crushed and twisted his already broken bollocks. He had been lifted before. First during internment in 1971 before he had joined, and a couple of times after he had raised his right hand and swore allegiance to the IRA. Promises, promises. He knew the drill. But the peeler didn't make a move.

'There's no Special Branch officer present in Strabane station,' he explained.

He shrugged but said nothing in response. The peeler drummed his fingers on the table. He could feel the cop's eyes on him. Silence ensued. The peeler pushed back his chair and left the room.

As soon as the door closed, he stood up and slowly started to pace, feeling the cold that seemed to have seeped into the bones of his feet, feeling the myriad of hurts, remembering them as they were administered, remembering all of them. When you torture a man, he will say anything, agree to anything, admit anything. First, he will beg for his life and then, he will plead for you to kill him. The men who had worked on his body in shifts with the thick wooden paddle, the iron ball on a chain, the electrodes rigged up to a car battery, had taught him this. Every man can be broken. It was a long time and he was no longer the person he had been, that the man who had ordered his torment had visited. His Officer Commanding in the Belfast Brigade of the IRA. He'd shook his head, a look of disgust on his face. As though being tied to a chair, looking like he did, and reeking of his own urine with his trousers and thighs smeared with his own faeces had been a choice.

'Someone's here to see you.' His OC had pulled his wife into view and clasped her face in his hands, forced her to stare at him. He'd felt the touch of an iron bar under his chin and he too was forced to see. Her eyes full of glass and fear and abhorrence. She had looked at him in a different way the last time they had met. But then, he had been a different man. She was released and she ran out of the barn in tears.

'There's plenty of tail in Belfast. But that one's out of bounds. Understood?'

'Yes.' It was only then that he realised he might actually survive this.

'Good. Then we're square.' He could not believe his ears. Not a question and delivered like a man paying a restaurant bill. His OC was staring at him, wanted him to reply.

'Thanks,' he'd said.

In Strabane station, he had retreated to a spot on the floor in the corner of the room when the blue-eyed peeler returned an hour later and set a plastic beaker of water on the table. If he was surprised to see him on the ground he didn't show it.

14

'I've made a call. To Belfast. Someone is on their way,' he said, and took a blister of aspirin from his shirt pocket. He popped four from the foil and put them on the table beside the water and then turned and made to leave.

'Thanks,' he said, not yet ready to move from where he lay.

The peeler nodded and left the room.

Time passed. He drank the water and took the pills. At first, he did not sleep. But he must have nodded off. It was gone six in the morning when the door opened again.

'So let's have a look at ye.' The man who had entered and now closed the door behind him did so on a wave of sparky energy, despite the hour. He was well over six feet tall, and unlike the peeler he wore plain clothes: a brown corduroy sports coat over a shirt and V-neck jumper combo, and a pair of expensive-looking slacks. He had a groomed beard and blonde hair that was almost flaxen and swept off his face. Like a Viking modelling for a clothes catalogue. The newcomer strode over to where he was curled up in the corner and hunkered down, face-to-face. His eyes were a blue-grey and cold, like the inner wall of a shell washed up on a northern shore. He smiled. 'Don't tell me, I should have seen the other guy,' he said and raised himself up. He clicked his fingers and pointed at a seat as he sat down at the table. Belfast accent but not plummy, despite his attire and swagger. He limped over to the table, sat down.

'Are you a Branch man?' A warrant card fell with a slap on the table. It said Special Branch.

Name: Samuel Royce Fenton.

'Read it and weep. That's legit. Now, to whom do I owe the pleasure of unpacking my cock from the arse of that wee WPC I left in bed, not to mention the death of a morning's golfing I had planned?'

He doubted whether the weather would permit anything in the way of golf unless things had changed utterly since he arrived here. He hesitated, but only for an instant, and thought, *This is what it is like to stand on the precipice of another world*, and then he spoke, told Fenton his name, where he was from.

'You're IRA,' he replied without hesitation. It wasn't a question, and he didn't confirm or deny, but he was correct. 'I've heard of you. Connected,' said Fenton, slowly pointing a finger at him, that cold smile on his face again. 'And here ye are. Not that your ma would recognise you.' Not an accusation, and no disdain in his voice. If anything, the big man seemed awed. He stopped pointing and thrust his hand over the table. They shook. And that was that. He knew it as soon as he took Sam Fenton's hand that he had crossed a divide and he could never, ever return. And he felt nothing at all. When he'd been dumped on a country road after they released him from the barn, he had just one loyalty left in the entire world and that was to himself.

Fenton stood up abruptly. 'Mon the fuck, this place is a shithole. Let's go for breakfast.'

He navigated them out of Strabane RUC station as though he owned it, and they accelerated west out of the town. The dawn was leaching the night from the sky behind them, weak grey replacing the blues and blacks that they pursued west. They approached the Lifford Bridge that would take them across the River Foyle. The river was the border with the Irish Republic and up ahead was a security checkpoint, manned by police and British

16

Army. All vehicles were being stopped. He turned in his seat and looked at Fenton, who returned a small wink. A big peeler with a hat on and wearing a thick bulletproof vest raised his hand, and Fenton slowed to a stop and rolled his window down. He passed his warrant card to the cop before a word was exchanged. The peeler took a few seconds to absorb it, his features moving from scrutiny to recognition to looking mildly perturbed. He handed it back quickly and barely glanced at the passenger seat, wishing Fenton a good day.

'Free State?' he asked as they left Northern Ireland behind them and entered the Republic, County Donegal.

'We need a bit of peace. To talk,' Fenton replied. Which was probably right, but here he had no jurisdiction, and the legally held personal protection weapon he no doubt had secreted was a criminal offence to possess. They drove along winding, high hedged country roads for almost half an hour, deeper into the green recesses of Donegal, the light of the new day awakening colour from the land. Fenton pulled in without indicating and stopped with a skid on a gravel clearing at the front of a whitewashed pub with no name. When they got out, he could smell turf smoke and saw a green An Post van and a white Ford Cortina with Garda emblems and a blue line down the side. Fenton rapped the closed door and gained entry. They sat in the snug, away from the smattering of uniformed Garda officers and postal workers who appeared interested only in minding their own business and drinking, illegally, without hassle.

'Early morning house,' he commented.

'The same,' confirmed Fenton, who sparked up a Dunhill filter and tossed the maroon box his way. He accepted the

17

flaming match and took a draw while Fenton ordered them both pints of stout, and bacon and eggs. '*Sláinte*,' Fenton said as they had their first sip, surprising him with his use of the Irish language. 'Oh aye, I know my Gaelic.'

Food arrived quickly and he surprised himself by eating the lot, though noted that his companion chased his round the plate. Fenton waited until he had finished.

'Talk to me,' Fenton said.

He did. Told him the whole thing, left nothing out. And then talked some more, like a man with a dam in his head that had ruptured. This man, he had a way. He made it easy. Charismatic was not a word he would have used at that time in his life, but Samuel Royce Fenton had it to spare. In fact, Fenton appeared, from his fallen perspective, as the unadulterated incarnation of it. When the words dried up, he checked his watch. He'd been talking for more than an hour.

'So, there it is. Everyone has their reasons. And now you want to come and work for us?' asked Fenton.

He shrugged. 'I'm done. My war is over.' He took a second smoke.

Fenton grunted at this, gave him a wry smile through the fug.

'Mate, it's not just your fight that's over. The IRA and the British have already fought this to a stalemate. Sooner or later the talking will start. Then there'll be peace, and sharing power, you can take that to the bank. I mean look at France and Germany, tucked up in bed together like the Second World War never happened. Someday it will be the exact same here between the Brits and the 'RA.'

'A man could get an OBE for that kind of loose talk,'

18

he observed. One behind the ear. Street slang for a single bullet in the back of the head.

'Oh, for a lot less,' said Fenton. 'But it's true. You've made the right choice today. For the first time in your career you're on the right side. The winning side,' Fenton said.

'I'm not interested in serving the Crown,' he replied.

Fenton threw his head back, laughed from his ribs.

'I didn't say you were,' he replied, and his face became sombre. He pointed the serrated knife that came with their breakfast at his chest and then across the table at him. 'This winning side. You and me.' Fenton jabbed the knife towards the low ceiling. 'The higher you go, the higher I go,' he explained.

'Sounds like I'll be doing all the work.'

'There's fifty large in cash every year for you. Anything you make on the side is your business, I'll not interfere. But you're going to need a new name, a codename.'

He thought for a few seconds and then pointed to the steak knife in Fenton's hand. Fenton shook his head, said that would not work. Then he stubbed out his smoke and clicked his fingers.

'Topbrass,' he said.

'Seriously?'

'It's exactly what you will be. Untouchable, my friend, you'll go all the way to the very top.'

The sun was fully up as they travelled in silence back towards the border. Fenton agreed to drop him off on the outskirts of Strabane and he would take the bus back to Belfast. They agreed on a story that would cover his absence. They crossed the Lifford Bridge as a mushroom of grey-black smoke rose in the distance ahead of them, followed a few seconds later by the sound of the explosion, like rocks rolling in a steel drum. Strabane had been bombed, yet again, and the IRA Christmas cessation was at an end. He watched the smoke drift in the wind, wondered absently if anyone had been killed and if the buses would be running. When he caught a glimpse of his reflection in the wing mirror, he almost didn't recognise the bruised mask that looked back. And the name that came to mind was not his own, it was Topbrass. Even though he had walked in and freely offered himself, he could not shake the feeling that he had been snared by this dark Messiah, a fisher of men who had called on him to drop his nets and had renamed him in his own image.

# PART ONE

## THE REPENTANT LUDDITE

# CHAPTER ONE

## Belfast, Northern Ireland
## Present Day

As the Liverpool ferry drew away from Belfast harbour on Thursday evening, DI Owen Sheen felt the buoyancy under his feet, and watched as the dockside slowly slipped past. He breathed in the sea air and raised his face to the dark sky, the stars bright and seemingly close enough to touch, if only he reached out his hand. Instead he raised the pint of Guinness he'd brought on deck and took a long, thoughtful pull. Sheen was off to London for the weekend. His old DCI's retirement party. And though he would miss the charms of Aoife McCusker, he was ready for a break. Hopefully he'd grab some kip on the overnight crossing and then it should be a straight drive down to London early doors. It was a long haul, but it was still better than flying.

As the boat picked up speed at the mouth of Belfast Lough his eyes found the twin yellow cranes in the Harland and Wolff shipyard and from there, tracked along the line of the coast to where he estimated the small district of

Sailortown had once been. The dockside community had been constructed on reclaimed land in Belfast harbour and had first housed rural families from across Ulster, fleeing the ravages of the Irish Famine in the 1840s. It also had been home for Sheen and his family, the place where he had spent most of his first decade. Until a car bomb had exploded on the street where he and his brother had been playing football. Sheen had survived. His brother, Kevin, had not.

Sheen closed his eyes, summoning memories from his childhood that he knew would not come. Like Sailortown and like his dead brother, Sheen's Belfast years had been erased from existence. All that greeted him from the darkness of his mind was the usual snippets: vignettes of violence from his brother's last moments and snapshots of the subsequent disintegration of his family. After his brother was killed and his mother drank herself into an early grave, Sheen and his father took a one-way flight to London. The start of a new life and the point at which a door closed in Sheen's mind, shutting off all access to the old. That awful journey had been his first experience of flying. Little wonder he associated air travel with anxiety and fear. He took another draw from his pint and felt his phone buzz in his jacket pocket.

Chief Constable Stevens. Sheen's boss.

The chief had taken a hands-on approach to his new role as senior officer linked to Sheen's unit, the Serious Historical Offences Team or SHOT. Sheen was still in charge, ostensibly anyway, but since things had restructured at the start of the new year the chief had been a constant presence. Regular visits, regular briefings and updates. To

24

be expected, Chief Stevens had positioned himself at the helm precisely to keep an eye on how things were being managed by Sheen. To help him 'steer clear of choppy waters' was how he'd phrased it.

To be fair, two of the cases Sheen had so far been involved in had respectively contributed to the devolved political parliament in Northern Ireland being suspended. As well as an embarrassing cross-border incident with the Irish Republic, followed by press revelations about historic child abuse and murder involving establishment figures in Belfast and Westminster. Put in context Sheen could actually accept the tighter leash, for a period of time anyway. But if the last couple of months were anything to go on, it seemed clear that the chief expected complete strategic control.

The first case the newly reformed SHOT had worked on this year was the death of a young woman in West Belfast some forty years before, who had been shot from a passing car while standing at a bus stop. Originally assumed to have been a case of indiscriminate sectarian murder, Sheen and the team had discovered an undercover unit of the British army was responsible. Soldier G, who had pulled the trigger, was now seventy nine years old and facing a murder charge. Sheen had wanted those in charge but came up against a brick wall. Convicting one retired squaddie was not his idea of success or justice for the family of the murdered woman. Sheen was not the only one who was pissed off. His team was buckling under the pressure, internal divisions starting to show. Sheen read the message on his phone and sighed.

*Get up to speed on the Cyprus Three before our meeting next week.*

The Cyprus Three. Sheen already knew enough without doing the homework task. And he also knew that the chief's text was as good as a written command to investigate the historic case. Which, no doubt, would be forthcoming.

The Cyprus Three was the name given to three IRA operatives, two men and a woman, who had been shot dead by the SAS in Cyprus in 1987. The IRA members had been in the process of planning a bomb attack on British troops stationed on the island. Though technically outside British territory, the SAS had been called in after local law enforcement had somehow got wind of a planned attack. The presence of the SAS was unusual. But given the fact that the IRA were targeting a British controlled Sovereign Base Area, the use of elite British troops had been given the green light by both Westminster and the Cyprus Government.

The real controversy as far as Sheen understood it was that the three IRA members who had been killed had proved to be unarmed. Plus, despite the claims about an imminent bomb threat, there were no explosives found at the scene. Although an original enquiry had judged the deaths to be lawful, there had been an international outcry, and at least one very publicised television documentary challenged the received version of events. Sheen had little doubt that the evidence which the chief would lay in front of him would confirm that the IRA members should not have been shot dead and that the conclusions of the original enquiry were flawed.

And Sheen knew why this had landed in his lap.

It had nothing to do with historic injustices. This was high politics. There were serious moves afoot behind the scenes to get the stalled Northern Irish parliament back in business. An investigation into the Cyprus Three would be a sweetener to encourage the main Irish republican party to play their part in getting the political system working again. No doubt something similar was in the pipeline to persuade their unionist and loyalist counterparts. And Sheen could see the logic, even the necessity, of getting the stalled parliament back on track. There was renewed violence from galvanised Dissident republicans, not to mention issues in Great Britain and Europe. The political vacuum created by the absence of the Northern Irish parliament, when added to these problems, meant there was a very real threat of a wholesale return to the violence of the Troubles. Sheen drained his pint and watched the dark clouds swirl in the dregs of his stout. He knew a man in the chief's position had to play the game, and Sheen understood as well as any how to play along. But he'd prefer the chief tell him it straight.

The ferry was far beyond the mouth of Belfast Lough now, and the lights along the shore were hazy and indistinct. Sheen set the empty glass down and closed the chief's message. He moved his fingers over the screen of his phone, tasting beer and diesel fumes. He opened his email and found the message from Graham Saunders that he'd received two days before. It had taken Sheen a few moments to place him. Graham Saunders, a spotty kid with a penchant for giving cheek to teachers and taking the lunch money from poor kids at their secondary school in London. Graham had never been Sheen's mate, and in fact, as he admitted in his email, had been a bit of a wanker. He'd given Sheen a pretty hard time about coming from Ireland and the accent he'd still had. Sheen had not said his name or thought about the guy in all those intervening years.

Sheen scanned the message, although he'd read it more than once already. Graham said he had been in and out of prison, which Sheen was ashamed to admit didn't surprise him. He didn't say what for but reading between the lines Sheen guessed petty theft and burglary. He was now working as a delivery driver for a local kebab place in Holloway and driving a minicab. Graham hadn't moved far, in every way, from his humble North London roots. But Graham Saunders had also shared a link to Belfast, just as Sheen did. And one that was a dark echo of Sheen's own childhood trauma.

His eldest brother had been killed in a booby trap explosion in West Belfast. It had happened in 1987, a few years before Sheen's own family had been torn apart by another bomb. Looking back, it explained a lot, the ill-concealed hatred he had shown Sheen, the anti-Irish abuse, his anger. Sheen had no idea at the time. Kids don't. Graham ended the email with both an apology and a request.

*I know I gave you a hard time, Owen, and that was wrong of me. I understand if you don't accept it, but I want to tell you sorry. And I am not just saying it because I want your help. But I do want your help is what I am saying. I saw you in the news when I was inside, and they said you are some kind of investigator in Belfast and find the truth on things. Nobody was ever sent down for my brother's*

*murder. Can you help find who done it? Like you*
*must want to know who killed your brother? I*
*thought Benny was so grown up, but he was just*
*seventeen when he was taken. He was a kid.*

He understood what Graham must be feeling: the
anger and helplessness. They had both lost big brothers to
Belfast's vortex of violence. The loss of a blood brother, it
was like a dark seam that cut through Sheen and his life
in Belfast, past and present. He pressed reply and started
to write, got as far as *Dear Graham* and then deleted the
words. He watched for a few seconds while the cursor
blinked at him expectantly before closing the message, his
reply unwritten. He'd promised himself that there would
be no more blurred lines.

In the past year Sheen had bent and broken too many
rules. He'd gone after John Fryer, the lunatic former IRA
man whom he believed, at that time anyway, to have
murdered his brother, Kevin, in the no warning car bomb in
Sailortown. In the process he had led DC Aoife McCusker
into harm's way and almost devastated her chances of
building a career. More recently he'd played a dangerous
game in an effort to regain Aoife's trust and to satisfy his
own desire for answers about a little boy's death. Once
again, he'd been lucky to escape with his life and the lives
of his team intact. The bridges he'd burnt with colleagues
in the Police Service of Northern Ireland's Serious Crimes
unit, Special Branch and MI5 would not be readily rebuilt.
And now he also had the chief watching his every move.

He pocketed his phone and picked up his empty pint,
his tongue ready for a refill. He would reply to Graham

Saunders, but not now. This weekend he wanted to forget. The job, the politics, the competing requests. But even as he savoured the tingle of the stout, Sheen couldn't shake the feeling that sometimes the past, just like our childhood, comes back and finds us, whether we're ready or not.

# CHAPTER TWO

Tom 'Tucker' Rodgers had a cracked ballpoint pen, an envelope, one second class stamp and no time left.

Well, that, plus a fair few regrets. The foremost of which right now being his stubborn refusal to own a computer or a mobile phone. Closely followed by the fact that the post had arrived late yesterday afternoon.

In the not so distant past Tucker had scoffed very self-righteously at pretty much every other person on the planet who felt so compelled to own an expensive mobile, especially one of the so-called 'smart' ones that could send an email or take a scan of a sheet of paper and whoosh it electronically to anywhere in the world. But he wasn't scoffing from a self-righteous perch any more. He was sweating, with his back to his living room wall this Friday morning. And his old police personal protection revolver was in the pocket of his dressing gown, when he should be snoring off the effects of last night's session.

Tucker pushed his glasses back up his nose and tasted the sweat that had formed on his upper lip. The bastard postie. If only he'd been on time, then Tucker would have opened the package before he had gone out yesterday and not when he stumbled through the front door at one o'clock this morning. Returned as drunk as a lord, in fact, from Roddy's funeral. Which was ironic. Given that it was clearly Roddy who had sent him the package. And also regrettable, given the information which it contained. But to suggest that the postman had been tardy was not entirely accurate. Roddy's funeral started at 2 p.m., but Tucker had actually gone for a few nips before, Dutch courage. Which was why he'd missed the post that had probably been delivered about the same time as usual. Either way, his head was pounding now, so much so that even the tepid light of a barely started Belfast March morning was almost too much to bear. The thought of his old drinking buddy now reduced to an urn of thin grey ash raised an unexpected lump in his throat. That and a fair dollop of booze-induced self-pity. But there was no time for laments, not when they come for you in the morning. They being whoever was in the car that Tucker had spotted slowing driving past his home more than once and who, Tucker knew in his gut, were shortly to pay him an unwelcome visit.

He'd been fond of a pint and a yarn with Roddy, not to mention the odd fishing trip over the years. He was a mate, a drinking mate. For the most part, he'd see him at the club from time to time and went over to his house for a takeaway to watch football on the odd Sunday. Tucker had always suspected that Roddy might be gay although it didn't concern him in the slightest. Matter of fact, it was helpful. It meant Roddy had no wife to complain about Tucker drinking with him until they both passed out, and the craic was always pretty good. Revolving anecdotes told as new, one round merging into another, but also weeks without a meet and then friends reunited, that kind of thing. Tucker had a fair few acquaintances like him. But could the same have been said for Roddy? Given what had arrived yesterday, it would appear not. Tucker rested the back of his bald head against the welcome cool of his wallpaper and tried to think. Instead, he cursed himself again for not having a mobile, and then he cursed himself for not paying more heed to Roddy's recent blathering at the club. His hushed, conspiratorial talk about a pension booster, nudge nudge, wink wink, a project he'd been working on for years that would pay him big bucks. The idiot must have been planning to use what was in the package to blackmail someone, someone who clearly didn't appreciate Roddy's entrepreneurial efforts. Finally, Tucker cursed himself for good measure for going out before the post had arrived, to soften the edges of Roddy's poorly attended sending off. Words echoed in his head, as though by another person, one more honest and clear-sighted than he had been in the years since his early retirement from the PSNI, and certainly braver than Tucker had ever been on the matter.

*I think you have a drinking problem.*

Tucker made a sound that could have started life as a laugh but died as a deep sigh. Right now, that problem would need to get in line, because the booze and the hangovers were far from his only issue. He wiped a palm down the front of his dressing gown and flinched as he spotted the dark hatchback, creeping past the front of his house for the third time. Tucker pressed his shoulders closer to the wall and tried not to shake. He glanced at the string-bound booklet of handwritten pages bearing the neat signature of Roddy's tidy script. That was what had been inside the package. No note, no explanation, but in a way, none needed. Thousands of words that spelt only trouble.

'Roddy, you stupid, dead fucking wanker. What have you got me drawn into?'

But Tucker knew that his problem wasn't ignorance. His problem was that he already knew too much.

After he'd got home last night from Roddy's funeral Tucker had sat on the sofa with a can, changing channels on the TV, but as usual had ended up watching the news. A local story had made the headlines, that cop Owen Sheen and his historical investigations team. Something about bringing charges against a retired British squaddie for an old murder, Soldier G they'd called him. Sheen was getting pretty well known; he'd cracked a cold case a few months past, had pointed the finger of blame at establishment figures. The previous summer he'd tracked down that IRA nutcase John Fryer. Tucker had to hand it to the guy, Sheen was one of those peelers who got the job done. And he didn't seem bothered if he made enemies or not. Tucker could drink to that, and he did. By the time he fell into bed he was plastered.

When he got up to use the toilet in the small hours, he initially thought he'd dreamt about opening a package the night before. He certainly had decided that he'd dreamt what was inside it. But the simmer of unease in his gut and sudden wakefulness at the thought had led him downstairs where he found the booklet on the small sofa, surrounded by empty packets of Tayto crisps. Tea in hand, he'd returned to it with that most cynical of all gazes, the dead-eyed stare of the hungover man. And though he was still half-pissed when he'd started to flick through the pages, Tucker was sober as a born-again at a Sunday service when he set it down and took a slurp of cold tea, swallowing three paracetamol with it. And hungover or not, Tucker Rodgers was a cynic no more. What Roddy had sent him looked legit. And that only made it worse. When he got up to make another brew, he also took his old revolver from the strongbox, checked that it was loaded and slipped it into his dressing gown. The weight of his old piece felt reassuring as he sat back down. Even so, Tucker's chest felt like a panel beater was hammering dents out of his ribs from the inside. And it wasn't just the hangover.

Roddy, a man who'd left no suicide note, had taken the time to send him this. Secret information on an IRA informer identified only by his codename, but with lots and lots of information about what he got up to fighting Special Branch's very dirty war. Tucker lifted the booklet and fanned through the pages, seeing the same name recurring time and again.

TOPBRASS

And shortly after he had sent it, Roddy had turned up dead, hanging from his bathroom door by a belt. Cue the small talk at the service about it coming out of the blue, about how you can never really know what's going on in someone's head. By the time he finished his second mug the birds had started to sing, though it was still dark out.

But Tucker's head was beginning to lighten at least and by then he knew what he couldn't do, which was a start. No point going to the press with this. He trusted journalists less than most of the scumbags he'd taken down over the years. Sooner or later his name would come out. No way was he going to the cop shop either. The peelers had more leaks than Northern Ireland Water. His name would end up in the papers anyway. Or something even worse would happen to him. Before the things in Roddy's wee book could see the light of day. Tucker's hand absently returned to his revolver, as he thought about Roddy's manikin-like face, framed with silk and flowers, dead and unreal. Even with the make-up, the undertakers couldn't completely mask the black bruises round his eye sockets. And then that voice spoke again, the one that was not his own, the one that said it true, like it or not.

*They murdered him.*

'Fuck's sake,' scoffed Tucker, but the panel beater was back on the job in his ribcage. He got up, started to gather the empty crisp packets off the sofa and straighten the cushions. He lifted Roddy's booklet and added it to the rest of the debris. He would bin it – better still, burn it – and just forget about it; pour a drink and go back to bed. Tucker paused. There was Roddy's face again, a livid waxwork in a horror museum, ruby-cheeked and smiling-eyed no more. Roddy was a bit of a gobshite, but Tucker had liked him. And now he was dead. But the last thing he'd done was send this to Tucker. Maybe because he had been a straight enough peeler. Or maybe because the poor bastard had no one else. Tucker felt a spike of anger at this, that ebbed quickly away, leaving only the cold facts of his predicament. The weight of his gun in his pocket said he well knew that destroying the book would not make this go away. He glanced at the blank television screen and remembered that he'd watched the news. Remembered the report about Soldier G and the detective who had uncovered the truth, consequences be damned.

Owen Sheen.

Not a man who toed the party line or cared about shaking things up a bit. As peelers come, this Sheen was a rare breed. Tucker had walked the beat for damn near thirty years, so he knew it better than most. And he knew that a rare breed of a peeler like Sheen was just the man for the job, and maybe, was the only man he could trust.

First Tucker tried calling directory enquiries, to get Sheen's office number. At such an early hour it was unlikely there'd be anyone working. But even so he could leave a message and find the address too. But when Tucker lifted the handset off the wall, his landline was dead. While he stood fruitlessly pressing buttons on the phone and lifting it in and out of its cradle, he spotted the car. For the first time. It was a hatchback, matt paintwork, undercoat grey and with the windows blacked out. It made a slow pass of his home before drawing away. Tucker waited by the window, keeping to the shadows, trying to keep calm. But all the while, the voice was having its say.

*Someone cut the line.*

He thought about Roddy, hanging from his bathroom door, his eyes blackening and tongue lolling.

*They murdered him. And they're coming for you too.*

Tucker kept his head low and one eye on the window

to the street, as he searched the downstairs, looking for anything that he could use. He was panicking but still thinking at least. He had to get Roddy's booklet to Owen Sheen. He found one envelope, one stamp and a ballpoint pen. Seconds later the same car passed again, from the opposite direction, moving slowly, before speeding off.

Tucker ran over to the coffee table, pen in hand, poising over the envelope. He didn't have Sheen's address. In fact, apart from Roddy's, there was only one other address that he knew by heart. He was about to search out his old address book, get the details of his old chief super, but then he heard the approach of a car from the dawn-quiet street, and scribbled the name and address he didn't want to use on the side of the envelope.

His son, David, who lived in Manchester.

Good thing he didn't need to lick the stamp, Tucker's mouth was as dry as kindling. He crept back to his vantage beside the window, envelope and pen in hand. Seconds later the same car passed, for the third time. The sun was all but up, and the street would soon be busy.

*Tick tock, Tucker.*

*You need to get out of here.*

Tucker dived into the hallway, searching frantically until he found his house keys which he stuffed into his pocket. He stopped, looked at the envelope. It was thin and long, the kind that could contain a cheque or folded letter, much too small for the whole booklet. He hadn't really thought this through. In fact, he wasn't really thinking at all any more, but he was getting the hell out of the house before that car returned.

He was half out the front door when he realised he'd

left the booklet on the coffee table. He ran in and grabbed the bound pages, stuffed them into his elasticated pyjama bottoms, securing them with a sharp tug of his dressing-gown cord. He was already out the front gate, sleety rain spitting down and stinging his bare head when he thought of his coat and hat, but he kept going. The dawn chorus echoed up and down the corridor of suburban homes. A car approached, and Tucker froze, eyes down, but it drove past without slowing. He picked up his pace, was breathing in hard rasps by the time he reached the post box another fifty yards down the street. Tucker leant one hand against its chipped, cold sombrero. That same voice now enquired why, though the object was, in fact, a cylinder, did we insist on referring to them as post boxes.

'Ah shut the fuck up,' he said.

He wiped the icy dew off the top of it with his sleeve and, after a quick glance up and down the street to confirm he wasn't being observed, he loosened his dressing gown and pulled the bound pages free, setting them on top. He removed the envelope from his pocket and stared at both, one rather thick, one very thin. Stark, white headlights glared, a car approaching from the opposite direction. Tucker lowered his head and searched to see if it was the same dark hatchback, but it was too far away, the headlights too bright in the gloaming. He made himself as small as he could behind the iron pillar, put his pen between his teeth and flicked open the bound pages, found one that was blank on one side and tore it free. He waited for his brain to kick back in with something useful, anything at all. The pen started moving.

*Dear David,*

Well, good to get the formalities right. The white headlights seemed to slow, getting closer, and now Tucker could hear the approach of a second car, this one coming from behind him. Not something he'd anticipated.

He closed his eyes, gritted his teeth and strained to recall some headlines about TOPBRASS from Roddy's book. Something that he could fit on a single page, that would give Owen Sheen a fighting chance to uncover the truth. The bastards who were right now scoping out his place had killed Roddy over this. And he would see them pay for that, but first he needed Sheen's help. Because right now he was in deep shit, and if he didn't get away, he would end up dead too. He opened his eyes, started to write as the wind flapped his pyjama bottoms against his legs, his face creased like a man attempting a particularly challenging bodily function.

*Dear David,*
*They killed Roddy and now they're coming for me.*
*Find DI Owen Sheen in Belfast. Only Sheen.*
*Tell him to look for TOPBRASS.*

*4th November 1981.*
*1st July 1984.*
*21st June 1986.*
*18th March 1987.*

*Trust nobody but Sheen. Watch your back.*
*I'm sorry.*
*Dad*

It was all he could manage. He stopped writing and dropped the pen. It would have to do. He folded the page, sealed it in the envelope and posted it. And then Tucker stood very still. The car with the white headlights was indeed a dark-coloured hatchback and it had stopped outside his house. Three blokes got out simultaneously from the back and passenger side. They were all dressed in dark clothing, one smaller than the others with a shaved head, one tall guy with a beard and one somewhere in between with his dark hair tied up in a small bun on top of his head. All three big-set, hard-featured. They were younger than Tucker, but not kids by any stretch. They looked like they were professional, and Tucker was glad he was not at his front door to find out what they specialised in.

Tucker watched as they approached his door. The men were partly concealed under the cover of his open front porch, but still visible from where Tucker now stood. One of them started to work on the lock. Fast, efficient. Open in under thirty seconds. Two of them slipped in, the tall one with the beard stood, his back to Tucker's open front door, his eyes on the road and opposite windows before he too back stepped into Tucker's home and closed the door. The dark car surged forward, coming his way. Tucker turned and started to walk. From his left, a woman's voice.

'Excuse me, are you OK? Are you lost?'

Tucker flinched, and then slowly turned around. The woman was half leaning out of the driver's window of an SUV, concern etched on her features, pity too. She was driving the car he'd heard coming from behind him. The woman repeated herself, slower this time, like Tucker was soft in the head or foreign. The wind drove a cold finger under his bedtime clothing, found his chest, and he gave an involuntary shudder. Not a bit of wonder she was treating him like a senile old fool, that was exactly what he looked like. The hatchback was closer now, but someone, sent by a god who at least deals shit luck out in more or less equal measures, had blocked its path. A neighbour had pulled out from their parking space as the car approached along the narrow road, like only a contrary shite will. And Tucker's neighbour didn't look like he was ready to blink first, good lad.

The woman was talking, asking him if he knew where he lived. Perhaps the divine intervened for the second time in as many minutes, or perhaps the shock of being out in the cold wearing slippers and watching his house get invaded by three dangerous-looking bastards with dead eyes is what did it, but Tucker's memory started working like a finely tuned machine. Something he'd heard at the club and now retrieved through the drunken curtains of countless same ending evenings.

It was an address that Roddy had told him, his beer breath on Tucker's ear as they stood at the pisser together, telling him that it was as true as God and not to breathe a word to another soul. Tucker took a deep breath and said an address but had the presence of mind once more to name one that was a few streets off where he needed to be. Whoever had come for him would keep looking. He told the woman he'd popped out to buy a pint of milk. And then he held his breath, listening to the car horns that had started to blare from a bit further down, where the dark hatchback's progress towards him was still gracefully blocked. The woman was out of her car. She slid open the back door of the people carrier, revealing a toddler strapped into a safety seat, who glanced at them, big crystal-blue eyes, full of surprise. The wee child offered Tucker a breadstick as he was helped into the seat beside her.

'You're all right dear. I know where you're going, I'll get you home,' said the woman, who had got back into the driver's seat and was now reversing back along the street. Tucker remained quiet, eyes fixed on the receding road ahead where he noted the stand-off had ended with the hatchback reversing at speed, stopping outside Tucker's home. He saw the three characters emerge and get into the car. The driver had probably been tasked with driving around the block a few times, to remain inconspicuous. Which he'd abjectly failed to do. By the look on the faces of the other three, their excursion into Tucker's residence had not exactly been a success either. The woman reversed around the corner and turned the car before setting off in the direction Tucker had named. Tucker dropped his eyes.

'Do you have anyone at home, someone I can call?' she asked. He could hear the concern in her voice. Absurdly, the lump had returned in his throat; the question had actually brought a prickle of tears to his eyes. 'Maybe I should call the police,' she said. Not a question this time. Tucker swallowed hard.

'It's OK,' he said, hoping that he sounded sure, and that he would convince her. 'I live with my son. He's at home. He'll give off to me for wandering off. Again,' he lied, with a small chuckle. It seemed to do the trick, the woman returned a thin smile from the rear-view and then gave the road her full attention. The wee one thrust another soggy breadstick at Tucker, who smiled, tears in his eyes.

'This is Alison,' said the woman. Tucker said hello. 'What's your son's name?' she enquired.

The smile fell from Tucker's face and this time he actually felt tears well up in his eyes.

'David,' he croaked.

'Well, we will see David soon,' she replied in a there-there voice.

Tucker looked out the side window at the passing details of Belfast streets beginning to wake to a new day. *I hope so*, thought Tucker. He'd just posted David information from a booklet that had clearly cost Roddy his life. The same booklet that had just sent Tucker running in fear of his own, dressed like Wee Willie Winkie. The hard faces of the hard men who had come to his door flashed before him and he shivered, despite the hot air that was blowing inside the car. David's was the only address that he could have sent his message in a bottle. But now it didn't seem like such an inspired idea at all. Tucker closed his eyes, but the tears started to fall anyway. He felt the firm edge of Roddy's booklet dig into his skin, and he willed for his only son to keep smart and stay safe.

Because he was pretty sure he'd just put him in the line of fire.

# CHAPTER THREE

Detective Constable Aoife McCusker picked up her pace as she felt the incline steepen, and let her legs do the running. She recalibrated her breathing and kept her eye on the bastard she was chasing. She was gaining on him, and she would catch him.

He was the man who had loomed over her several months before; a shotgun in his hands and murder in his eyes.

He was the psychopath who had kidnapped her adopted daughter, Ava, last summer and driven her away with a primed bomb strapped to his back.

He was the addict ex-boyfriend who had betrayed her and set her up. The man who had caused Ava to be taken away from her and almost destroyed her career.

He was every waster who had crossed their threshold when she was a little girl. The jackals who had come to prey on her vulnerable mother until she had got really sick and then, of course, they were nowhere to be seen.

One by one she ran them down, faster and stronger than them all. She pressed the button on the running machine to increase the speed, really sweating now, her arms pumping. The pounding of her feet on the rubber treadmill was the slamming of cell doors as one by one they were locked away and disappeared from her mind. Aoife reduced the incline and then the speed, her thoughts now turning to the specifics of the syllabus from the Police Manuals she had been revising for the last six weeks. The details of legislation and law which she knew by heart, and the various scenarios she had already committed to memory, plus the rationale for justifying the correct response.

Next week she would sit her Police Sergeants' Exam. And she would be ready.

By the time Aoife had unplugged the running machine in the garage, and re-entered the kitchen of her home in Randalstown, to the north of Belfast, it was 6.45 a.m., and Ava was still asleep, none the wiser. Which gave Aoife three quarters of an hour's revision before attempting the comparatively daunting task of waking her daughter up for another school day. Thirty minutes in and she was distracted by the buzz of a calendar alert on her phone. She stopped writing mid sentence and picked it up.

'Deirdre Morelli's birthday,' she read. Aoife quickly texted a birthday greeting, plus a suggestion that she and Deirdre meet up for a glass of wine. But not until her Sergeants' Exam was completed. She turned her attention back to the scenario question she had been working on, but after a few moments Aoife dropped the pen and got up to put the kettle on.

Deirdre Morelli started as a professional acquaintance who had since become a friend. And she was someone that Aoife felt she had failed miserably. Deirdre had come to the SHOT offices and asked them to investigate the death of her father who had been murdered in 1983. Not one of their assigned cases, and not an investigation that had been authorised by Chief Stevens. What was known in the trade as a walk-in. Strictly forbidden. Aoife had agreed to help her anyway. The woman was distressed, and she had come to the police to help uncover the truth about her father's death. Given that she was from the strongly nationalist Ballymurphy estate in West Belfast, Aoife respected that. It was not a place that traditionally had much trust or respect for the cops. Aoife should know, she had grown up not more than a mile away from where Deirdre's father had been killed. Historically, no matter what the problem, the last thing people did in her area was speak to the police. Aoife could still remember what had been painted on walls when she was a child:

WHATEVER YOU SAY, SAY NOTHING.
INFORMERS WILL BE SHOT.

What's more, Deirdre's father had been an IRA veteran from the long-forgotten campaign along the Irish border in the 1940s. 'Red' Giuseppe Morelli had been the son of Italian immigrants and, his nickname implied, was well known for his Marxist leanings as well as his IRA record. Morelli had been sixty-two years old and no longer an active IRA member when he was shot dead in his Ballymurphy home by loyalist paramilitaries. According to his daughter

47

there had been collusion in her father's death. In Belfast parlance that meant one thing. The authorities, police and British Army, conspiring with paramilitaries. She said that the usual police presence on her estate had evaporated in the hours before her father was killed, only to reappear again after the murderers had made good their escape.

Aoife dropped two teabags into an oversized mug and poured the boiling water.

She had no idea if Deirdre's claim was true and she did not get much of a chance to investigate it. Chief Stevens had got wind of her little project and read the riot act to both her and Owen Sheen. To Sheen's credit, he took responsibility, and said he was at fault as senior investigating officer and team leader. Deirdre had been nothing but thankful, despite the disappointment she must have felt. It was after their dressing down that the chief had pulled Aoife aside and asked her if she had considered trying for the Sergeants' Exam. He had reminded her that her colleague Sergeant Geordie Brown would retire sooner rather than later, but also told her that achieving such a promotion meant being trusted with responsibility. Which in turn meant respecting the chain of command and ensuring other colleagues did the same. Aoife knew what he was getting at. *Stay in line and help make sure that Owen Sheen does the same and you will get a promotion.* Aoife had neither agreed nor objected, but later that day she had started revising. Like every hard-won advancement in her career, if she passed the exam and moved up the ranks it would be first and foremost because of her hard work. She didn't think she could control Sheen and had no interest in going there, but the fact remained that she had walked away from Deirdre Morelli's questions just as the chief had ordered. Sometimes in this life you had to play the game, even if you wished you could change the rules.

Aoife blew on her tea, took a sip and then closed the revision materials. As she laid out the bowls for her and Ava's breakfast, she looked at the third space at the table and her mind turned once more to Owen Sheen. It had been just Ava and her for so long that she'd got to the point where she no longer really imagined how anyone else could share in that, or how she could trust a man enough to join their little team. The chief was probably right that Sheen was a loose cannon at times, but he was damn good at his job, and despite his reckless streak, Aoife believed she could trust him. Though he quite clearly was still stealing the odd smoke behind her back. But all in all, Sheen was different to the other men in her life. A lot of fun, certainly, but also perhaps the bloke that she could take things to the next stage with. Career goals aside, she was still young enough to think about having a baby someday, but time would not always be with her. She'd resolved not to push it with Sheen. If he was ready, it had to come from him. Plus, Ava remained her number one priority. The child had, to her eternal shame, spent a number of months in care last year when things in Aoife's life had spiralled completely out of control. The foster carers had been tremendous, and Ava had settled back into normal family life without too much friction – though there had been one or two incidents at school, and she had been in one fight which was very unlike her. If she and Sheen decided to get more serious and move in together, Ava would be consulted first.

Aoife took Ava's mobile phone from the top shelf in the kitchen and put it beside her glass of orange juice. She had bought it for her at Christmas, which was sooner than she had planned and Sheen had made his reservations clear more than once without having to say much at all. But Ava had been moved up a year after being assessed by teachers while she was in care, which meant she would begin secondary school this coming September. And kids today were growing up in a very different world. She could not insulate her child from the realities of the connected, media-filled life she would live in, but she could manage and regulate it. As well as having an app that allowed Aoife to monitor her location, she also had access to her communications with friends online, a form of snooping that Aoife did not feel in the least bit ashamed of engaging in. Most of it was harmless, though she did have a chat with her daughter about one post, thankfully sent only to a verified private group of same-aged friends. She'd got her hands on Aoife's make-up and manufactured a bruise on her face, and then posted the picture with the headline 'Stop Domestic Abuse'. Earlier that week Ava had asked the meaning of the term and, as always, Aoife answered as candidly as she dared, and tried to explain some of the warning signs to be aware of when it came to healthy and unhealthy relationships. Much as she lauded her daughter's sense of emerging social conscience, her PR skills needed a lot of work.

As far as Aoife could tell, kids her daughter's age rarely communicated via written sentences any more. Rather, things seemed to be done through the medium of an endless river of exchanged images with overlaid graphics and tricks that morphed faces into animals, older versions of themselves, gender swaps. The days of being a young teen and feeding silver into a phone box to speak to a friend or a first boyfriend were gone and gone for ever, and Aoife was under no illusions. She was in a race to keep up, even with a child who was just shy of twelve years old. Aoife took the phone off Ava in the evening and returned it to her before she went to school. Weekend access was strictly controlled, and she was duty-bound to abide by the school's rule that all devices remain switched off and in bags during lessons. If Ava did not comply, she would lose her phone, and Aoife made it clear she would not budge on that.

Aoife checked her watch and saw that it was time to wake up grumpy lumpy. Her daughter was not a morning person, even on a Friday. Aoife took a breath and braced herself. Here was one scenario that they didn't prepare you for in the Sergeants' Exam. Still, she had her personal protection weapon. But what she really needed was riot gear.

# CHAPTER FOUR

In the end, Tucker had to run off from the woman who had stopped and helped him. Which he had felt bad about, but there was nothing he could do. She'd driven him to the street address on Stockmans Lane in West Belfast as requested and then insisted on walking him from the car, all the way to the front door. Tucker had hoped she would leave him at the corner, meaning he could have doubled back on himself, cut across the forecourt of a petrol station and made his way to the actual address he wanted. But the woman had been more diligent than he had anticipated. Besides, when they'd passed the petrol station on their way into the area Tucker noted that it was now vacant and overgrown with weeds, its forecourt set up as a drive-through hand car wash, closed for business at this hour, and the perimeter secured with high steel fence panels fixed in place with zip ties. As they passed the site, he noted that there was a gap in one of the grilles, close to the main road. This was something he might have known if he had a car and had travelled into the west for any reason. But Tucker Rodgers had as little interest in owning a motor as he did in owning a mobile. The woman had offered Tucker an arm to help him get out of the car which he didn't need but accepted anyway. When she had turned her back on him to get the child from the car Tucker had made a dash for it. As he turned the corner he heard her surprised call.

'Hey, wait! Stop!'

But Tucker didn't stop, and he didn't turn round. One of the gardens on the road was yet to be reduced to a double parking space and Tucker ducked through its open gate, not stopping until he had positioned himself behind the wheelie bins, the biggest of which more or less covered him entirely if he bent his knees and waited. No sooner had his laboured breathing calmed a bit than his heart spiked in involuntary panic. Roddy's booklet. He drove his hand into his dressing gown, could not locate it, and then he found it. It had slipped down his leg. His dressing-gown cord had loosened a little, but the booklet was still there. Tucker stayed still, and he listened. He thought he heard the woman shouting again, and one of the cars that drove by as he kept watch might have been her people carrier, but he wasn't sure. After a number of minutes, he emerged, looked both ways and found the street bereft of people. He took a right and made a line for the bottom of the street. It was a dead end with no through road, but beyond the grassy mound with small saplings he could, he hoped, get access to the rear of what had been the petrol station. Tucker reached the steel fence panel sweating and wheezing

53

and feeling like death. He took the metal grille in his hand and shook it. Dew rained down, cold and unpleasant. But it held firm. His feet were already damp from trudging across the long grass. He would have to go up and over if he wanted to reach the exit gap. Either that or retrace his steps and follow the streets back the way the good lady Samaritan had driven him. Not an option. The sun was more or less fully up now and if he wanted to get to his place of cover before West Belfast street life cranked up this was the only way.

He started slowly, shaking with the exertion of maintaining toe and finger holds to sustain his weight, and slipped once, tearing a fingernail and landing on his backside. He set back to work immediately and second time lucky he actually managed to get to the top. Tucker swung one leg over, careful not to rest his weight on the thin seam of the fence top, not with only his pyjama bottoms and the fabric of his dressing gown to guard his tackle. It was all going to plan, he'd managed to get his other leg over the top and had only a dignified descent to complete, and then his weight-bearing foot slipped. Tucker dropped and his dressing gown caught on a sharp edge above his head.

'Fuck – me – in – the – night!' he commented, his words punctuated by the ripping free of a big portion of the back of his dressing gown. He landed on his rear for the second time in several minutes, but softer this time than previously. In fact, the snagging of his dressing gown had acted like a kind of parachute which now hung in a strip from where he'd been caught. It reminded Tucker of those old photos of people who had tried to escape East

Berlin during the Cold War and ended up suspended by barbed wire in no man's land. And no man's land was exactly where he felt he had landed this morning. Roddy's booklet was on the grass. He picked it up, wiped the dew off it and rolled it tightly before securing it with a double knot of his dressing-gown cord.

Tucker glanced furtively about, saw nobody and headed for the hole in the wire he had spotted on the far side. Beyond was the busy main road that led from west to south, and without checking or allowing himself to wait Tucker stepped out and walked with his head down, taking advantage of a lull in early morning traffic to get across a slip road and then walk the curving length of an underpass with the M1 motorway burring and echoing above. Lots of shadows here and no artificial lighting. Cars passed him, but at speed, and showed no interest. In the psychological geography of a modern city, there could be few places where the average punter going about their day could naturally claim less personal ownership and responsibility than the damp concrete cave world of the motorway underpass. Which was good news as far as Tucker was concerned, who emerged unchallenged by help or harassment and thirty seconds later crossed into the sheltered overgrowth of Musgrave Park's perimeter shrubs. There he stopped and took a breath and took stock.

He skirted the boundary fence, stayed hidden until he was in a concealed position near a park gate, and most importantly now directly opposite the location he was searching for. The traffic had already picked up considerably. Tucker waited for a lull aware of how parched and dry his throat was. The ebb in passing vehicles was a while coming, but at least he was able to survey the homes on the far side. Big, three-storey detached homes, set a good bit back from the wide pavement and a comfortable distance from the busy thoroughfare. He didn't need to see a house number to be pretty confident that this was the place that Roddy had described to him many months before. All the homes on this stretch were well separated from one another, could boast a wide buffer of land to each side, and probably much more to talk about out back. All but one looked like they were occupied, modernised and well-maintained. Not multimillion-pound homes; those sort of mansions were found further into South Belfast, places like Malone, Newforge Lane. But all the same, very nice, much better than the house Tucker lived in. Or, perhaps it was more accurate to say the house he *had* lived in. He shooed the thought away. That sort of negativity was a first cousin of self-pity and he had no time for it. It would do no good.

The house that drew his attention and on which he now rested his gaze was the odd one out. The second to last in the line of eight that stretched from west to south. It was a ruin, no other word for it, and exactly as Roddy had described it. The front garden was overgrown and the bay windows on the ground, first and second floors were either smashed or missing. The roof was a patchwork of broken and missing slates. The front door was a piece of industrial-looking steel, that Tucker had seen used to secure homes from looters and squatters in the past. He imagined that the well-heeled neighbours looked on it with disdain and dismay, and had doubtless made more than one attempt to have the eyesore dealt with over the years. The fact that it had remained as it was filled Tucker with a little hope that what Roddy had confided to him was in fact true.

The traffic cleared, and Tucker made a dash for it, praying that his slippers would stay on his bare feet and he that he didn't trip up and fall face first into the road. He reached the shelter of the overgrown front garden and he was virtually hidden from the adjacent homes and well shielded from the road. Tucker walked slowly, feeling the long grass saturate his shanks with ice cold dew, fallen rain and sleet. That he didn't mind, but what he wanted to avoid was stepping on dog or fox shit, or the business end of a broken cider bottle. When he reached the side alley that ran down the side of the house, he stopped and leant against the moss-encrusted brickwork, tall vegetation on two sides, a clean, brittle blue March morning sky straight above. He felt light-headed, and suddenly overwhelmingly tired. He'd been up since well before dawn and apart from a couple of mugs of tea, his stomach was empty and in the cavern of a deep sugar crash, courtesy of his mostly lager hangover.

He pushed himself off the wall, forced his feet to move, focusing on his next step through the overcrowded side alley, trying to recall Roddy's words. When he trampled his way round to the back of the place his heart gave an involuntary leap. Exactly as Roddy had promised, the old coal scuttle was there, about twenty feet from the metal panelled back door to the house. It was a squat, concrete shed of sorts, about ten feet by fifteen, but instead of a door, it had a dog-kennel-sized opening at the front where a wide shovel could be slotted in and a load of coal removed. In its slanted roof was a slightly wider opening, secured with interlocking wooden doors, not unlike the bulkhead doors of a cellar. Which was enough to make Tucker break the first smile of what was already feeling like a very long day.

The doors were rickety but intact. The old padlock that had once secured them was rusted solid and open. Tucker eased it out of the latch, tossed it aside and opened the doors on stiff hinges which crunched and flaked rust yet thankfully didn't squeal. Inside was black and uninviting as the disused old coal scuttle it was. Tucker could see one or two chips of slag that presumably had fed a furnace in the bowels of the big house at some point. Coal dust coated his fingers as he gripped the door frame and peered inside, tasting the carbon, earthy ghost of the coal, hearing the hollow echo of his breathing return from the concrete container. If what Roddy had told him was true, Tucker needed to get inside this. He glanced at the overgrown garden, the sad shape of the abandoned mansion, and was very close to pushing himself off the coal shed and getting out of there, getting back to a world of passing cars and public phones and normal behaviour, when he stopped. He thought of what he'd seen this morning, four horsemen of the Apocalypse, who, even if the driver was shite, had invaded his home and were probably sent to murder him. He thought about Roddy's dead body and his bad death, and then he thought about that package and what it had contained. All of Roddy's loose talk had turned out to be golden after all. He was a man who had managed to get acquainted with dangerous secrets, and now his old buddy had brought him on board. Tucker braced himself, heaved one leg up and over the low edge of the coal shed hatch, and followed with the other. He lowered his head and descended into the dirt and the darkness.

After a couple of minutes scratching about on his hands and knees in the damp coal dust, he was ready to call it quits. That was when his fingertips felt the outline of the hinge. He brought his face closer to the spot, closed his eyes tightly and blew as hard as he could in a line from the hinge point, choking and sputtering at the dry dust that was raised. His fingers traced the seam of the concealed hatch and he was able to follow its perimeter. It was a one metre square block of toughened plastic with no handle. Tucker found his house keys and used the serrated edge of one to dig away at the earth. His fingers widened what the key had started to reveal and finally found purchase under the plastic seal. It took him three attempts, white sparks cascading in the dark before his eyes, but the hatch opened on its hinges with a crunch, and a draught of stale air wafted into Tucker's face from below. It smelt like it had come out of a car's tyre.

Tucker used his feet to keep the hatch ajar and rested his back against the cold stone of the coal bunker. He was sweating and he was thirsty, but he resisted the urge to wipe his face with his hand; he'd end up looking like a miner at the pit head. So far, so good. Tucker found a couple of big bricks of coal and used them to wedge the hatch open, and then he slipped inside, feet first, slowly. His slippers found steps and he cautiously entered the bunker, going deeper, arms to his side and palms wide on what felt like poured concrete walls. The air was dank and still, the only sound was the scrape of his slippers on the steps, one at a time, and the amplified noise of his own breathing. It was very dark. He turned and looked back up, saw a weak stream of daylight coming from the opening above, seeping down to him, but only barely. He turned and closed his eyes, hoping to adjust his vision, but all was the same when he opened them. He took another step, but instead of going deeper, his toe touched a solid wall. He reached ahead with one hand and felt what had to be a door.

This was good. This was what Roddy had said. He inched his hand across to the right, found what felt like the edge and migrated his fingers north and south, but found nothing. He was sweating again and could hear the blood beating in his ears. He moved his left hand from its steadying position and wiped the sweat from his face that was stinging his eyes. Unanchored, he was suddenly disorientated, half stumbled like he was on a ship braving rough seas. Tucker cried out, his voice sounding alien and afraid as it briefly echoed up the stone stairwell. His right hand sought the wall and instead found an object, hard and cold and metallic. He had almost keeled over when it blinked to life, white and luminous. The ethereal numbers glowed from the keypad. The sudden light gave form to his cramped surroundings and he calmed almost instantly. Tucker raised a finger to the keypad and inputted the six numbers he knew and didn't need to try to remember. He knew it by heart, just as Roddy had. It was the phone number of the club.

There was the mechanical sound of something unlocking. Tucker smiled, gave the door a small push and it nudged opened an inch or more. It was heavy, felt like steel. But the hinges were smooth and gave no resistance. Tucker stepped through and fluorescent lights blinked to life, making him at first flinch and then briefly shield his eyes against their hard glare. A hallway the size of a broom cupboard with a door straight ahead, and one to his right. Tucker stood, one foot holding the entrance door open; perhaps because of its weight, or maybe by design, he could feel the pressure of it, pushing back against the side of his slippered foot. He reached over and turned the handle of the door to the right. It opened and similar overhead lights blinked on. A small room, maybe eight by nine feet, no bigger than the holding cell in an average cop shop and similarly fitted out. A double bunk of moulded plastic was fixed to one wall with a rolled mattress and folded blanket on each bunk. The walls, ceiling and floor were finished with the same grey concrete screed. Not far off the colour of the hatchback that had delivered the raiders to Tucker's home earlier. Though the temperature inside was adequate, the decor created a psychological chill. Tucker pulled his dressing gown round him. In one corner was a small toilet, the same moulded plastic, no lid. No bog roll either. He craned his neck to see if there was any water in the bowl but could not. His mouth was arid; he'd never felt thirst like this. Tucker backed out, tried the other door. Once again, the motion sensitive overhead lights came on and revealed a room identical in size to the first. This one had a table and chair attached to one wall, composed of the same moulded plastic as the bed and toilet in the other cell. A standing cupboard occupied the entirety of the adjacent wall, its contents, if any, concealed behind two closed doors that, though secured with a latch, did not seem to be locked. Tucker continued to scan across the small room.

His eyes widened.

A sink was attached to the wall opposite the seats, moulded plastic once more, but serviced by two silver taps that glinted under the lights. Tucker licked his lips, his thirst ravaging for release from inside him. His legs moved without bidding. As his hand closed over the cold head of one tap he heard it.

*Twwook*

The gentle sound of the armoured door closing. Tucker spun around, his mouth a wide grimace of realisation and despair. And then another sound filled the cell, coming from the small keypad he now saw was on the inside wall beside the door.

*BEEP BEEP*

Tucker dashed for the door, blundering through three long steps that he had no recollection of having made to reach the taps in the first place, the slowly stretching stuff of a nightmare come true.

*BEEP BEEP*

The tail of his dressing-gown cord caught under one of his feet and he knew he would fall before he started his sprawling descent. He landed on his right knee, announced with a lightning flash of pain, and then skidded forward, shielding his face with his right arm, as his glasses spun off and clattered on the hard floor.

*BEEP BEEP*

Tucker was up almost as fast as he'd fallen, gritting his teeth against the bolt of agony that emitted from his knee and he managed to get one hand on the cool burnished steel of the door, but didn't manage to reach the handle positioned halfway up.

*BEEP*

And then the mechanical sound of bolts engaging, followed by a crunch that was very final indeed. Tucker grabbed the handle and tugged, but he knew the outcome even before he started to yank fruitlessly at the locked door which remained oblivious to his exertions. He let go of the handle and upped his game by slapping his hands against the door as hard as he could until his palms tingled and danced with pain to compete with his knee and he stopped, panting. He focused on the keypad, slapping its face indiscriminately. Tucker forced himself to lower his palms and take a breath and then he punched in the six digits that would release the lock. Only they didn't. The keypad emitted a disapproving drone. He must have done it wrong. He steadied himself and slowly re-entered the numbers but got the same result. He was halfway through a third, clearly futile attempt when he stopped, his distressed breathing half full of tears. He found the red X and pressed it. To cancel his attempt. Tucker didn't know a lot about technology, but he knew enough to be aware that computer-related things would go into lockdown if you put the wrong code in too many times. And this was one machine that he didn't want to upset more than he already had.

He dragged himself away from the cell door and went back to the tap. He closed his eyes and turned the one with the blue plastic eye that should give cold water. A man could survive for a while on only water. It wouldn't be pretty, and he would die eventually. *Food was good, water was essential. Without it, a person would last days, and death would be very ugly indeed.* Once more, these words were voiced from a different side of him, the one that had been dormant but seemed to be regaining some kind of control. These were facts and had terrifying implications. But spoken in a matter-of-fact way, a voice that would broach no gurning or panic, a man who had walked a beat during the height of the Troubles and always, always come home to hang up his holster. The tap screeched, and nothing emerged.

'No, please no,' pleaded Tucker, now trying the red-eyed tap. This one didn't even screech; it turned freely as only a prop will. Tucker groaned and carefully lowered himself to the concrete floor, crying out as he had to bend his knee and ask it to momentarily take the strain of his weight. He pushed his head against the cool wall and strained to see behind the sink. It was dark, but he could just about make out two pipes. One fat drainage pipe and one thin copper inlet. Which was something. He blinked sweat from his eyes and looked again, dry tongue on his top lip. There was something else in there too, but his eyes were shot. Tucker crossed the cell on his hands, dragging the leg with the damaged knee as he went and got his glasses. The left lens had a thick crack that crossed it at a diagonal, but otherwise they were intact. He set them on his nose, got back to the sink and looked again. He could see it now.

There was a stopcock. And that meant there would be water, if he could open it.

He stretched the first two fingers of his left hand behind the moulded plastic and pushed them against the T valve. It did not budge. After three attempts it squeaked and moved, but it took another minute of managed careful manoeuvring and nudging to turn it two complete revolutions. At first nothing at all, and then he heard a rattling from deep behind the sink followed by a gasping and spitting from the sink over his head.

Tucker emitted a cry of victory and got off the floor in time to see clean water cascading from the mouth of the cold tap. He cupped it and inhaled a mouthful, choking it back out and instantly repeated the process. After he drank his fill Tucker took one more cupped scoop of water and splashed his face, watched as the coal-black water briefly filled the small basin and drained away. He turned off the tap, shuffled across the cell and collapsed into the picnic seat, panting, but no longer thirsty. Tucker raised his face to the harsh glare of the fluorescent lights and let out a rueful laugh. How long had it been since dying of thirst had been literally true for him? How long since he'd been quenched, ecstatic in fact, by a skin full of water, just cold water? In response, as he raised his hand to his chin and flicked off a few stray cold drops of water, he noted he was shaking, the tremors moving up his arm and making his teeth chatter. He surveyed the cell into which he had been born again. Maybe it was the water he'd just guzzled, but it did seem colder now. And it was very, very quiet. An air vent was located high in one corner, and it looked incredibly secure, steel and bolts fixed into concrete. Tucker clenched his fists against the shaking and it subsided. He had water, and water could be enough to keep him alive, but not for long. He sat still, letting the time pass, listening for any sign of life, any sound at all but there was nothing, no distant hum of traffic, no sounds of passing aircraft, only the almost imperceptible buzz from the overheads, and after a few minutes he had begun to wonder if he was imagining that. And how long would the lights last? Fluorescents could survive for years, which was a lot more than he could say for himself right now. In response, the overhead switched off and the living cell – this was the name he had now rested on – was plunged into a darkness so thick Tucker felt like he could tear lumps of it like black sponge from the space in front of his eyes. He extended his arm and waved it in a wide arc in front of his face. After two or three sweeps, whatever sensor there was picked up his movement and the lights blinked back on.

Tucker loosened his dressing-gown cord and removed Roddy's booklet. He dropped it on the table. It was the cause of all of this, and it needed his attention, but it would need to wait. He groaned as he raised himself off the seat. His knee felt tight and hot and painful, but he'd been lucky. It wasn't broken, otherwise he wouldn't be able to move at all. With any luck, in the cupboard there might be some medication and not just tinned food, though the food was what was really important now that he knew he had water – anything that he could survive on here while he worked out how to get out of this mess. These were the lies spoken in his brain, as he moved slowly towards the big plastic storage unit that stood against the back wall of the cell. Spoken by the same voice that had concocted the rationale for leaving early to go to Roddy's wake. When in fact then, as now, there was only ever one reason for Tucker doing anything at all. The beast of addiction fantasized that a bottle of good hard liquor would be waiting in the cupboard, even as the other man inside saw, in not altogether unwelcome sobriety, that there would be no booze there. The beast was wilder than any rabid animal of this world and had a thirst that nothing but his own destruction could ever slake.

# CHAPTER FIVE

Sheen had arrived back in Belfast on the overnight ferry from Liverpool. He had left London the previous afternoon and driven up to catch the boat which then took eight hours, arriving in Belfast a little after 6.30 a.m. Monday morning. The Irish Sea was choppy on the crossing and he'd not caught much sleep. Most of his former colleagues at the Met had been pleased to see him, especially his former DCI whose retirement party it had been. One or two had treated him differently, as though he had changed in their eyes. There was a truth in that.

He'd spent almost a year now as an armed officer of the PSNI, and he had used that firearm and had taken fire. Sheen had seen a hell of a lot more action in the last eight months in Ireland than he had in as many years working homicide at the Met. Even if he resumed his old job at the Met tomorrow, he would step back into it as a different man. And he had gained some unwanted fame – or notoriety, depending on how you looked at it – in the process. The smell of sour grapes had been mixed with the wine and cocktails at the party, he knew it. But that was their problem. His old DCI and the few good mates he kept in contact with were diamonds, and their banter had always been exquisitely abusive and personally insulting. The tough love of true mates.

Sheen yawned as he climbed the narrow stairs up to his Laganside loft apartment and reflected that Saturday evening had been a large one and there'd been little rest yesterday before he set out on the long journey back. He had been sensible to book this Monday off work. A shower and few hours' kip would set him right. Or, maybe just straight into a few hours' kip. Aoife McCusker was working today so he'd have to wait to see her, but it would be worth it. He'd been too distracted on the Friday and Saturday to feel any pangs of separation, but as soon as he hit the long road north through Sunday emptiness, Sheen's mind had turned to her. They'd spoken for a time as he drove, and though it was a good imitation of having her in his company, it was still a poor substitution for the real thing. She'd asked him if he had been smoking – no, he was bloody proud of that, lots of opportunities for a fag and hard to refuse after a few drinks – whether he'd rolled some old flame into bed – certainly not, though he'd had to roll his old DCI into a black cab and ended up paying for his fare in advance – and whether he missed her.

Yeah, yeah, he did, and he was more than happy to admit that.

Aoife said she had a nice spa thing planned for when he came back. The thought of it gave Sheen a lustful rustle of desire, his sudden need exacerbated as always by the rough edge of fatigue. But he would have to bottle it up and save it. It would be hours before she finished her shift, but at least she had promised to be with him tonight. The prospect of having her between the sheets in the comfort of his own big bed after what felt like a century apart made his heart spike and his stomach dip. He set his overnight bag down with a small groan and found his keys. Sheen snapped out of his reverie as he raised them to the lock.

Someone had been here. Or was still here.

When he left he'd double-locked, and he knew the difference by looking at the door. With the security lock engaged the door sat more snugly in its frame than it now did. He slowly put his ear to the wood. Sure enough, there were sounds coming from within what should be his silent and empty apartment. Not of discord and rampage. Music. Sheen frowned, the hours of sleep deprivation pouncing on him like a pack of hyenas, tearing chunks and strips off his rational self. Had he locked up? As a matter of fact, he could not say for absolute certain that he had. If someone had walked in after finding the door open it was arguably not even a crime. But burglary was not his only concern. They'd had an urgent memo sent round just the week before. Dissident republican terrorists were stepping up their game. They'd managed to secure a shipment of arms and had consolidated their disparate groups into one leaner and better disciplined outfit. And killing police officers was one of their primary goals. Sheen reached for his personal protection weapon, but his hand found thin air under his left arm where it was usually holstered.

He'd left in locked in the strongbox inside his flat. Couldn't travel to London and go drinking with his mates with it strapped under his jacket. Sheen gritted his teeth in silent frustration. He listened for another couple of seconds. Dissidents didn't traditionally attack to the accompaniment of background music. And there was a smell, pleasant but strong: lavender. He raised his fist to rap the door but then stopped. What the hell was he thinking? This was his manor. He slotted the key home carefully and turned it in the Yale lock. He gave the door a good kick and it swung open.

'Police officer, you're under arrest, don't move!' Sheen stood with his fists at the ready for whoever might now try to make good his escape. Nothing for a couple of seconds, and then a voice.

'Oh, Detective Sheen, please, don't arrest me,' it implored. Silky, teasing, and a voice he knew. Sheen's mouth opened in surprise. She stepped into view. And then his mouth dropped open all the way. Aoife had a small bathrobe on, showing off her long legs, a slice of cleavage. Her eyes were smoky and heavy-lidded. Sheen waited for his brain to catch up. This was not what he had expected. 'Are you ready for your spa treatment?' she said.

Sheen smiled and nodded, feeling partly a fool but mostly a lottery winner. Aoife had a key, something he had not considered. She reached out and drew him into her by the buckle of his belt. 'I thought you had to go to work?'

'I do, but I have childcare issues this morning, won't make it in until nine.'

'Is that a fact?' said Sheen, stealing one kiss, and then another, feeling his tempo rising like mercury.

After, Sheen watched from the bed, half-dazed, as Aoife went through the motions of getting ready for a working day, apparently enlivened and all the more energised by their lovemaking than she had been before. As he'd got older, Sheen had found he was less inclined to drift off to sleep after sex, but it still took an effort. In contrast, for the most part, the women in his life had been the opposite, and Aoife was no exception.

'Hey, thank you,' he croaked.

'Get some rest, old man. I'll see you when I finish work,' she said and kissed him, leaving an imprint of her glossed lips, the apple scent of her perfume. 'And Sheen, it's time to get a cleaner and some food in the fridge,' she said from the door. 'I'll do anything for your love, sexy man. But I won't do that,' she said, and closed the door with a soft click. Sheen thought that sounded fair enough, as the darkness enveloped him and he finally submerged into the depths of deep sleep.

# PART TWO

THE CYPRUS THREE AND MINT CHOC CHIP

# CHAPTER SIX

*Officious, political-game-playing prick.*

'Got a question, DI Sheen?' asked the chief.

'No, sir,' replied Sheen.

Chief Constable Ronnie Stevens nodded and rose from his chair; his signal to Sheen that their meeting was now concluded. They were in the cramped office Sheen shared with Aoife McCusker which was one of three rooms used by the SHOT at Grosvenor Road police station in West Belfast. They had been allocated this space because of its close proximity to the city centre and main motorway links. Sheen had rather hoped that being this far from the PSNI Serious Crimes HQ in Ladas Drive in the east of the city would keep Chief Stevens at arm's length. No such luck.

'Good. Then make a start on the Cyprus Three. First priority. You can expect delivery of Security Service documents pertaining to this case in the next couple of days. Things are about to get busy.' Sheen nodded, tight-lipped, and then replied that he would get on to it. Matter of fact, he already had. Thus, the dossier of information he had compiled on the three IRA players who had been shot dead: their original home addresses in Belfast, family members, that kind of thing, was in Sheen's desk drawer, awaiting his attention. Copied in duplicate. If he was going to be press-ganged into this, he wanted Aoife leading the case with him. 'Be sure to keep me updated. And thanks for the coffee,' added the chief.

'Sure, we'll see each other soon, sir. And you're welcome, by the way,' said Sheen, unable to retain a neutral tone. Neither of them had touched their drinks during the course of their twenty-minute conversation, though Sheen could have sipped his at leisure. The chief had done most of the talking. Sheen's boss flashed him a strong look.

'For the coffee,' added Sheen, and the chief's arrow stare softened. Sheen got off his seat, they shook hands.

'Don't worry about seeing me out,' said the chief, already on the move. Sheen picked up his cold coffee – filter, from the French press, not the muck from the vending machine adjacent to the holding cells – and took a gulp. It was good, even cold, but he could feel it burn. He set it back on his desk. Sheen had a bitter enough taste in his mouth without adding to it. He heard the hasty scrape of chairs from the other room: his team getting to their feet as the chief travelled unannounced through their shared office. Sheen should follow after him as it was the time to go and tell his team the news about the Cyprus case. Instead, Sheen collected the cups and French press, and took his time emptying the contents down the drain of the small sink in his office before returning them to the kitchenette, adjacent to the main working space where his SHOT waited.

Jackson Stevens looked up from a computer. The newest addition to the team and the chief's nephew. He was in his twenties but still looked like he was completing his A-levels, an impression exacerbated rather than diminished by the crop of fluff he'd been cultivating for the last month on his chin and top lip. As usual, he wore a too-large, off-the-rack suit with a collar and tie. When the chief had introduced Jackson to the team, Sheen had assumed he would be the big man's eyes and ears, someone to treat like a mushroom at all costs. In other words to be kept in the dark and fed shit.

It turned out Sheen's fears were unfounded: delegation wasn't the chief's style after all. Jackson's appointment appeared to have been a case of good old-fashioned nepotism, something the Irish north and south did better than anyone else. Sheen had warmed to him and could see his qualities, but nonetheless remained a little wary.

'Coffee up to scratch, sir?' he asked. Sheen told him it was quality, and Jackson puffed up. Jackson was the one who had brought the French press and a supply of decent filter coffee into the office. Sheen quickly looked round the office, noted that Geordie Brown, the old-school detective he had plucked out of an alcohol-soaked retirement, was at one desk, partly visible behind a rather large stack of letters. Aoife McCusker was not around.

'Chief just gave me the run-down on a new job,' started Sheen, speaking to the room.

'Long as it's a better one than the last,' commented Geordie. His surly tone warned of a bad mood, which wasn't unheard of. Sceptical impatience was pretty close to Geordie's default setting. He was sweating, dark patches visible from under the armpits of the short-sleeved shirt that was tightly stretched over his thick shoulders and chest. Today, however, Geordie's displeasure was more targeted.

'What's all this?' Sheen asked, momentarily distracted from his would-be announcement. The sound of rapid typing from Jackson's keyboard stopped and then Geordie replied, sounding as agitated as he looked, which was very.

'Hate mail,' he said. Geordie was almost buried in post. The plastic sack that the letters had been delivered in was beside him and had more inside it.

'Sir, it's not just the letters.' It was Jackson. 'You're trending on Twitter, and we have made the top story of BBC NI News. Well, you have,' he said. Sheen glanced at the screen of Jackson's computer on which he had opened the BBC News page.

### SHEEN'S SHOT: SOLDIER G TARGETED

Sheen sighed and then spotted something at the bottom of the page.

*DI Owen Sheen was asked for comment but declined,* he read. He was going to let fly with a few choice expletives but gritted his teeth and swallowed the vitriol. The chief. The bastard was speaking on his behalf now to the press. Sheen was lucky he hadn't read about taking on the case of the Cyprus Three in the news.

'Lot of comments about this,' said Jackson quietly. Sheen put a hand on his shoulder, before stepping away. The kid was feeling awkward. He'd put the pieces together, a clever lad, but this wasn't his fault. His uncle was a man best suited to the reptile house in London Zoo.

'Emails as well, Sheen. The general enquiries inbox is full of complaints,' said Geordie, slicing open another envelope and dropping the empty sleeve on the floor where a large number had already fallen.

'Do people still write hate mail? I mean actual letters?' asked Sheen.

'Boss, I can confirm that the good people of Northern Ireland still trust the Royal Mail to deliver dog's abuse,' replied Geordie. He nodded to the table in front of him, almost shoulder-high in opened post. The phone rang and switched immediately to answer facility. Sheen noted the green light on the machine blinking with stored messages. 'And our Jackson here was just about to start listening to the phone messages,' said Geordie. Sheen nodded. He wanted to say something to Geordie that would make this better, but he had nothing.

'Don't bother,' Sheen said to Jackson. 'What's the point of listening to people's messages who probably don't have the courage to leave their own name and number?'

'Like trolls, sir,' Jackson replied.

'Indeed, but I prefer the old-fashioned name. Spineless losers,' replied Sheen. He turned back to Geordie. 'Will you just leave it, mate? You've read one, you've read them all,' suggested Sheen.

Geordie shook his head and tipped more unopened letters on the floor at his feet, plucked one from the pile and went to work slicing it open.

'I'll read the lot,' he said. 'Unless you have something a bit more tasty for me to get tucked into, Sheen?'

This was the moment. Time to break the news about the chief's latest dictate: they would be investigating the case of the Cyprus Three, an IRA active service unit.

But Sheen had neither the heart nor the bottle. 'Nothing pressing,' he said.

Perhaps committing to a full year in charge of the SHOT had not been so well thought through after all. His stubbornness meant he'd instinctively told the chief he was in, despite the stranglehold he knew the boss had on the team. And he was in too deep to turn back now anyway. His London gaff was rented out and his Met job, at least the one in the Homicide team, was no longer there for him to return to. Still, it wasn't just stubbornness and ambition that had inclined him to stay, with or without the chief trying to pull his strings.

'Where's Aoife?'

Geordie answered without looking up. 'Secondary school visits. Though why I know that and you don't is a tad worrying,' he said. Sheen had known, or at least he now remembered Aoife telling him. Ava, Aoife's niece and adopted daughter, was due to make the transfer from primary to secondary school at the start of the next academic year. In Northern Ireland, the grammar school system was alive and well, and although the Eleven Plus examination had been abolished, the academic segregation of children was still decided by entrance exams and non-compulsory taking of the old test. Religious divisions still abounded too, with most young people opting for sectarian segregation too, or rather their parents making that decision for them. Sheen wondered at what cost, given the deep and still raw divisions that marked this society. He stared at Geordie's stack of opened hate mail. Sheen grabbed his leather jacket, finding the office and the job suddenly too pressing and too much. He took out his phone and wrote Aoife a quick text.

*The chief has spoken. We work the Cyprus Three case, March 1987. Don't tell Geordie, let me. I'm out for lunch. Hope the visits went well.*

'Where you off to?'

'Something else that the chief asked me to look into,' he replied.

Geordie nodded, not listening. He was reading another letter with a scowl.

Sheen signed out at the front desk and watched Aoife McCusker enter through the first set of sealed security doors. She was wearing a pair of tight-fitting jeans, low-heeled suede boots and her lightweight Puffa coat. The inner door buzzed as she touched her security pass to the electronic lock.

'This man's been asking to speak with you,' said the sergeant on the desk. He turned to the man who was sitting on one of the three plastic chairs in the reception area. Chequered shirt, large beard. Aoife approached. She nodded, flashed Sheen a smile, and he caught a waft of the fresh, apple-like scent of her perfume.

'DI Sheen, can I have a word with you?' The man stood up. He looked to Sheen like he was in his early thirties, but it was hard to tell. His face was mostly a block of brown beard. The sleeves of his shirt were rolled up revealing one heavily tattooed lower arm, a Koi carp and swirls of water. One of his earlobes was enlarged with a fitted ring, wide enough for Sheen to put a doubting finger through it if he had wanted. He didn't, but he couldn't stop staring at it.

'Sorry, but we don't accept walk-ins,' Sheen said. *Especially not today*, he thought.

'My name's Dave Rodgers,' he persisted. Sheen detected a hybrid accent, north of England, maybe Manchester, but definitely with some roots in Northern Ireland. Sheen took his offered hand and shook but was simultaneously shaking his head.

'Mr Rodgers, I'm sorry, but to say this is a busy time is an understatement and we have a very strict policy of not accepting cases in this way,' he said.

Aoife now stood beside Sheen. 'DC Aoife McCusker,' she said, and shook Rodgers' hand.

'This is about my father. He's gone missing,' Rodgers continued, all his attention now directed at Aoife.

'Then you'd best report it to this man,' countered Sheen, nodding in the direction of the uniformed officer at the front desk. 'We don't deal with missing persons.' Dave pulled out a folded envelope from the back pocket of his jeans and offered it to Sheen, who did not accept. Aoife took it from him and gave Sheen pointed a look.

'May I?' she asked. Dave nodded, and his ear lobe sort of flapped. Sheen wondered what he would do when he was an old man and retired with a super-sized earlobe. They got larger as you aged anyway apparently, like the scrotum. Aoife took a piece of paper from the envelope and started to examine it.

'I take it you have checked the hospitals. It's usually a safe bet,' offered Sheen.

'Spent most of yesterday on the phone. Checked them all; he's not been seen. I think it's more serious than that. I think he has been kidnapped. Or something even worse has happened to him,' he said, a thread of the frantic now colouring his words. Sheen sighed, the guy was clearly distressed and probably believed he had fair reason to be. Sheen felt for him, but what could he do? Take in every anxious relative who had lost someone or been victim of a crime? Sheen tried a different approach.

'Dave, listen. I'm going to put you in touch with someone who can actually help you with this. Someone who will listen to you and take your father's disappearance seriously. I know you've probably read things in the news about how I have found people who were lost and disappeared, but honestly, mate, I really think you've got the wrong end of the stick here.' Sheen began to move towards the door.

'My father was a police officer,' said Dave. 'One of you. First he was RUC and then for a while he was PSNI too.' Sheen stopped, the new information giving him pause.

'Sheen,' said Aoife.

'Just a second,' replied Sheen.

'You need to take a look at this,' she persisted. Sheen turned to her, prepared for her blue eyes, that imploring look that would both melt and shame his resolve to turn the young hipster Dave Rodgers away. But instead he found Aoife was all eyes for the sheet of paper in her hand. It looked like it had been handwritten, both sides. Whatever it was, Aoife knew better. They'd had a walk-in off the street in early January, their first week at Grosvenor Road and just when the new team was finding its feet. Aoife had brought the woman in and made a start on the case of

83

her father's death. And then the chief had found out what was going on, closed it down and threatened Sheen with a formal disciplinary. He'd taken the rap, which was the least he could do for Aoife, but he'd promised himself and made it crystal to her: never again.

'Aoife, you know what we agreed,' said Sheen quietly, private business now edging into public view.

'This is different.'

Sheen gave her a patient smile, but it took some effort.

'And why's that?'

Aoife handed him the sheet of paper.

'Because his father has asked for you, by name,' she replied.

# CHAPTER SEVEN

Sheen hung his jacket on the coat stand in the main office. Geordie and Jackson glanced up as Aoife walked Dave Rodgers past them.

'Back so soon?' asked Geordie, but he was looking at the stranger who now walked into Sheen's office. Sheen grunted something non-committal. He desperately wanted a smoke. Even if he allowed himself one, he couldn't smoke here, so he homed in on the next best thing.

'Jackson, is there any danger, mate?' he asked, nodding towards the small kitchenette where the French press stood on the shelf. Jackson said he would be happy to, and he looked genuine. Geordie was reading aloud yet more creative abuse from a member of the tax-paying public when Sheen closed his office door and took a seat behind his desk. He asked Rodgers for identification and his driver's licence checked out. Sheen noted his age, twenty-five, and the place of issue, Manchester. He handed it back.

'The beard puts years on you,' said Sheen. And it did. Rodgers was a good few years younger than Sheen had placed.

'Least I can shave, DI Sheen,' he replied curtly. That accent again, a tinge of Belfast, but almost entirely diluted. Sheen appraised him unsmiling. Then he nodded, offered Rodgers a seat across the desk from him which he accepted. Aoife remained standing, one hand on her hip, the piece of paper Rodgers had brought with him in her other hand. She was reading the page intently, the frown that meant trouble forming a dent between her eyebrows. She handed the paper to Sheen.

'Your licence says Manchester. What age were you when you moved there?' chanced Sheen.

'Fourteen. But my mother took me to Rochdale, that's where I lived, where I'm from, I suppose. She had a sister who lived there, but she's passed now,' said Dave.

Sheen nodded. Manchester made sense. The largest city in the immediate area, more work.

'What do you do, Dave?'

'Got a job in MediaCity, with the BBC. I work on app design, customer interface,' he explained. Sheen had heard of MediaCity but had never visited. A massive business park by the Manchester docks, designed to attract investment from digital and creative businesses. Explained the hipster look.

'So what brings you back to Belfast? If your father's gone missing, surely you should begin in Manchester,' suggested Sheen.

Aoife came to his side and set the piece of paper down on the desk in front of him.

'My father's still here. Or was. I said that my mum

and I left for Rochdale,' he clarified. Sheen could hear the contempt in his voice, maybe for his mother, or his father, or perhaps the whole messy family implosion that had resulted in him being uprooted in his teens and forced to start anew. 'I came back here because my old man sent me this message in the post,' he said.

Sheen glanced up quickly from the scrap of paper on which there seemed to be a poem or a song written in neat script on one side.

'A letter?'

Dave Rodgers nodded, said that his father had refused to own a mobile and didn't use a computer. A letter. After the avalanche of post that Geordie was currently sifting through, after the email message he had received from his old school mate Graham Saunders, this bloke turns up asking for help and what is it that prompted him? A letter. Rodgers was still speaking. 'Being a Luddite meant he had another excuse for not keeping in touch.'

'You and your dad not see eye to eye?'

'We didn't see one another at all. There was no real beef, just no relationship to speak of,' said Rodgers. He ran his lean fingers up and down the tapestry that covered his lower left arm. Sheen somehow doubted that. The edge to Dave Rodgers' voice when he had mentioned leaving with his mother and the note of concern when he was asking for Sheen's help to locate his father said something different.

'Last time you two met?' The question came from Aoife.

Dave shrugged, shook his head. Sheen noted his fingers has become restless. Sheen guessed Dave Rodgers wanted a smoke. Sheen understood.

'Maybe a year ago. Me and my girlfriend had moved in together. She kept asking about him, so I invited him over to our new flat,' he said.

'How'd that go?' asked Sheen.

'We got as far as the local on the corner for a quick drink, you know, while Lisa got the roast prepared? He got blattered. I couldn't move him, so I left him there, had to explain that to Lisa,' he said.

'So, he's never actually been to your place?' asked Sheen.

Dave shook his head. His fingers had found a stray paperclip and he was straightening it back into a silver wire.

'Look, I'm not sure why you're asking me these questions,' he said.

'Your father has never been to your apartment, but he remembered your address, drunk or not, and saw fit to write and send you this. Why? And why not just call you or text you?' Sheen asked.

'I told you, he refused to own a mobile. I dunno why he didn't call me on his landline; he had my number,' said Dave.

Sheen had more questions but before he dug any further into the case of the drunken Irish dad, he needed to see what had Dave Rodgers so spooked, and how his name had anything at all to do with this.

'I don't think that my father wrote that poem. His message is on the other side.'

Sheen turned the page. There was a scrawled note, written in what looked like a blue ballpoint pen, the same pen and handwriting that had been used to write the name and address on the envelope which Dave Rodgers now slid across the desk for Sheen to examine. The envelope had a blue second-class stamp with a Belfast postmark, dated four days previous.

'No expert, but yeah, it does look like two different people wrote each side,' said Sheen. 'You can verify that this is your old man's handwriting?'

'I'm certain,' he said.

To be fair, it didn't take forensics to see that two writers had been at work. He was ready to accept Dave Rodgers' certainty.

'Dave, what is your father's full name?' asked Aoife. She was at the computer on the other desk.

'Thomas Rodgers. Tom, but he was called Tucker as a nickname. He encouraged it,' said Dave.

Aoife started to type rapidly. A few moments later Sheen heard the printer hum to life and then Aoife handed him a sheet of paper with Tucker Rodgers' home address. Killeaton. It was in the south-west of the city near Dunmurry. Pretty nice place; it had at one time been a little village that was part of the rural hinterland, but had been gradually subsumed into Belfast as the industrial revolution caused the city to expand. In terms of the political and sectarian topography of Belfast, where Dave Rodgers' father lived had once been almost one hundred per cent Protestant and loyalist, but now was more mixed. Still, it was a safe enough location for a retired police officer to live in terms of the threat posed by Dissident republican groups who still thought they were at war with the apparatus of the state. But then again, such complacency had been the death of many men and women in the past. Sheen gave his full attention to the short, handwritten letter, taking the time to read it twice.

*Dear David,*
*They killed Roddy and now they're coming for me.*
*Find DI Owen Sheen in Belfast. Only Sheen.*
*Tell him to look for TOPBRASS.*

*4th November 1981.*
*1st July 1984.*
*21st June 1986.*
*18th March 1987.*

*Trust nobody but Sheen. Watch your back.*
*I'm sorry.*
    *Dad*

'Roddy?'

'No idea. His mate?' suggested Dave.

'This mean anything to you?' asked Sheen. He turned the page around and pointed at the word TOPBRASS.

Rodgers shrugged. 'I was hoping you would know. He told me to come to you after all.' Sheen sighed. He hadn't a clue. Belfast was the global epicentre for shortening names and giving people nicknames, which at a guess this appeared to be. He asked Aoife if anything jumped out.

'Dave, did your father have enemies, criminals that he helped to put away over the years that might have held a grudge?'

Aoife's idea was solid. Sheen had seen it before: cases where cons who had spent years inside and who then made it their life's mission to take some measure of revenge when they were released. His old DCI in London had told him about one bloke who had systematically targeted every prison warden he had spent time under, and he'd managed to do a bit of damage too. It was when he moved on to hitting the judges that they'd nabbed him. But unlike High Court judges, people like Tucker Rodgers didn't have round-the-clock security protection.

'I'd assume so. But if you mean whether there was one old nemesis who always wanted to get even with him,' he said and shrugged, 'not as far as I knew. But then, I didn't have a lot to do with him,' he conceded.

'Let's assume that TOPBRASS is a group, or a gang, or an individual. The dates must be significant, a common thread. Otherwise, why would your father be so specific?' persisted Aoife. Again, a fair point, but Sheen needed more.

'Like unsolved crimes? Something that Tucker had been working on in his spare time,' Sheen mused. But to what end? A police pension was healthy, but the returns involved in blackmailing criminals using evidence accumulated across a long period of time could be a lucrative bonus. But it could also backfire catastrophically. Sheen turned his attention to the dates and spoke each one slowly in his head, casting a fly on a stream, catching nothing as he moved from 1981 to 1986. He stopped at the last date on the list.

Aoife must have caught the change in his expression.

'Something?' she asked.

Sheen stood up and walked to the shelves which contained box folders of case files and PSNI policy documents. He reached up and heaved a hefty tome off the top shelf. *The Bradley Index*. It was a meticulously detailed, harrowing chronicle which recorded the death of every single man, woman and child who died in what was remembered as the Irish Troubles between 1968 and 1998. It was compiled by a professor of history at the Ulster University who had given his name to the chronicle. Although the catalogue did not include those murdered by Dissident republicans and loyalists since the late 1990s, there was no other compendium which so comprehensively told the story of the death of over three thousand six hundred people in the conflict. Here in this book was Kevin's name, Sheen's only brother, listed with the other children and the woman who was murdered by the same no warning car bomb in Sailortown in the early 1990s. Sheen found the date he wanted, 18th March 1987. He walked the book over to his desk where Aoife joined him.

'Look,' said Sheen. He pointed to the page. Three IRA volunteers shot dead in Cyprus by members of the SAS.

'Isn't this what you texted me?'

'The Cyprus Three. Chief's orders,' he agreed. Sheen enjoyed that familiar flutter of excitement, the certainty that he'd picked up the scent, and the anticipation that there was more to follow. He scanned the details of the other deaths listed on the page. Some dates had multiple casualties, others had a single name listed. That month had seen a flare-up in violence because of an internal feud that had taken place between factions of a socialist republican splinter group, the Irish National Liberation Army (INLA). Two of their members had died that day in separate attacks. But Cyprus was way more significant. It had to be the reason why Tucker Rodgers had included this date.

Which meant TOPBRASS must be significant too. This was Sheen's chance. He could honour the chief's orders by investigating the Cyprus Three as instructed, but this angle could offer him more. The chief blatantly had his eye on a preferred outcome, namely that the three IRA operatives had been unlawfully killed by the SAS, and well they might have been. But here was an opportunity to make the Cyprus investigation his own. And it could be even bigger than that. If March 1987 switched on a light, then perhaps the other dates Tucker Rodgers had listed could also be linked to significant events of the Troubles.

'Does this mean you're able to help?' asked Dave Rodgers.

Sheen passed *The Bradley Index* to Aoife and walked over to the large dry wipe board where he had a staff rota, weeks out of date, sketched out.

'There might just be a way, Dave,' answered Sheen. But that was a lie. Sheen was hooked. He wanted to see where the rest of Tucker's dates led him. He spun the board to reveal the clean side and first tacked to it the print-off with Tucker's personal details that Aoife had given him and then wrote 18th March 1987 with the details of the Cyprus Three bullet-pointed beneath on the right side of the board. '4th November 1981,' he said, writing the date on the left side of the board, forming a timeline.

Aoife flipped through the pages of the book.

'Got it. Bernadette Bell. She was executed by the IRA. They said she was informing to the British authorities. Originally from Belfast but her body was found dumped on a country lane in South Armagh.'

'1st July 1984,' said Sheen.

After a moment searching the book, Aoife again summarised what she had found.

'Dennis Lamont, off-duty RUC, murdered while serving behind the counter at his wife's ice-cream parlour in South Belfast. Claimed by the IRA,' she said.

Sheen glanced at Tucker Rodgers' note and said the next date. 21st June 1986.

'Eight British Army soldiers murdered by a roadside bomb attack on the bus they were travelling in. It happened at a place called Ballycarrick, County Antrim. They were on their way back to their barracks after taking part in a charity fun run in Bangor.'

Sheen wrote the details on the board. He knew Bangor, a lovely little seaside town about fifteen miles out of Belfast, but he was not familiar with Ballycarrick. The final date, which marked the death of the Cyprus Three was 18th March 1987 and was already up on the board. Sheen could feel his mood darken and his heart become leaden in his chest. These were mere snapshots of what had been an unceasing procession of death. So many people, so many wasted lives, each death rippling pain and devastation to untold family and friends. What a fucking awful time it had been. How could a society that had endured this ever really heal? Could things ever really be normal again?

He stood back and surveyed what he had come up with. His instinct that the dates were connected because of historic crimes looked right. But what was the common denominator? Aoife spoke, giving Sheen an answer.

'All linked to the IRA,' she observed.

94

'Two dates are IRA attacks, one against the police, one against the army,' said Sheen.

'And two are cases of IRA members being killed, including the Cyprus Three,' confirmed Aoife.

Sheen scanned through the details on the board once more. In Belfast, history usually spelt the Troubles and this case, it seemed, was no exception. Still, while he could see the woods, he was not yet able to see the trees. But as these were no ordinary crimes, it made sense that TOPBRASS would likely be no ordinary criminal.

'Dave, have you gone to your father's home, or tried to call him?'

Rodgers said he had come straight from the airport to the police station.

'I phoned his house, but the line is dead,' said Dave. Sheen's eyes narrowed at this. 'I also tried to call you here but spent an afternoon going straight to voicemail.'

'Yeah, I'm sorry about that. Don't suppose you have a key to your father's place?'

'No chance.'

Sheen thought about the postmark on the envelope. Four days already since Dave Rodgers' father had put pen to paper, a man who had stated that he feared for his life. And who had claimed that a murder had taken place. Sheen walked over and wrote one word on the board and underlined it.

TOPBRASS

'So, what do you think?' asked Dave.

'I think we'd best take a run up to Killeaton and pay your father's house a visit.'

He wanted to find out all he could about this

TOPBRASS, how he or it was connected to the Cyprus Three case, and how the other deaths in Tucker's list fitted in. With any luck, he might even be able to help Dave Rodgers find his missing father in the process. Tucker's home was as good a place as any to begin.

# CHAPTER EIGHT

On the first night in the bunker Tucker had dined on tinned sardines in brine and dry oat biscuits, all washed down with cold tap water, which had a slightly rusty aftertaste he had decided. His shakes had got a lot worse and were accompanied by the sweats and the shivers. He tired of pacing the walls of the living cell sometime around early evening, if his internal clock was to be believed, and curled up on the bottom bunk with a blanket wrapped over him. The sweats got so bad that he ended up tearing it off his body, and instead clutched it like a very pathetic teddy and let it soak up his perspiration, which had already seeped through his thin pyjamas. His stomach joined the party after about an hour on the bed, had knotted and cramped, and despite his best efforts, he ended up emptying its contents into the toilet basin. His supper was ten times worse coming back up than it had been going down, not that he would have ever believed it possible while he'd forced himself to eat it. But that was just the beginning. His guts had kept on giving, and greenish-yellow bile chased after his evening meal until at last he had no more to give. He had slumped to the cold concrete floor, his hot cheek on the cool, smooth cement. He lay there for a time and fell into a fitful sleep in the darkness that ensued, but woke up with a start as his involuntary spasms triggered the sensor and filled the bed cell with stark fluorescence. Tucker had crawled back to his nest and this time covered himself, face and all, in the blanket, imagining it was a funeral shroud, and hoping he would die of a heart attack as the room was sucked into total blackness once more. Fitful, terrible dreams that meshed with feverish alertness, pain and then welcome oblivion. At last he came to, a slowly surfacing sense of himself rising up from the deep. He was alive. Then the granite slabs of the hard facts fell into place: the package, the escape, the accidental self-incarceration. All of that had happened then, and this was now. How long ago that had been Tucker had no real way of knowing. Perhaps a night, or perhaps much longer.

When he opened his eyes, the darkness was so complete that Tucker was overcome by a sense of vertigo. His arms and legs flailed in panic, triggering the overhead light which illuminated his sparse cell. His heart gave an unpleasant wallop in his chest that sent a dull throb of pain from his eyelids to the base of his neck. He struggled to free himself from the blanket, stale and slightly dank with his sweat and turned in the bed, eyes blinking, and peering into the small room. He focused on the doorway that led to the darkened mini hallway and unlit living cell beyond, searching for movement and danger. He saw nobody and nothing. Tucker's tongue was a desiccated lizard in the sarcophagus of his mouth. He worked it around his gums, glad he couldn't – yet – taste anything as he eased his legs one at a time off the cot, exhaling a small moan as his bad knee was put to work.

He ached. Like he'd been fed into a mangle. Like he had at the end of his first week as a raw, teenage recruit into the British Army where he'd served three years to escape the poverty of Belfast's Lower Shankill Road, an experience that had given him something where previously he had had nothing at all. And that had been enough to get his foot through the door with the RUC, in 1969 to be exact. The year the Troubles had sparked off in a proper way. He had seen more war and conflict and death and horror in his first year as a community police officer in Belfast than he had in the previous three years as an armed soldier of Her Majesty, travelling the world. Which was almost funny, now that he took a moment to reflect on it.

Almost, but not really. Not at all.

He hobbled through to the living cell and splashed cold water on his face at the sink. His hangover headache had subsided some, but his shakes had got a lot worse. And now his brain and body were crying out not just with the awfulness of his toxic comedown, but for a drink, any drink whatsoever. Tucker's let's-pretend-we-really-need-and-want-food ploy, that he'd used while searching, fruitlessly, through the big storage cupboard was now gone. His dry mouth remained parched even as he sucked water from the tap to at first rinse and then force himself to swallow as many cold gulps as he dared. He glanced at his wrist and saw only the too thin lower arm of a man with more white hair than dark, but no watch. He'd gone to sleep in the evening but had no real idea of how long ago that now was. And, really, nor did it matter, not when it came to boozing. Tucker was a Bloody Mary for breakfast and beer for elevenses sort of retiree, and had been for a quare while before he finally took his pension for that matter. And now he'd been without a drink for at least a day and likely a bit longer by his reckoning. Though, in his defence, he was rarely drunk. That had been one of his go-to excuses; his favourite actually. Only once in a blue moon did he ever manage to get as hammered as he'd done at Roddy's funeral, and let's be honest, folks, who didn't cut loose once in a while? Another one of his sayings which he liked to keep at hand. But the truth was that he was almost always drinking, and ordinarily, he would have serviced and renewed his hangover by now.

The funeral was now an eternity ago, in a different universe where things had not gone so completely down the pan and he was locked inside a safe bunker under the streets of West Belfast. He looked about his new home and unexpectedly burst into tears. He let it come, not really knowing or caring why, and stopped the self-pitying gurning only when he thought of his son and of the letter he had sent him. The danger he was most likely now in. That had been stupid, inconsiderate and irresponsible. Which more or less summed up his parental style and achievements in a sentence. He sniffed back the snot and tears. He'd never cried as much, not in his whole life, and this was the first time he had let it out sober, maybe ever. Tucker took a few deep breaths. The truth. There seemed to be an abundance of that at present too.

'I don't fucking care about the booze!' he bellowed, and drummed the sink with both hard balls of his palms.

He chanted it again, building up energy and volume, not caring if he was heard or not, though he was fairly damn sure he would never be heard in this bunker. He stopped when he'd had enough, the blows still thrumming in his hands and wrists, and his head continuing to bang, the latter no less than he deserved. He was breathing hard but actually smiling now, and as Tucker turned his face to the ceiling, eyes closed, he laughed. Against all the odds and the panic about not having a drink – people died when they stopped suddenly, or so he had assured himself many times in the past as he braved the first of the day – there was a part of him that actually felt all right. Not good, he doubted he would ever be able to wake up in a good mood again, but if he had a mirror he would look himself in the eye, despite what he'd done writing the letter to David and the mess he'd helped create by missing the post and going to Roddy's wake early for a drink. But there was, possibly, just one saving grace to all of this. For the first time in a long, long while he'd gone for a day without the sauce. And he'd survived. Which also meant that he could do more than one day if he absolutely had to. And locked up in here, he probably would. He was not dead. In fact, in an odd kind of way, he'd been freed.

'I'm alive, you murdering fucking cunts ye!' The small cell filled with his cry and then drowned it, back to silence. 'Alive,' he whispered.

He breathed in stuttering rasps, as he pushed off the sink and exercised his painful knee. He had the feeling of a man who had left the sun and commotion of a piazza and entered the vast coolness of a barely lit cathedral. His senses were stunned, humming at the novelty of not being oiled and warmed by the lubricant of drink. But he also felt like he was sharper, despite the pain and shock being processed by his barely adjusted brain. Co-piloting with the angry, frantic voice in his head that was screaming for a cure, there was now also the other part of him, the thinking and sober part of Tucker's mind that was sense-checking the dials and instruments in the cockpit, back in the chair after a long sabbatical. This Tucker was calmer and more confident, had evaluated the stock of food and found it, and the single plastic beaker and knife and fork set, to be adequate. There were at least two months' worth of high-calorie bars, tinned fish and powdered supplement drinks, but no alcohol and no medication. If the water kept coming, and there seemed to be no reason to think that it would suddenly stop, he was in no immediate danger of starving to death or dying of thirst.

He looked for a washcloth or towel but there was nothing there, so he ran his hand down his wet face and flicked away the residue. Both his hand and arm were shaking so badly it took three attempts before he could grip on the side of the sink. He poured a beaker of water and decided this was vodka and lime, plenty of ice. He took a sip and savoured the bite of the voddy, Ketel One, real quality. He felt it singe the back of his throat in a way that announced he'd had a good knock of what mattered, but appreciated its smoothness as it made its way down, the mark of a quality vodka in Tucker's estimation. The fresh lime juice flavoured the neutrality of the spirit perfectly, and he enjoyed the gentle glow that began to pulse and emit from his core almost immediately. The sour belch that returned in a mouthful of cold water was full of acid and tasted like off fish. Tucker set the beaker down, swallowing hard, refusing to vomit any more. His hand was steadier now. He slumped into the hard plastic seat attached to the opposite wall and picked up Roddy's scrapbook, notebook, or whatever the bloody hell sort of book it was.

'Time for the truth, eh, Roddy, my old muck,' he said. He read the front cover:

TOPBRASS: A SECRET HISTORY

# CHAPTER NINE

Aoife McCusker was in the passenger seat as Sheen pulled up outside Tucker Rodgers' house on Killeaton Park in outer West Belfast. Dave Rodgers sat in the back. She took a moment to scan the surroundings. Residential, middle-class homes with well-maintained facades and front gardens in the main, with many of the latter paved and used for off-street parking. The cars she could see parked in front of homes or on the street were quality European brands with number plates no older than three years. Young professionals, spending their lives in relative comfort. The flotsam and jetsam of family life scattered in the drives of the two semi-detached properties which flanked Tucker Rodgers' address. A child's tricycle lay on its side, a weathered basketball against a fence, a baby doll in a little pram was abandoned in a front garden. Tucker Rodgers' house was a spacious terrace, no side entrance in contrast to the two adjacent homes. Aoife could imagine that his neighbours had a view on the state of their shared neighbour's home. Tucker's house was poorly maintained to the point of being dilapidated. The window frames were flaked and peeling, and a drainpipe had detached itself from the side of the house at some point in the past and was prostrate on the overgrown lawn. The windows looked like they had not been cleaned for years. Aoife could just about make out the lank net curtains that hung inside. Her eyes followed the telephone line from the telegraph pole to Tucker's house, noted that the black wire was tacked to the brickwork and led to the open-fronted porch.

'Not exactly house-proud,' she commented as they got out of the car.

'He's got no pride at all. And less shame,' replied Dave.

The front gate was old, an original wrought iron with a rising sun emblem, very seventies, but perhaps not painted since the end of that decade. They crossed the garden, and Sheen found where the telephone wire emerged within the small covered porch before it continued its journey through the frame of the front door. He took the cleanly severed wire between his fingers and showed it to Aoife, who nodded her recognition. There would be no calls made from this line. She watched as Sheen unclipped the gun holster under his left arm where his personal protection weapon was waiting. Aoife adjusted her jacket to reveal her own weapon.

'This has been cut,' Aoife explained, for Dave Rodgers' benefit, and then asked him to hang back. He did as asked and stepped back into the front garden. Aoife joined Sheen, who had moved closer to the front door. Red paint, blistered and warped, now weathered to a faded pink. The letterbox and knocker were tarnished and dull, barely returning her reflection from the shadows of the porch. They waited, listening and trying to absorb something from the home behind the door but there was nothing, only the faint hum of background traffic from the surrounding streets, birdsong and their breath. Aoife watched as Sheen raised his fist and knocked. The door relinquished without a fight. It creaked open slowly under the pressure of his rap, exposing a dark crease of the unlit interior. Aoife took a small step backwards and gently slipped her gun from its holster, holding it at a low angle with both hands, ready to point and use if needs be. Sheen, now slightly in front of her, had done the same. Aoife's eye fell on the Yale lock. Scratches. Clean cuts had scored the weathered brass. The lock had been picked. She slowly pointed one finger at what she had discovered to ensure Sheen had noted it.

'This is the police,' he said, loud enough for his voice to carry into the house. 'Mr Rodgers, are you there?' he called, and slowly edged the front door open a little wider with the side of his foot, to give them both a view into the house. Aoife edged forward and blinked in an effort to adjust her eyes to the relative gloom, and then Sheen shouldered the door open abruptly, moving three paces inside, his gun pointing straight ahead and then tracking up to his right where the stairs rose to the first floor. Aoife followed, spinning on her heels as soon as she entered, covering Sheen's back and the blind corner behind the front door.

'Clear here,' she said, softly, and Sheen glanced back. He pointed to the stairs which she took with stealth, two at a time, the gun trained on the darkened passage at the turn of the stairs as Sheen advanced along the small entrance hallway. She blinked, demanding that her eyes adjust, and then turned onto the small landing, her gun rotating between ten and two. Empty, and very quiet. She could taste dust and stale body odour in the air. Four doors, all closed. She turned the handle of the one to her right and kicked it open. Stark white daylight flooded out as she stepped in, squinting and moving her gun into all corners.

'Jesus,' she whispered. She'd seen some disgusting bathrooms in her day but this one took it to another level. She grimaced at the awfulness of the unflushed toilet, and then turned and tried the other doors. A shout of 'Clear!' from Sheen downstairs, helped confirm what her gut had already told her after she entered and checked what must have been Tucker Rodgers' bedroom. The place was empty. A tangled mess of sheets had half fallen from the stained, lumpy-looking mattress, and she could see that the carpet was littered with beer cans and bottles. The front bedroom was empty, just built-in wardrobes, but no bed or other furniture, and the small box room was exactly that. Piled up with cardboard storage boxes, a rolled-up duvet and bric-a-brac. Aoife returned her gun to its holster and walked back downstairs where she found Sheen standing in the middle of the downstairs lounge. To her right it led into a smaller dining area and beyond that was a little kitchen, partially hidden from view.

'Upstairs is clear,' she confirmed.

'Anything out of the ordinary?'

'Toilet's a crime scene,' she said.

Sheen went to Dave Rodgers, who was still waiting in the front garden.

Aoife slipped on a pair of latex gloves from a supply in her coat pocket and tried the kitchen door which led into a back garden, taking care to use the very tip of the handle so as not to smudge potential prints. It was locked, and the overgrown garden beyond with its moss-covered wooden table and chairs looked like it had not been traversed in recent memory. She returned to the lounge. Sheen was now in the process of snapping on his own gloves. Dave Rodgers wandered in.

'Don't touch anything,' Sheen warned him.

'Bloody hell,' Dave said, surveying what she too could see. The place was a tip. Empty beer cans on the mantelpiece, more on the low coffee table, most of them extra strong lager. There was a rising tower block of takeaway pizza boxes on the floor beside a sofa that had, perhaps, once started off as tan or cream but was now faded off-grey with dark and threadbare shoulders. Aoife's eyes focused on the coffee table. A single mug with the remains of milky tea, surrounded by countless empty cans of beer, like an erratic of domestic normality in a landscape of excess. It did not look like there had been a struggle here, though it was rather difficult to tell. Something had caught Aoife's eye, something on the floor. Dave was still lamenting.

'Man, this is bad. This is worse than I would have believed.' He paused, still surveying the wreckage of the house with a look that was the hybrid offspring of dismay and disgust. 'Hold on, he's not, like, here, is he?'

'No, the house is empty,' replied Sheen from the dining area.

Aoife took a pen from her pocket and hunkered down beside the coffee table. There was a white, A4-

size padded envelope on the carpet. It looked like it had been ripped open in haste. She flipped it over and read Tucker's given name, Thomas, and this address. The letter had been correctly stamped, and the postmark told her it had been processed in greater Belfast, but it was dated exactly two weeks previously. She looked at the tight, neatly printed script which detailed Thomas Rodgers' name and address. The last line of the postcode had been scratched out and replaced with new numbers and letters, different ink and different hand, absolutely no doubt about it. Aoife called Dave Rodgers over.

'Do you know the postcode here?'

'Not off the top of my head. BT17,' he said, and then he produced his phone, his fingers working. He read out the last three digits.

'Thanks,' said Aoife. She was right. The original address had been completed incorrectly. Which meant the package must have experienced a delay. Most likely it had found its way back to the main sorting office where someone had taken the time to correct the error. Aoife carefully lifted the envelope by its corners. The script that had been so carefully written by the person who had originally addressed this package; she had seen this distinctive calligraphy before. She stared at it for a few seconds, and then it came to her. It was the same handwriting as the scrap of poetry which was on the other side of the letter Tucker Rodgers sent to his son.

'Aoife, come and have a look at this.' It was Sheen. She did as asked and brought the envelope with her. Sheen was standing over what looked like a small safe that was inside an open drawer in a cabinet beside the dining-room table.

'What's this, a safe?' Aoife asked. Dave Rodgers joined them.

'Strong box,' Sheen clarified. Inside was a police warrant card, two bullet casings and a photograph. Sheen lifted the card out, and Aoife read Thomas Rodgers' name and noted the red retired stamp that had been imposed over his picture. Her eyes lingered on the face of the young Tucker. He could not have been older than his early twenties when the mugshot was taken, probably when he'd first hit the streets. Dark hair, copious but feathered quite short, a neatly trimmed moustache so redolent of the time and not one speck of grey in it either. Handsome guy. And his eyes looked clean and clever, his head was held high, Aoife could see the pride that he clearly still had back then. In his job, his protective role, and Aoife suspected in his young family too. She mentioned this to Sheen, who said that he totally agreed, and then he set the card back.

Aoife picked up the photograph. Same man, but this time wearing too short shorts and a vest, his moustache now gone and his hair thinner, but in great shape and well tanned. He was standing beside a rudimentary barbeque that was billowing smoke, holding a big can of beer now. There was a woman with a pinny and highlights, pretty, leaning on his shoulder. A little boy in a bright yellow T-shirt was pulling a face and pointing to a can of Coke in one hand.

'That was taken here. In the back garden. I remember that day,' said Dave Rodgers, from over her shoulder. Aoife had forgotten he was there, noted the wistful, slightly taken aback look in the man's eyes, and felt like she'd been caught snooping on another person's memories.

Dave slowly walked into the kitchen, his head bowed, a man lost in thought.

'Where's his gun?' Sheen asked.

Aoife returned the photograph to the box and examined the bullets. Sheen had a point: it was the next obvious question. Aoife knew that many former police personnel in Northern Ireland were licenced to own a personal protection weapon, and if Tucker had bullets it was a safe bet he must have owned a gun too.

'Dunno,' she conceded. 'But I hope Tucker has that gun with him rather than pointed at him right now.' Despite what was still nebulous, part of a picture was slowly emerging here.

'Take a look. This was on the floor, beside the sofa,' she said. Sheen scrutinised the envelope. He quickly picked up on the discrepancy with the date.

'My take is that it actually arrived quite recently,' offered Aoife.

'Like four days ago?' Sheen replied, alluding to the date that was stamped on the other envelope, the one that Dave Rodgers had received from his father with the cryptic message and appeal for help. Aoife nodded and asked Sheen to take a look at the handwriting.

'That's the same script, Aoife. Like the poem, on the other side of the letter that Dave gave us,' he confirmed. Aoife nodded her agreement. She walked back to the sofa where she'd found the envelope and Sheen followed her.

'I see Tucker Rodgers opening this white envelope while sitting down here with his tea. And this is a guy who liked his beer, but for some reason, he wants to keep straight, even for a little while,' said Aoife.

'Something in the envelope must have spooked him. Enough for him to open the strong box and take out his gun,' said Sheen. He asked Aoife if there was a return address or a sender's name on the white envelope, but of course, there was not. In that case, it would never have reached Tucker, not with the address incorrectly detailed. Sheen pointed to the hallway beyond the lounge door.

'I'd say he tried to call first. Maybe planned to phone Dave, but most likely us.'

'Discovers the phone's dead, decides to put pen to paper,' said Aoife.

'Whatever arrived in this envelope was larger than a single page,' observed Sheen.

'Probably, but perhaps that was all he could send. Or had time to send,' said Aoife. 'Think about the cut phone line, Sheen. And the picked front door lock. Assuming someone really did come for Tucker Rodgers, then they were no amateurs.'

'We need to find out who Roddy is, the man who Tucker said had been murdered. If Tucker believed that he was in danger, there's a fair chance the penny dropped after he read what was in that package. And he linked it to the death of this man,' suggested Sheen.

'You think this Roddy sent Tucker whatever was in this?' she asked.

'It's a place to begin. We can start by checking police records for any sudden deaths, might get lucky.'

Dave Rodgers' voice called out from the kitchen. 'Roderick "Roddy" Grant, died two weeks ago tomorrow,' he said. Aoife and Sheen joined him where he was reading from what he initially took to be a remembrance card

112

that was attached to the fridge with a *Lovely Las Vegas* magnet. 'Don't worry, I didn't touch it,' said Dave. Aoife read the card. It was an invite, to Roddy Grant's funeral service at Roselawn Crematorium and a drink's reception after at the Shandon Park Golf Club. She moved out of the way and let Sheen see it.

'I know that place. It's way out in East Belfast, the other side of town,' Sheen said. Aoife nodded to Sheen and he followed her out of the kitchen to where Dave Rodgers could not overhear.

'Lots of cops from Ladas Drive are members,' she confirmed.

'Which means Roddy could have been a cop,' said Sheen. Something she should have thought of, though of course without the luxury of Roddy Grant's full name the hunch would have remained exactly that. Sheen took out his phone and seconds later he was speaking to Jackson. Asked him to dig up everything he could find on Roddy Grant.

'What now?' asked Aoife. She was of a mind that there was enough here when added to Dave Rodgers' letter to suggest a crime had been committed, at the very least to have concerns for Tucker's safety. Which meant that technically this should be reported. The chief's stern words from earlier in the year replayed in her mind. The need to respect the chain of command, to play by the book and ensure that colleagues do the same, should she hope to gain a much-deserved promotion. Sheen chewed his bottom lip.

'If we call this in, make it official, there's a good chance this case and the chain of evidence will end up in Paddy Laverty's lap,' he replied. Laverty was DI with the Serious Crimes team in Ladas Drive station. Not Sheen's number one fan. Not someone who would readily kick the case back their way. 'And Tucker asked for me, by name,' he reminded her. 'I have a moral obligation.' That was part of it, but hardly the whole picture.

'Sheen, think about the professionalism of whoever came for Tucker Rodgers, and the way those dates in his letter match IRA deaths across decades. And that name: TOPBRASS. This could be big. We don't want to risk losing control of the case by breaking the rules,' she argued. *Or risk Tucker's life*, she thought.

'I agree. It certainly feels bigger than a missing person case and that's exactly what an overworked crime desk will quickly relegate it to if we call it in.' He took out his phone and started to photograph everything they had found.

'This is a mistake,' she said quietly.

'The house has been left undisturbed for a few days. We close the door and leave it as we found it, and with any luck that will not change.' Aoife caught his eye, gave him a look. 'If the postman accidentally opens the door and reports it, that would be unlucky, but we have what we need,' insisted Sheen, holding up his phone on which he had photographed the evidence. Despite his words, he didn't sound convinced by his own logic.

*And what then?* she thought. *Then we make it worse, for ourselves and probably for Tucker, by investigating this behind the chief's back? Not if I can help it.*

Dave Rodgers emerged from the kitchen and he and Aoife followed Sheen out. As they left, Sheen pointed out that Tucker's shoes and a pair of trainers were by the front door, a coat and a jacket still hung on the hooks. Aoife thought of something.

'Dave, did your dad drive?'

'Yeah but he didn't own a car,' he replied. They exited Tucker's home, and Sheen did his best to pull the front door closed as he had found it. No phone, no computer and no car. Seemed like their man had cut himself off from the world well before disappearing. Aoife glanced down the street as Sheen and Dave got into the car and she saw a red Royal Mail post box halfway down. Tucker had made it that far, but was he at home when someone had entered his house quietly and with ill intent? As Aoife got in she caught sight of a car pulling quickly away. It had been parked close to the post box. She nodded to Sheen, who also watched as it accelerated off, too fast for her to make out much more than it was a hatchback, matt grey and with a blacked-out back window.

# CHAPTER TEN

Sheen had dropped Dave Rodgers at the front of the three-star chain hotel in Belfast's fashionable Cathedral Quarter where he had reserved a room. In response to Dave's enquiry about whether Sheen was willing to help him, Sheen had replied that he would do his best and that Dave should stay in Belfast.

'Was that a yes?' Aoife McCusker was observing Sheen from the front seat of the car as he exited the city centre and headed west towards Grosvenor Road.

'I'll be interested to hear what Jackson has to say about this Roddy Grant,' he said in reply.

She went quiet for a few seconds and then said, 'Either way, we have one missing and one dead man. And Tucker's house is not secure. The chain of evidence is open to contamination. If your answer to Dave Rodgers was yes, then we need to make this official.'

'Yeah, I get it,' answered Sheen. Too abruptly; not how

he'd hoped his response would emerge. She was right of course. 'I know. I just want to get a better picture of what we are working with, that way I approach the chief better armed.' Which was barely true. He was walking the line yet again, on a razor's edge between complying in a professional way with actioned commands and galloping off the reservation and pursuing his own bounty. His hand absently went to the part of his lower arm that had been grazed with a shotgun blast a few months ago. He looked to Aoife, who had been left staring down the barrel of that gun while he lay helpless. Sheen found the chief's personal number on his dash display and hit call. The boss answered after two rings. To his credit, he always did, even if he was in a meeting, in which case he usually told Sheen he would return his call unless it was an emergency.

'Sir, something has come up that's relevant to the Cyprus case,' he said.

'Already? Carry on,' said the chief.

'It's actually related to a concern about a missing person, a former police colleague,' emphasised Sheen. He purposely avoided the term 'walk-in', which doubtless would have resulted in this conversation ending abruptly and not in his favour. 'It's a bit complex, might be better to try to explain it face-to-face and show you what I've got,' he said. A thoughtful sigh emerged from the car's speakers.

'It more often than not is, Sheen. I'm back at Ladas for the rest of today, but I'm in and out of meetings,' he said to the background sound of turning pages. 'Three-fifteen, I have a ten-minute window,' he said, not in a consultative way.

'Thanks, sir. I'll see you then,' replied Sheen, and the chief killed the call.

'There,' said Aoife, visibly pleased. 'That wasn't too painful, was it?'

Sheen didn't reply. Next, he picked up the police radio and requested a uniformed response to Tucker's address at Killeaton Park and asked for the house to be sealed pending examination.

'Can't see him agreeing to this,' commented Sheen as they approached Grosvenor Road station.

'Positive thinking, young man,' she said.

'How'd the school visit go?' he asked, in reference to the secondary school visit Aoife had made earlier that morning.

'I liked it. Ava said she hated the uniform and didn't take to the headteacher, but she loved the art facilities. A long way for her to travel, mind. If we had a place in town, might make it easier,' said Aoife.

This was another thing. They had talked around the idea of maybe buying or renting a place together in Belfast, a way of shortening Aoife's fairly long commute into town from Randalstown, the small town on the outskirts of Belfast where she and Ava lived. And of course, it would take their relationship to the next stage. Sheen enjoyed his time with Aoife but was less thrilled by the prospect of giving up his loft apartment by the river, or indeed by living with a soon-to-be teenage girl. That and saying a final goodbye to the very occasional cigarette he still stole out his skylight window when he couldn't sleep. Or, perhaps, he was being phobic about engaging in a more meaningful way than their dalliance at his place the day before. Fun was fun, but he understood that at some point things were going to become more serious or the wheels would start spinning. And after the months he had spent rather fixated on the possibility of getting close to her, it was now she and not Sheen who was behaving in a more emotionally honest and mature fashion.

'We should look into it,' he replied, and that seemed to do the trick – for now, but it would not last for ever. Aoife shivered, and turned up the heat in the car. Sheen's mind returned to Tucker's house where his overcoat and shoes waited in the hallway. He hit the brakes and pulled to a stop in a bus lane before finding Jackson's name on his display screen and calling the number. The bleat of the ringtone sounded through the speakers.

'Something?' Aoife asked.

'Maybe.'

Jackson picked up.

'Sir, I was just about to look up Roddy Grant's details—' he began.

'Drop it for now, Jackson. If I wanted to search through 999 calls made in the Greater Belfast area, say in the last four days, based on specific criteria, how hard would that be?'

'With respect, sir, if you were to try it might end up being a drag on your time,' he said. Sheen said he had expected as much. He honestly had no idea how the emergency calls were filtered and fielded; most likely it had been outsourced. 'But it shouldn't take me very long if you want to give me some specific search details,' he said.

Aoife smiled at Jackson's jibe and Sheen joined her, but only momentarily.

'Right, I want to know if anyone called in with safety concerns for a pensioner who might match Tucker Rodgers' description in the last four days,' he said, and told Jackson to check out the bullet-point description of Tucker Rodgers he had added to the whiteboard in his office. 'I think if he left his home, he probably did it in a hurry and he was unlikely to have a coat, maybe not even a pair of shoes on his feet. That's the sort of thing people pick up on,' said Sheen. Animals, old people and children in confusion or distress, the public could, mostly, be relied on to have a go, and in that order. Jackson said he was on it. Sheen pulled out from the bus lane but took it slowly, silence and anticipation replacing conversation between himself and Aoife.

Jackson's call came through as Sheen turned on to the Falls Road in West Belfast, headed back towards Grosvenor Road station.

'Go ahead, Jackson,' Sheen said. Jackson's reply arrived through the car's speakers.

'Sir, three calls pertaining to emergencies involving a male pensioner were processed over the past four days that may be a fit. The first from a male caller in the Ormeau Park area this morning. He claimed to have seen an old man staring into a kiddies' play area in a way described as menacing,' said Jackson.

Sheen knew Ormeau was quite far south and east, off the River Lagan. Given Tucker's home was on the opposite side of the city he didn't like it.

'Don't think so. Next?'

'Just a moment, please.' Jackson explained that the system was slow. They waited, Sheen counting the seconds until Jackson spoke.

'A woman called for police and ambulance last night after her father took a fall down the stairs in his home near Tates Avenue.'

West, but clearly not their man. Sheen slowed to a stop in heavy traffic, their progress on the road mirroring Jackson's efforts to pick up any sign of Tucker Rodgers.

'No dice, Jackson.'

'This one might be interesting. Police and ambulance called to Chapel Lane late yesterday evening. Pensioner attacked after leaving Mass,' said Jackson.

Aoife nodded from beside Sheen. Chapel Lane was on the hinterland of West Belfast leading into the city centre. Not beyond the bounds of reason that Tucker had made his way there, and certainly not unlikely that an old boy looking lost and vulnerable might take refuge in a church, and then be attacked by someone later. It was a rough area, especially at dusk.

'Mugged,' continued Jackson, but slowly, clearly reading from a computer screen that was giving its information one sentence at a time. 'Refused medical assistance and was not interested in making a police statement.'

'Jackson, please tell me you have a description.'

'I do, sir,' replied Jackson, his response stretched and slow as the words he was attempting to access.

Sheen's fingers drummed the steering wheel, willing this idea to float. But no, Jackson burst his bubble.

'Sorry, sir. Female pensioner,' he said.

'Never mind. Forget it, Jackson, get back to digging what you can on Roddy Grant, we are on our way back. And thanks, mate, you—'

Jackson spoke again, this time Sheen could hear a thread of excitement in the young detective's voice.

'There's one more here from four days ago. A woman

reported picking up a pensioner whom she said was confused and lost. He got out of the car near Kennedy Way in Andersonstown and she said he then ran off. The woman had a child in the car with her and could not pursue,' he said. Sheen focused on Jackson's words. This could be what he was looking for.

'Name of the street?'

Jackson read him the street address and postcode, and Aoife jotted it down in her notepad. Stockmans Lane, in the west of the city.

'Sir, the woman also said this man was wearing a dressing gown and slippers,' said Jackson.

Sheen thought of Tucker's coats and shoes that were at his home. He felt a tremor of excitement but kept it under control.

'Jackson, is there a note to say where she found him?'

Jackson asked him to hold for a second and Sheen heard a tapping of keys, and then silence.

'Got it. She reportedly picked him up in the Dunmurry area,' confirmed Jackson.

Sheen clicked his fingers.

'That's him; it has to be. Jackson, please tell me that there's City Council CCTV close to Stockmans Lane, or an ANPR camera nearby,' said Sheen. Automatic number plate recognition. He could hear the rattle of keys over the car's speakers as Jackson set to work.

'There's ANPR on the M1 motorway, and that's less than a hundred metres from Stockmans Lane. But it's directed at motorway traffic.' Of course it was. 'And no CCTV masts in the immediate vicinity. There's one about half a mile west, but on the Andersonstown Road,' confirmed Jackson.

Which made sense: it was a main artery in and out of the city centre. 'Stockmans Lane is mostly just residential, but you might find domestic CCTV cameras on the street. Sometimes they can pick up things,' suggested Jackson.

'What about near Tucker's place at Killeaton while we're at it?' asked Sheen. More rattling keys and more of the same response. No CCTV masts overlooked Tucker's suburban street. But perhaps no matter. What Jackson had just dug up could already be the key to understanding where Tucker Rodgers had gone after posting his letter to Dave, and how he managed to travel there.

'Thanks, Jackson. You done well, mate,' he said, and ended the call. It looked like Tucker Rodgers had made his way into West Belfast and so far, he had not turned up dead or in a hospital. But questions remained. Who was he running from, and how had he managed to disappear and remain hidden?

Ten minutes later they stood on Stockmans Lane in West Belfast, quiet and residential with semi-detached homes located between the Andersonstown Road and the motorway. The original trajectory of the street had been bisected by the later construction of the M1 which Sheen could hear in the background, an undulating throb and hiss of passing traffic.

'What now, Sheen?' asked Aoife.

Sheen surveyed the street which was unremarkable in every respect. And no domestic CCTV cameras that he could see. The way they had entered led back on to the Andersonstown Road. Busy, populated and well policed. Not a place he would opt to scarper to if he was hoping to avoid detection. The end of Stockmans Lane was buffered from the motorway underpass by a small copse of trees and shrubs. Sheen walked that way, Aoife behind him. He pushed his way through low-hanging branches and stamped the long grass to gain passage. Dead beer cans and a pair of boxer shorts. Sheen glanced at the shorts, thought they might be relevant to Tucker, and immediately wished he had not. They didn't fit their time frame anyway; they had clearly been there for a long while. Aoife asked him if he knew what he was looking for.

'Yeah, and that's it,' he replied. They emerged at a wire mesh fence, its sections held together by zip ties. The clearing ahead looked like it had been a petrol station at one point but was now being used as a car wash. The forecourt opened up to the underpass and, beyond that, the extension of Stockmans Lane. There, on the fence a little to Sheen's right, was what had caught his attention.

'What's that?' asked Aoife.

Sheen trudged his way to the spot and touched the brown-coloured cotton material through one of the mesh windows.

'Unless I am much mistaken, I think this is a strip of Tucker Rodgers' clothing, maybe a dressing gown,' he replied. Sheen surveyed the strip of material. It was snagged on a protruding bit of metal that stood proud at the top of the fence. But the fabric was draped over the other side from where he now stood.

'How can you be sure?' Aoife asked.

Sheen admitted that he could not. But he could take it with him, send it off for analysis. The chances of there being useable DNA on it were probably slim. Plus, he'd need to have a comparable DNA sample to match Tucker Rodgers.

Perhaps a hair sample from his home? At a stretch, they could always get a mouth swab from his son; any match would at least help determine the probability of a family link. Science aside, this was nothing more than a hunch, but it felt right. Sheen thought again about the coats and shoes that still waited in Tucker's hallway, ignored by a man who had left in a hurry. And this spot fitted the facts so far and was hidden and private. Also, a tick. Aoife spoke as she squinted up at the way the fabric was draped.

'We can also ask Hayley to give it the once-over. Assuming that this is something she can read,' Aoife suggested. Hayley White was a close friend of Aoife, and one of the most unusual people Sheen had ever met. A year ago he would never had thought he could accept it, but the truth was she had a gift. Psychic intuitive was how she described herself. Sheen didn't really know what to call it, but she'd been instrumental in helping them crack a very cold case not so long ago and there was no denying it. That said, Sheen's gut still told him that police work and reading minds were two different things. And should be kept well separated.

'Maybe we shouldn't bother her. Last time took a lot out of Hayley. She might not want to get involved again,' he said.

'Sure she would,' she replied, but absently. Aoife was examining the torn strip of cloth with a tell-tale frown. As expected, she saw what he had. 'Looks like someone went up and over, snagged this as they did. And they were headed that way,' she said, pointing at the open entrance of the car wash. Sheen spotted a gap in the wire close to the open gate. Even if this place had been closed for business, a person could have found their way through. With enough effort and determination. And despite the son's belittlement of his father, what Sheen had gleaned about Tucker Rodgers so far was that he was a man to be reckoned with, albeit not without his demons.

Aoife snapped on a pair of latex gloves and handed Sheen a plastic bag. He watched as she scaled up the fence, lithe and strong, and he waited as she unsnagged the fabric and lifted it over the fence before dropping it into the evidence bag. It would need to be transferred to a paper bag to eliminate the risk of condensation and mould spores contaminating it as evidence, but for the time being this would have to do. Aoife jumped down from the fence, and Sheen leant into her as she steadied herself and kissed her. She returned his unexpected advance and he followed the sweet relief of her back, found the swell of her tight butt as she flicked her tongue exploratively between his lips before breaking off, suddenly matter of fact, but eyeing him like he was an incorrigible schoolboy. Which was precisely what she had the power to make him become in seconds.

'Can I see you tonight?'

'I promised Ava we would have a night together,' she said. 'But you know, if we had a place together . . .' She let her words tail away but held him with her eyes suggestively. He'd purposefully avoided office romances in London while with the Met, had assumed it would be a distraction from the job and a way to make enemies at work as well as on the streets. But Aoife was different. It was easy, both to get the job done and to be with her. Maybe this was it, the way people who grew old together and moved through the world in a dance with one another, maybe this was the simple truth of it. It worked because it really wasn't hard work, that life apart was unbalanced and more difficult after you met the person you knew was right, the fabled 'one'.

'Then, let's do it,' said Sheen.

'Seriously?'

'Yeah. Seriously,' he said.

Aoife kissed him again, and this time held him and did not let go. It was Sheen who reluctantly broke their bond.

'Well, Sheen, I'll say this, you choose your moments,' she said, and nodded at the soiled boxer shorts close by.

'Life's romantic, you know me. The chief,' he reminded her.

'Knew you'd be late,' she replied. 'Sheen, if Tucker came this way, then where was he going?' asked Aoife as they stepped their way back across the overgrown grass, headed for the car. The big question. She probably didn't expect him to give an answer. And Sheen did not have a definitive one.

'Wherever he was headed, I think he had a plan. He knew where he wanted to go,' said Sheen. That much, and the fact that Tucker Rodgers was almost certainly alive, Sheen was willing to run with. Whatever Roddy Grant had sent to Tucker, the old copper had realised he needed to get off grid and get safe. And by now, whatever had been gifted to him could make Tucker the best informed person in this investigation. Tucker's guile and experience had served him well, but Sheen could only hope that for this clever and resourceful man, luck would not run dry.

# CHAPTER ELEVEN

Tucker noted the frayed edge of the second page in Roddy's booklet. He had torn it out to scribble the note to David. There had been a poem of some kind on the other side of it, but now he couldn't remember what it had said. He strained to recall exactly what he had written to David. He closed his eyes, trying to see it again. He remembered starting it with 'Dear David', and he had ended off telling him to be careful, not to trust anyone but that London copper, Owen Sheen. That was good, that was something at least. Had he written dates, other things? He felt sure he had but try as he might, he could not summon the details. Tucker ran a finger over the capitalised words on the front page. He was also pretty sure that he had mentioned the name TOPBRASS, but again he was unclear about how much he had said, or what value it could hold. What he could recall was that TOPBRASS spelt very bad news indeed. For Roddy, and for him, and now maybe for David too.

After flicking through the first few pages, he now recalled that Roddy had been less than methodical. Nothing seemed to be in chronological order. And Roddy's booklet was not simply facsimiles of leaked documents. He had pasted in old newspaper stories, written poems – most didn't really rhyme, but even Tucker could see that a few were not half bad – and transcribed his thoughts in that signature neat print of his about what he thought had gone down, though the latter was pretty cursory. And there were also crosswords, some part-completed, same for word searches which likewise seemed to have been snipped from newspapers over the years. The crosswords made some sense too, because Roddy had always been a man for doing puzzles. Tucker could still see him on the end of the bar scribbling away, working quickly through them.

Chaotic or not, Roddy had been playing detective. The Tucker who now set to work, slowly turning pages and scanning the details, had left all thoughts of booze and self-pity behind him. He searched for the transcribed document that his peeler's nose told him would be most vital here. And then he found it. Before he dug deeper, however, he took time to check the booklet once more, until he was satisfied that this was the one. The source, the beginning. Which, despite Roddy's inane system, Tucker Rodgers knew was the only safe place to start.

TOPBRASS was a walk-in, had literally appeared at an RUC police station in Strabane near the border with Donegal and the Irish Republic in December 1979 and offered his services to Special Branch. According to the record TOPBRASS was a member of the IRA, Belfast Brigade.

Clearly, whatever his rationale for turning and working

for his enemy, TOPBRASS was nobody's fool. The document mentioned that he was Belfast IRA. But to walk into a police station in the city, or even within twenty miles of his home town, ran the risk of being spotted and compromised. By choosing Strabane TOPBRASS had travelled as far as he could from his home turf without leaving Northern Ireland. And Tucker knew that shifts between Christmas and New Year could be quieter than most, especially if the IRA had called an annual ceasefire as they were apt to. Though the document confirmed that TOPBRASS was part of the feared Belfast Brigade it did not mention which command area. Which was a shame as that information could have helped Tucker narrow down where this double agent actually lived. The First Battalion was Andersonstown and Lenadoon; the Second Battalion was the Falls Road and Ballymurphy areas – all West Belfast. The Third Battalion was a conglomeration of nationalist enclaves in the north and east of the city which included Ardoyne, the Markets and Short Strand.

The name of the officer who had submitted the first report was Detective Sergeant Samuel Royce Fenton. It meant nothing to Tucker, who had walked a beat for most of his policing career and rarely rubbed shoulders with Branch men. He'd had little time for the secret police and their superior ways and dark arts. Those guys spent too long staring into the abyss and letting it stare back at them as the old saying went. But he'd bet his last beer that having his name on these documents would mean a bit more to this Fenton boy. Enough to try to dam the leak if he had discovered one. Tucker pushed his glasses up his nose and flicked through the pages, searching for the next Special Branch document. He stopped when he had found what he thought he was looking for, but not before he had read enough to begin to see why Fenton may want to keep his work with TOPBRASS under wraps at all costs. Including murdering a clerical worker like Roddy Grant, who had quite clearly got in way over his head.

Roddy had included a series of newspaper cuttings, with stories of interest neatly framed in red ink. In early 1980 a series of arms finds were made by the police in areas of North and West Belfast, believed to have been hidden by the IRA. Two weeks later an IRA active service unit travelling in a car was rammed on the Grosvenor Road by an undercover RUC police team. The IRA member who was driving the car was killed, three others arrested. Guns and masks were recovered. Police stated they believed the IRA team were en route to carry out a murder. Into 1981. An IRA team failed in their attempt to murder an off-duty prison officer at his home in Bangor County Down, about fifteen miles from Belfast. Tucker could clearly see that TOPBRASS was earning his money and supplying Special Branch with valuable intelligence that was damaging the IRA.

But it was not all good news. In August of the same year a young man from the Clonard area off the Falls Road was reported as missing by his family. A news article quoted his mother who admitted he had been involved in 'a wee bit of trouble' – Tucker translated this as joyriding and petty theft in the area – but he was a 'good boy'. Her little angel had been instructed by the IRA to attend a 'meeting' at a disused factory in the district. Tucker knew what that meant. The guy had been told to turn up and take his punishment, most likely a knee-capping. Street justice, the old Belfast way. The young man had done as instructed but had since disappeared. Tucker turned the page and read the next newspaper clipping. He frowned. The youth had turned up dead a week later, his body dumped on waste ground, shot in the back of the head and with a signed confession in one of his pockets. The IRA had claimed responsibility, said that the guy was a Special Branch informer. Tucker's old copper's nose creased. He didn't buy it. The young man was a hood, a criminal, not the sort of individual that Special Branch would waste their time on. He would have nothing to give them; in fact, he had probably done all he could to keep out of the IRA's way. Hardly a rich mine of information. Roddy had picked up on it too. One page had nothing but two neatly written sentences.

*The young TOPBRASS learns about give and take. But for what he takes others must give.*

Tucker's mouth was suddenly dry. In 1980 and '81 TOPBRASS had gifted the Branch dead Provos, and access to IRA arms dumps. But these things had come at a price. The street criminal had been used as a scapegoat; he had been killed to protect TOPBRASS. No doubt the losses that TOPBRASS's treachery was inflicting on the IRA had aroused their suspicion and anger. They had started to look for the tout. And quite clearly TOPBRASS had given them one. Which meant this Special Branch agent had likely been permitted to torture and kill a low-life criminal to protect his own skin. And Fenton, his handler, must have known about it. Tucker didn't have cast-iron proof of course. But once he read the next stolen document, he didn't need it.

# CHAPTER TWELVE

Sheen had parked up in his spot, behind the blast-resistant walls of Grosvenor Road station.

'So, how are we going to play this?' Aoife asked.

'Assuming I can get the chief on side, we run with the dates in Tucker's letter, Cyprus included. Treat them as an interconnected case. My suspicion is that if we can unlock one, we can make sense of them all.'

'TOPBRASS in other words?' asked Aoife.

'Exactly. The team will work separate strands, but TOPBRASS will be key. You and I will work the Cyprus Three case from March 1987 but this afternoon, I want you to start with Roddy Grant, Tucker's mysterious pen pal. His sister's number was on that invite, so she might be able to help.'

'OK.'

'I'm going to set Geordie and Jackson on the case of Dennis Lamont,' said Sheen. The murdered police officer, the man who had been serving ice cream at his brother's shop in 1984 when a lone gunman had entered and killed him. 'Depending on how this pans out, I'll also ask him to focus on the bus bomb attack in 1986 that killed the British Army squaddies.'

'He'll be a bit happier with that,' commented Aoife. 'And the other date?' She meant the case of Bernadette Bell, the IRA member who had been killed by her own people as an informer and dumped on the side of a road in rural South Armagh.

'We will get to her, but the Cyprus Three case has to come first, and then we begin to work backwards from there.'

Back inside the SHOT main office space, Geordie was still opening letters. Sheen told him to forget it, and gave both he and Jackson a potted summary of the morning's events and then their orders.

'Christ, you mean to say that from having nothing to do this morning but read love letters we're now working four separate cases that are likely all linked? Never rains but it pours in this town,' said Geordie.

'You're not wrong about that,' agreed Sheen. He asked Geordie if he remembered the death of Dennis Lamont. Geordie stood up and shook his head.

'Afraid not, there was just so many,' he explained. Sheen's question probably had sounded naive. In London, the death of a police officer as a result of violent crime had always been big news; plaques were erected, names were readily recalled for years to come. But in Belfast, the catastrophic had become normalised, the stuff of everyday teatime news bulletins. He thought about Tucker Rodgers' slide into evident alcoholism and the implosion of his

134

family life. It was a wonder that there were not many more like him. Probably, there were. 'This is more like the sort of case we should be working, Sheen. What about you?'

'Aoife and I are focusing on the Cyprus Three. Chief's orders,' he replied.

Geordie was stony-faced but didn't voice an opinion.

'But as said, the Cyprus case and the murder of Dennis Lamont might well be linked.'

'The chief on board with this?' asked Geordie.

Aoife spoke as she exited Sheen's office and joined them. Sheen had heard her on the computer and then speaking on the phone while he had filled Geordie and Jackson in.

'Matter of fact he is. Or, he will be,' she said.

Geordie didn't look convinced, and Sheen hoped she was correct.

'Is there something specific I'm looking for?' asked Geordie.

'For now, I just want you digging. Treat it as a standard historical case, a cop's murder that wasn't solved. But don't forget, TOPBRASS is probably key,' replied Sheen. He pointed to the large whiteboard where Dennis Lamont's name and date of death was visible. 'Feedback what you find and hopefully, we can begin to join the dots,' he said and thought, *Until the chief closes this down and kicks us all back in line.*

Geordie said he was on it and then told Jackson to get him the case records and anything else he could find. Jackson's fingers started to work rapidly. Geordie had taken two equally bad ties from his desk drawer and eyed them judiciously.

'I just spoke to Janice Stewart,' said Aoife. 'Roddy Grant's sister,' she clarified.

'Which reminds me,' said Jackson, searching for a sheet of paper on his desk and passing it to Aoife. 'I found some background as requested.'

'Roddy one of us?' asked Sheen. He meant police.

Jackson shook his head.

'No, civilian. But Roddy did work *for* the police. He was a clerical officer. There was not a lot of specifics, but I know that he worked at several different police stations until he retired last year.'

'Same position throughout?' queried Sheen.

Jackson shrugged.

'Clerical officer in the PSNI covers a range of possible jobs. I did it for a summer between school and uni, and it was everything from delivering internal mail to making my uncle tea and fetching records from the archives. I've listed the stations,' said Jackson, nodding at the paper he had passed to Aoife.

Aoife spoke, her expression serious.

'Roddy committed suicide, hung himself,' she said.

Sheen nodded, quickly assimilating this. Tucker's letter had claimed that 'they' had killed Roddy. He thought about the state of Tucker's place, the evidence of a destructive drinking habit, a life in freefall. Not exactly the context from which reliable testimonies tended to emerge. The coroner had clearly released Roddy Grant's body for burial, which meant that the inquest had concluded the cause of death to be suicide. But then Sheen recalled Tucker's photograph on his warrant card, the sharp, perceptive-looking gaze of the younger man who had survived two and a half decades on the beat in the most dangerous city in Europe. So far, the dates Tucker had sent seemed to be meaningful. If they had validity, then perhaps what he had claimed about Roddy Grant's death was also true.

'A police clerical officer could get access to sensitive information,' reflected Sheen. And by definition Roddy must have mixed with police personnel as a matter of course. His friendship with Tucker was evidence of that. No doubt that also explained why Roddy's sister had selected the Shandon Park Golf Club to host his remembrance event. If Roddy mixed in police circles in Belfast it was probably one of his watering holes.

'I asked her about access to Roddy's home. Janice lives in Ballymoney and said she will not be able to come down to Belfast until tomorrow at the earliest. She has a key to the property and seemed willing to help but was definitely a bit perturbed to hear from us,' said Aoife.

Ballymoney was a small town about fifty miles north of Belfast. Sheen could appreciate the woman was being asked to come out of her way and was perhaps at risk of having her life unsettled even further.

Geordie was shrugging on his grey woollen overcoat. Sheen watched his face contort; the guy was still in pain after breaking ribs and ripping his shoulder from its socket when his car was attacked by Dissidents several months back. He'd been hospitalised for more than a week, and of all of the team, he'd been most seriously hurt. And Sheen could vouch that the older you get, the longer the body takes to heal. Not that Geordie ever complained, not about that anyway. Sheen winced too. Geordie had opted for a tie that looked to Sheen

137

like Christmas wrapping paper from the 1970s, which was probably when he'd bought it. Jackson was at the printer. He handed Geordie a sheaf of printouts, which Sheen took to be the case details for the murder of Dennis Lamont, and then returned to his desk.

'What do you think you're doing?' Geordie asked him.

Jackson had started to listen to yet another abusive answer machine message. He put the phone down.

'But Sergeant Brown, you said—'

'Never you mind what I said. School's out. Time to do some proper police work. Get your coat on, Detective Constable Stevens,' he answered, flicking the papers that Jackson had given him and heading for the door. Jackson followed as ordered.

Sheen went to his desk and took out the two copies of the Cyprus Three dossiers he had compiled and handed one to Aoife.

'The Cyprus Three. Names, addresses, family connections. All three members of the IRA unit were originally from West Belfast. Their leader was a guy called Danny Caffery. His brother still lives in the family home. I want both of us to pay him a visit tomorrow,' said Sheen.

'Thanks, I'll read over this,' Aoife said. 'You're going to be late for your meeting with the chief.'

'No, I won't. In fact, time permitting, I'm also going to call into the Shandon Park Golf Club. See if I can shed any light on what happened that night. It looks like it was Tucker's last outing before he sent that letter and disappeared. Enjoy your girls' night with Ava,' he said, grabbing his jacket.

'We will. And you are going to be late,' she said.

By the time Sheen rapped on the door of the chief's office at Ladas Drive station he was ten minutes late for his three-fifteen meeting.

'Come.' Sheen entered. The chief was on a call and raised a finger as Sheen closed the door behind him. The chief made his excuses and ended the call. Sheen braced himself for a bollocking, but the chief asked him to take a seat and whether he wanted anything. Sheen wanted a cup of tea and a smoke, but his eye fell on an expensive-looking coffee machine and the chief took that as a request. He set to work with a lever and coloured capsules. A minute later, after a lot of humming and dribbling, the chief gave Sheen a black coffee and sat opposite with one of his own. Tasted a bit weak despite the theatrics of its creation, but Sheen had skipped lunch and appreciated it.

'So, DI Sheen, explain. You said something about a missing person and it being complicated,' prompted the chief.

Sheen took a breath and started talking. For the most part, the chief listened, his eyes focused on the desk and fingertips supporting his chin. He stopped Sheen only twice. First to confirm that Tucker Rodgers was definitely a retired member of the Police Service of Northern Ireland, and to ask Sheen if Roddy Grant's death was the subject of a current investigation.

'No, his body was released for burial. His sister told us he committed suicide,' said Sheen.

The chief gave him a small nod in reply.

'Those dates, run them by me one more time,' asked the chief.

Sheen again consulted his notepad, which he had used to relay the details. Sheen had given the chief an executive summary first time round, months and years, rather than detailing specific days. He was conscious of having arrived at his scheduled meeting late, so his abbreviated version amounted to a measure of expediency only. But now Sheen's gut told him to hold back, even just a little, and keep his powder dry on this. He had resisted the temptation to ask for forgiveness rather than permission by coming clean with the chief in the first place, but nice boys came last. To overburden his boss with details would risk turning him off the idea. He needed to sell it as a clear pathway, stepping-stones that made sense and would be logical to follow. Which, of course, was what he hoped he had here.

'March of eighty-seven is certainly a match for the Cyprus Three,' he said. 'But the others,' he said, and raised both palms, showing them to Sheen, his implication clear. They were as empty as the case Sheen was suggesting he might have. 'Your remit was Cyprus. I understand that you are intrigued, as am I, but we can't have our energies diffused. And we have an understanding, no walk-in cases,' reminded the chief. On the latter point, both Sheen and the chief were in firm agreement. In general.

'My thinking is that we could be working on related events, historical crimes that link together. If we can make sense of that then we shed light on the individual cases, and most pressingly the Cyprus Three,' argued Sheen.

'Sheen, this is not London. Belfast in the 1980s was in the grip of what amounted to a slow-burning civil war, and the police were caught in the middle of it. There are just too many cases, some will never see the light of day. You know that's the reality of the task that faces your team. What you're proposing is to start a crusade of some kind that we have neither the time nor the resources to win,' said the chief.

'Not at all, sir. In fact, we have already isolated likely crimes from the era that seem to match Tucker's dates. The execution of an IRA informer, a policeman who was murdered while off duty, a busload of squaddies who were blown up.'

The chief was shaking his head.

'Which will spread you and your team paper-thin. No.'

'Sir, not if we aim to find the common denominator. I have a hunch that if we can unlock one then we will unlock them all. And think about the turnover. This could amount to three or four well-publicised historical cases put to bed for the price of one,' offered Sheen.

The chief went quiet. He clearly was thinking about Sheen's spin on this, and the potential public relations windfall that could be harvested. On the other hand, the opposite was also true as Sheen knew all too well. Rather than just one case going belly-up and the PSNI being dragged through the mud by the media, Sheen's proposal held the potential for a multiplication effect when it came to bad press.

'The common denominator you refer to being this so-called TOPBRASS person? If indeed this even refers to an individual,' said the chief.

Sheen could feel this slipping from his grasp again.

'Yes, sir. But we also need to think about Tucker Rodgers in this. He's one of our own, and there's no doubt at all that he was terrified enough to run from his home with nothing more than the clothes on his back. For what it's worth I believe he is alive, but I think he's in danger,' Sheen said.

'According to his son, the man's a drunk. How can we even be sure all of this is not some kind of alcohol-induced psychosis?' said the chief, now getting to his feet. His usual sign that the meeting, and the discussion, were at an end.

Sheen stood up too and quickly explained what they had discovered when they visited Tucker's residence: the phone line cut, the door open and evidence that the lock had been picked.

The chief exhaled and raised a hand for Sheen to stop.

'You did the right thing bringing this to my attention. I'm aware you had a choice. And I am going to admit I am torn on this,' said the chief, who then lapsed into silence. Sheen had made his best pitch and speaking now would serve only to rile the man. He waited it out. The Chief turned to him. Sheen braced himself for the worst.

'But because of your transparency and the fact that drunk or sober Tucker Rodgers risked his life every day of his career as a serving officer, I am going to give you the green light. Missing person's cases have a tendency to gather dust.'

'Thank you, sir. I appreciate this,' replied Sheen.

'But Cyprus comes first. Do not disappear on a treasure hunt, DI Sheen. I expect results. And regular updates,' he said.

'Sir,' Sheen agreed. 'By the way, does the name TOPBRASS mean anything to you?'

'Not a thing,' replied the chief without any hesitation as they exited his office. 'Given what you have told me about Tucker Rodgers' phone line being tampered with and home entered, tread carefully, DI Sheen.'

The chief took a left and disappeared in long strides down the corridor, leaving Sheen to think about who or what might be out there. A common denominator in numerous deaths across many years. Someone highly placed and highly proficient who had caused Tucker Rodgers to run and hide. Tucker's words, written in haste, repeated in Sheen's mind as he navigated his way out of Ladas Drive.

*Trust nobody*
*Watch your back*

# CHAPTER THIRTEEN

'How you doing, mate? Mind if I have a quick word?' asked Geordie.

He flipped open his warrant card so the man behind the counter of the small vaping shop on the Dublin Road on the south side of Belfast city centre could see. This was the commercial property where the off-duty policeman Dennis Lamont had been murdered in 1984. Jackson, who had joined him, now did the same. Geordie frowned as he glanced at his rookie partner. He looked like a Mormon in that suit, and as soon as they were done here, Geordie was taking him for an Ulster fry. The guy was built like a jockey's whip. And Geordie was more than peckish. That said, there was no denying that Jackson had a good eye and an ability to get things done. As soon as they'd parked up, Jackson had noted that the property was partitioned. Namely the vape store where they now stood and a mobile phone shack next to it, the sort of unit that unlocked and sold second-hand phones no questions asked. It had taken Jackson two calls and less than three minutes to run a check on the address. According to police records the property should be a single business unit, not two. In other words, somebody had partitioned it into two separate enterprises but neglected to let Belfast Council know or ask for planning permission.

The bloke behind the glass counter of the vaping store eyed him warily but nodded.

'Why do you want to speak to me?'

Geordie estimated early forties, but the guy was carrying a bit too much weight, and it put a few years on him. Not that Geordie could really throw bricks in that particular greenhouse. It was only because the stubble that coated the guy's chin and flabby throat were still dark that Geordie was ready to place him under fifty. He wore a cheap, ill-fitting tracksuit with a food stain down the front.

'Well it's nothing to do with the fact that you're subletting that unit to the man next door,' said Geordie. The guy's eyes widened. He looked like he was about to deny it, but Geordie cut him off. 'I'm not messing with you. I don't care about that, but the council will. I'd declare it if I was you.' The man's expression morphed from caution to confusion, mixed with a shot of irritation. No helping some people. Geordie asked his name. He hesitated and then spoke.

'Alex Lamont,' he said. Which was the same name that Jackson had dug up as the owner of the property. Dennis Lamont's son. The man he needed to speak to, but Geordie needed to step carefully, he'd read the case notes.

'Look, we work for SHOT, the historical investigation team. We're looking into the murder of Dennis Lamont in 1984,' said Geordie. Alex Lamont flinched, as though Geordie had prodded him in the ribs. He could have said more but instead, he waited, gave the guy a bit of take up time.

'That's my da,' he said quietly. Geordie noted he was looking down, into the corner. 'Was,' he qualified.

Geordie sighed, he hated this.

'I'm sure this is torture for you, but if you can it would help us if you'd answer a few questions,' he said.

Alex Lamont sniffed and shrugged. He lifted a vaping pipe that looked to Geordie like a refashioned car exhaust and inhaled, the vapour filling the space between them. It smelt of bubblegum.

'What's the point? They looked into it and found nothing. The bastard that done it's probably dead by now,' he said. Geordie had no answer to that, but at least Lamont was speaking.

Jackson replied, 'Even if he's dead, there is still a point. No matter how much time has passed, we won't give up on victims. This is what we do.' Geordie nodded in agreement.

'What would you know about it? You boys have it easy doing this job today. Back then it was carnage,' said Lamont, taking another draw from his pipe.

'I do know. My father was in the RUC, and my uncle is still a police officer. I remember watching my dad leaving for work and saying a prayer that he would not get killed. Every day. I understand what it was like, and I know how things can stay with you.'

Alex Lamont remained quiet, his eyes lowered. Good on Jackson, he'd spoken well. Geordie hoped that Lamont would not ask who his uncle was, might take away from Jackson's efforts to be someone he could relate to. It seemed like a good time to push ahead.

'It happened here, right?' Lamont looked up at Geordie and nodded. He pointed at the partition that divided the premises. And suddenly, Geordie understood why it was there. The case details that Jackson had provided said that Dennis Lamont had been murdered in front of his seven-year-old son. No wonder the guy wanted to make the old property unrecognisable.

'Can you tell me what you recall from that day?'

'You mean what the killer looked like? I wish I could,' he replied.

'He didn't wear a mask?' This was unusual by the standards of the time. Especially as Dennis Lamont had been killed during business hours, and on a long Belfast July day too.

'No, that much I do know. But all I can remember was his voice, what he ordered. And then the shooting started. After that . . .' Lamont's words trailed off and Geordie could see he was struggling to keep his composure. 'After that, all I can remember seeing was my da, on the floor,' he said.

It felt like he was twisting the knife by asking him more, but Geordie knew that sometimes small details could be key, and they could remain overlooked after investigators got into a groove of thinking about a case.

'What was it he said?'

'He said, "Do you have any mint choc chip?" We did,

but it was not in the trays. My da turned around and said he'd grab some. And then I heard the shots,' he said.

Geordie thanked him, though he felt like a bastard making the guy unpick the scab from a wound that would likely never really heal.

'Is there anything else? Anything at all that you can remember from that time that your da might have said, anything that was going on in his working life that stands out? Maybe, if I could have a chat with your mother?'

Alex Lamont shook his head, hit the vape pipe again and exhaled two jets of white vapour from his nostrils.

'Mum's dead. Breast cancer, a couple of years now. That's when I inherited this place. It's a living, but it's weird working here,' he said. 'You know Da hardly ever did shifts in the parlour. It was only because Mum had a summer flu that he stepped in, rather than close the place in July like,' explained Alex. 'She never stopped thinking about that.'

A thought came to Geordie.

'Did your da keep any documents, anything that might have detailed people who he was wary of at the time, people he was scared of?'

Alex shook his head, but then stopped.

'I still have his old RUC diaries, you know, the notes he kept about his day-to-day duty. It was something he liked to do. I never understood it as a kid, it was like self-inflicted homework as far as I could see. But I get it now. I think every day he came home alive was worth recording, maybe it made the madness more manageable?' suggested Alex.

Geordie said he understood, and he did. He knew a lot of guys who did the same over the years and Alex's analysis sounded spot on to him. And this was precisely what he needed.

'You don't have them here by any chance, do you?'

Alex slid off the stool on which he sat, asked Geordie and Jackson to hold the fort and then disappeared behind the counter. A couple of minutes later he returned with a white plastic bag. Inside were four A5 notepads, each as thick as Geordie's thumb. Geordie thanked him and flicked through one. It was filled with handwritten notes, all dated.

'I live in the apartment upstairs,' he explained.

'Mind if I borrow these? I'll return them to you,' assured Geordie.

'Long as you do,' he said. Geordie packed the notepads up and thanked him. 'Listen, the first investigation said that the gun used to murder my da was a police pistol. Were you aware of that?' Geordie stopped. He shook his head. He glanced at Jackson who was already jotting the information down in his notepad.

'That's a fact,' said Alex. 'And they still never managed to get the guy.'

Geordie wanted to tell him that he would be the one to find out the truth and that he would leave no stone unturned. But he'd learnt long ago not to make promises that you could not be certain of keeping. As they left the shop Geordie noted that he no longer had an appetite. A big gust of wind blew along the Dublin Road, raising a gyre of fallen leaves and litter which circled them before collapsing to the pavement. He wasn't prone to flights of fancy, but that felt like the ghost of Dennis Lamont, calling on him to remember the fate he had endured. A cop, who had worked to keep the darkness at bay in Belfast city, murdered in cold blood in front of his son, with a police-issue weapon.

# CHAPTER FOURTEEN

After Sheen had left for his meeting with Chief Stevens, Aoife received a text from Ava to say that she wanted to stay on for an after-school debating club. It gave her an hour to play with, probably more. She scanned the list of police stations where Roddy Grant had worked over his career. One in particular caught her attention, and she used a yellow highlighter to emphasise it.

Castlereagh RUC station. Also known as the Holding Centre.

It was a well-known interrogation centre with a grisly reputation and also a place where RUC Special Branch and British intelligence officers crossed paths and sometimes crossed swords. Both groups had been at the cutting edge of an intelligence-led war against the IRA. The information provided by Jackson did not say exactly what Roddy's job had been, or how long Roddy had been employed there. She made a note to pass this onto Sheen and also to mention it when she met Roddy's sister at his home the following day. Aoife turned her attention to the pages of information Sheen had left her about the Cyprus Three.

The main man was clearly Danny Caffery, the Officer Commanding of the IRA unit who were killed by the SAS. But it was the woman who Aoife wanted to learn more about. Monica Gleeson had been the only female member of the IRA unit and one of a minority of female IRA volunteers in the organisation. Aoife knew that IRA units in the 1980s operated in a closed cell structure or active service units. Secretive and insulated from one another, many of these small teams had proved virtually impossible to infiltrate. Which was exactly the point: it was a precaution to guard against informers and spies in the ranks. So how had this young woman earned her place in what must have been an elite IRA active service unit? Aoife read the first few lines from the summary Sheen had put together and found her answer.

*Early records suggest she was involved in the transportation of arms and explosives over the Irish border. She was so good at it that the soldiers on sentry duty knew her by name and used to chat her up.*

Aoife could immediately see the benefits of having a female member of the IRA team. While men in the area were being frisked and harassed by the army, Monica Gleeson could walk on by pushing a pram, with a bomb under the blankets, not a baby. It gave them an edge, but it also spoke volumes about what sort of character this young woman must have been. Cool, very cool. But also, as Aoife read on, Gleeson was incredibly ruthless too.

*In 1985 Monica Gleeson was caught in a car with a man known to be in the IRA near the Donegal border with the Irish Republic. Police believed she was driving him over the border to be interrogated and probably killed as an informer. She did a few months on remand and the case fell apart, and then Gleeson went to ground.*

No doubt she had been welcomed by Danny Caffery into his unit, Aoife surmised. Shooting someone in the heat of a firefight was one thing, but luring a person to certain death, and probably not a good one, that required even more, a cold commitment. And look how it had ended. Here was a woman who had faced a bloody and violent death at an age not much older than Aoife was now. It was arguably the final outcome of the choices she had made. But then again, Aoife also knew that sometimes life was not so clean cut. Children growing up in places like West Belfast in the 1970s and '80s did so at a time when many accepted norms and values had been put on hold and nobody really played by the rulebook. In some ways, it was a miracle that anyone managed to get out of that time alive and in one piece.

And yet, Aoife had been raised in an intensely nationalist district, one where the IRA had held sway. Her own mother had foolishly got entangled with one of the most dangerous members of that organisation, a man who had left an indelible mark on her family in ways that made Aoife shudder. She pushed the thought of this away. She had opted for a different path, albeit under very different political skies, with Northern Ireland transitioned from civil war to a hard-negotiated peace. She had become a police officer, something she was proud of, something she knew her daughter could see, a model for the right path. But the question of nature versus nurture was always there, and maybe the argument would never really be resolved. Aoife grabbed her car keys and headed for the door. Sheen's information included an address for Monica Gleeson and as he was apt to tell her, if you want to be a detective, you have to rap on a lot of doors.

As she parked up on the steep incline of Hillhead Drive in West Belfast, Aoife's first thought was that nurture had just taken a hit. Although this little district was very much in a nationalist, working-class heartland, it was clearly a small oasis of middle-class exclusivity. Neatly presented detached and semi-detached homes with spacious gardens, the street was quiet and looked like it would have been populated by small business owners or publicans forty years ago. Aoife approached the front door of what had been Monica Gleeson's address and pushed the bell. But all the same, Caffery had selected Monica Gleeson to join his elite cell of IRA volunteers. A young woman who had grown up in this home, but who had been prepared to ferry a man to his death across the border, and to risk her life and liberty by shipping guns and ammunition through British Army checkpoints. A curtain moved behind the glass front door and then it was opened. A woman, probably in her seventies, appeared. Almost luminous green eyes and short feathered hair that was dyed a bold coppery red. She had a great complexion and was dressed in a patterned jumpsuit that would have been more appropriate for a woman a third of her age. But, like the daring hair, she managed to carry it off. Aoife showed her warrant card and introduced herself, then asked the woman if she was a relative of Monica Gleeson.

'I am Mairead Gleeson. Her mother,' she said, and one hand moved to where a small gold medal rested at her throat. 'Police?' she said, and then, her moment of slight disorientation seemed to pass. 'What's this about?'

'I work for a unit called SHOT. We investigate old cases, likely miscarriages of justice—'

'I know, I heard about your team. On the news,' she interrupted. Mairead Gleeson opened the door and beckoned Aoife inside. 'You don't mind removing your shoes, do you?' she asked.

Aoife popped off her shoes and set them on the mat, a little self-conscious of her yellow socks, and suddenly feeling a little exposed as she followed Mairead Gleeson into the first room on her left. The carpet was a myriad of orange and yellow swirls like Van Gogh had dropped acid and went into interior design. The wooden dining table and chairs where Aoife now took a seat and the small brown sideboard all confirmed that Mairead Gleeson had not redecorated since the early seventies. The place was impeccably clean, however, and though the carpet was a little worn and the chair on which she sat was a bit lumpy, Aoife knew that this was doubtless the 'best room' in the house, a place to entertain special guests and show off. It was also likely to have been as it was when Monica Gleeson was growing up. She thought again about her police record, and what it had said about the ruthless young woman who had ended up shot to death in Cyprus.

Mairead Gleeson said she would fix them both a nice cup of tea before Aoife could object. Five minutes later she was sipping good strong tea from a china cup and eating a cherry scone covered with butter and jam. She'd missed lunch.

'So, you finally got round to investigating Cyprus?' asked Mairead Gleeson, pouring herself a cup of tea and adding a slice of lemon using silver tongs. She stared at Aoife; her eyes were so green it was almost unsettling. 'There was an enquiry at the time, I mean,' she added.

'Were you happy with the outcome?' countered Aoife. The original inquest concluded that the killings were lawful.

Mairead closed her eyes and shrugged.

'It was no surprise,' she answered, and glanced at a framed photograph that hung on the wall to Aoife's right. A schoolgirl, smiling in a posed portrait, hand on her lap. She looked mildly embarrassed, her head held slightly to one side as though to deflect the attention of the camera. Her long brown hair covered one side of her face and flowed in a middle parting all the way to her shoulders that were slightly hunched.

'Is this Monica?'

Mairead gave a small smile and nodded.

'She was fifteen when that was taken. I didn't know it then, but she had been more or less recruited into the IRA by that time. She left school a year later,' she said.

'You don't seem to approve,' commented Aoife quietly.

'Of her joining the IRA? We were never that way inclined. I mean, look,' she said, motioning at the decor, as though her dining room was evidence of a life free from all corruption and taint.

'If you're not a republican family, then how did Monica become involved?'

'Bad company, teenage rebellion?' offered Mairead Gleeson. 'She was strong-willed. And she had a nose for injustice. She could see what was happening in the streets. I think she got intoxicated with the idea that she could fight for a romantic cause,' she sighed and raised a scone to her lips but then returned it to her plate. 'What I'm saying probably doesn't make sense to you.'

Aoife thought about her own daughter, Ava's already ingrained need to oppose the injustices she perceived in the world. Her child was being coached in an after-school debating club, but what if she was forced to witness burning barricades and armed soldiers on the streets? What if she was exposed to revolutionary idealism instead of memes on social media?

'I think it makes a lot of sense in fact,' she said.

'Maybe it was my fault. I had an old uncle who used to visit. He'd fought in the Irish War of Independence in 1920, liked to tell tall tales of the old IRA,' Mairead said.

'Ms Gleeson, we intend to be very thorough, cover all angles. If the facts point to unlawful killings by the British authorities, that will be our conclusion. You mentioned that Monica got led astray by bad company, the wrong kind of people. Does the nickname TOPBRASS mean anything?'

Mairead Gleeson paused in the process of stirring her cup of tea, a frown creased her otherwise impressively flawless forehead.

'No. Why do you ask that?' She was observing Aoife with that same intensity as before, and Aoife could tell that she was discreetly computing.

She paused for a beat before answering. She opted to give Mairead Gleeson a straight answer. There was no other way she could see that might encourage the same from her, assuming she had something of value to tell.

'We suspect there may be a link between this name and the killing of your daughter in Cyprus. But we need more to go on, we need the families to step up and help us if they can. Did Monica have a friend, someone she may have mentioned in passing? Did she ever discuss the Cyprus mission with you or another family member, or say anything that at the time you may not have felt comfortable sharing with the police or the inquest?'

Mairead scoffed humourlessly, her eyes back on the portrait of the girl she had lost.

'My daughter was quite the urban guerrilla,' she said, but there was no pride in her voice; it was suddenly thick with reproach and old hurts. 'She told me nothing. It took the peelers to kick in my door looking for her, for me to find out she was up to her neck in it in the first place.' She was no longer really speaking to Aoife at all, her eyes had darkened and her jaw was clenched. 'The humiliation of it,' she spat. 'She was smart, and she could have been anything, done anything she set her mind to. But she fell in with that lot. And the only way the Brits could stop her was to shoot her like a rabid dog on the street,' she said. She turned to Aoife, blinked away tears which threatened but which she did not permit to flow.

'Who was it that led her astray? You mentioned bad company.'

'That bastard Danny Caffery got her involved. I know it,' she growled, and what had been simmering beneath the surface a few moments before briefly boiled over in a show of real anger. She may hold her middle-class gentility in high regard, but Mairead Gleeson, like her hair and probably like her daughter, also had some real fire.

Aoife nodded and thanked her, then stood up to leave. So far nothing. If Mairead knew what or who TOPBRASS was she was not for telling, though Aoife's instinct told her she probably did not. And apparently Monica Gleeson's closest comrade had been Danny Caffery, who was also dead. Like Monica, he would never tell his secrets.

'Thanks for your time, Ms Gleeson. I appreciate that me dragging all this up is not easy for you,' said Aoife, and she meant it. She could see that Mairead Gleeson was still seething at her mention of Danny Caffery but seemed to have it under control. 'I just hoped that TOPBRASS might ring a bell for you.' One more try, while her blood was up.

Mairead Glesson glared at her and lifted the tray of crockery with enough force to make it rattle.

'You want to know what bloody bell it rings for me? A police call sign, or an army code. I remember them parked up on my street, right outside this house for hours at a time, their idiot codes barking back and forth on their radios, driving everyone to distraction,' she said.

Aoife's eyes widened. Mairead Gleeson quickly glanced away. She took a breath and apologised, her previous decorum re-established. Aoife told her there was no need and that she would see herself out, but Mairead waited as she put her shoes back on and wished her luck at the door.

Aoife checked underneath her vehicle for improvised explosive devices favoured by Dissident republicans, and found none. She gave the process the due attention it required, but as she got into her car her mind was on what

Mairead Gleeson had said. That TOPBRASS sounded like a codename, not a nickname, and one that had military connotations. Again, she thought about Roddy Grant, who had worked at Castlereagh, the infamous Holding Centre that housed spooks and Special Branch secret police. She quickly sent a text to Jackson and asked him to get some specifics on what Roddy's work as a clerical officer entailed and how long he had been there. Aoife glanced at the Gleeson home as she pulled away. Mairead Gleeson stood alone at the front window. Aoife could not be certain, but she appeared to be weeping. Aoife needed to collect her daughter, and she needed to hug that child and tell her that she loved her, and that she was proud of her. And first thing in the morning she needed to speak to Roddy Grant's sister, Janice, and check out the house where, if Tucker Rodgers was to be believed, Roddy had been murdered.

# PART THREE

BERNADETTE BELL, BAD LUCK AND BUDDHA

# CHAPTER FIFTEEN

He'd drunk the water.

The heat and thirst had got the better of him, and he'd done it without thinking. But he knew it was a mistake as soon as he had set the glass down on the counter and tasted the mineral, odd aftertaste. Bit earthy, like soil. The cramps had started soon after and then nausea had followed. He didn't tell the others; the slegging they'd give him. He would never live it down. His three mates had already been in the holiday apartments for a week, had managed to get a base tan and, of course, knew to stick to bottled water. After the initial wave, Brian Maguire's bad tummy had settled down and he'd been fairly sure that all would be fine. By the time it was obvious that he was wrong, it was already too late.

His guts twisted and rolled as he cracked a cold sweat under his sun hat and shades, struggling to keep up, but failing, falling further behind the others. PJ turned and gave him a nod, his eyes enquired if Maguire was all right, if he should be concerned. Maguire nodded and returned a thumbs up. He pointed to his stomach and then made a wave with one hand but shooed him on. PJ shrugged, hurried and caught up with the two other Irish holidaymakers who had strolled a few lengths down the street. This was just a dry run, recon. If it had been the real thing then Maguire's response would have been enough for them to abort. Maguire would have been the first to call it. As it was, he persevered, what odds? The others were talking loudly, sharing some joke or other, their flip-flops clapping on the dry concrete of the sunlit street. Monica and Danny were linked arm in arm, and PJ, the tallest now, walked a little further ahead of them. He had a can of lager in one hand, the rolled-up towels under his other arm. The beach was at the end of the road. But the towels contained bags of flour, weighing seven pounds exactly, not swimming togs and cans of beer or lemonade. Seven pounds was what PJ had calculated would be needed to do the bandstand and anyone on it. Brit soldiers were scheduled to perform there in two days' time, for the Queen's official birthday. Today walk by and select. Tomorrow was to assemble, prime and position. The day after they would be long gone. Maguire gasped, then he stopped dead and held onto the hot iron railing of a garden gate. He was going to shit himself; he was sure of it. He turned slowly, testing whether he could walk without pebble-dashing his shorts, eyes frantically searching for a garden bush, anywhere he could swing his arse into and let it go.

Which was how he spotted the fella in the milky yellow short-sleeved shirt as he walked across the street. There was nothing at all on the surface to make Maguire suspicious, but his eye was drawn to him all the same. The bloke's arms were well tanned and thick as a leg of lamb. He had dark brown hair that was almost black and barbered to a short back and sides style. He wore white trainers, tightly laced, like a man on the starting line of a race. Maguire had only seen him from behind. In years to come, he'd replay this moment again and again in his mind's eye, trying to capture what it was that raised his hackles, and why it was he never saw fit to call the alarm. Maybe the way the guy moved: he was stealthy and precise, not a guy on his holidays. Maybe it was the way his shirt was not tucked into his trousers. More than anything, it was the trainers. The guy wore them like they were functional as boots, not a recreational option. That was the thing about plain-clothed soldiers, they always looked exactly that. Soldiers who were trying to appear like civilians, but who always ended up looking like men in uniform, of a sort, nonetheless. Exactly the same way Provos on the streets of Belfast were easy to spot for those with their eyes open and who lived on the inside. They wore their trainers and Doc Martens in the same way the guy in the yellow shirt wore his civilian disguise. In the dreams, nightmares, that would haunt Brian Maguire in the years to come, he tried to cry out and warn his mates, only to find his throat clogged with burning tar, and his feet stuck in quick-drying cement. In reality, he'd remained silent, with suspicion blossoming in his brain like poison weeds, but in the main struggling to control his cramping intestines, still half a block behind them. Even if he had managed to shout out, there was no guarantee that it would have changed a thing.

Aside from the fact he would be a dead man.

The bloke in the lemon shirt pulled a snub-nosed semi-automatic gun that was concealed in his waist and accelerated around Maguire's comrades until he was standing adjacent to PJ, with the piece pointed at him. It happened so fast. PJ's eyes filled with a momentary recognition, and his smile bled away. People who claimed to have lost memories of traumatic events were full of shit as far as Maguire was concerned. PJ's face was branded in Maguire's brain and it would die only when he did. At least, that was Maguire's hope; that things like this did die and didn't haunt your soul, walk with you along the roads of the night.

PJ dropped the roll of towels and moved, fast for a big guy. He stepped in front of Monica, tried to use his frame to block the lemon-shirted assassin's line of sight. He must have known it was all over, for him anyway. But his final act of selflessness was squandered. To the right three other men had materialised, dressed in the same casual manner, with identical semi-automatic handguns raised and their faces hard and set. PJ was hit first. Maguire watched his body dance a jig before collapsing like a boneless puppet to the concrete. No blood, not in that instant. Just the bark of the gun, three quick and controlled bursts in a savage diagonal across PJ's torso, a track that guaranteed total annihilation of his vital internal organs.

The slickness of those men, the way they emerged as one and, until they'd permitted themselves to be spotted, how they had managed to blend in so very well, it should have been enough to tell him they were not dealing with ordinary cops or even bog-standard Brit soldiers. But it was those clipped, controlled bursts from the semi that confirmed it for Brian Maguire. He knew that managing that kind of gun could be tricky. But lemon shirt made it seem easy, his leg of lamb forearms flexing as he rotated the barrel. PJ was dead before his body had hit the deck. The gunman stepped towards PJ's body and plugged three more rounds into the back of his neck.

Maguire stayed still and then slowly edged backwards along the fence. A woman emerged from the house opposite, and heads appeared over balconies to his right, confusion and questions. Maguire said nothing, sweating harder now but thoughts of foul water were gone. His stomach was a dry walnut, and his guts numb, no longer his concern, no longer even really there. It had been three seconds since the lemon shirt had opened fire. His two accomplices moved on Danny and Monica. Danny turned and ran but remembered to criss-cross the street rather than dart in a straight line. His training on how to avoid a sniper's bullet there for him, despite his panic and terror. The killer with sandy-coloured hair and wearing a blue T-shirt tracked him with his gun for a split second and then started after him, arms pumping at his sides rapidly making ground. And Danny was a fit guy, still played Gaelic football and trained hard. Maguire melted around a corner that led to a narrow street, dark and cool in shadows. As he heard the slap of Danny's flip-flops on the concrete, approaching fast, Maguire slowly crabbed along the wall but something made him freeze. Another drill of semi-automatic gunfire and two clipped shots that ricocheted up and down the stone-fronted street.

Monica.

Ripped in half by a scourge of bullets.

Finished off where she had fallen.

Danny careered past. Maguire was a statue. He was moss on the wall; he was sun-baked brick, cold in the late-morning shade. He caught a glimpse of the side of Danny's face, a mask of fear and adrenaline, and then he was gone, the assassin in the blue T-shirt almost on top of him. Seconds later another fierce burst of gunfire and after a long pause two more shots. And then nothing at all, just the beat of Maguire's pulse in his ears and the rasp of his breath. Now he ran, made it most of the way down the alley and nearly fell over a pair of bare feet that were sticking out from behind a bin. Maguire stumbled on, but then skidded to a halt. In the far distance, he could hear a wail of sirens.

He turned and searched the darkened doorway for the owner of the dirty feet. The guy looked up at Maguire, startled, bright eyes lit like lamps in the worn leather hide of his face. Maguire spoke little Greek, so instead he pulled out his wallet and showed him a Cypriot fiver. The tramp's eyes widened and then narrowed as he returned them to Maguire, suspicious of what he wanted for the money. Maguire managed to break a smile, mimed drinking from an imaginary bottle. He pointed to the empty bottle of Ouzo on the ground and then signalled to him; one for you, one for me, what you say? The tramp didn't need time to think. He scrambled to his feet, and Maguire forced a laugh, embraced him like an old mucker and accepted the man's arm around his shoulder in return as they staggered towards the sunlit mouth of the entry that led into a small shopping district. Maguire had parked the day before on the other side. Over the border and into Northern Cyprus.

Two uniformed cops skidded to a halt as Maguire and his new mate rounded the corner. The tramp had given Maguire his empty bottle and was waving the five quid note in front of them like a pass, repeating something over and over and patting Maguire's shoulder. Maguire had untucked his shirt and now raised the sticky mouth of the dry Ouzo bottle to his own. The cops paused, but for only a moment. Maguire felt the heat of their stares as they assessed him and his companion. The ruse had worked. One of the cops shoved Maguire out of the way and then both were running hard along the alley, back the way Maguire had come, where the screech of tyres and much louder sirens could be heard.

Maguire kept his head down and walked away from the tramp who was shouting something and still holding his loot. Good luck to him. At that moment, Maguire would have given anything to change places with the down-and-out. And really, how far was he from that man? He had the clothes on his back and the little cash that was in his wallet. And he was alone, with the three most trusted friends and comrades of his life cut down and lying lifeless on a foreign street. He was a dead man walking. But even as Maguire summoned to mind the memorised details of a contingency plan he'd hoped he would never have to use, questions fired and blasted in his brain like so many gunshots.

*How did they know?*

*How did I escape?*

*Who sold us out?*

# CHAPTER SIXTEEN

Brian Maguire blinked away the memories and checked his watch. He'd been lost in thought about what had happened in Cyprus for over ten minutes. That was when he had heard the tell-tale latch and screech of a gate opening across the street. And not just any gate. Somebody had opened what Maguire still referred to as PJ's gate, though of course his former comrade was dead and buried. Back in the old days, he and PJ had agreed to keep their front gates unoiled so as to be forewarned of an uninvited approach and ensure that each could be ready to offer backup to the other. This was before the advent of CCTV, or indeed cameras in doorbells that broadcast to your mobile phone. His nephew had recently tried to explain the latter to him, but he'd left Maguire behind at the doorbell. And besides, the original alarm worked just fine. PJ's gate pulled old wires in Maguire's head which rang a bell. Unfortunately, his reflexes were less responsive. He'd made it off the yoga mat in time to see PJ's front door close. But he had noted a dark saloon car that didn't belong was parked outside. Question was, who was the stranger that had come to visit, and what did they want at PJ's house?

Up until that interruption, he'd been doing Buddha proud.

The steeple of ash on the incense stick that had been burning on the windowsill toppled into the brass saucer. The little that he had taught himself about physics was enough to conclude that in this world, it was the inescapable way of things. The movement from order to chaos, the transition from structure to dissolution. Nothing had been lost, of course, only the form. The incense stick was still here, but in a different way. Now it was molecules of smoky odour, the bead of light that was gently fading from its hot tip, the warmth that exuded as it did so, and the ash that dusted the dull brass saucer and powdered the glossy windowsill. His mind returned once more to the way PJ had collapsed, cut in two with a rain of high-velocity bullets and already dead before he hit the hot pavement of a Cyprus street over thirty years before. Physics was physics, but Maguire was pretty convinced that PJ, Danny and Monica had been lost, snuffed out in those moments. He didn't know for certain whether they still existed elsewhere or not. Sometimes, the ash is all we are left with, and our certainties grow from it. And for Maguire, the death of his comrades, his friends, had been the beginning of a new world of problems he had never foreseen. First the whispers that had followed Maguire about and then the writing on the wall – literally, on more than one occasion. And all because he had been the only one of the four to survive and make it back alive.

171

Maguire closed his eyes, tasted the last of the incense and tried to clean his mind.

*Do not dwell in the past, do not dream of the future, concentrate the mind on the present moment.*

He had to hand it to old Buddha. He had a go-to saying for damn near everything. Matter of fact concentrating on the moment was exactly what Maguire had been straining to achieve as he had meditated in the small front bedroom of his terraced home in Andersonstown, West Belfast. It was a contemplative space for him, a safe space. Sometimes used as a spare room or office depending on the need and also where he most liked to work on his yoga. The wee room had an excellent view of the cul-de-sac street on which he lived. From its window, Maguire could see people coming and going. The residential equivalent of sitting with your back to the wall and a view of the door in a pub. In fact, perhaps that was why he found this room so conducive to his moments of meditation. In a previous life, it had been necessary to wait, and remain watchful. First on the lookout for the Brits and peelers, and then for his former comrades who no longer met his eye.

As well as offering an excellent vantage point, sounds were also funnelled down the terraced street and arrived clear and clean at his home, here on the end, nestled in the corner. And there it was again. That tell-tale latch and screech of PJ's gate opening. Maguire peered between the partly closed Venetian blinds, making sure he remained cloaked in shadow. He watched as a man emerged from what had been PJ's home. He walked towards the dark saloon that Maguire had clocked. Maguire silently quantified him. Tall, but not gangly. Well set, but not bulky. He wore a tan-coloured leather jacket that looked like it might have been fashionable around the same time Maguire managed to escape with his life across the border to Northern Cyprus, but this fella was younger than Maguire. He reminded him of photographs he had seen of the 1916 revolutionary Michael Collins, the big frame and the set of his jaw. But, unlike Collins, this guy didn't sport that unruly Irish mop of hair that would reappear on JFK fifty years later, and nor did he have the plumpish face that Collins never quite managed to shed. Maguire watched the man as he performed a well-rehearsed security check on his motor, running his hands under each wheel rim and quickly checking under the car for a pipe bomb booby that would explode as soon as he turned the key in the ignition. The checks told Maguire what he needed to know. Big Mick Collins was a peeler.

As Maguire gazed unblinking at him, the peeler suddenly turned and looked directly at Maguire's home, stared intently at the very upstairs window from which Maguire looked back. Maguire stayed absolutely still, even though he knew that he could not be seen from his vantage point. The cop's eyes were alert and intelligent. Mick Collins was bang on the money. It was all in the eyes, as it always is. But now, as he faced him and searched Maguire's house with that probing, questioning look, he knew the cop had a name of his own. This was Owen Sheen, that guy from London, the one who had been in the news last summer and then again a few months ago. Something about a missing boy from the '70s. There'd been articles in the paper about it. Ruffled feathers, a lot of them.

Sheen stared for a few seconds more and then glanced at the adjoining houses before he turned to his car. Quickly, like a blade returning to its scabbard. He hadn't seen Maguire, but this guy had sensed him, he was in touch with his gut. Maguire thought about that as the cop unlocked his car and got in, his back brain working overtime to recall what else it was he knew about Detective Owen Sheen. Maguire heard the dark saloon growl to life and then seconds later Sheen tore away. That car. He knew the make and the brand. On the surface, you could be forgiven for assuming it was nothing special but it had sounded like a caged tiger and the way it sped off confirmed that it had something pretty mean under the hood. Maguire thought about this too. The incense had died in a thin line of white smoke. Maguire waited until its transformation was complete and then he nudged open the door and called his nephew's name.

'Pearse!'

A moment later heard the creak of the stairs as the big beast climbed up.

'You friendly with wee what's-her-name across the road there?'

'Who, India?'

Maguire nodded. PJ's wife had flown the coop and remarried years ago. But the niece now lived there. Belfast was a city with a fair few transformations in recent years, but in West Belfast some things never changed. A Housing Executive home was like a family heirloom or a season ticket for a Premier League football club. They were never really given up, even after the original occupant had long gone. They were passed down the line. Pearse rocked his head from side to side in a 'sort of' gesture.

'Just to talk to, say hello like,' he clarified. His nephew was gay, though he didn't appear to be. Not to Maguire, but what did he know any more, or ever? Part of him sort of expected gay men to wear perfume and be into flower arranging. Which his nephew was definitely not. It seemed like homosexuality was everywhere these days. Which of course was only to say that people were no longer scared to be who they were. It did make him question how many of his former comrades, not to mention the Brits and peelers who hunted them, had also kept their sexuality a secret. A good few, if the law of averages was to be respected. Maguire didn't have a problem with his nephew's sexuality. His terseness and Pearse's timidity were rooted in another wee problem, which was first Pearse's and now Maguire's by association. That was another thing about West Belfast families, not so much my house is your house, but my shit is your shit. The joys.

'Wait a minute and then away over and talk to her. Say hello and find out what that peeler wanted at her door,' ordered Maguire quietly.

'What peeler?'

Maguire took a deep breath and steadied himself before replying. He'd told Pearse to be watchful, to note strangers and strange cars on the road. God knows twenty years ago he would not have needed to issue such a reminder. And given Pearse's massive gambling debt and who he owed the money to, he really should not have needed to remind him now.

'You didn't even clock him, did you?' Pearse said nothing for a few seconds. Maguire felt a pang of regret. Anger, it was like lifting hot coals and hurling them at someone else. No matter what happened, you always ended up with your hand burnt. These were things that he tried to repeat to himself. For he was better than this; he had transformed.

'I-I'm sorry, Uncle. I was in the kitchen,' said Pearse. Which was at the back of the house.

Maguire nodded, told him to forget it. What Maguire meant was that he was sorry, and was about to say that too, but he didn't.

'What's this about?'

'Probably nothing,' said Maguire, his eyes again resting on the open gate across the street. 'I have to go to work soon. If I'm gone by the time you come back, remember to lock the security gate and the front door,' Maguire cautioned him. He turned to his nephew, but Pearse was already going down the stairs. Maguire heard him gathering his things and a few moments later the sound of the front door and then the security gate opening and closing. As he observed his nephew walk towards PJ's, his phone out and fingers working it, Maguire's own mobile glowed, silently announcing a call. He stared at the screen for a few seconds, his expression grim. How very timely. He picked it up.

'Maguire,' he said.

Forced laughter on the other end. And then the voice from the speaker was suddenly serious.

'I know it's you, Brian. Sure, isn't it your number I just hit?'

'Winky. What can I do for you?' A long pause. The bellend was trying to create some kind of suspense. Maguire watched as his nephew hugged PJ's niece on the doorstep across the street, and then kissed her on both cheeks. There was another thing that had crept in over the years. Handshakes were gone these days; people wanted to hug you. Well, some people did. Maguire had not been embraced as an old pal for some time. Winky did them both a favour and decided to break the tension.

'You know what you can do for me,' he replied. Grit in his voice, and Maguire understood that this anger was not manufactured, any more than the threat of violence which he intoned was a pretence. Winky MacDonald had been a quartermaster in the loyalist UDA for over twenty-five years, a man whom Maguire would have disposed of as readily as a cockroach in his former life, a sworn political and military enemy. These days Maguire's former Provo comrades arranged tea and buns with Winky's like, to police the peace and, Maguire was pretty certain, politely carve up protection rackets and drug distributions across Belfast and beyond. Not that he had any proof, but there was a lot of money still sloshing about and it had to have come from somewhere. Winky had, in a manner of speaking, moved from the business end of conflict to that of peace and was now Commanding Officer – for the want of a better term – of almost every betting establishment in the east and north of the city. Which was where Pearse, Maguire's nephew, entered the fray. The big, greedy, blundering, fucking gabshite supreme.

'I'll have the money. I'm working two all-nighters this week, off the books. I can drop it to you,' he offered.

'Or maybe I'll come up west and drop in on you and that thieving faggot nephew of yours?' suggested Winky.

Maguire gripped the phone, his heart starting to snare. Pearse was an airhead, but it was not for the likes of Winky

177

MacDonald to call him out. Or to threaten him. Pearse was the closest thing Maguire had to a boy. He breathed in and out, searched for the peace inside, refused to let Winky change his world. Though right now, in a more practical sense, Winky was lord and commander of it.

'You're always welcome,' replied Maguire, his voice as rich and warm as a freshly baked fruit bannock.

Another burst of laughter now from Winky, and not altogether forced this time.

'Christ, Brian, you have got some set of balls on you, you really do. Not a bit of wonder nobody's ever put you out of that house. Who would have the bottle?' he asked.

Maguire said nothing. More reasonable from Winky now:

'You do know that there's easier ways to pay me back than taxiing up and down to the airport at all hours,' he said.

'No thanks,' returned Maguire, faster and a little harder than he'd intended. Truth was he would never pay back what Winky claimed that Pearse owed. And they both knew it. At some point, things were going to come to a head. But not today. 'I'm on a different page now. But thank you,' he added. After Cyprus, Maguire's career in the IRA took a hiding. Watchful looks from former comrades turned into being blanked and ignored. Invitations to join secret operations against the Brits and peelers ran low, and then dried up. For the last five years of his time as a soldier of Ireland, Brian Maguire was tasked with dispensing street justice to joyriding car thieves, granny muggers and small-time drug dealers. And he'd been good at it too. Just as he had been a respected volunteer in an active service unit, so Brian Maguire had become a feared man by those who crossed the line in West Belfast.

Winky sighed gravely.

'Shame, really. I'd say there'd be a clean slate in a matter of months. Less, if the jobs turned out to be dirty enough. And your nephew's hole is not the deepest on my books, Brian. I have a ton of work waiting. Not everyone's got the skill set I require, know what I mean?'

Maguire closed his eyes, heard the snap of an arm bone as he wrenched it again and again against the hinge of the elbow while it was jammed between the iron railings of the City Cemetery. He saw the hard edge of an ash hurley stick connect with the splayed fingers held on a table in front of him, turning the bone and tendons to pulp. He heard the screams of those he had hurt, so shrill and agonised, the pain stripping humanity away until Maguire had reached the animal inside. He knew exactly what Winky meant.

'Respect the offer, Winky. I'll have this week's with you the morning after next,' he said.

The line went dead without a goodbye. Maguire set the phone down, his hand shaking lightly. He decided that he was going to do a bit of yoga, but instead he made his way downstairs and out the back. The inside of his shed was dry and smelt of last year's cut grass. He cleared a space and heaved the bag on the hook, slapping the dust off its surface. The gloves were tight and frayed, but as he started to punch and move, he felt them loosen up, his muscles waking to the demands of the bag and giving more power to each punch.

His mind was back on Mick Collins, a man the might of the British Empire had failed to beat, but who was then gunned down as a traitor by those he had once called friends. So often the centre could not hold. His mind skipped to Owen Sheen, the mystery peeler who had sensed Maguire's gaze. He stopped punching, breathing hard and with sweat on his forehead and face. Sheen was in charge of that historical offences unit – what was it called?

'SHOT,' answered Maguire, nodding, and then he started to work on the bag once more, pleased to note how much he still had in the tank, even though it had been a long time, even though he'd gained more than a few pounds and lost most of his hair. The dull impact of his punches, his energy transferred through his fists, wanted to tug his mind to darker thoughts. Maguire blinked them away, ordered himself to remain in the present as he repeated Buddha's mantra until he could give no more.

*Just as a snake sheds its skin, we must shed our past over and over again.*

# CHAPTER SEVENTEEN

Aoife's first stop of the day was Clonard Monastery, a Catholic church less than a mile off the Falls Road. Though not strictly accurate, the church was known to most as Clonard or the monastery. Aoife had spent time working as a lay assistant there not so long ago and still lent a hand when she could. It had been a period of her life that had coincided with traumatic upheaval and the murder of Clonard's resident priest, Father Phil Rafferty in the sacristy of the church that he had served. A small chill fluttered through her as she entered the cool shadows of the church and breathed in the smell of burning wax, polish and incense. But as she walked up Clonard's magnificent central aisle she spotted the person she had come here to see. As well as losing a friend when Father Phil had been murdered, Aoife had also found a new one. Hayley White was busy removing the spent tealight candles from the iron shelves in front of the statue of St

Gerard which was adjacent to the main altar.

'Here you, police, drop those candles and put yer hands up,' she jested.

Hayley turned to greet her with a smile.

'Oh my God. Will you look what the cat just dragged in,' she said, and took Aoife in her arms in a huge hug. Hayley gave a great hug. And as always she was immaculate, her angular hair sporting streaks of blue and pink that she somehow managed to make look cool, offset by a wool cardigan and skirt combo with hints of the same hues, perfect for the long road they still travelled from Belfast's winter into spring. If Aoife had tried her outfit on, she would doubtless end up looking like a librarian who had a sideline in serial murder. As usual, Hayley wore a small silk scarf around her throat, and Aoife knew why. Her Adam's apple. It was, like Hayley's large, wide hands, one obvious giveaway that she was transgender, and a source of great self-consciousness for her friend. And it was not the only aspect of Hayley White that set her aside. Hayley said they should head into town for a coffee at their favourite breakfast joint, Harlem's Cafe.

'I'd love to, but I'm working,' explained Aoife.

'Oh, I see. You're here for business aren't you, Miss Prim?'

Aoife smiled, and took out the plastic bag that contained the fabric she and Sheen had taken from the wire fence next to Stockmans Lane the day before. The fabric that Sheen believed could be a piece of Tucker's dressing gown.

'I was hoping you would have a look at this for me,' she said. But of course, that was not really what she meant. Aoife had no idea how Hayley's gift worked. But just like the CBD oil she had recently started to take for the old gunshot wound that she carried with her from her first case working with Sheen, she was utterly convinced that it did work. Hayley nodded, suddenly a little more serious and invited Aoife to sit with her on the pew facing the wide altar.

Clonard felt vast in its emptiness. It was only the two of them. The hard wood of the pew was cold and smooth as ancient bogwood. Hayley took the plastic bag from Aoife. She didn't ask her anything about the fabric inside, and Aoife told her nothing. Hayley opened the seal. She slipped one hand into the bag and closed her eyes. Seconds passed, and Hayley's breathing became slower, more shallow. Aoife watched as her friend's pupils bobbed and twitched beneath her lids, like a woman in a dream sleep. Finally, she spoke, her voice a little softer and more detached than it had been before.

'The man who wore this was scared. But . . .' Her voice faded away a little and Hayley frowned, as though in pain or confused. 'Scared of getting hurt, and that he might hurt someone else, someone he wants to protect. He has to get someplace. He . . . he has numbers in his head, numbers he keeps repeating.' Silence from Hayley, and then she exhaled and opened her eyes. She took her hand off the fabric and placed two fingers on the bridge of her nose, lowering her head.

'Hayley, are you OK?'

'That is so not fair. You definitely owe me that coffee now, McCusker,' she replied.

'Are you hurt?'

'I'm hungover. The man who was wearing that' –

183

she nodded to the brown fabric in the plastic bag – 'is a wee drinker. Wee as in very big. And he was rotten with a hangover. Which I've now a taste of. Even though I abstained last night knowing I'd be up to help with the dawn Mass,' she said, but with a weak smile now that told Aoife they were cool.

'What you said fits in with what we think we know about this,' said Aoife, who then offered a potted summary to Hayley, including what had happened to Tucker Rodgers.

She nodded her agreement.

'Yeah, that makes sense. He was anxious about someone, lots of guilt, lots of self-loathing,' said Hayley, and gave a little shudder.

'You mentioned numbers. Do you remember them?'

Hayley shook her head, looked apologetic.

'It wasn't as clear as that, more like the feeling of having to recount and repeat a series of digits, you know. There was a six, at the beginning. I am pretty certain of that,' said Hayley.

'A phone number?' Many older numbers in the Greater Belfast area started with a six after the area code.

'Could be. But you're the detective. I'm just a freaky antenna,' said Hayley.

Aoife gave her hand a squeeze.

'You're my best mate,' she said. 'And Ava wants you up for the next girls' movie night.'

'Count me in. But no horror movies. Wine's on you. Seeing as you already gifted me the hangover.'

Aoife couldn't help but laugh, and Hayley joined in a chuckle, but it quickly dried up. When she glanced up, Hayley had become suddenly more sombre. She nodded to the scrap of fabric that Tucker Rodgers had left behind as he fled.

'Aoife, hungover or not, this man was running scared, scared for his life. I hope his lucky numbers worked for him,' said Hayley.

# CHAPTER EIGHTEEN

Sheen found a parking space in the grounds of Shandon Park Golf Club in East Belfast a little after two in the afternoon. After leaving his meeting with the chief yesterday evening traffic had been absolute murder and he had decided to put off his planned visit. Not that it had made a great deal of difference. It was as bad this afternoon and it had taken him over an hour to make his way across town. When he called Aoife last night to give her the good news about his meeting with the chief, she'd told him she had taken the initiative and spoken to Mairead Gleeson, the mother of the only female member of the Cyprus Three IRA unit. Ms Gleeson had been cooperative but not particularly helpful. Aoife had asked her straight up if TOPBRASS meant anything to her but had drawn a blank. Sheen had to agree that the direct approach, asking about TOPBRASS and then gauging reactions, was probably the best line in. When pushed,

Mairead Gleeson had lost her cool and said it sounded like a military call sign, something that Sheen had not considered. And worth looking into given that Aoife also confirmed that Roddy Grant had spent a portion of his career working at Castlereagh. Sheen had asked Aoife to raise it with Roddy Grant's sister, Janice, when she visited Roddy's home today. Hopefully she might get a break. So far, the direct approach had yielded nothing for Sheen.

Earlier, he had driven into Andersonstown and knocked on the door of the family home of Paul Joseph Wilson, who was known as PJ, the second member of the Cyprus Three. Sheen opened the relevant dossier and scanned the details he had gleaned about Wilson. He had been the technician, the man responsible for putting together the bomb that the unit had planned to use against the British Army – and anyone else unfortunate enough to be close to them at the time. The council house was still in the name of the Wilson family, and the young woman who answered the door said she was PJ's niece. She'd told Sheen that her auntie, PJ's wife, had emigrated and remarried, and she had taken PJ's little boy with her, decades before. The only thing the young woman could remember about the Cyprus Three was that she had been at the funeral and recalled the masked men shooting volleys over the coffins that had been draped in the Irish tricolour.

TOPBRASS meant absolutely nothing to her, and in fact she seemed pretty much oblivious to her family's significance in the IRA roll of honour. Despite that, she had invited him in and offered him a smoke – very, very tempted, but one small victory of the day thus far was that he had declined – plus insisted on making him tea and feeding him fruit bread and talking to him anyway. The breakfast was appreciated, but Sheen had gained nothing of any value in Andersonstown. Though he did get a weird feeling of being watched as he had left the house. Something had set him on edge immediately. He had waited to see if the grey-coloured car both he and Aoife had spotted at Tucker's place would emerge, but nothing had.

The barman at the Shandon Park Golf Club delivered a half of Guinness and a packet of posh-looking cheese and onion crisps to his spot at the end of the bar. In the dim light of the interior Sheen was one of a small handful of punters and the youngest. There was skiing showing on the large flat-screen television with the sound on mute and Dean Martin crooning low and velvety over the speakers. Sheen thanked the barman, opened his phone and found the image of the invitation to Roddy Grant's funeral reception which he had photographed while in Tucker Rodgers' kitchen.

'Were you serving at this event a few days back?' asked Sheen, holding his phone so the guy could see. The barman looked to be in his fifties, small-framed and with crooked teeth. He probably needed to admit defeat and shave off the last wisps of hair that formed a veil over the top of his head. He scanned the image and lifted a finger to the screen to reposition the picture a little. Sheen noted his name on the small badge on his shirt. Austin. He also noted that his first digit was yellowed with nicotine. Another reminder of why quitting permanently was the correct decision.

'Aye, I was here.'

'Do you remember seeing a man called Tucker Rodgers?'

The barman's gaze became more hooded, and then he averted his eyes from Sheen and started to buy himself time by collecting empty pint glasses from the end of the bar beside them.

'There's a lot of people pass through. I wouldn't know many by name though,' he said.

'Let me start again, Austin,' said Sheen, and he set his phone down and took out his warrant card. The guy was being circumspect, and he was right to be. If the Shandon served a lot of coppers the last thing they wanted was the staff running their mouths to any new face who turned up with questions. The press was one possibility, but so too was the very real threat from Dissident terrorists who had recently proved they had the means and intent to murder. The barman took a few seconds to study Sheen's ID.

'A peeler. Now why am I not surprised?' he commented with a small smile.

'Tucker is one too, retired. Do you know him?'

Austin shook his head again, seemed a genuine answer this time. Sheen moved his finger across the screen of his phone, sifting through images he had snapped until he found what he wanted. Tucker's old warrant card. He enlarged it to show only the younger Tucker's face and held it up for Austin. The man took a few seconds to assess the picture, and had started to slowly shake his head but then he stopped, his eyes flickering with recognition.

'Yeah, I know this guy. But this is a properly old photo, right?'

'Correct,' said Sheen. 'But you recognise him?'

'Aye, I do indeed. He's not a regular, or a member. Roddy used to sign him in as a guest, but only occasionally. I remember him now. Same guy was here for the funeral drinks, drunk as a lord.'

The door to the gents' toilet opened and an old boy emerged. He was dishevelled but dapper in a tight-fitting sports jacket with a luscious head of silver hair swept off his face to showcase a nose that said he was fond of a drink. He found a spot further down the bar and Austin set about fixing him a pint of lager and a large measure of Scotch without being asked.

'So, Tucker and Roddy were good mates?'

The same wry smile as before from the barman.

'Depends who you ask. If you asked Roddy the pair of them were best mates, maybe even more. It used to be Tucker this and Tucker that,' he said and then glided to the other punter and gave him his drinks. No payment was forthcoming or requested. Sheen guessed a tab, no doubt a large one.

'What do you mean by more?'

'Look, it's not for me to judge, but I always got the impression that Roddy was, you know, queer,' he said, dropping his volume to reflect the evident gravity of the revelation. 'For this guy Tucker,' he explained.

'But the feeling, friendship or romantic attachment, was not mutual?'

'No idea. But between you and me, people used to laugh when they heard Roddy going on about planning a fishing trip or a day away with Tucker. You know, like people would have asked him if he'd ever gone camping in Brokeback Mountain,' said the barman. 'Roddy wasn't married.' In Sheen's experience that meant very little, but he respected the barman's instincts even if he didn't appreciate his use of the term 'queer'.

'Roddy have other people in the club he was friendly with, people he would have talked to?'

'He was a wee barfly, the guy talked to everyone,' said Austin. And in a club where most of the clientele were cops, what were the chances that Roddy Grant had said the wrong thing to the wrong person? A person who could be connected to the top brass of a very murky underworld. Fairly high as far as Sheen was concerned. Another snippet from Tucker's panicked letter to his son came into Sheen's mind.

*They killed Roddy and now they're coming for me.*

The barman's face grew suddenly sombre. 'Real shame about what happened to Roddy. He was a bit of a metler but no real harm there. But then, they say it's hard to see it coming.'

'You seen Tucker since?'

Austin's face deepened from serious to grave.

'Jesus, is that what this is about? Do you think this bloke Tucker topped himself? Broken-hearted? They say it's contagious, you know?'

Sheen thought about the hard stare from the young Tucker captured on his expired warrant card, and about the strip of dressing gown that had been left while Tucker had evaded and disappeared.

'No, not at all, mate. This is totally different,' he assured him. A thought came to mind and Sheen reached into his wallet and handed Austin his card. 'But if anyone else comes through here and asks about Rodgers, even if they mention his name, can you give me a call on this number?' Austin said he would. Sheen thanked him and paid up, noted that the old boy had vacated his stool, though his pint still fizzed in the shadows. Sheen turned to go, and then another thought came to him. Maybe he didn't have to wait for Austin to call him.

'Is there any chance I could get a copy of the member's list here at Shandon?'

'Well, um, you know, I'm not sure about that. I'd need to run it past the manager. Do I have to?' Austin meant was he legally obliged to. Not unless Sheen had a search warrant, and he didn't.

'It could really help. One man's dead and another who liked to drink here is missing. The sooner we get to the bottom of it, the less the risk of bad press, know what I mean?' By the look on Austin's face Sheen thought he knew exactly. In fact, Sheen could see this going his way. And then the bottom fell out of his little scheme.

'Is everything all right here?' The owner of the plummy-toned voice was behind Sheen. He turned around. There was a bloke wearing a God-awful navy blazer with gold buttons and a pair of red chinos. He introduced himself as Carwyn Greechan, the manager. Greechan clearly had his own opinions when it came to fashion. He eyed Sheen's leather jacket like it was a bit of roadkill that had crawled off the kerb and died on Sheen's shoulders. Sheen asked about the member's list again, and somehow Greechan's expression of disgust actually deepened. He quickly ushered Sheen into a back office where the little jobsworth had politely explained that he could not oblige and that Sheen would need to return with a search warrant if he wanted a copy of their confidential club records. His membership valued their privacy and security, he explained. All the while looking down his nose in a way that said if it was up to him, Sheen would never join that hallowed list. Sheen's reminder that he was also a police officer held no sway.

In theory, Sheen could have hung around and questioned punters as they came and went but that was a fool's errand and lacked discretion. Besides, the bar was as empty as a ghost ship. All of which meant Sheen, or someone else, was going to have to waste time putting together the tedious application for a court order. And even with a copy of the membership list, it all felt a bit tenuous. Austin the barman had said Roddy was a barfly and had talked to everyone. That could include guests, as Tucker Rodgers had been, or a one-time visitor who may have signed in under a false name or not signed in at all. And if Roddy ran his mouth at Shandon, there was every chance he did the same elsewhere.

As he left, Sheen spotted the old boy who had left his beer on the bar. He was standing alone under a gazebo on the other side of the car park, shrouded in blue smoke. Sheen paused, and almost turned in that direction with a mind to bum one off the old-timer but forced himself back on course and instead set about giving his car the cursory security checks.

Under the gazebo, Samuel Royce Fenton crushed his Dunhill into the ashtray and immediately lit a replacement, all the while observing Detective Inspector Owen Sheen as he first checked his car for concealed booby trap devices and then got inside. Fenton's cold stare remained on Sheen as his powerful car growled to life and then followed him as he drove off. He drew hard on his smoke and took out the burner phone which buzzed from his back pocket. He read the message from his team and killed his smoke. Not the news he had hoped for. Which was unfortunate. And that meant Owen Sheen was about to learn that bad luck keeps bad company.

# CHAPTER NINETEEN

One of Maguire's colleagues from the minicab firm was next in line but the woman with no luggage walked straight to Maguire's car, opened the back door and got in.

'Where to, love?'

'Hillhead, please,' she replied.

Maguire sized her up in the rear-view as the toll bar lifted and he accelerated away from the airport, joining the two-lane country road towards the city. She was looking out the window, her face partly obscured. A pensioner. She wore a large woollen scarf, browns and oranges, that was wrapped around her shoulders like a shawl, her hair was set and dyed an unnatural shade of bright copper. But it suited her. He could smell the heavy scent of her perfume. It was cloying, the type older women seemed to insist on wearing.

'Been any place nice?' he continued. Banter, small talk, meaningless, of course, he didn't care. The woman did not reply. Maguire accepted the silence. It was sometimes part of the work. Hillhead was located on the outskirts of Andersonstown, near the Stewartstown Road in West Belfast. Nice little place, detached bungalows and semis with big gardens. But also close to much more densely crowded estates like Lenadoon, a place that had seen a lot of action over the years. Close, in fact, to where Maguire's own home was located.

'Small world,' offered Maguire, eyes back on the open road ahead. 'I'm from down that way myself,' he confided. Belfast was a tapestry. It could put a person at ease when they knew you were from their part of the patchwork. Stupid really, but no getting around that. Nothing in return from the woman. He decided to shut up. If she didn't have the decency to answer him, why should he care if she was relaxed or not?

'I know where you're from, Brian,' she said. Maguire's hands tightened slightly around the wheel and his heart spiked. His name was on his badge which was displayed on the dash, possible that she'd seen it. But she said she knew where he lived. He slowed down and turned in his seat as she moved her face from the window view she had been enjoying and stared back at him. Green eyes, like an owl. He saw them transposed, over thirty years before, watching him from the tanned face of a much younger woman, one who would never have the chance to age with the grace and beauty of her mother. Monica. Monica Gleeson who had died in Cyprus. He heard the shots that killed her, that drill of semi-automatic fire and two clipped shots to complete her execution, action replay, a horror show just for his ears. She had come from Hillhead. Maguire returned his attention to the road. He was sweating now.

'Listen, Ms Gleeson, I don't know what this is, but I want no trouble. If that's what you're here for, you can get out of my taxi and walk to Hillhead,' he said.

'Take the road into Templepatrick, Brian, then go down the M2,' she instructed. Maguire had been planning on cutting into West Belfast using minor roads and following the slope of the Black Mountain through what had once been the rural parish of Hannahstown. Gleeson's route was much longer. But it also meant they would avoid being seen together as he drove into the West.

'We need to have a chat. I have a proposal,' she said.

'What about?' he replied. He had still not entirely rejected the possibility of pulling up and getting her out of the car.

'The only thing we have in common. The murder of my daughter in Cyprus,' she said. And so there it was, the ghost that had haunted him most of his adult life was here in his cab. He felt an old well of anger bubble and heat deep inside, catching him by surprise every bit as much as this woman had done.

'What gives you the right? Out!' he yelled, and Maguire hit the brakes hard enough for the tyres to squeal. A big haulage lorry that had been on his tail blared past, ball-shrinkingly close, with a massive blast of its horn.

Gleeson remained impassive and did not move.

'You asked me earlier whether I had been anywhere nice. In fact, I have not been anywhere. I took the bus up to the airport from Great Victoria Street in town and waited half the morning until you finally showed up at the taxi rank. I missed you initially and I decided to wait. If I had simply wanted to give you a hard time, Brian, I could have come to your front door and saved myself the effort.'

Maguire let his heart subside, forced the unwelcome intruder of his temper back inside its cage. This was not him, not any more. He did yoga; he focused on chakra bells.

'Ms Gleeson, I know what you've heard, but I had nothing to do with the death of Monica, or any of them. They were my friends.'

Maguire rejoined the traffic and took the car in the direction she had suggested.

'Call me Mairead. I know that now. I doubted it at first. Everyone did,' she said.

'Oh, you know that for sure, do you?' he said, the anger was rattling the bars of the cage, still contained but he could feel it, like a black vibration in his mind. 'Maybe you'd be so kind as to tell me why,' he said.

'Because you're still alive, Brian,' she observed.

'So what? Why come to me now, after all this time?'

'Yesterday afternoon I had a visit from a young thing who works for the PSNI. McCusker her name is. She works for the historical investigations branch.'

'SHOT,' said Maguire. Owen Sheen's team.

'I knew it was only a matter of time before Cyprus was investigated,' said Mairead Gleeson. 'And what she said made me think they've got a sniff of something rotten. They're on the hunt,' she said.

He hesitated but decided to speak.

'I saw your man Sheen, the London peeler who's in charge. He was rapping on PJ's door, earlier.'

Mairead nodded as though it proved a point. She asked him if he knew what had been said.

'Na, not yet. I sent my nephew over to have a word, but I've not had a chance to catch up,' he explained. Maguire had gone directly out after sending Pearse on his errand. But of course he'd called Pearse for an update. PJ's niece had confirmed Sheen was indeed asking questions about the Cyprus Three. And he had mentioned a name, one that Monica's ma had thus far not said. 'What do you mean by rotten?'

'When that McCusker, came to speak to me I expected promises that Monica's death would be investigated again impartially, some assurance that the SAS would be brought to account if the killing was deemed unlawful,' she explained.

'And?'

'There was a bit of that. But that wasn't what had got her goat. She tried to downplay it, but I could see there's another angle,' said Mairead. 'Like it wasn't the Brits they were interested in digging up dirt on,' she said.

Maguire's eyes widened. The cage rattled and slammed, smash, smash, smash.

'They think the Cyprus job was a set-up,' Maguire said slowly. 'By a tout?'

'What's TOPBRASS mean to you, Brian?' she asked.

Maguire simply shook his head. Not a lie. The name meant nothing to him. But he recognised it. TOPBRASS was the same name that Sheen had said to PJ's niece.

'I want you to find out. And I want justice for my daughter,' said Mairead Gleeson.

'Sheen and his team will do it. He's capable,' retorted Maguire.

Mairead punched the back of his seat hard enough to make him flinch.

'I want the bastard dead,' she hissed.

Maguire absorbed this.

'I left that behind me. A long time ago. Shed it like a skin,' he said.

'Have you got children?'

Maguire told her he had a nephew, but he was like a son.

'If he is, then you'll know why I came to you and not Owen Sheen. I don't blame the SAS. She took her chances. But not the other way,' she said, shaking her head.

'No.'

'I have money,' she said. Maguire's ears pricked up at this. 'The IRA paid me her money every month. Like a death tax. I have over fifty grand, all in cash. We never used it; I couldn't bring myself to touch it, but no matter what I said, that money was delivered every month without fail,' she said.

He thought about Pearse's debt, his debt. That cash would cover it even with the interest that had been accrued.

'The answer's no,' he said. 'Come on, I'll drop you home.' Maguire had arrived in the city centre, and now pulled to a stop outside the Europa Hotel.

'You can drop me here,' she said.

'How did you know? About me, I mean? Not everyone does,' he said. He meant about his role in Cyprus, the fact he had escaped and the bad reputation he'd been left with in the IRA.

'Oh, Brian, do I really need to explain it?' she asked, stepping out of the car and settling her green eyes on his through the passenger-side window. 'This is Belfast. People talk. At bus stops, in the supermarket, outside Mass. Over the years, I heard it said more than once. But the first time was one of the IRA's delivery boys. He mentioned your name when he dropped off the money.'

A call from Pearse bleated through the car's loudspeaker. He dismissed it.

'This is my number, in case you change your mind,' said Mairead.

Maguire took the piece of paper that she offered.

As he did, a text alert flashed up on his phone. Pearse again. He felt a flutter of unease at this; Pearse was not usually the persistent type. He glanced at the number she had given him and saw there was a small note written on the back.

*Back seat. Down payment.*

He turned and saw a plastic supermarket bag was on the seat behind him. He pulled off the elastic band and opened it, already knowing by the feel what it was she had left. A thick bundle of used notes.

'Ah, for fuck's sake,' he said. He craned his neck, trying to find her but she had gone. He flicked through the wad. There was five grand here. He wrapped it and put it in the glove compartment when his phone rang again through the speakers.

It was Pearse.

He pulled away and answered it using a button on the steering wheel.

'Gabshite,' he said amiably, but despite that, his heart was cantering a bit.

Nothing from the other end. Scuffling sounds from the

speakers, and then laboured breathing. Maguire frowned. A sobbing voice: Pearse's.

'Uncle.' One word, but it was all Maguire needed to be sure his nephew was hurt, or scared, or both.

# CHAPTER TWENTY

CONFIDENTIAL
ROYAL ULSTER CONSTABULARY
SPECIAL BRANCH
10th Day of September 1981
SPECIAL REPORT
SUBJECT: TOPBRASS

TOPBRASS continues to feed high-grade intelligence which has led to a thwarting of IRA operations and the recovery of many dumps of arms and munitions. His work, at significant personal risk, has helped to safeguard the lives of both non-combatants and security force personnel.

Gains have been offset by a rise in suspicion from those in similar ranks that a spy may be operating in their midst and TOPBRASS has reported a perceived 'cold shouldering' by some fellow Provisionals and a 'freezing out' of certain planned operations. Though overt suspicion is not at present directed at TOPBRASS by more key players in higher ranks, he feels it will be only a matter of time before scrutiny turns on him in a more direct way.

Suggest an offering which will allow TOPBRASS to both impress the IRA Internal Security unit and in doing so achieve the flexibility to continue to act as a valuable asset by safeguarding his position for some time to come. The regrettable reality is that not every intelligence asset in our employment is of equal standing or value. Although we should feel personally bad about this, I feel compelled to up the stakes as required by the realities of this very dangerous conflict. Our business is espionage, not selling insurance.

Submitted to the chief constable: Detective Inspector S. R. Fenton

Tucker set the booklet down on the table and slowly exhaled. Fenton, already promoted from sergeant to inspector, was openly proposing to forfeit an active Special Branch agent. One agent's life surrendered to spare another. Or, more accurately, to bolster the career of another and ensure the uninterrupted flow of valued intelligence. Tucker was reminded of the mind-bending philosophical conundrums that he had come by from time to time. Is it better to save a baby from a burning house or an elderly person? If you could go back in time would you murder Adolf Hitler as a defenceless child? Is it morally justifiable to push one man off an overcrowded boat in order to stop it sinking and killing scores of people? These were the meat and drink of the decisions faced by those in positions of power and control during the Troubles. Right and wrong got muddied, no two ways about it, and the moral high ground was obscured by dark clouds, heavy with a poison rain.

Tucker was a realist. He'd walked the beat; he'd seen what had gone down. Over the course of decades of unceasing conflict, society in Northern Ireland had circled the drain. The fight against an enemy as ruthless as the IRA could not always be conducted according to Queensbury Rules. And yet, there was something cold and cynical about Fenton's report. This was a man who must have started off as a rank and file peeler just as he had. A man who had promised to keep the peace and preserve life as his primary duty. But here Fenton made his so-called offering sound like a cash bonus the chief would need to sign off. Which, as Tucker read the next newspaper clipping and Roddy's script, it was pretty clear he had done.

'Bernadette Bell,' read Tucker, before quickly scanning the rest of *The Irish News* article that was dated 5th November 1981. Bell had been a twenty-three-year-old member of the IRA. She had been taken from her home in Fallswater Street in the west of the city a week before, and her body was found on a lane in South Armagh with a black plastic bag over her head and a bullet through her brain. The IRA admitted that she was one of their members and claimed she had confessed to being a Special Branch informer. According to the newspaper report her body showed signs of torture, with evidence of cigarette burns on the soles of her feet and her fingernails removed.

'Jesus wept,' said Tucker, running a hand over the glassy stubble that covered his cheeks and chin. On the next page he found the woman's obituary. She had been unmarried at least, no children, but was survived by both parents. Roddy had penned a short poem to her memory called *Did You Look Back?* It was about the moment that Bernadette Bell was driven away from her Fallswater Street home, never to return again. Tucker felt a twinge of sadness after finishing the last stanza, transmitted across time and space by dead Roddy Grant, who surely felt the same sense of hopelessness and despair when he had drafted the poem. But Tucker clenched his fist and resisted the allure of tears and pity. If this woman was an agent for Special Branch then she was a damn brave person, and one whose work may well have saved lives, maybe even had saved Tucker's life for all he knew. He had been a cop on the same streets and at that time. And what was her reward? To be thrown to the dogs and ripped apart by the so-called Nutting Squad, the IRA's internal security unit. For where better to conceal the king of touts than within the very unit tasked to root out traitors? A unit feared by all, and thus virtually beyond reproach. He flicked back to the Special Branch document.

*Our business is espionage, not selling insurance.*

But if Tucker was in Fenton's shoes, he'd make sure that he had his back covered. And Fenton was not the only problem. TOPBRASS had even more to lose, that much was clear. A shiver worked its way up Tucker's back and made the hair on his arms stand up. Now he knew who it was that had likely stiffed poor Roddy and had come close to getting him. Fenton, or TOPBRASS, or maybe both in cahoots. Tucker closed his eyes and tried to think. How did they discover that Roddy had a saucerful of secrets in the first place? Tucker grunted. If there was one thing that Roddy liked to do it was talk. It was a small wonder he managed to keep a lid on this for as long as he clearly had. The golf club, if Tucker had to take a guess. But then how did they manage to connect Roddy to him? Tucker only rarely frequented the golf club; it was way out on the other side of town. Maybe they watched Roddy send the package and photograph the address? Or perhaps they simply put a gun to the poor bastard's head and he told them? Either way, they had found him, and that meant that Samuel Fenton had become as adept at insurance over the years as he was at espionage. And if they had traced Roddy's stolen secrets to Tucker, it stood to reason that they could trace his son, David, especially if he turned up in Belfast looking for Owen Sheen. Exactly what Tucker had encouraged him to do. Tucker closed his eyes and wished he knew a prayer, but all that came to mind was the black and white photograph of Bernadette Bell's hooded body, dumped in a ditch, and Roddy's mournful lament.

*Did You Look Back?*

Tucker cleared his throat and turned the page, his face set and his mind ready as he continued to read.

# CHAPTER TWENTY-ONE

'Pearse! What's happened? Where—?'

'Uncle, you have to come home,' he said.

Maguire swung the car into the oncoming lane and pulled it through a tight U-turn as other vehicles skidded to a stop or swerved out of his path. He left the chaos and an elephant's herd worth of blaring horns in his wake and accelerated hard before taking a left turn on to the Grosvenor Road. He was headed for the junction with the Falls Road and into West Belfast. As he passed the police station he fleetingly considered calling the peelers and telling them to go to his home. But the part of him that never had, also knew that he never would.

When he entered his estate he was sweating and on alert, but had calmed sufficiently to retain the presence of mind to park the taxi well away from the mouth of his cul de sac. He slowly walked around the corner and took a look down the street. No foreign cars. He knew who owned each motor that was parked up. Maguire tracked his eyes along the row of houses, searching. Nobody concealed in a front garden. Nobody loitering on the footpath. He focused on his own house and growled when he saw it.

The iron security gate was wide open.

Maguire squinted and noted that the front door was ajar too. Not good. If someone had come for Pearse they could still be in the house. He wished that he had his Beretta Stampede revolver. But the old piece was hidden under a floorboard in his shed with a box of bullets and it had been there for many years. Buddhists like him had little need for guns. Until this week. Maguire jogged back to his car and popped the boot. He removed the hurl and returned to the corner of his street. The hurl's fine ash wood was weathered and darkened with age but still solid, incredibly strong. Around its spoon-like leading edge Maguire had four steel bands machined in place. Ostensibly a measure used by hurlers to improve the durability of their stick in the heat of a clash on the pitch, but utterly illegal to have more than one according to Gaelic Athletic Association rules. That had never been Maguire's concern. Of all the things he'd hit with his hurl over the years a ball had not been one. He started down the street, staying close to the parked cars for cover, never taking his eyes off his front door.

He nudged the door open with the head of his hurl. Listening. Ready. A single voice, speaking from within. Sobbing, hysterical, coming from his front room. Maguire slipped inside the house. He resisted the urge to barge in, his gut response on hearing his boy in distress.

Instead, Maguire took two tentative steps further along the hallway and stopped. Still only Pearse's voice, and from the way he was speaking, Maguire could tell he was on the phone. Maguire stayed still, absorbing the sounds from the front room that was behind the half-open door to his right. Pearse's hitching sobs as he listened on the phone, and then his words, clotted with tears. Pearse was saying that something hurt. Maguire felt his shoulders tighten, and his fist gripped the hurl. No other sounds from within.

'Pearse!' shouted Maguire. His nephew stopped speaking. 'Are you alone?'

'Yes.'

Maguire kicked open his living-room door and spun in a tight circle, his shoulders hunched, the hurl raised. The living room and kitchen beyond were empty. Pearse was on the sofa. He stared up at Maguire. His eyes were puffy and red with tears that still coursed down his cheeks. He had his mobile held up to one ear. Pearse had evacuated his bladder at some point. The dark stain of urine was visible down the front of his light blue jeans. And then Maguire saw the problem. Pearse's other hand rested on his thigh and quivered as though searching for a divine tempo beyond man's reach. His thumb was blackened and swollen and crooked in a way nature never planned. Maguire asked him what had happened.

'Winky sent someone. Said you invited him,' said Pearse, and then the crying started again.

Maguire walked over to him and laid a hand on his shoulder. His mouth, he should have controlled it. He'd told Winky earlier that he was welcome at his home anytime. On cue, his phone rang. Maguire threw the hurl to the floor and answered it, feeling very far from under control.

'Sorry I missed ya,' said Winky.

'His fucking thumb. Seriously? After I told you I would pay?' he said. The thumb was plain sadistic, without the use of your thumb you could do nothing. Maguire had read somewhere that the loss of a thumb in an industrial accident paid more than almost any other body part.

'He's lucky it was only the one. And so are you. Otherwise you'd be wiping his arse for him as well as paying off his debts,' said Winky.

'No, it was your man who was lucky. That I wasn't here.' A pause from Winky at this. He must have detected the change in Maguire. That he meant what he said. 'I have a good mind to find him and show him what a proper hiding looks like.'

'Brian, now listen. It's fair to say that we both got out of line. A bit. But—'

'I'm dropping five large to the bookies at the bottom of the Shankill Road. And you can thank King Billy that I'm about to get very preoccupied, otherwise I might turn my attention your way. The debt will be paid. I'd like you to accept my word on that this time,' said Maguire.

More silence. Maguire was about to hang up when Winky spoke.

'Why? After all this time, all my offers? And today's the day you decide to go back in business?' He didn't even sound angry; in fact, he sounded like Maguire had hurt his feelings. 'Was it the thumb, is that what did it?'

Maguire ended the call. He turned to Pearse.

211

'Did you leave that front door unlocked with the security gate open?'

The gabshite lowered his head and didn't reply. He told Pearse to get his boyfriend, Conor, to come round and take him to the Royal Victoria Hospital.

'What if they come for me again?'

'They won't. But I want you to stop over at Conor's for a few nights anyway.'

Maguire reached for a bottle of Jameson that was on the shelf and took a slug, and then took one more. He'd tried, but sometimes enough was enough. Maguire took out his phone and started to text as he walked through the kitchen and out the back door. He added Mairead Gleeson's number using the bit of paper she had left him and paused outside his shed, before pressing send.

'Ms Gleeson, it's me. I'll take that fare.'

Maguire closed the shed door behind him and waited as his eyes adjusted to the dimness of the interior. The air was still and dry, with a bass note of bicycle tyre rubber. He shoved a toolbox out of the space that it had long occupied in one corner and then used a penknife to first scrape away the dirt and oil in the seam of one of the floorboards that had been revealed before levering the point of the blade under it, prying it open. Beneath was black and cool, but Maguire didn't need a torch. Even though it had been many years since he had checked this place, his arm disappeared with surety into the cavity he had created. He felt the slab of lead under his fingers, gritted his teeth as he took its weight and edged it out of the way. Maguire's hand closed around the cloth-wrapped contours of the Beretta revolver and a box of bullets. He lifted them free and then sat on the shed floor and unwrapped both, the greasy cloth unfolding to reveal cold, oily steel.

The Beretta Stampede. It was an Italian-made exact replica of the Colt Single Action Army Peacemaker. Its cylinder had the capacity to hold six rounds and could fire .45 Long Colt bullet cartridges. Fixed front sight and dark walnut grip, Maguire's piece had a five-and-a-half-inch barrel, which meant his gun was just shy of eleven inches all told. Maguire had always subscribed to the wisdom that you're best hung for a sheep as a lamb. And although some of his former comrades in arms had relied on smaller guns that could do a lot more talking, the Stampede had always been a voice of authority on the streets for Brian Maguire when West Belfast was a wild place indeed. As his fingers plucked cartridges from the box and started to slot them home into the Stampede's cylinder one by one, his phone buzzed. It was Mairead Gleeson.

'Thank you for letting me know.'

But Maguire knew what she meant. And he knew what he was agreeing to.

*I want the bastard dead.*

TOPBRASS. The tout. The person who had somehow sold out his unit in Cyprus and killed Maguire's name and reputation in this town too. He'd managed to stay hidden for all these years. But now his time had come. Yet Maguire was not the only person hunting him. Owen Sheen was on his tail too. So, keep it simple: follow Sheen, find TOPBRASS. That famous poet Rumi's words spoke up in his mind as he put a loaded gun in the pocket

213

of his old US Army surplus jacket for the first time in many years.

*Forget safety. Be notorious. I have tried prudent planning long enough. From now on I'll be mad.*

# CHAPTER TWENTY-TWO

Janice Stewart, Roddy Grant's sister, was waiting in her car outside her brother's home a little after 3 p.m. as she had promised. Aoife returned her phone to her pocket and quickly processed what Jackson had just sent her. An update. Roddy Grant had spent the single longest stint of his clerical career working at Castlereagh Holding Centre. The hub of Special Branch and the home for spooks who fought a secret war against the IRA. And Roddy had one job there. He had been an archivist. Sheen had mentioned yesterday that a police clerical officer could get access to sensitive information should he have a mind to. In Roddy's case he was likely up to his neck in it on a daily basis. Which gave him means, but Aoife needed to remain dispassionate. She had no real evidence that he had done anything wrong.

Aoife took stock of the street as the elderly lady got out of the vintage VW Polo, handbag in hand and wearing a pair of white gloves that complimented the starched collar of her high-necked dress. The red-brick terraced homes just off the Ravenhill Road in mainly Protestant East Belfast were not unlike those on the housing estates she had frequented while on various jobs in the west of the city. In terms of income, education and life chances, there was likely little difference from one working-class side of this town to the other, from Protestant to Catholic. But Aoife guessed, based on what she knew about the sectarian geography of Belfast, that there would be some residents on both sides that would never in their lifetime have the cause or interest in covering the four or so miles that separated these worlds. Roddy's home was an end of terrace, with a dark slate roof and sparse but immaculate paved little front garden.

'I'm DC Aoife McCusker,' she said as the lady approached the front gate where Aoife waited. She offered her warrant card. Janice Stewart nodded at but did not examine her ID. She felt a pang of guilt at dragging this woman down the motorway to revisit the home where her brother had died in tragic circumstances of one kind of another. God knows, she had probably been the one who had found Roddy's dead body. She looked strained and tired. 'Thank you for agreeing to meet me,' she added.

'Janice Stewart. Can you tell me what this is about?' she said, and took a set of keys from her bag.

Aoife stepped aside as Janice took a few moments to unlock the door. Aoife waited for her to enter and then followed her inside but took a second to glance at the lock of the now open door. Fresh scratch marks, very similar to those she had spotted on Tucker Rodgers' door lock at Killeaton. Her stomach took an involuntary dip. What had initially seemed likely to be the drink-induced psychosis of a washed-up old copper now seemed way too plausible, and incredibly sinister. Aoife thought once more of Tucker's scribbled note.

*They killed Roddy and now they're coming for me.*

'I'm afraid that we seem to have misplaced one of our old boys,' said Aoife. The small entrance hallway was covered in dark green wallpaper, a faint odour of dampness and dust in the stale air. 'A man called Thomas Rodgers, Tucker for short. A friend of your brother's we believe,' she said. Janice had led Aoife into a dim back room that opened out to a small kitchen. The Formica-topped table and chairs must have been 1970s originals, and pine kitchen units and deep sink were probably even more retro. Aoife was reminded of mock-ups, staged rooms she had seen while visiting the Ulster Folk and Transport Museum. She almost expected to see a vintage bottle of Fairy Liquid on the windowsill and a branded packet of cigarettes on the tabletop, but the half-finished bottle of washing-up liquid was Asda own brand and there was no ashtray, and no smokes.

'Yes, I know who you mean. I sent an invitation to Mr Rodgers. He was at Roderick's funeral, and at the reception afterwards. He was very inebriated while at both,' she said, the disapproval clear from her tone.

'Good friends with your brother?'

Janice Stewart did not reply. But she opened one of the

kitchen cupboards and took down an address book. She opened the first page.

'I can't say that I knew much about my brother's private life. He was a life-long bachelor. I don't believe he had many close friends,' she said.

Aoife nodded. There were two names and addresses on the page. The first was the Shandon Park Golf Club, and the second was Tucker Rodgers' name and address at Killeaton. A thought came on the back of this.

'Janice, when you arranged the reception for your brother, did you use a list of people, names and addresses? You said yourself that he had few friends you were aware of.' If Janice Stewart had a list of names that corresponded to regulars at the golf club, it could be a starting point to begin the process of cross-referencing.

The woman shook her head.

'No, this was the only name and address I found. I requested that the golf club advertise the gathering which they agreed to let me organise. I am not sure whether they sent the invites to members in the post or simply handed them out to those they knew to be Roderick's associates. In the end, it was reasonably attended. But Mr Rodgers was the only guest to whom I sent an invitation personally.'

Aoife studied Roddy's address book entries once more. The distinctive script was a match for the handwriting on the large envelope they had found at Tucker's place and also for the scrap of poetry that had been written on the other side of the hurried letter that Tucker had sent to his son. And there was more. Tucker's postcode. The last three digits and letters as recorded in the address book were incorrect. She had found exactly the same error on the padded envelope on Tucker's living-room floor. Which confirmed it. The package that she and Sheen surmised must have sent Tucker Rodgers into a blind panic had been sent by Roddy Grant. Aoife's mind returned to what Jackson had dug up about Roddy and his place of work, Castlereagh. And the dates that Tucker had managed to communicate to them, drawn evidently from whatever Roddy had posted to him. Dates that corresponded to IRA attacks and the killing of IRA volunteers.

'Your brother was an archivist at Castlereagh. Did he ever speak to you about his work there, or mention Special Branch in any way?'

'Ah, are you kidding me?' Janice said, raising her eyes to the ceiling and then resting a weary look on Aoife. 'Sure, he was never done talking about his links with Special Branch. On the rare times we met up.'

'Though you said that you knew little about his private life,' countered Aoife.

'I would never speak badly of him. Especially not after what happened. But he was a bit of a Walter Mitty. Tall tales and imaginary adventures. That's what I meant when I said I knew little about his private affairs.'

'What do you mean by tall tales?'

'He'd get a few drinks in him and then it would start. Special Branch this, operation that. He even told my daughter's wee lad that he was a double agent, working undercover.'

'Was he?'

'If you'd known him, you wouldn't have to ask me,' she replied, shaking her head slowly. She went quiet for a few seconds. Aoife asked if she had permission to look around the house and Janice agreed. Janice excused herself, said she would wait in the back garden.

The front room was sparse, a television, sofa and a bookcase beside the fireplace. She turned her attention to the bookshelf. Aoife didn't know for sure, whether Roddy Grant was a fantasist as his sister had claimed, but he was definitely interested in the secret world of spycraft and espionage. Every single book on the shelves was related in some way or other to intelligence agencies and counter-intelligence. Much of it was linked to the Cold War but there were a fair number of books on the Troubles too. She noted two out-of-print books by the late Dylan Martin, a well-known investigative journalist from Belfast who had been murdered under suspicious circumstances decades before.

Upstairs was as dated and weary as the ground floor, but clean, albeit a bit dusty. She did a quick check in the wardrobe, under the bed, looking for anything that seemed out of place, but nothing jumped out. And then Roddy's bedside table drew her attention. There was a framed colour photograph, two blokes with their arms around one another's shoulders, standing beside a small river. One she recognised: Tucker Rodgers, his free hand holding a massive bottle of super-strength cider, half of it gone. The other man she assumed must be Roddy Grant, cradling a fair-sized trout that looked to be about to break free of his hold. She thought about what Janice had said. That her brother Roddy's private life was a mystery, despite his silly talk. How many men had a framed photo of their drinking buddy beside their bed? Maybe a few, but most of them were more likely to remain lifetime bachelors, Aoife assumed. And perhaps a man who may have kept his sexuality under wraps had other things that remained hidden from public view?

Beside the photograph was a book. Hard-backed and hefty.

'The Mitrokhin Archive: The KGB in Europe and the West,' she read. This book was different from the rest. Not on the shelf downstairs. But, also, it didn't look as though it was a bedside read, despite its location. It was standing on a wooden plinth, placed in fact. Just as the framed photograph of Tucker and Roddy was quite evidently elevated and hallowed. The co-author was an academic called Christopher Andrew. A quick scan of the back cover told her he was a man who had made his career writing about spies and intelligence agencies. Another history, and another study of the shadowy world of spies and counter-intelligence. But what made this book so special, as it very clearly had been for Roddy Grant? She set the weighty volume down and opted for her phone. A quick Google search told her what she needed to know. And it set her heart beating.

Vasili Mitrokhin had worked for almost thirty years in the foreign intelligence archives of the KGB. Unknown to his superiors, Mitrokhin had spent over a decade noting and copying highly classified files about KGB agents in the West and had stored them under his dacha floorboards. She thought about Roddy's job. An archivist, just like Mitrokhin, but with access to Special Branch documents that would detail the names and activities of their agents at work within the IRA, rather than KGB spies. If Mitrokhin had copied and stolen documents, then perhaps Roddy, who had evidently viewed Mitrokhin as some kind of hero, had done the same? Some or all of which he had posted to Tucker in that white envelope. Aoife thought about the dates Tucker had sent them and the events they corresponded to. So far, they suspected that TOPBRASS might have a high-level IRA link. But what if TOPBRASS had been someone who was not just a player, but also an agent who had played both sides? Mairead Gleeson's comment the day before about military codenames and call signs suddenly seemed incredibly pertinent.

Aoife stepped back from the bed and scanned the room with fresh eyes. Mitrokhin had stored his stolen documents at his home. Under the floorboards. Aoife walked from one bedroom to another, noting that all three were carpeted. Back in Roddy's bedroom she searched the floor for any sign that the carpet had been recently lifted but found none. Aoife sat on the bed. And then looked again at the bedside table. It had a stone top, framed in dark wood. It looked heavy, and after clearing its contents and attempting to move it, she found that it was. Aoife put her weight behind it, and carefully rocked the table from side to side until she had shifted it about fifteen centimetres to the side. The carpet beneath was fuller, and deeper coloured. She got down on her knees and felt around the newly exposed space, searching. It was smooth; there was nothing here. And then Aoife felt it. A seam, right at the line where the worn, faded carpet met that which had been covered by the floor of the table. She used her nails to get purchase and then she gave it a tug.

The small square of carpet lifted to reveal the floorboards beneath. She could clearly see that one of the boards had been sawed, though some time ago. It didn't look fresh. Aoife found her keys and used one to lever into the space between the boards until it popped up. Her heart was racing now, as she fumbled for her phone and found the torch function. She took a breath and shone the white light into the dark cavity below. There was something there. She reached in and took out a plastic wallet, and then found a couple of plastic ring binders, plus a few pencils, a sharpener and an eraser. But there was nothing else. No documents as she had hoped. But she was sure that her hunch was right. Roddy Grant must have been thieving, and, just like Mitrokhin, stored the stolen documents here beneath his floor. Perhaps until relatively recently. Whether he had managed to send everything he had to Tucker was impossible to know. But he had sent him something. The fact that shady characters had come to Tucker's place in search of him, and presumably the secret documents, certainly suggested that Roddy had managed to pass his information on before he died. Or, perhaps, before he was *murdered* as Tucker had claimed.

After replacing the bedside table as she had found it, Aoife went to the small downstairs bathroom that was adjacent to the kitchen. This was where Roddy Grant had died, apparently by his own hand. Though from what she had found here today, she was far from convinced that was true. Aoife glanced at the back of the door. She saw the strong hook that was screwed into the wood and, as expected, black scuff marks, too numerous to count, a foot or so off ground level. This was where Grant's shoes had scraped and knocked the white-painted door in their ghastly death jig. One that would not have ended with the quick snap of his neck. A slow, painful way to go.

Whoever had done this had been shrewd and cynical enough to ensure they passed this man's death off as a suicide. Grant's body had been released by the coroner and was buried. There was no live murder investigation and no evidence aside from the marks on the lock that a crime had been committed. In terms of forensics, the place had been contaminated beyond useful value. Any evidence she might retrieve could be readily discredited. If Roddy's death was to see justice, it would have to be at the business end of cracking Tucker's disappearance and finding out the truth about TOPBRASS. Aoife left the bathroom and joined Janice Stewart in the back garden. She was finishing a cigarette and quickly stubbed it out when she saw Aoife.

'If my husband knew I was smoking he would not be happy,' she said.

'I won't tell,' replied Aoife. 'Janice, you said that your brother used to talk about spies, agents, that kind of thing. Did he ever mention someone called TOPBRASS?'

Janice Stewart took her time before shaking her head, that weary look on her face once more.

'No, never that. But it certainly sounds like it might be from one of his stories,' she said.

*Not this time*, thought Aoife. TOPBRASS was for real. And so was the danger that knowledge of the truth about him brought to those who got too close.

# CHAPTER TWENTY-THREE

'Please, come on in.'

Aoife followed Liam Bell into his small Fallswater Street home in West Belfast. This was her last stop of the afternoon before she would meet up with Sheen to speak to the brother of Danny Caffery, the IRA leader of the Cyprus Three gang. The octogenarian was still wide-shouldered and straight-backed under his woollen V-neck sweater, and Aoife noted approvingly how neat and tidy the hallway of his home was, a fastidiousness that extended to the rest of the house she suspected. The smell of lemon air freshener pervaded, but below its high scent was a deeper layer of tobacco smoke, maybe cigars, that was not altogether unpleasant. He offered her a cup of tea, but she declined, and he beckoned her to take a seat on the two-seater sofa in his back room. It was humble. A small bookshelf which included dated paperback volumes of *The Godfather* and the Native American classic *Bury My Heart at Wounded*

*Knee*. And heavier reading too. A copy of Marx's *Das Kapital* and *The Communist Manifesto*. Both had well-creased spines and were clearly not on the shelf for show. Beside the bookshelf was an old portable television with a small table lamp in the corner next to it. The walls were similarly sparse, the only pictures being two small framed photographs that hung above the mantelpiece. One was of a young girl on a bike with stabilisers, chubby legs astride, smiling with glee at the camera. The other was a black and white wedding snap, Liam Bell as a much younger man, straight-backed and poker-faced, his bashful-looking bride in white clipped to his arm. Aoife noted that the house was devoid of the sort of religious iconography that was typical for homes in this very Catholic and nationalist district of the city. No gilded print of the Virgin Mary, no holy water font at the front door.

As Liam Bell settled slowly into a high-backed, well-upholstered chair, he nodded at the photographs at which Aoife had been looking. 'You say this is about our Bernie?' Bernadette Bell, the twenty-three-year-old IRA volunteer who had been executed by the organisation as an informer in November 1981. Her name had been the first match for the dates scribbled by Tucker Rodgers. Aoife had read up on her case before she came here. The young woman had been missing for a week before her body was dumped miles from home. But the photograph Liam Bell had nodded towards was that of the little girl with a brand-new bicycle.

'Yes. Was this her?' she asked.

'Aye. She loved that wee bike,' he replied simply. Liam Bell surveyed Aoife, his dark eyes watchful, distrustful behind heavy lids. The skin on his face was soft and pale as unproved dough and she now saw that his knuckles were badly swollen with arthritis, the joints red and angry on both hands. Aoife explained her background, the role of SHOT and that they were interested in re-investigating the case of his daughter's murder.

Liam Bell raised one gnarly hand and she fell silent.

'What do you mean, re-investigate? There was never any investigation in the first place. And besides,' he said, as he produced a pipe and pouch from the side pocket of the chair and started to pack the bowl with strings of tobacco, 'I already know who killed her. And I know why,' he said.

'The IRA,' she confirmed. Liam Bell nodded once and set the unlit pipe between his lips. Aoife took a breath, thinking about how best to proceed, trying to see a way forward that would not force an old man who had lost his daughter to a violent death, the pain of reliving the loss. But there was no other way. 'The day that Bernie was taken away, were you here?'

'Yes,' he answered, without hesitation.

'Did you see the people who took her?'

'No.' But less emphatically this time. Aoife waited, and Liam Bell watched her, unblinking and hard-eyed, with the pipe set in his mouth. He extracted it and spoke again. 'It was dark. Night-time. All I saw was that a car pulled up outside. People in it, more than one.'

'Mr Bell, were you aware that Bernie was in the IRA?'

He gave a throaty laugh, sharp, like he was clearing gravel.

'Of course. And until her demise, I was proud of her. They weren't ideal, but the Provos were the only means to achieve a revolution. And this place was overdue one. Still is,' he said, and set the pipe back in his mouth, nodding slowly. Aoife thought about the books on his shelves. Recommended reading for little Bernie, the chubby-kneed girl who once loved her bike and ended up suffering the death and infamy of an IRA tout.

'Did she know that she was under suspicion, that she was in danger?'

Bell's eyes flicked to the photo over the mantelpiece for a second or two and then returned to Aoife. Some of the hardness had melted.

'Probably not. Otherwise, she'd never have got into that car,' he observed.

'What about her comrades, those she ran with? Did you meet them, did she ever confide any details, anything at all from that time that comes to mind?'

He nodded twice.

'I knew a few. One got shot dead the year after Bernie was killed. He was murdered by loyalists. The other one blew himself up while trying to park a car bomb outside the Ulster Hall in town.' Aoife said she understood, but this was frustrating. Too much time had expired, but what did she expect? 'There were others of course, but I kept my distance, and she didn't talk about it, which was as it should have been.' Another gritty laugh, as devoid of real humour as the first. 'Not to me she didn't anyway,' he said.

'So, you believe she was an informer?'

Nothing from Liam Bell. His mouth turned downwards and one of his inflamed hands closed into the nearest thing to a fist as he could now manage.

'I don't blame the IRA for killing her. She knew what she was getting involved in,' he said.

Aoife blinked. His own daughter. Someone had once

told her that the Latin roots of the word 'fundamentalism' translated as 'a place without reason'. She had no idea, despite her convent education, whether that was true or not. But it was clear that for this old atheist, revolutionary politics was his religion, and what he'd said made him as much of an extremist as the men who ploughed into innocent people on London Bridge and then went on the rampage. 'But they should never have tortured her. There was no need,' he said, his voice cracking on the last word.

'Maybe she was innocent?' said Aoife.

Bell shook his head emphatically.

'I've spent my life thinking about this. I was an idiot. I missed the signs, or probably just didn't want to see them. She had too much ready money all of a sudden and she was edgy, even by the standards of an IRA volunteer,' he said. 'And anyway, what's this all about? Why my Bernie? And why now?'

'We have reason to think that there may be more to your daughter's death than was concluded at the time.'

'Meaning what?'

'That it may be connected in some way to a number of other crimes. And that a degree of collusion may have taken place,' she said, thinking about what she had discovered at Roddy Grant's home. His obsession with spies and informers. The hidden storage hole where he had likely stashed copied Special Branch documents just like his KGB hero had once done in Russia. Only Roddy Grant had clearly collected evidence about a Special Branch agent in the IRA. TOPBRASS. And if TOPBRASS, an agent for Special Branch, was implicated in Bernadette Bell's killing, then at the very least those running him may have turned a blind eye to the crime. Or worse, had for some reason given him a licence to murder.

Liam Bell's face darkened. He got off his chair and asked her to wait as he left the room. Aoife wondered what would have happened if Bernadette Bell's father had discovered her secret treachery. Would he have demanded that she stop selling secrets, or would he have delivered her to the IRA for execution? Bell re-entered the room, carrying an ancient tape recorder with a faux wooden finish. He sat down and set it on his lap.

'Listen,' he said and pressed play.

The static crackle of an old recording was followed by the rasp of what sounded like fabric rubbing against the microphone. And then, a voice. Female, shaking with fear and doubtless full of pain too.

'My name is Bernadette Bell. I am an IRA volunteer and have been working as a Special Branch informer for two years. I have sold secrets and betrayed my comrades. I—' Here her voice wavers, as though unsure or unable to continue and another voice can be heard. This one is male, speaking in a little over a whisper. 'Keep going, keep going,' he commands, and Bernadette Bell obeys. 'I have caused the death of fellow volunteers and I accept the sentence that has been passed on me.' Her voice cracks and there are tears. The recording is stopped and then begins again, possibly at some point later. 'Daddy, I am sorry for the shame I have brought on you and my family. I want my death to be a lesson to others. Never trust the promises the British and Special Branch make. May God have mercy on my soul.' The recording ended and Bell stopped the tape with a click. Silence descended, but Aoife could still hear the voice of that young woman, speaking from a hopeless place and still caught somewhere in time. Liam Bell was impassive. He'd heard this recording before. But Aoife could not fathom how he could ever be able to listen to its horrors more than once. Perhaps this was his revolutionary penance, a punishment for the shame his daughter had spoken of in her dying words?

'Collusion or not, it doesn't change the fact that my daughter turned,' he said.

'Perhaps not, Mr Bell. But it may well have influenced her murder. If you don't mind, I will need to take a recording of this. I can do it on my phone, but it means we will have to play it again.' Bell pressed rewind and asked her if she was ready.

Afterwards, he opened the front door and Aoife stepped out into the small front garden. The air was fresh and breezy, the sky above a rolling parade of white fluffy clouds with little gifts of brilliant Belfast blue sky showing here and there. There was a forecast of rain and despite the early spring hiatus, she believed it. When you could depend on nothing else in this life, sooner or later the rain would still fall in Belfast. She drank in the clean air, suddenly aware of how glad she was to be out of Liam Bell's still and sterile abode.

'Would you mind?' he asked, handing her a large box of safety matches. He wanted her to strike a match so he could light his pipe. A little finesse was needed, and his hands could not oblige. She stepped into the doorway and touched a flame to the bowl of the pipe as Bell inhaled. It was sucked into the tobacco which immediately glowed a deep amber and then they were both enveloped by a veil of sweet cherry smoke. The man thanked her and took his place on the threshold. He pointed the stem of his pipe towards the far end of the street where Fallswater Street joined the Falls Road.

'You asked me about our Bernie's comrades. There was one other fella. I never met him; he kept his distance. Bernie would have hooked up with him at the corner. He had dirty ginger hair, I remember that. But I never saw him close up.'

'Was he IRA?'

Bell nodded, slowly.

'You said she didn't talk about it, and that you kept your distance. How can you be sure?'

He glanced at her and then returned his eyes to a point further down the street, or perhaps somewhere in the past.

'I'm not sure. But he might have been the guy who was driving the car. The one that picked her up the night she was taken away.'

'Did you ever check it out?'

He shook his head through a fug of smoke, his old jowls quivering slightly as he did so.

'How could I? Why would I? The last people in the world I wanted to get near was the IRA's Nutting Squad. But if you're right then one of those boys was as bent as Bernie. So now, aye, now I wish I had gone looking for him,' he said.

# CHAPTER TWENTY-FOUR

Sheen parked up a few doors away from where his satnav told him he could find Danny Caffery's address in Beechmount, West Belfast. He could see the green hummock of the Divis Mountain framed at the bottom of the road where it sloped out of view and would lead into the grounds of Belfast Heights Psychiatric Hospital. Sheen had driven through a dense network of terraced, industrial-era red-brick streets to get here and had checked his rear-view more than once. He'd been looking for the grey hatchback with the blacked-out windows that he and Aoife had spotted near Tucker Rodgers' Killeaton home the day before. There had been no sign of it, but still Sheen could not shake the pervasive sense that he was being tailed and being watched. Movement, a car turned the corner, visible in Sheen's wing mirror. He tensed, ready to reach for his weapon should he need it, but then he dropped his shoulders. It was a taxi, one of the cabs that worked the

International Airport. The car slowly passed. The driver was thin on top, big set and wore a vintage army surplus jacket. He ignored Sheen completely, his eyes searching the homes adjacent to where Sheen waited, as though looking for an address. After passing Caffery's place he accelerated and disappeared down the road.

Sheen texted Aoife McCusker to tell her he was waiting, and then picked up his dossier on the Cyprus Three. He glanced in his rear-view once more. No wonder he was a bit on edge. This place had been an IRA stronghold at the height of the Troubles. He had passed a large mural on a gable wall which celebrated the one hundredth anniversary of the Irish republican 1916 Easter Rising. In many ways the rows of terraced houses here were no different from their duplicate nineteenth-century industrial cousins in northern English towns like Bolton or Sheffield. But of course, those similarities were superficial. The writing on the walls was symptomatic of how much history, and indeed blood, had been loosed here. In previous decades IRA men like John Fryer, the psychotic killer Sheen had faced down last summer, had prowled these streets like lions in the night. He flicked through the pages until he found what he wanted. Information about Danny Caffery.

Caffery had been a notorious IRA gunman, thought to have been personally responsible for killing seventeen British soldiers on the streets of Belfast. When the IRA introduced a cell structure in the late 1970s, Caffery used it as a chance to form his own elite team. He had hand-picked Monica Gleeson and PJ Wilson. And all three had died in a hail of SAS bullets in Cyprus. His brother, Peadar Caffery, who now lived at the address, seemed to have been cut from a different cloth. No criminal record, and no suggestion that he was ever a member of the IRA. He was, however, a member of the main Irish republican political party who, until recently, had shared power with unionists in the Northern Irish parliament. And of course, Sheen was of a mind that the chief's main motivation for ordering him to investigate the case of the Cyprus Three in the first place was to appease the interests of such people as Peadar Caffery. Sheen's investigation would likely gift Caffery's party the opportunity to highlight a historic injustice that the British were guilty of, win points with their voters, re-enter the power-sharing parliament on a propaganda high and, in doing so, keep the chaos that threatened to return, at bay.

A sharp tap on the window. Sheen flinched and then unlocked the car. Aoife McCusker got in, bringing a waft of cool air and a greeting.

'How's it going?' she asked.

Sheen gave her a potted summary of his day's work so far. Nothing of note from PJ Wilson's address in Andersonstown and nothing but headache from Shandon Park Golf Club.

'You?'

'Oh, I did better than that,' she replied, and Sheen could see the glint of excitement in her blue eyes. She'd found something. Aoife gave him a run-down. First, that Hayley White had been able to confirm the man who owned the piece of fabric they had found had been running scared, just as they believed Tucker had been.

'Did she suggest where he might have gone?'

'No, sorry. But she did mention something about him

repeating numbers, like a phone number.' Sheen nodded and asked her to continue.

Aoife explained what Jackson had clarified about Roddy's position as archivist at Castlereagh. And then she told him what she'd found at Roddy's home. The obsession with spies and agents, but most tellingly the hidden compartment under his bedroom floor.

'Bloody hell, that's great work, Aoife,' said Sheen, and then fell silent for a few seconds, piecing it together. 'We felt confident that Tucker's dates point to TOPBRASS having an IRA link.'

'Oh, I'm pretty certain he does. But I think he's much more than that.'

'TOPBRASS is a Special Branch double agent,' confirmed Sheen.

'Who has clearly got a lot to hide,' replied Aoife. She told him what she had learnt from Liam Bell. That he did not dispute that his daughter was an informer and watched as she was driven off to her death.

Sheen was silent for a long moment, absorbing what Aoife had told him about Bell's cold attitude to his daughter's murder but also what this meant for their investigation into TOPBRASS.

'If TOPBRASS was an informer and was also involved in killing Bernadette Bell, then this is much darker than we initially thought.'

'One Special Branch agent permitted to murder another,' confirmed Aoife. 'And Roddy's door had the same scratches on the lock that we found on Tucker Rodgers'. No way of being certain but I'd say forced entry.'

'Suggesting foul play in Roddy's death, just as Tucker claimed,' said Sheen.

'And if Tucker's dates are to be believed, maybe TOPBRASS was permitted to do a lot more than kill Bernadette Bell,' replied Aoife.

'You read the file?' asked Sheen, nodding to the information about the Cyprus Three. Aoife nodded. 'Then let's go speak with Danny Caffery's brother. See if he can tell us anything more about this,' said Sheen, getting out of the car.

Danny Caffery's home had a plaque fixed to the wall above the door. His name was printed in Irish, as was his IRA status as an *óglach* or volunteer. The Irish tricolour and the blue and white motif of the starry plough flag which dated from the 1916 Irish Rebellion adorned the plaque, as did Caffery's date of death.

### MURDERED BY A BRITISH ARMY DEATH SQUAD
### WHILE ON ACTIVE SERVICE
### 'IRELAND UNFREE WILL NEVER BE AT PEACE'

Sheen pressed the doorbell and the deep bark of what sounded like a very big dog came from within. A man in his early sixties with a neatly manicured white goatee opened the door. He was average height, average build, and eyed Sheen and Aoife from behind a pair of dark-framed reading glasses. Sheen held up his warrant card and made a quick introduction for them both.

'Yeah?'

'We work on historical cases,' said Sheen.

A little glimmer of recognition from the man when he said

this. There had been a fair bit of news coverage last summer and, of course, most recently about the Soldier G case.

'You the ones that brought that soldier to trial?'

Sheen said that they had.

'I'm investigating the deaths of Daniel Caffery and the Cyprus Three in 1987.'

'Danny was my brother. I'm Peadar. Come in,' he said, and opened the door. 'Princess, get in there and calm down,' he said. Princess, a very large, sandy-coloured bitch that looked like she might be a pit bull cross, went obediently into a steel cage in the small front room into which he led them. Peadar Caffery pushed the door closed, but Sheen took note that he did not bolt or lock it. The dog had pink jowls, and green eyes. It stared at Sheen and Aoife as it started to pace the small space it had been confined to. Its tail moved back and forth like a small horse whip. Caffery gestured for them to take a seat as he helped himself to an armchair adjacent to Princess's cage.

He and Aoife sat down on the small sofa at the window. There was an oversized framed reproduction painting of the Virgin Mary over the mantle. On a small table next to it stood an A4-sized framed colour photograph which caught Sheen's attention. It was the heads and shoulders of three young men, long hair, beards and smiles. They could have been art students, but Sheen recognised the face of the man at the centre as Danny Caffery. This must have been the original image from which his headshot had been snipped. The latter had been used by news reports and articles at the time of the Cyprus killings and ever since. Sheen had seen it painted on more than one gable wall too. He didn't look like a killer and neither did the small group of men he must have called friends. But then bitter experience had taught Sheen that few murderers, if any, fitted the stereotype. Peadar noticed him staring at the photo.

'That was taken in Long Kesh, after internment,' he said. Long Kesh was the original incarnation of the Maze Prison or the H-Blocks, the purpose-built, maximum security prison which housed Irish republican and loyalist paramilitary inmates.

Peadar asked him if he recognised anyone else. Sheen studied the faded print, the original from which it had been copied had been almost sepia with age, and the whole effect very much shouted the 1970s.

'Is that guy on the left who I think it is?' The men in the photograph were similarly long-haired, but the man he had focused on with his distinctive black curls and dark beard stood out. He looked more Sardinian or Sicilian than Irish. And like Caffery, his was a face that Sheen had seen before.

'One and the same. That's Brendan Kielty,' said Peadar. He was clearly pleased to be able to tell Sheen and proud too. Kielty was the candidate for First Minister of Northern Ireland and the leader of the same Irish republican party of which Peadar Caffery was a member. But, unlike Peadar, it was well known that Kielty had been an active IRA member in the past, a one-time street Provo from the republican heartland of Ballymurphy who had never denied his involvement.

'Were they friends?'

'Comrades,' corrected Peadar.

A hush fell on the room. Princess and her owner watched Sheen. There would be no offer of tea.

'Peadar, we have been asked to investigate the killing of your brother and his associates,' said Aoife.

Peadar glanced at her, a look of incredulity.

'Don't you mean their murder? If so, 'bout time. But it's not me that you need to talk with. Go to Somerset, or Canterbury, or the Costa of wherever the SAS go to keep tight-lipped and drink warm ale. Ask them why they thought fit to do my brother in cold blood.'

'You can rest assured that we will conduct a thorough investigation,' replied Aoife. 'The original inquest heard testimony from the soldiers involved in which they claimed your brother and the other IRA members appeared to make threatening movements, as though going for concealed weapons,' continued Aoife.

'And the first news reports that probably were written by Whitehall said they were armed and a bomb was found at the scene. But was there a gun found at the scene? No. And there was no bomb either. Seven pounds of sugar was dropped by PJ Wilson that he had wrapped up in beach towels,' said Peadar. He was growing red in the face, his eyes beginning to bulge behind his glasses. Princess started to growl low and deep like a racing motorbike idling in neutral. Sheen needed to change the course, or this would end doing more harm than good. 'The Brits killed them the way the Brits know best, unarmed and defenceless.'

'Peadar, I'm going to request unrestricted access to MI5 documents and police records. If the official version doesn't stand up then I'll call them out,' Sheen assured him. 'You can trust me, us, on this,' he said. Peadar sat back in his chair, gave Sheen a small nod. 'And you were right. I don't need to check what happened on the ground with you; it's not really why we are here,' he said and turned his head towards Aoife, hoping she would pick up on his message. 'But I do need you to cast your mind back to that time, tell me if you can recall anything at all that your brother said or did, any detail which might have been missed or never picked up on in the first place,' suggested Sheen.

Peadar sat quietly for a few seconds, his head lowered. 'Look, my brother was an IRA volunteer, and a great one. The kind of operative that earned the respect of other fighters because he never asked them to do anything he wouldn't. And that was how he died, side by side with those he led. But he never discussed his work with me, not with anybody as far as I knew. He worked in a secret cell. Until Cyprus, I didn't even know who was in it,' he said, but Sheen noted that Peadar's animation and conviction was gone, and his eyes were lowered.

'What if I told you that your brother and his unit might have been betrayed, sold out?' risked Sheen. If TOPBRASS murdered Bernadette Bell, then perhaps the Cyprus Three were killed on the back of information he had provided too?

'I'd tell you to get real,' snapped Caffery, but a little too quickly for Sheen's liking. Caffery's right eye twitched. 'That's not the message that we want to hear. That's the kind of whisper that MI5 likes to start, a good way to deflect blame from the Brits, when it was them who killed my brother in cold blood. They could have arrested him,' said Caffery. *We*. He meant his political party. Caffery was only interested in one version of the truth. The truth that would further his side's governmental agenda. A revelation that IRA volunteers were cut down in cold blood by imperialist Britain was one thing. But to suggest they were sold out by one of their own number did not have the same PR value. This was going nowhere, but Sheen decided to have one more try.

'Did Danny ever mention someone called TOPBRASS?'

Peadar's eye continued to twitch.

'No, I've never heard that.'

Sheen had nothing more to ask. He stood up, and Aoife followed his lead. Princess traced their moves with wide eyes.

'Thanks for your time. I can appreciate that this probably isn't easy,' he offered.

'You did the right thing in your last case. This time go further, follow the truth all the way to the very top,' suggested Peadar Caffery at the front door, pointing skyward with his thumb for emphasis.

*I will*, thought Sheen, *but unlike you I'll be looking for the other kind of truth, the one that does not change depending on your politics.*

Back at his car, Sheen quickly conducted the required security checks and found the vehicle clean. 'Well,' he said as they got in, 'even if he does know something about TOPBRASS he certainly won't be telling us,' he said.

'He got a bit rattled, though, when you mentioned it. You think he knows who it is?' replied Aoife.

'I saw that. Impossible to say. But it doesn't change matters. So far, we've got nothing to show from the Cyprus case. Mairead Gleeson, pleasant but unhelpful; PJ Wilson's family was a non-starter; and Peadar Caffery is only interested in one outcome,' said Sheen.

'We still have the MI5 documents to go through, when they arrive,' offered Aoife. Which was true.

'Yeah. And I'll be interested to hear what Geordie has dug up on the case of Dennis Lamont, the cop who was murdered in the ice-cream parlour,' said Sheen.

'Plus, we still have the bus bombing to look into,' said Aoife. She meant Ballycarrick, eight dead squaddies, another of the dates on Tucker's list. 'If we can't unmask TOPBRASS by investigating Cyprus, we might still get to him through the other cases.'

'I hope so. One thing about Cyprus confuses me, though,' said Sheen.

'Go on.'

'So far there's agreement that Danny Caffery ran a tight unit, handpicked. One of the points of the IRA cell structure was to prevent informers getting access to information. In an active service unit of three or four, there was nobody on the periphery. Everyone was known and trusted.'

'And all three members of the Cyprus unit died together,' said Aoife.

'Which begs the question: how could anyone have got close enough to betray them, without ending up dead in Cyprus too?' said Sheen.

# CHAPTER TWENTY-FIVE

Sheen had asked Aoife to join him for some food, but she declined. She wanted to get back and put a few hours' revision in for her Sergeants' Exam which was coming up in a matter of days. It was close to seven by the time Sheen had parked in his space in the underground garage at his Laganside apartment block. The rent he was getting off his Russell Square apartment in London more than covered it and the view from his small penthouse was breathtaking. But of late he'd taken the concept of a bachelor pad way too far. There was nothing in the fridge, and Aoife was right about what she'd said: he needed to clean the place up or pay someone who could do it for him. He exited his garage and headed for a small place near the City Hall, AMPM. A great little bistro that reminded him of the sort of place he used to enjoy on the outskirts of Soho in London.

An hour later he was back at the apartment building, slowly climbing the narrow staircase to his penthouse. His hands were laden with two bags of groceries that he had picked up at the Today's Express convenience store, and his head felt a little furry with the half carafe of claret he had enjoyed with the oxtail stew at the bistro. He felt his phone thrum in his jacket pocket but ignored it. The stairs were steep, four flights in all. Twelve steps a piece, each flight followed by a sharp right turn on a small landing before he started climbing again. Sheen stopped where the stairs took one final turn. Twelve more steps to the door of his apartment. He rested the bags on the carpet and flexed his fingers. Sheen's eye zoomed in on the door to his apartment, just above his line of sight.

It was open, but barely. As though enticing him to come and see. His heart picked up a beat and a shudder of anticipation ran through him. Aoife had forsaken the revision after all. And now he knew why his phone had been buzzing. She was waiting for him. Sheen smiled and picked up his shopping bags, taking the steps to his apartment door one at a time on tiptoe. He was halfway up when he heard the sharp crack of a floorboard coming from within. Sheen's smile faltered and then fell. He knew which board made that sound. It was in front of the fridge in the small kitchenette. But there was one problem. That board complained when Sheen put his not inconsiderable weight on it, like a snap of disapproval that asked him whether he really needed to visit the fridge for another can. But when Aoife stayed over she didn't get the same response. Not enough weight. Sheen climbed another few steps, his eyes on the door, listening intently. Now his heart was drumming much faster, all appetite for carnal pleasure gone. He slowly set the groceries down on the step above him, the rustle and crunch of the plastic bags suddenly cacophonous.

Sheen waited. Not a sound from behind the partly open door and the sliver of the room beyond was all shadow. Then he focused on the keyhole. There were fresh scratches on the brass. Similar to those that he had spotted on the lock of Tucker Rodgers' home. Same as the marks that Aoife had found on Roddy Grant's front door. He reached for his gun, managed to get it halfway out of its holster before his phone rang, loud and impossible to muffle. In the same instant, there were sounds of movement from inside his apartment.

'Shit,' said Sheen. He managed to position his right foot down one step and pull his Glock free. In the same instant, his apartment door swung open, incredibly fast, and Sheen was rammed by a figure dressed in black who exploded from the shadows within. He felt a vice grip on his right wrist as he was shoved backwards, twisting his hand into an unnatural position, making it impossible to pull the trigger. As Sheen fell, he caught a glimpse of the man who had charged into him with the force of a skip lorry carrying a full load. Small but very stocky, wearing black, with a ski mask over his face. His eyes were keen and composed as he watched Sheen fall.

Sheen landed on his rear on the square of carpet at the base of the stairs. The back of his head slammed hard against the plasterboard wall. If it had been solid brick he would have been knocked out cold. Instead the wind was instantly knocked from him and a firework of pain exploded from his skull, joined a second later by another from his coccyx. He sucked air into his lungs and raised the gun, which had become suddenly heavy in his hand. The dark figure bounded down the steps, made the distance up in two big jumps. Sheen squinted and tried to aim for his squat centre of mass, but his finger on the trigger refused to cooperate. The man sliced at Sheen's extended arm with the edge of his hand. A sharp stab of pain above the wrist. Sheen dropped the gun. The assailant followed through with his elbow which connected with Sheen's left temple, snapping his head back and to the side, and spraying his vision with stars and billowing blackness. Rough hands quickly frisked him then this man's hot breath on Sheen's face, laced with the phantom of a recent cigarette. Sheen sensed him depart. He shook his head, ignored the pain from both temple and crown, and lunged after the moving figure. Sheen managed to get a hand on one of his booted feet as he jumped away from his grasp, and Sheen pushed him with a growl of anger and frustration, using all his available strength in an attempt to topple him over.

Sheen scrabbled to his hands and knees, absurd elation filling him as he watched the attacker unbalance and then tumble. He snatched his Glock off the ground and got to his feet. In the time it took him to do so, the bastard had fallen into a forward roll down the stairs and landed on his feet in a moving run. He disappeared around the corner, and Sheen could hear his rapid descent. Sheen took a step in pursuit and instantly had to grip the bannister to prevent himself from toppling over. He slowly sat on the step feeling the world rotate, tasting the sour prelude of his supper's encore as it now threatened to reappear. He managed to keep it down, and very slowly descended the stairs, any possibility of pursuit and apprehension now gone. He exited the door to the street and turned in a circle, eyes wide and his gun ready.

The street was empty. The only sign of life was the chorus of seagulls from the harbour and the drone of a plane passing overhead. He lowered his gun, much more aware now of the competing pains that vied for his attention: his lower back, his right wrist, his head. To his right, he heard the screech of tyres and raised his weapon once more. Maybe two hundred metres away a small grey hatchback with matt paintwork had stopped. A figure dressed in black slowly got in and the car sped off. It was too far away to ascertain details but Sheen knew two things: that was his man – the same frame, the same unhurried casualness that he had exhibited while almost getting shot at point-blank range by Sheen before diving headfirst down a flight of stairs; and he knew that car. It was the same motor that had pulled out and driven off when he was leaving Tucker Rodgers' home in Killeaton. He was right. They'd been following him, watching.

*They*.

Sheen's phone rang. He holstered his weapon and answered.

'Sheen,' he said. It hurt to talk.

'Sheen, something's happened,' said Aoife. 'I've been trying to reach you.' He heard the concern in her voice, thought about what he'd just experienced.

'Are you hurt? What's wrong?'

'I'm fine. It's Dave Rodgers. Someone broke into his hotel room this afternoon. He must have either been there or interrupted them. He's alive but he's been hurt.'

'Where is he?'

'Royal Victoria Hospital. They've put him into an induced coma,' she explained.

Sheen went silent for a long moment. Aoife asked him if he was still there.

'Yeah. I had a visitor too.' He gave her the run-down.

'Christ, Sheen,' she replied, and she didn't need to say anything else, he heard it in that one phrase. He'd been lucky. This could have ended a lot worse for him, for them. 'I'm going to check in on Dave Rodgers.'

'No. I'll ask Geordie to take a hike over to the Royal, see if Dave's likely to wake and be in a position to talk anytime soon. You stay with little Ava. And be careful.'

'Dave's hotel room was turned over. Police at the scene assumed robbery,' she said.

Sheen now remembered that his attacker had searched him, no doubt in much the same way he had searched Sheen's apartment. Sheen reached into his pocket. His warrant card was there, but something was missing.

'Aoife, the bastard who broke into my place stole my notepad,' he said. Sheen quickly summoned to mind what he had written there. He had definitely written the first three dates that Tucker Rodgers had sent them, and he may have also scribbled 'Cyprus Three' in lieu of the date in 1987 but he wasn't sure. Maybe it was the knock on the head, or maybe it was because the whole point of the notepad was not to have to keep things in mind as well as recording the actions of the case. But one thing he was certain of, he'd written the name that Tucker had told him to investigate: TOPBRASS. Tucker's letter was safely locked in Grosvenor Road station. Whoever had attacked Dave Rodgers did not get that at least. But now, it barely mattered.

'What will they get from that?' asked Aoife.

'Everything we know,' replied Sheen.

# PART FOUR

## RED GIUSEPPE AND EIGHT DEAD MEN

# CHAPTER TWENTY-SIX

'*A chara*,' said Fenton by way of greeting. *My friend.*

He was speaking on a burner phone which he would later dispose of. This one was number three and had a brother of the same number, on which the man he called now listened. Phones one to ten, and when they were finished, a replacement set would be bought and numbers exchanged. In recent years, it had been very rare indeed for them to work through a full set of phones, but in the last two weeks, they had gone through three. In the many years that they had worked together previously, they had trusted other ways of communicating in total secrecy. A small laugh from the man on the other line. Fenton's use of Gaelic was an old, old joke, but somehow it always managed to tickle. When he spoke, the man's voice had no trace of humour.

'Have you got good news?'

Fenton put a flame to the tip of his Dunhill and inhaled furiously, feeling the smoke ignite a forest fire in his tired lungs. The colostomy bag that was secured to the bottom of his calf was uncomfortably full and he shifted on his feet in discomfort.

'Not the news we wanted.'

'Fuck's sake, Fenton.'

'But we have something,' Fenton hurriedly added.

'Go on.'

Fenton quickly summarised what they had discovered in Owen Sheen's notepad. Not a lot, but at least they now had an idea of the extent of Sheen's knowledge, where previously they had not, and Fenton said so.

A friend of a friend had told Fenton that Roddy Grant had been overheard at the golf club saying he was going to get rich selling Branch secrets back to them. Fenton lay low, but sent one of his boys to approach Roddy, and to show him a fat wad of fifties. Which was when Roddy Grant said the Special Branch codename of the man Fenton was now on the phone to. Which, of course, changed everything. When his boys visited Roddy at home there were no Branch documents in sight. And he had proved unexpectedly resistant to questioning, even with a gun to his head. Fenton had dug around a bit, discovered Grant had a sister in Ballymoney. It was only when they explained that she would be dealt with that he started to spill the beans. He admitted that he'd posted a secret stash of copied files to Tucker Rodgers, the only name in his address book. Grant had given them just a few details of what he'd stolen and copied, but it was enough for Fenton to know he had to go. So they strung the bastard up, made it look legitimate, and turned their attention to Tucker. Who, against all odds, had managed to escape and stay well hidden. Fucking shitstorm extreme.

'This is good news. We assumed the worst, that Tucker might have sent everything to his son. But Sheen's team only have four dates, and there's no way they can make much sense of anything with that. We need to keep calm. This we can contain. We just need this bastard Sheen and his pals to back away. And then we find Tucker.'

'But what if he doesn't back away? What if they get to Tucker Rodgers and those Branch documents first? Our names are all over those fucking things.' Fenton crushed his smoke, thought again about what he'd read in Sheen's notepad. He had to tell him. 'Sheen already has your codename.' He waited. Complete silence from the other end. 'But they don't know your real name. And they never will.'

'They have my name,' said the man. Fenton said nothing. 'I'm in charge now.'

Fenton fumbled for a fresh smoke with his eyes squeezed closed and found the pack was empty.

'No. You need to leave this with me. I'm dealing with it. My way. Discreetly. We took a risk with that clown Roddy Grant. We can't go leaving a trail of dead bodies. I have a plan.'

'No. We have a problem. And as someone once said, death solves every problem. No man, no problem. You do it your way. But don't cross paths with me, Fenton, be warned. Your wee pack of guard dogs don't impress me.'

'Will you just listen for a second? Don't do anything stupid. This is in hand.'

A growl from the very dangerous, very agitated man speaking in Fenton's ear.

'What did you say? Stupid? Who's the stupid fucking cunt who allowed this to see the light of day?'

Fenton felt woozy. It was his bag, mostly that.

'Move on to phone four. Keep me informed. You'll hear from me,' he said and then the line went dead.

Fenton was sweating. For the first time in his long and illustrious career, he was behind the curve, a long way short of catching a wave that now loomed over him as dark and menacing as a leviathan from the deep. He made a call. His man, his most trusted guard dog, picked up and listened without even a greeting. All business, and as Fenton spoke, he felt his pulse settle and his calm restored. His man said he would sort it, as ordered. No, he didn't need Fenton to give him the where or how, he would find a way to make it work. Fenton agreed. The less he knew, the less it would likely come round and nest on him afterwards. Then Fenton thought about the heavy-handedness that had left Tucker Rodgers' son incapacitated. That had not been his man's fault. The bastard had put up a fight. Still, discretion.

'Remember: alive and awake,' he warned, and then he ended the call and set to work dismantling burner phone three. Alive yes, for the time being anyway.

# CHAPTER TWENTY-SEVEN

Sheen took two more anti-inflammatory painkillers, even though he should have waited another hour before doing so, and washed them down with cold coffee at his desk in the SHOT office. First thing this morning he'd managed to visit Dave Rodgers at the small high dependency ward in the Royal Victoria Hospital by showing his warrant card. But despite the formality, his visit was personal, not just police business. Dave remained in an induced coma, hemmed in by a hissing respirator and intermittent beeping from various monitors. No change since the previous evening when Geordie had reported that Tucker's son was unconscious but stable. The nurse on duty suggested that he had suffered a form of strangulation, most likely the result of a chokehold. Sheen understood the dangers. It was an effective but potentially very dangerous move that posed the risk of stopping blood and air flow, and had resulted in the death of a number of suspects. It led Sheen to think that Dave had perhaps disturbed an intruder, possibly more than one, and that he was lucky to be alive. Sheen made a mental note to check that Geordie had contacted Dave's partner in Manchester and told her what had happened. That said, if a thug had wanted to disable Dave with several hard blows to the head it was surely always an option, and in Belfast it was more often the first one that was selected. Meaning that whoever Dave had challenged had exercised at least a modicum of restraint and moderation. As only a professional can.

Sheen again considered the man who had invaded his home and attacked him the night before. Likely the same crew. He'd been capable, well-trained and controlled. Another element of this that seemed to whisper spooks, Special Branch, or some combination of the two. After a late night waiting for the SOCOs to finish at his apartment they had given him nothing of value. Not a fingerprint, and nothing in the way of a trace sample for DNA testing. Sheen had also run a check on grey-coloured hatchback cars but without a registration detail or certainty about the make, he'd come back with the phone book. Spooks were also proficient at leaving little trace and disappearing.

Sheen had been left bruised, though still breathing. And he had been the one with the loaded gun. Roddy Grant had not been so fortunate. And Sheen was pretty sure that Tucker Rodgers, a man who now likely had access to the secrets about TOPBRASS, could expect the same treatment if they caught up with him. Sheen hoped that allowing the intruder to get his notebook and the information it contained would not put Tucker in even greater danger. But it wasn't all bad news.

If Aoife's hunch that Roddy had copied Branch documents like his KGB hero was correct, then Sheen's logic told him that the originals must still be out there, in an archive. So, dig up Branch files linked to the dates Tucker had sent and Sheen could find the originals. The next challenge would be to get the chief's permission to access them and then he could potentially break this case. Probably. He'd been down that line before with Chief Stevens and it had not ended amicably. Not long after Sheen had arrived in Belfast the chief had made it clear that digging up dirt on the intelligence community and Special Branch was not his idea of productive police work. Sheen would cross that bridge as and when. But in theory, if he could find the same documents that Tucker had been sent and go public with names and details, he'd have the upper hand. Exposing things would take the heat off Tucker and nail the bastards behind Roddy's death. Plus, he'd get to the truth about what TOPBRASS had been sanctioned to do, including how he fitted into the Cyprus Three case. Many birds, one rock.

Problem was, Special Branch records were not available for public viewing in Belfast Central Library and Castlereagh had been demolished in 2005. Sheen had spent over an hour on the phone trying to get a clear picture of how historical police files pertaining to PSNI cases, and those of the RUC before it, were organised, only to reach the frustrating conclusion that for the most part they were not. There was no one unified and cross-referenced system. Many records remained in their original paper form and were warehoused in large storage units where they would likely remain and rot. Funding was tight for officers on the street, let alone clerical staff who would scan and input dead files into databases. Other records remained in their respective police stations and were organised in systems that best suited the staff who filed and used them. Digital records existed for the modern era, but the information Sheen wanted was from the past, assuming that records had survived at all.

In the end, he'd decided that it was a job for Jackson, and he emailed him the remit. If anyone could dig up what he needed, Jackson could. Sounds of life from the main office. His team had arrived, and as he checked the time, he noted that the morning had already worn on. Sheen yawned and then winced at the pain it caused in his head. His phone vibrated and he read the message. It was from Dermot Fahey, the investigative journalist whom Sheen had befriended while investigating a previous case. Fahey's insight and ability to give Sheen insider information that few others could provide had been invaluable. And in exchange, Dermot got an exclusive scoop on the corruption and crimes which Sheen had unearthed.

*Book launch tonight, starts at 8 p.m. Free drinks.*

Sheen messaged him back with a congratulations and said he would drop by, hoping he could be good to his word. Fact was he could do with sitting down and having a pint with Dermot. He got up and headed for the main office space from which he now could hear laughter. As he opened the door Sheen was greeted by another massive roar from Geordie, who was reading from a notebook of some kind and turning purple.

'Here, listen to this one. 11th August 1980. "Man arrested. He stole a bottle of wine from an off licence, drank half and topped it up with water. He returned it and claimed the wine was corked, and requested a refund."' Geordie started laughing again, tears in his eyes. Sheen smiled, but Aoife shook her head and raised her eyes to the ceiling. This had clearly been going on for a while. Jackson was busy behind a computer, apparently oblivious. 'One more, one more. 4th December 1982. "Reports of a drunk woman flagging down cars outside Lavery's Gin Palace on Bradbury Place and then flashing her breasts. Six units attended."' Geordie sniggered and shook his head. He glanced up and noticed Sheen. He turned suddenly sombre and asked him if he was all right.

He was referring to the intruder at Sheen's apartment. 'Yeah, just a bit bruised, nothing serious,' replied Sheen. 'But we all need to be careful. Listen up. Everyone.' Sheen summarised where he felt the investigation was now at. Roddy Grant's involvement in copying Special Branch documents, his suspicion of foul play surrounding his death and the likelihood that Tucker Rodgers had found himself in possession of documents that pertained to a high-level agent in the IRA: TOPBRASS.

'So, we think that it was spooks who came after you and did Dave Rodgers over?'

Sheen again thought about the professionalism of the guy who had invaded his apartment and attacked him. About the fact that he was the one who had been armed but had ended up knocked almost unconscious. And about his various overlaps with Special Branch and the security services since he arrived in Belfast the year before, none of them good.

'Yeah, I do. I suspected I was being followed,' answered Sheen, thinking about the sense of being watched in Beechmount near Danny Caffery's home and the car they saw outside Tucker's place. He gave the team a description of the vehicle and the attacker, for what it was worth.

Geordie nodded, tight-lipped.

'And what's more, it looks like the same people were responsible for breaking into Tucker Rodgers' place and quite likely the death of Roddy Grant too,' added Aoife.

'If that bloke had wanted to kill me last night then he could have. But a dead copper is maybe a step too far, even for this lot. But be careful. All of you,' warned Sheen. He gave them a quick run-down on his idea to locate the original Special Branch documents he presumed that Tucker had received. He asked Jackson if he'd got the email he had sent.

'Yes, sir. In fact, I just had a bit of luck in a related area for the case you assigned to Sergeant Brown and me. I've managed to locate the original investigation records in the murder of Dennis Lamont in 1984. They are stored in a basement in Antrim police station. I'll set to work on your request now,' he said. Sheen thanked him.

'Good man, Jackson,' said Geordie. 'I'll go there now. See what more there is to learn,' he said. Sheen asked him about his current thinking. Geordie gave the room a quick overview of his interview with Alex Lamont, the son of the murdered police officer.

'I take it he can't help us with a description?'

'Na, the kid was traumatised. He couldn't help then,

and he can't remember now.'

Sheen understood that, much better than most.

'This?' He gestured at the books, the source of Geordie's amusement.

'There might be a serious side to these,' replied Geordie. He explained about the diaries, and how in his experience officers often noted details that could have a bearing on cases which they would otherwise forget, as well as being a form of catharsis in a job that was dangerous and incredibly stressful. 'Oh, and there's more. Alex Lamont told me that his da was murdered by a police-issue gun and that the original investigation knew about it. The impression I got was that the case had been mothballed,' explained Geordie.

Sheen raised his eyebrows. If so, it would be incredibly unusual in his experience. The death of a cop was something that fellow officers never let go, at least in the Met, and he'd be surprised and dismayed to learn that the same was not the case in Northern Ireland. Alex Lamont was a child at the time of his father's murder. Maybe, hopefully, he was mistaken about this. Geordie said he wanted to make a start on the documents stored in Antrim and asked for permission to leave.

'Of course. But I have one more job for you. It'll keep until tomorrow morning, but I need you to draw up a court order to search the records of Shandon Park Golf Club,' said Sheen.

Geordie groaned, told Sheen he'd do anything, anything at all, but not that.

'I'm really sorry, mate, but you can see what we are up against,' said Sheen, and then explained his thinking about checking Shandon's records against Special Branch or other names that might set off an alarm.

'I still don't want to think that one of our own, even if they are the Branch, might have been behind Roddy Grant's death,' said Geordie.

'I know, but the worst mistake we can make right now is refusing to believe what the evidence tells us is true,' cautioned Sheen.

'Jackson, I need you to go through these diaries, fine-tooth comb, especially in the months leading up to this man's murder,' said Geordie.

Jackson said he would. Sheen nodded. The young man continued to impress him. The role he was performing with SHOT was neither glamorous nor always interesting. Plus, he was stuck behind a desk and not out in the thick of it most of the time. But he did not quibble or put his feelings first as Sheen had known other ambitious young officers to do in the past. Sheen also noticed that there was a map of Greater Belfast now stuck to the board. Jackson saw him observing it and spoke.

'That's mine, sir. My thinking is that these events, if they are linked, could also be understood spatially. There might be a pattern which could emerge that may otherwise be lost in the detail.'

Sheen told him to crack on and noted that three pins on the map corresponded to the street addresses of the Cyprus Three that Aoife and he had already visited. He'd adopted a similar strategy in the past while working homicide in London and more than once it had proved effective. Even though the four cases they were working on that linked to TOPBRASS bridged big gaps in time, there was always a spatial context. And often criminals left traces this way which were every bit as revealing as forensic evidence. He turned to Aoife and asked her to give the team a quick update on what she had discovered the day before at the home of Bernadette Bell.

'Predictably not a lot to go on. Similar story to what we found out about the Cyprus Three. She was secretive, so not a lot of sharing of information with family members. Her old dad's a piece of work. I'd say he would have shot her dead for informing himself if he'd been asked. He shared this,' she said, and produced her mobile. After a few seconds swiping the screen, Sheen and the others listened to the recording she had made of Bernadette's final confession. When it ended Sheen felt the atmosphere in the room turn heavier.

'We have a second voice on that recording,' he noted.

Aoife said she had heard it too, and agreed it was likely the man who had killed Bernadette. And it was probably also the same person who had put her through a week of medieval torture.

'And there's one other thing. A very small detail that her father recalled.' Sheen listened as Aoife relayed the new information given by Liam Bell. That an IRA man with dirty ginger hair met with his daughter and who may also have been the man who drove her to her death.

Sheen thanked Aoife and pointed at the board where she now added her findings to the information about Bell's murder that was there already. There was one name and date on the board that had yet to receive any attention.

21st June 1986.

'Which leaves our squaddies who were blown to pieces after taking part in a charity fun run,' said Sheen.

Aoife nodded and handed him two pieces of paper from the desk adjacent. As usual, she was one step ahead of him.

'I've been on the phone. There's not a ton of information to go on, but the original files from the investigation had been scanned and I was able to access most of them digitally. A television documentary was made ten years ago about the murders. Apparently, one of the lads who was killed was due to leave the army shortly afterwards and had been offered a place in the British national athletics squad.'

'Awful. What about the lines that we can follow?'

'Two that jump out. The first is Darren Howes, the corporal who was driving the bus. He survived. In his statement, he said that he had been directed onto the road at Ballycarrick by what he described as a police diversion. However, the inquest heard that police denied placing any signs and that the road was known to be off limits due to the threat posed by the IRA. Howes left the army a short time later, but not sure if he jumped or was pushed.'

'Sounds like it's worth looking into further. Don't suppose there's any chance we can find him?'

'Finding him was easy but getting him to agree to speak was the challenge. I've arranged a Skype call with you, but it's not until nine this evening.'

'Because you're simply amazing.'

'I know.'

'You said two lines?'

'The second is Patrick Glenholmes. Forensic evidence found at the scene linked him to the two-hundred-pound car bomb that was detonated remotely as the soldiers' bus slowed to take a sharp corner. He served ten years before being released under the terms of the Good Friday Agreement.'

Sheen thought about this. Glenholmes might have been the technician responsible, but from what Sheen already now understood about IRA active service unit cells, he was very unlikely to have completed the operation single-handed. 'This guy got sent down, and took the rap,' he said.

'I would say so. But I plan to ask him myself. He lives off the Glen Road, West Belfast. His home is not in his name,' she said. Which meant it was, beneath layers of cleanly laundered cash, probably owned by the IRA and the republican movement. Glenholmes was being taken care of, a pension of sorts for time lost and loyalty proved.

Sheen thanked her again, a little fizz of excitement now replacing the heaviness about allowing his notebook to be taken and seeing Dave Rodgers in an induced coma earlier in the day. Things were beginning to move and, despite the number of different strands they were working with, they had a common denominator. TOPBRASS. An IRA double agent who had been allowed to murder, and who had almost certainly sent others to their death. And now Sheen wanted his real name and those who colluded with him. The phone on the desk next to him rang and he picked it up.

'Sheen,' he said, and listened to what the duty sergeant at the front desk explained as Geordie left

269

the office. 'OK, thank you. Can you send him up?' He turned to Aoife. 'Seems that MI5 have a better filing system than Special Branch. The documents the chief promised us about the Cyprus Three have arrived.'

# CHAPTER TWENTY-EIGHT

Tucker's hangover was long gone. He'd tried to estimate how long he had been in the bunker, but the time he lost at the start of his stay and the lack of natural light made it almost impossible to keep track. One thing he did know was that the sleep he did get was of a different breed. Better, deeper and more dream-filled than he had enjoyed for years. For as long as he could recall, in fact. Cold turkey was no easy ride but drying out had its benefits. That said, he still dreamt of the booze, and he still had the shakes, though they had subsided quite a bit. And if he had access to beer, a cold pint of cider or a big glass of red wine, would he succumb? Tucker licked his lips and got off his bunk. The light in the living cell blinked on as he entered, but by now his feet knew the route and he could navigate in the darkness if he needed to. He filled up his beaker at the tap, and then found a chocolate chip and peanut energy bar in the supply cupboard and ate it while standing up. He looked over at the little table where he'd left Roddy's booklet the night before. Drink? There was enough in there to make anyone want to hit the hard stuff.

Tucker eased himself into the hard, plastic seat and flipped the booklet open at the last page he had read. Following the death of Bernadette Bell at the hands of the IRA, the good times rolled for Special Branch and TOPBRASS. Document after document detailed his exploits as an asset and agent of the RUC. IRA active service units were caught red-handed with guns and masks at the homes of police officers who miraculously had decided to vacate. No sooner had Colonel Gaddafi gifted the IRA guns and explosives than the arms dumps were found by chance. In response, bottom feeder street criminals and green recruits into the IRA were interrogated and killed by an organisation that was growing more paranoid and unsure of its bearings day by day. And all the while TOPBRASS continued to rise, trusted and used by the inner clique of the IRA's so-called Nutting Squad, and a feared commander in the Belfast Brigade. And TOPBRASS was not the only one riding the wave. By late 1983, Samuel Royce Fenton had risen to the rank of Detective Chief Inspector. But at some point, the piper would have to be paid for the tune that TOPBRASS and Fenton wanted to be played.

CONFIDENTIAL
ROYAL ULSTER CONSTABULARY
SPECIAL BRANCH
14th Day of November 1983

SPECIAL REPORT
SUBJECT: TOPBRASS

TOPBRASS is arguably the most influential asset currently in our employ within the IRA. My previous memos have detailed his achievements which include thirty-two convictions and the seizing of over five hundred pounds of explosives, seventy ArmaLite rifles and two thousand rounds of ammunition. His intelligence has saved the lives of security personnel and innocent civilians alike, and he remains keen to continue his dangerous work on our behalf.

He has learnt how to skilfully avoid detection and feels there is no strong suspicion directed towards him. A small minority who may have questions about his loyalty lack the support needed to give voice to their concerns. TOPBRASS is popular and has built something of a cult status amongst younger recruits, many of whom would willingly suppress dissent against him.

It has come to my attention, however, that loyalist paramilitaries in the Ulster Freedom Fighters (UFF) are aware of a leading IRA man living in TOPBRASS's district and plan to assassinate him. This information has been verified by an asset in place in the UFF who has been tasked with gathering the intelligence necessary to target and kill TOPBRASS.

There are a number of options. The least preferable being the safe extraction of TOPBRASS and the effective ending of his career as an asset. The alternative, feeding misinformation to the UFF, is equally unpalatable. To do so would place our other valued asset in grave danger. There is, however, a third way, which we have discussed in some depth and now seems inevitable. Such decisions are not made lightly and never as our first choice. But the dangerous game we are forced to play can only be won if we adhere to the 'big boys' rules' which our dangerous enemies, rather than we, have set. The greatest mistake we can make is to assume that we can afford to be less ruthless than our enemy, or that our opponent is any less intelligent than us.

Submitted to the chief constable: Detective Chief Inspector S. R. Fenton

A week before Christmas, the same year, Roddy had written one word in large letters at the top of the page: SCAPEGOAT. Under it was an article from the *Belfast Telegraph*.

*Veteran Irish republican Giuseppe Morelli, aged 62, was shot dead in his Ballymurphy home late last night as he sat with his two grandchildren watching television. Morelli, the first-generation son of Italian immigrants who arrived in Belfast in the early 1900s, was interned in the 1940s for suspected IRA activity. Known as 'Red Giuseppe' because of his distinctive hair colour and communist leanings, the veteran republican was interned without trial once more in 1971 but later released without charge. In a statement claiming*

274

*responsibility for the murder, the UFF said they had*
*'executed a known IRA commander' in the area and*
*would '. . . continue to bring the war to the enemy'.*

There were a few well-known Italian families in Belfast, mostly settled in Catholic areas, and Tucker knew about the Morellis. They were strongly linked to republican politics, even from before the advent of the modern Troubles in the late 1960s. And Tucker remembered hearing about Giuseppe Morelli's murder. His heritage and age had made the case distinctive, even by the standards of Belfast at that time. Hard to be certain, but if Morelli was an IRA man in 1983, he was very much of a previous generation. An elderly man by the standards of that time. In other words, Giuseppe was no TOPBRASS. But he'd been a close enough fit, an IRA member who came from the same district in which loyalists were hunting for TOPBRASS.

Morelli had been selected for sacrifice because he happened to be in the wrong place, wrong time, and next in line. And though it didn't give Tucker much more to go on, he now knew that TOPBRASS was active in the Second Battalion of the IRA's Belfast Brigade, and was from Ballymurphy. A relatively small place, but an estate where IRA membership was not exactly unusual at the height of the Troubles. But it was better than nothing, another piece of a puzzle that he might just manage to crack.

If the depressingly cynical history of TOPBRASS was not enough to turn Tucker to an imaginary drink, then Roddy's blasted incomplete crosswords would do it. Words were really not his thing, and Tucker usually kept away from such puzzles. They usually left him feeling frustrated and inadequate. Especially the cryptic variety which were a mystery to him. But time and energy bars were all he had.

'Three across. Six letters,' he said. Tucker didn't have a pen, but if he did, he'd be chewing it. 'Artistic dance. Waltz!' Six letters, his heart sank. Tucker knew nothing about dance, but now he could not let it go. 'Polka,' he said after another minute, with a purr of victory which quickly died away. He closed his eyes, tried to see dancers, thought about break-dancing and cleared the stage. A spotlight, and in it a beautiful young woman, so lithe and slender that she didn't look real. He'd taken his wife to Sadler's Wells Theatre in London, on their first wedding anniversary. They'd watched *Swan Lake*, her hand resting on his and David asleep in her womb. When he had thought that life could be as graceful and choreographed as the movements on that stage. 'Ballet!' he shouted. Tucker counted the spaces with his finger to be sure. That was it. Roddy had managed the rest, but he had completed it. He stretched his arms above his head with a satisfied sigh. He thought about eating, but he wasn't hungry, he just wanted something to do. So instead, he turned the page, hoping for another crossword, and started reading. As TOPBRASS's story continued into 1984, the small smile of contentment that had lingered on Tucker's lips gradually fell away.

# CHAPTER TWENTY-NINE

Dr Shaun Maitland was a little guy with two very large cases. Sheen helped him with one and Aoife took the other. He was dressed in green corduroy trousers that were worn thin in patches and held up by a pair of red braces and faded blue shirt which had started to turn white at the collar and cuff. The white-haired man with the tweed jacket and dazzling, alert blue eyes could have been a gentleman farmer. Or the kind of shabby chic character that Sheen had seen shopping for wine and cheese in Fortnum & Mason on a Saturday afternoon. In fact, Maitland was a fellow of Corpus Christi College, Cambridge University, and one of only two official historians of MI5. His status meant he was a trusted bridging point between the secrets and shadows of Britain's domestic security service and the outside world.

When the chief sent through the request for British records on the operation that led to the death of the three IRA operatives in Cyprus, it was MI5 who eventually picked up the call. While technically MI6 should have taken charge as the secret intelligence service tasked with overseas work, Operation Severus, the codename used for the military operation against the IRA unit who would become known as the Cyprus Three, was an MI5 job. Cyprus was largely English-speaking, and the British soldiers who were at risk from the IRA bombing unit were stationed on bases on British-controlled land.

Maitland thanked them as Sheen and Aoife set the cases on two desks and, after introductions were made, he continued. 'These are the documents which have been requested. Copies, of course, but accurate in every respect,' he assured them. Lancashire accent, which surprised Sheen. He had been expecting marbles in the mouth. And he had also expected to wait much longer for their arrival or be asked to travel to London. The latter would probably have entailed a flight. So, on both counts, Maitland's visit was a blessing.

'Quick service,' said Aoife, her thoughts clearly mirroring his own.

'Oh, not at all, Detective McCusker. This process has taken me several weeks of meticulous searching and cross-referencing,' replied Maitland.

Aoife turned to Sheen, open-mouthed. Of course. Sheen had been a fool to assume that the first he would hear of the chief's plans and dictates would be when he was given his job. This had been in the pipeline for some time. Part of the bigger job of reinstating the fragile Northern Irish parliament and playing into the chief's political agenda, which was no doubt set by those even higher up than him. Sheen was being used, a puppet on a string that would dance as asked and at the agreed time. This week the respective political players had re-occupied their offices and administrative quarters in Stormont on the outskirts of East Belfast for the first time in many months. Sheen would offer his conclusions about the death of the Cyprus Three at a point when the First Minister was preparing to take office. Brendan Kielty, a republican IRA veteran seated in partnership with his former enemies, for the first time in the driving seat.

'No offence, Dr Maitland, but I'd have much preferred to see the originals with my own eyes and make a decision about what was relevant and what should be left out,' said Sheen.

'None taken, DI Sheen. But I'm afraid the system is very simple and the same for one and all. I can assure you that I am not a court historian, and I am very thorough. What you see is exactly what is available. Though it must all return with me when you're done. And you'll understand if certain names and other details are redacted to protect the identities of those involved and safeguard officers who are still active in the field,' he said.

'Of course, this is an investigation, not a witch hunt,' Sheen replied. He'd browsed through some of Maitland's published work and read his official history of MI5. The guy was no stooge, and he didn't pull his punches when it came to holding the security service accountable for its actions. But the evidence before him was only as valid as that which Maitland was given in the first place. And Sheen was sceptical about how open and transparent the spooks would ever really be. His experience with them since arriving in Belfast had taught him that a long spoon and eyes on the back of your head were essential equipment if supping in their presence. He called to Jackson, who was studiously working through the old RUC diaries given to him by Geordie.

'Sir?'

Sheen handed him twenty quid. 'Pop into town and see if you can grab us a few paninis from that little Italian place we like,' he said.

Jackson took the note and started to put on his coat.

'Cathedral Quarter?' Sheen nodded and asked him to get extra pesto. Jackson wrote their orders down. 'Sir, I think there might be something here,' said Jackson, nodding at the murdered police officer's diaries.

'More jokes?'

'Some of it is very humorous,' confirmed Jackson.

Sheen tried to imagine what it would have been like as a beat cop in Belfast at that time and concluded that he really could not. He had nothing in his world that was comparable. But he could understand that trench humour was likely as essential to survival as a bulletproof vest. But for Dennis Lamont, it had only shielded him for so long.

'But this is not a joke. There's something that doesn't sound right,' continued Jackson.

'Go ahead,' said Sheen. He could see Shaun Maitland unpacking ream after ream of documentation and his heart sank. This sort of thing was one of his least favoured parts of the job. But given that he was in charge of a historical offences team, it was inevitable that at some point it would be the meat and drink of their work. And today everyone was having to take a bite. Geordie was ankle-deep in the old case files in Antrim and Jackson was working through a dead man's diary. He should crack on and start looking at the Operation Severus files, but Jackson was sharp and in Sheen's experience it often paid to listen to a colleague when something had made their copper's nose twitch.

'Not from the immediate time period of Dennis Lamont's death, but about four months prior. He says' – and now Jackson pocketed his lunch order, lifted up one of the diaries and started to read aloud – '"Have spotted the 'red menace' near the junction of Castle Street and Royal Avenue two days in a row while staffing a UDR vehicle checkpoint. Known Belfast IRA volunteer and a very dangerous man. Acting suspiciously. Have reported this and will attempt to apprehend on next sighting. I have never fired my weapon in anger, but I would have no hesitation in shooting this person if it came to it."'

The UDR was auxiliary British Army, a sort of home guard that was composed mostly of soldiers from the six counties of Northern Ireland.

Jackson kept reading.

'And then, later. Here. "Had the flu, battled on and finally took two days off. Blessed with the virus. The vehicle checkpoint I was working this week was attacked by IRA gang. Two soldiers killed, and one RUC colleague. Yet more funerals to attend. Suspect 'red menace' and have reported this to Special Branch. No response, what's new?"'

'Special Branch,' said Sheen.

'That's what made me think,' said Jackson.

Sheen clapped him on the shoulder. Jackson flinched.

'You're damn right,' he said, and now walked to the board with the emerging timeline of events and Jackson's map. He pointed to Bernadette Bell's name. 'Her father said that the IRA man she used to meet in secret and who probably took her away to her death was ginger. And now' – Sheen pointed at Dennis Lamont's name – 'we find that Lamont also spotted an IRA man he called the "red menace", and later his colleagues were murdered in an IRA attack.'

Aoife was on her feet and had also approached the board.

'And then Lamont gets gunned down while off duty after telling Special Branch about it,' she said.

'And his son tells us that whoever killed him used a gun that had once been police issue,' replied Sheen.

Jackson asked Shaun Maitland if he wanted something from the Italian deli. And that was when the firework that had been smouldering in Sheen's mind since Aoife had recounted what Bernadette Bell's father had told her, ignited and shot into orbit.

'Something?' Aoife asked.

'Aoife, the walk-in. The one at the start of this year that you tried to take but the chief put the stops on it.'

'Giuseppe Morelli's daughter?'

'Red Giuseppe,' agreed Sheen. 'IRA and Marxist, but also red-haired, the daughter claimed that his murder had involved collusion.'

'Morelli was murdered by loyalists in 1983, I think. Definitely before Dennis Lamont wrote his diary entry,' she replied. Sheen wrote Giuseppe Morelli's name and date of death on the board.

'I know. But it's a hell of a coincidence.' He paused, looking at the timeline, and then he spoke again. 'And I'm not suggesting that he is our man. Morelli was murdered by loyalists. But he was an old timer, not even in the game as far as I remember.'

'The "red menace", as Dennis Lamont called him,' said Aoife.

Jackson was at the door, about to leave.

'Ha, I get it. TOPBRASS, you see? Top brass,' he repeated, with a smile, now pointing at his own hair to help them see.'

'I think I finally do see,' said Sheen, but he wasn't smiling.

# CHAPTER THIRTY

Shaun Maitland had left them to it at 6 p.m., under the strict understanding that the documents would not be removed from the office. The paninis were long gone, and Jackson had made two batches of coffee. The rookie was still busy in Sheen's smaller office trying to root out the location of the Special Branch documents that pertained to the dates they were interested in, but so far with zero success. He had already confirmed that there was nothing on storage records that corresponded to the case of Bernadette Bell. Which meant that either there was no Special Branch knowledge or involvement at any level, or the documents had been made to disappear. Sheen was stiff, his brain was turning numb and he had a lot more to do. This would likely end as an all-nighter. He and Aoife were swimming in paper, but at least he was beginning to get a sense of the narrative as told through the MI5 documents which Shaun Maitland had delivered. Sheen wanted TOPBRASS, and he hoped to find something important about the agent in these files. But he also had his remit from the chief. And like it or not he needed to get a clear picture about what happened on the ground in Cyprus in 1987 and come to an objective judgement as to whether the killings were lawful, as ordered.

If the MI5 records were to be believed, the authorities were caught flat-footed and, so far, Sheen had found nothing to indicate TOPBRASS's involvement. In fact, the British knew nothing of the planned attack until Caffery, Gleeson and Wilson flew into Larnaca under assumed identities. It was then that British authorities requested the Cypriot administration track their movements. Two days later control of the operation was handed over to the SAS after a military bomb disposal officer checked a white Renault which had been hired by Danny Caffery. He concluded there was a chance that it did contain a bomb. The car was later destroyed in a controlled explosion but found to be empty. The decision to hand over matters to the SAS based on this evidence seemed to Sheen to be flimsy as explanations go. A car which contained a bomb with the potential to kill a platoon of troops would be quite easy to spot and difficult to get wrong. That kind of weight showed on the suspension and the car would be riding low. Sheen thought again about Peadar Caffery's anger and indignation over his brother's death when they visited him at his Beechmount home. The SAS were rarely called on when the outcome that was hoped for was the arrest of an enemy. He checked his watch. It had gone 7 p.m.

'Sheen, I'm taking a run up west to see if I can get a word with Glenholmes,' said Aoife. She meant the man who had served time for his part in the bus bombing that killed the eight squaddies at Ballycarrick in 1986. 'I'll come back when I'm done. I managed to arrange a sleepover for Ava with my mate Marie. Don't forget to Skype call Darren Howes at nine. He's expecting to hear from you,' said Aoife. Sheen said he would not, but in fact it had pretty much slipped his mind. She wrote the necessary details down and passed it to Sheen. Yet another piece of paper. Aoife squeezed his lower arm and then she was gone, leaving him with a pleasant residual tingle, like she was electrically charged. Which, in a way, she was.

Jackson emerged from his office and added more pins to the map. Aside from the bus bomb at Ballycarrick, the events they were interested were clustered around the West Belfast area. Bernadette Bell was just off the Falls Road, the original homes of the Cyprus Three were in Andersonstown and Beechmount, and although Dennis Lamont was murdered on the Dublin Road in the south of the city, he reported seeing the so-called red menace near Castle Street, on the edge of West Belfast. And then there was Red Giuseppe, shot dead in Ballymurphy.

'Jackson, call it a night. Go and get some food and rest,' he said. Jackson thanked him, didn't argue and then explained that Special Branch documents that may link to Dennis Lamont's death were not recorded in any of the storage centres he had been able to speak to. The same with Bernadette Bell's case. Either there was no Special Branch involvement, or the paper trail had been destroyed. He said he'd pick it up again in the morning but sounded sheepish like he'd failed in some way. The phone in Sheen's office rang and Jackson returned to answer it.

'Sir, it's Sergeant Brown,' he said, and passed the phone to Sheen who sat at his desk. Geordie, hopefully with something to tell.

'Sheen,' he answered.

'Burning the oil I see. Your mobile's going straight to voicemail,' said Geordie.

Sheen took it out of his pocket, saw that it was dead, and made a mental note to plug it into the charger.

'Sorry, mate. Tell me you've found something, but first listen to this.' Sheen relayed what Dennis Lamont's diary had revealed and the likely significance of their man being a redhead.

'So, what you're saying is you've managed to narrow down the hunt for TOPBRASS to IRA men who had ginger hair? That might be helpful if he was running around Lagos, but this is Belfast. Ginger central,' said Geordie. Always a man to see the upside.

'Go on, then. Have you got something more?'

'I do, but you might not want to hear it,' said Geordie. 'So, found the files. Looks like Alex Lamont was right about the gun that was used to murder his da. Forensics confirmed that it was very probably a Ruger Speed-Six and once part of a batch issued to the RUC. Matter of fact I recall using the same side arm around about that time.'

'Any reference to Special Branch in those files? Any note that Dennis Lamont had reported this red menace character as a suspect in the killing of the soldiers and police at the checkpoint he was supposed to be staffing?'

'Nada. But I did get some stuff on the murder investigation. The gun angle was being followed up but then the plug was pulled. The SIO called it time and that's where the trail went cold,' explained Geordie. SIO, the senior investigating officer.

'Who? Why?'

'No idea why, but I know who. And in fact, so do you,' said Geordie.

'What do you mean?'

'I mean the SIO was a Detective Inspector Ronald Stevens.'

'Ah shit,' said Sheen, his tired brain suddenly reeling, trying and failing to calculate the implications and the fallout of what Geordie had just said.

'Shit is right. Chief Stevens, our boss. Why the fuck can't things just be simple for once?'

Sheen had no answer to that.

# CHAPTER THIRTY-ONE

'What about ye, Mr Bell?' he said as Liam Bell opened his front door on Fallswater Street. He gave the old todge a name, not his own of course, and said he was calling from Clarke House. Which was broadly true. Clarke House was the HQ of the Irish republican political party on the Andersonstown Road, a place that he had frequented often over the years and been accidentally locked out of more than once. Which was a bastard, because it was as secure as Alcatraz and nobody answered the door. Liam Bell squinted into the darkness of the late evening in which he now stood, smiling.

'What do you want?' Bell's eyes moved over his features and as they did, he assessed his reaction, looking for a glimmer of recognition, and seeing none. Which was not that surprising. His appearance had changed a lot over the years. And he'd always kept his distance from this door. Still, he had to be sure.

'Do you mind if I come in? We've had a few reports that the peelers are harassing families of volunteers who served in the conflict. We're not a bit happy about it. I'm just trying to get the record straight before we issue a complaint to the ombudsman.'

Bell nodded vigorously and beckoned him inside with a hand that looked like a swollen claw. He clicked the front door closed with the heel of his shoe and did not take off the gloves that he was wearing against the chill of the evening. The old boy had walked into a back room where a light glowed, and he followed him. By the time he joined him, Bell was sitting down in a big chair that looked like a well-upholstered throne. He was drawing on a pipe that was filled with dark tobacco but unlit. It stayed in his mouth as he now spoke.

'Peelers were here. McCusker her name. Asking about our Bernie,' he said, and his eyes moved to a small photo of a kid that was framed on the wall. Bell's eyes remained lowered. 'She was executed for informing,' he said quietly.

'It was a terrible time, Mr Bell. And too many people died. There's nothing we would like more than for you to have Bernie seated here this evening by your side. And the Brits and the RUC were to blame. They used and abused her,' he said with the right trace of melancholy. Almost funny because it was, in this case, pretty much true. 'And they've no right coming here and opening old wounds.' Soundbites; tried and tested and interchangeable for a hundred different situations requiring mock sincerity and political one-upmanship. He asked Bell what McCusker wanted to know.

'Who it was that our Bernie used to run with.'

'And you said?'

'That I knew nothing, and that her former comrades were dead, just like her,' he replied.

'Good man,' he said. He'd spent his life separating truth from lies as men and women watched him in fear, hoping that what they said was what he wanted to hear. And Bell seemed sincere. So far.

'I played Bernie's confession. Let her hear it for herself,' he said.

'Anything else?'

A pause. Too long, too staged. A lie.

'No, that was it.'

He nodded, said that he'd make them both a quick brew and leave him in peace. As he stood in the small kitchen, trying to find the teabags, Bell spoke again.

'Say again,' he called.

'I said your woman mentioned collusion. Said that Bernie's death could be linked to other stuff.' His gloved hand squeezed the handle of the kettle he had just filled up.

'That a fact?' he said, his head turned to make sure the old man could hear.

'Aye. Make the tea, I'll explain what she said.'

'No, keep going, keep going,' he encouraged, and switched the kettle on.

But Bell did not continue. There was only silence. He waited and then slowly re-entered the back room. Bell had turned in his seat and stared at him. His eyes had changed. They were full of something that he found very alarming indeed. Recognition. It must have been something that he said, something about his voice. And then he understood. He'd said that he played the confession tape. Bell raised one trembling hand and pointed a knotted and misshapen finger at him.

'You,' he said, his voice hoarse. And now a boiling rage had filled the old man's eyes too. He stepped into the room, his face impassive, not taking his eyes off Bell. 'You tortured her and killed her. Even though you were on their payroll as well, you bastard!'

'Couldn't write it, could ye?' He lifted a cushion from the small sofa.

Bell moved as though to raise himself off the chair, but he was old and slow and choked up with anger.

He pounced, the cushion held in both hands and his teeth bared and clenched. He shoved the old man back into his seat and pressed the cushion over his face. Liam Bell jerked and spasmed and, despite his age, nearly succeeded in wriggling free. Bell wanted to breathe. More urgently than he wanted him dead. But not quite. He stuck his knee on the old man's chest and pinned him against the chair then leant with all his strength on the cushion. The muffled sound of his cries faded first. Then Bell's arms, that had been pushing fruitlessly against his shoulders, fell slack. Finally, his legs stopped kicking and he felt the old man deflate under him. He sniffed, his nose creasing at the fresh stink of shit coming from under him. He slipped off one glove and held a finger beneath the old bastard's nose. No heat, nothing. Bell's eyes were open, dark and lifeless as shadows on the moon.

He walked into the kitchen and quickly turned the gas on at the hob, made sure each switch was fully open. An immediate hiss filled the air, followed by the gagging, familiar stench. He returned to the back room, found the old man's lighter, lit his pipe, and reluctantly gave it three or four strong pulls. The bowl soon glowed fiercely. Blueish smoke engulfed him. He left it smouldering on the chair, close enough to a hanky that had been resting on the arm for it to likely take hold. Even if it didn't, the pipe would be enough. He walked to the front door and carefully opened it, checked that the street was quiet and slipped out, into the darkness. One date covered. He should never have trusted Fenton to be able to deal with this. He knew what needed to be done. Death solves all problems. No man, no problem.

# CHAPTER THIRTY-TWO

As Aoife parked up on Gransha Park in West Belfast where Patrick Glenholmes lived, it was already dark. Fat drops of rain splattered her windscreen. She checked her notepad for his house number and counted along the homes on the other side of the street until she reached his abode. Detached, red-brick with a garage. The big house was set well back from the road and a BMW saloon was parked in the expansive driveway. A large cherry blossom tree which was beginning to push out its leaf, would offer privacy from prying eyes when it bloomed. Even now, she could not see the details of the home's front entrance due to its shielding branches. The iron gates that fronted the property were closed, but not locked as far as Aoife could tell. She was momentarily blinded as a car turned into the street and then drew to a halt behind her, its white halogen headlamps stark in her rear-view until they were extinguished. Aoife waited, thinking about what her best approach for this man would be.

Glenholmes had spent a long stretch in a cell in the H-Blocks. The guy had done his bird, missed out on the important years as his children grew, and he'd kept his lip buttoned. Aoife didn't feel sorry for him. The eight young men who had been blown to pieces by the bomb he'd constructed had never arrived home. He had, and by the looks of it, was now living in considerable comfort. Something she knew was not always the case for IRA veterans who left prison with their material goods in a shopping bag and then went home to sit with only their demons for company.

She got out of the car and checked up and down the street. The impending downpour had apparently sent any remaining kids on the street after dark back indoors and even put the usual West Belfast dog walkers off. Glenholmes' place looked dead. When she approached the front door a security light switched on but several presses on the doorbell and raps of the letterbox produced no response. She pushed the letterbox open and used the torch on her phone to illuminate the porch. Letters and junk mail were scattered on the mat. She withdrew her hand and then glanced down to her right. Next to a flowerpot and partly obscured by shadows cast by the security light was a small cardboard crate that had been folded flat and wedged behind the pot. Poking from one side was a handwritten note. Aoife recognised the box. Fruit and vegetable delivery service, organic produce to your door. Not cheap. Glenholmes was certainly eating well. She removed the note and read it.

*On holiday for two weeks. Please cancel our next two orders.*

The note gave the date requesting when deliveries should resume and was signed off from the Glenholmes family. Two weeks' time. If Patrick Glenholmes had anything useful to relay, they would either have to wait or find out where he'd gone. The thought of being flown out somewhere hot to track him down and have that word was a sacrifice she'd be willing to make. Aoife pulled her coat round her as the rain started to fall in cold, heavy drops. Sheen wouldn't be flying if he could avoid it. But she doubted Chief Stevens would agree to it. Not when the Cyprus Three was their core remit, and not with funding stretched like it was. Back to Grosvenor Road it was, empty-handed. She closed Glenholmes' front gate and ran towards her car, one hand shielding her face from the rain as she searched in her pocket with the other for her keys. She was about to open it and get in when she remembered her security checks. How long had she been at Glenholmes' door? No more than two minutes, and the street was deserted.

All the same, she started to inspect the car as trained, rainwater plastering her hair to her head and falling hard enough now to trickle down her neck. She'd done the front of the car and was inspecting the back on the roadside when the white halogen headlights on full beam blinded her and a car revved and then skidded from its parking space, hurtling towards her. She had a second to register that it was a hatchback, maybe grey. Same as the vehicle Sheen had described. Aoife found her gun and raised it, double handed, the rain blurring her vision, already half blinded by the glare of the lights. She aimed for the space above the glare and cursed herself for her complacency. She'd clocked the car when she had first arrived. That had been her chance to speed away. But she'd wanted Glenholmes, wanted to bring something to Sheen that would unlock the jam they were in. The car was close. She compressed the trigger, braced herself for the kick and got prepared to dive and roll into the hedge beyond the pavement to her right.

Sudden movement, and the crash of snapping twigs, coming from her right, coming from the place she'd planned to use as a foxhole. In that instant of unanticipated distraction, she hesitated, for no more than a nanosecond, but on such islands of time fate can turn. Something hit her like a high voltage guillotine blade impacting on the back of her neck. A fury of pain exploded in her head and a light, brighter than the blaring headlights that were on top of her, filled her world. She had no time to breathe and no time to scream before the light was vanquished and the darkness consumed her.

# CHAPTER THIRTY-THREE

Sheen almost forgot to Skype Darren Howes, but managed to make the call, albeit ten minutes later than Aoife had arranged. As he did so he also remembered Dermot Fahey's book launch which he'd now missed. But no time to call and apologise. No time on his side whatsoever it now seemed. Darren Howes' image appeared on the computer screen alongside the smaller window where Sheen could see, quite disconcertingly, a very tired-looking projection of his own face. Howes was in his late fifties and had lost most of his hair. He wore a roll-neck woollen jumper and looked to be speaking to Sheen while seated at a desk in what appeared to be a cosy office or study. Behind him, Sheen could see shelves filled with books and Howes had a big mug in one hand. Sheen excused his tardiness, and Darren Howes waved his apology away.

'I'm sure you're a very busy man, DI Sheen. Your partner said this is related to Ballycarrick?'

'Yes, it is. I appreciate it may not be easy for you to discuss it, so thank you for agreeing to do so.'

The old soldier nodded. His emotions apparently firmly boxed up.

'There is not a day that goes by that I don't think about it. Talking won't make it any harder. Who knows, it might help.'

It was not for Sheen to presume, but Howes didn't strike him as a man who would have opted for the therapist's couch.

'Then I'll cut to the chase, Mr Howes. I understand that when the bombing was investigated you claimed to have followed a diversion?'

'I did follow one.'

'And yet the police denied having set one up.'

Howes nodded, grim-faced.

'They said that the road I took was out of bounds.' And although not subjected to any form of disciplinary action, Sheen knew from Aoife's printed case notes that Howes had left the army after Ballycarrick. He'd been a corporal with a distinguished record up until that point. The man said he thought about what happened every day. Perhaps he blamed himself. Or perhaps he had been saddled with responsibility for an error that had cost eight young men their lives.

'And was it?'

'Not officially. It wasn't the designated route I had been given, granted, but I've spoken to other lads that were tasked to drive troops back to base from the Belfast area and none of them recalled Ballycarrick being officially out of bounds. In fact, one remembers actually being diverted down that same road the week before we were ambushed,' said Howes.

Sheen sat up in his seat. It was pretty clear that the police did not set up the diversion, but his gut feeling that Howes was not fabricating was now reinforced by what he had said regarding the experience of another squaddie. What the other soldier had described could well have been a dummy run on the part of those planning a deadly attack, assuming that whoever had diverted Howes that night had also been responsible for setting up the ambush and explosion. When the first diversion had gone unchecked and unchallenged the week before, the IRA team knew they had a green light for the real thing. But to be effective, such a diversion must have been believable.

'Mr Howes, what was it that made you convinced the diversion was legitimate?' he asked.

Sheen could see Darren Howes visibly bristle, his hand gripping the handle of his mug.

'I know what you're thinking, that I lost concentration or invented it after accidentally taking a wrong turn.'

'I'm not insinuating that at all,' assured Sheen.

'It was dark. As per bloody usual it was raining. But there was an RUC Land Rover parked up in a passing place with its hazard lights blinking. There was a police checkpoint sign that reflected the headlights from the bus and cones placed on the road ahead. And there was a uniformed police officer with a torch who directed me to take a right turn onto the Ballycarrick Road.' Darren Howes had not raised his voice, but Sheen could feel the heat of the man's anger.

'How did your superiors in the army and colleagues at the RUC account for this?'

'They said that I was mistaken. That my story didn't

make sense. I had my statement ripped up in front of my face and a fresh sheet of paper and a pen set down in front of me.'

'And?'

'And I told the truth. Again. It won't change. It's like I told you, I think about it all the time. But of course, that was not the answer they wanted. After that, things changed for me in the army. Punishment duty for the slightest thing and then for things that I had no part in. And finally, I was brought into an office and told the army life was not for me.'

'Jump or be pushed?'

'Pretty much. A dishonourable discharge would haunt me for the rest of my life. At that time, I wanted to join the fire service, so I walked away. But I never changed my story.'

'I'd like to hear it, as much as you can remember.'

'When I took that right turn the lads were singing that song "One Man Went to Mow"; it was driving me up the wall. The cop who waved me right could hear them. I remember he shook his head as though to say that he understood my pain.'

The man's memory seemed fine to Sheen, and he had no reason to assume that the RUC had lied about there not being a diversion that night. Which meant that whoever had waved Darren Howes to the right must have been an interloper, and a man with the means to masquerade convincingly as a police officer. And didn't Geordie say that Dennis Lamont had been murdered by a police issue Ruger Speed-Six? Sheen felt his guts convulse.

'Mr Howes, can you describe this man? The police officer.'

'I can only remember what I saw, and as I said it was

dark and it was raining hard. He wore the uniform, or the long raincoat, bottle-green. The hat too. His face was mostly in shadows, under the peak of his cap. But he had a moustache, and I could see his hair went over his ears. I remember thinking that he was pushing it. In the army, he'd have been sent to the barbershop.'

Sheen held his breath.

'What colour was his hair, Mr Howes?'

'Darkish red, not really bright ginger, more of an auburn.' Dirty red. Same as the man who had taken Bernadette Bell away. And Sheen was willing to bet that it was the same IRA volunteer that Dennis Lamont had spotted before the checkpoint he was stationed at had been attacked. The red menace. TOPBRASS. A Special Branch agent it now seemed very clear, who had direct access to two very contrasting universes. The world of the IRA, but also the inner sanctum of the RUC's secret division. Darren Howes must have read Sheen's expression, and he asked Sheen if he knew who the person was.

'No, not yet. But I want you to know that I believe you, Mr Howes. And I am sorry you were treated that way. It wasn't deserved. I'd like to be able to tell you more, but it's a live investigation. But please know that you've been a great help tonight,' Sheen assured him before they exchanged a polite farewell and the screen went dead.

Sheen found the sheet of paper with Patrick Glenholmes' information, the man who had been convicted of making the bomb that had destroyed Howes' bus. After a minute of searching he found what he wanted. Glenholmes had been living in Dermott Hill at the time of his arrest in 1986, a little district close to an interface point between

302

Catholic and Protestant areas at the foot of the Black Mountain. It was bang in the heart of West Belfast where several of the other points of interest had been added to their map by Jackson. Close to Ballymurphy where Red Giuseppe, the veteran IRA man had been killed in his home by loyalists. A man who may have been set up to take a fall for TOPBRASS.

Which meant Sheen had a choice. He could begin afresh and search all known IRA suspects who fitted the bill and lived within the geographical points of interest they had plotted. Labour intensive and potentially fruitless, especially given what Geordie had correctly said about the proliferation of both IRA suspects and red-headed males in the vicinity. Or, a more targeted approach. Glenholmes clearly did not work alone, and if they could get him to talk, he could be the only person so far that might be able to give them the name of the man who remained hidden behind the title TOPBRASS. He doubted Glenholmes would be willing to cooperate, but Sheen trusted that Aoife would get the job done. Glenholmes could say something that might switch another light on for them or betray an important detail without knowing it. Which was why knocking on doors and speaking to suspects and witnesses mattered so much.

Sheen yawned, found the French press and rinsed it out, then looked for biscuits while the kettle boiled. As he filled the coffee maker to the top and chewed a stale custard cream, Sheen thought about the implications of what Darren Howes had just suggested to him. If TOPBRASS had been sanctioned or in some way excused for his part in the Ballycarrick ambush, it painted a truly dismal picture. A world where the moral compass of those in positions of authority had ceased to work. Sheen could only guess that if TOPBRASS had been permitted to take part in Ballycarrick, then something big must have been given to Special Branch in return. Like three of the IRA's most ruthless operatives shot dead in Cyprus. If true, TOPBRASS and those he worked for had done a good job at covering their tracks too. The facts were known in snippets and shared by the few. Men like Darren Howes, miraculously lucky to survive, but penalised unfairly. Men like Glenholmes, who spent long years behind bars and remained loyal to a cause that had been well and truly sold out. And people like Bernadette Bell and Dennis Lamont. Sheen cleared his desk and again reached for the Cyprus Three folders. If they or Lamont or Bell could speak, Sheen might hear the truth about TOPBRASS. But that didn't mean Sheen was ready to stop asking questions, and he wouldn't stop until he had the answers.

# CHAPTER THIRTY-FOUR

Tucker was making progress. With the crosswords. In fact, he could not really grasp why Roddy, always a legend at them, had not managed to complete the three that Tucker had now done. But Tucker could definitely see the allure of them, now that he had the time and a sober eye. There was a lot of satisfaction to be had from getting the answers, even if he didn't have a pen to physically complete the puzzle. If he ever got out of this hole – no, *when* he got himself out or Owen Sheen worked out a way to find him – Tucker was definitely planning to take up crosswords in a more serious way. The thought of a change of clothes, a hot shower and a cup of tea with a fresh, untouched crossword puzzle sounded like a dream. Small pleasures. Things that had always been masked and overwhelmed by the single pressing priority that had dominated his world before the bunker. Namely, where his next drink was coming from. And the one after that.

The thought of his old nemesis, though, was not entirely unpleasant. He opened the storage cupboard, still replete with supplies, and saw the dry biscuits and energy bars, the vacuum-packed astronaut meals that needed only cold water and the cans of fish in oil as twinkling bottles of high-grade booze. The bourbon and the Scotch, the Irish and the Baileys. The white spirits too; clean and clear rum and the triple distilled vodkas, the aromatic gins and the silver label tequila. The mixers were all there too, anything you wanted and a big tub of ice in which lounged an open crate of quality European beers. His mouth was suddenly parched, even though he'd guzzled enough cold water to make himself feel seasick.

Tucker grabbed some oatcakes and sat down on the plastic seat. He'd flicked ahead to find more crosswords and grunted in approval at his two latest conquests. He wished he had a pen. The act of filling in the void boxes would crown the satisfaction in a way that he could not completely account for. The first one had just come to him, no hesitation; he didn't even have to think. Six down, seven letters. Tendency or partiality. Leaning. Had to be. Simple. Spurred on by that he had searched out the next one, but this had taken much longer. Five down, seven letters. Sod's adage. Tucker was not entirely sure what an adage was, but he'd persisted with sod which he was familiar with. It took him three cups of water, two toilet breaks and an oat cake, but at last he got it.

'Murphys,' he said, savouring a repeat of that same tingle of exhilaration he had enjoyed when he'd cracked it. And Tucker needed something to keep his spirits up. He'd discovered that he was not claustrophobic. Being in the close confines of the bunker did not fill him with panic or anxiety. But it was a bit cold and the information he was working through did nothing to warm his spirits. Although there was no smoking gun when it came to the case of Dennis Lamont, Tucker could wire the circuit. TOPBRASS had complained to his handler that he had been clocked more than once by a RUC officer in the city centre while undertaking an intelligence gathering mission. Fenton referred to the operation as 'essential to maintain necessary credibility for TOPBRASS, despite his ascent in the IRA hierarchy. His reputation as an operative who does not shirk active service (properly managed) is indispensable.' TOPBRASS, however, had subsequently been advised by Samuel Fenton to try to lie low, but to avoid attracting suspicion from fellow IRA members.

Tucker turned the pages of Roddy's book that followed the copied memo. A gun attack on a joint UDR and RUC checkpoint in the city, three were killed. And then, the reports of the murder of an off-duty RUC officer who was working in the family ice-cream parlour on the Dublin Road. Dennis Lamont. The press releases mentioned that a police-issue revolver was believed to have been used in the attack and then, the story just dried up. Tucker remembered what it had been like. One death or tragedy dominated the news and captured the imagination and sympathy of the majority of the public, until it was eclipsed by yet another, sometimes even more horrific, happening. Like a firework display in a bad dream that exploded live rounds and real bombs, and awed spectators with ever greater destruction of human life. A line from one newspaper report, however, had been neatly highlighted by Roddy. The reporter explained that in a tragic twist, Dennis Lamont had earlier escaped an IRA attack that was launched on a city centre checkpoint after falling ill with the flu, only to be singled out later while off duty. Roddy had written another poem here, this one titled *Mint Choc Chip*. One of the cuttings had mentioned that Lamont's little boy had witnessed the murder but could only remember that the killer asked for that particular flavour. It was bloody touching.

Tucker cleared his throat and turned the page. His spirits leapt and then plummeted. There was another crossword, dated from the time and with one clue remaining. But it was a cryptic one. Tucker cursed and slammed the plastic table with the flat of his hand, hard enough to hurt. He let his breathing calm down a bit, took a trip to the toilet that he didn't need and returned to his seat. That reaction was disproportionate. But then again, the proportions of the normal world had warped and bent out of all recognition this week. He looked at the clue.

'Ten across. Two words,' he calmly instructed. 'Three letters and four letters. The clue is "Rusty-looking locks".' Tucker chewed his thumb nail, and then stopped. 'Set lock,' he said. But that was a stretch, and it didn't sound right, and besides the last letter of the second word must be an r. Roddy had not filled it in but it was the only thing that feasibly fitted with 'rasher', and it made sense for that clue which was 'Piggy with no self-control'. Tucker reread the clue for rasher. He could see how this worked now. Not the same as the quick crosswords. The clues needed to be interpreted. And they sometimes seemed to rely on word plays and double meanings. Tucker stared at the clue he needed to solve and tried to let his brain swing like a double-hinged door, to visualise the multiple meanings which the potential play on words might evoke. He saw a padlock, seized up and needing oil. His heart spiked in excitement. First word, Oil? 'Oil need!' he shouted, and then his shoulders slumped. Need didn't end with the letter r.

He growled and turned the page. There, like a ghost, a pasted photograph of himself as a younger man waited. In fact, it was a copy of his mugshot from when he had first joined the police, which Roddy clearly had managed to dig up. Tucker stared at the youthful, good-looking guy who gazed unblinking and undaunted back at him. A young fella coming from not a lot but expecting it all. A boy really, who had very little idea about what the early 1970s would show him as a peeler in Belfast. How the things he took as certainties in his world were really built on sand. Roddy had crowned him with the altogether dubious title of 'One Good Cop, One Great Mate'. The photo, like some other elements of this booklet, lacked a rationale, it just was. Which, Tucker absently reflected, was a little bit like life at times. But Tucker didn't need to be a detective to see that Roddy had actually viewed him both as a 'Great Mate' and maybe even something more. The camping trips. And how he'd insisted that he give Tucker the odd gift, like that watch for Christmas one year. And what had Tucker ever done in return?

'Damn all, as per usual,' he commented. He'd pawned that watch before the new year for drinking money. Tucker shook his head in disgust, as though recounting the past crimes of a different man, one who had cared little for anyone or anything beyond himself and his next drink. He moved on from the crossword that had stumped him, for the time being.

There followed a request from Fenton in the summer of 1986 that all surveillance that may hamper TOPBRASS's IRA cell in West Belfast and beyond be lifted. Tucker assumed that there would be a way of doing this indirectly, without naming TOPBRASS to units as a man to be left alone and thus arousing suggestions that he was protected and blowing his cover. Fenton claimed that TOPBRASS was close to delivering a 'sizeable setback to IRA operations and morale in Belfast'. Tucker then read the newspaper cuttings about the Ballycarrick bus bombing that left eight British Army soldiers dead and many injured. If Roddy had evidence from Special Branch to suggest that TOPBRASS was involved, he had not included it in his booklet. Tucker assumed that something like that, if it involved some level of collusion, would likely never be written. But he could see the gist of Roddy's thinking, by reading the highlighted snippets from the reports he had collated. And the very fact that it had been included told Tucker that there must be a link. When it came to TOPBRASS, Roddy had so far been coherent and meticulous. Tucker surveyed the facts. The fact that the driver had claimed to have followed a police diversion, the fact that the police had denied it, the fact that only one man was convicted and that he came from Dermott Hill in West Belfast. Very close, in fact, to Ballymurphy where Tucker had already deduced TOPBRASS to likely be living at that time, based on the fact that Giuseppe Morelli, another IRA man from the district, had been set up for assassination to save TOPBRASS's skin. It stank like raw sewage in high summer. And the next copied Special Branch correspondence explained what TOPBRASS had apparently gifted in return.

CONFIDENTIAL
ROYAL ULSTER CONSTABULARY
SPECIAL BRANCH
14th Day of August 1986
SPECIAL REPORT
SUBJECT: TOPBRASS

TOPBRASS has struck a major blow against the IRA. Intelligence and advance warning over several months resulted in an attack on Andersonstown police station being foiled. Three known IRA terrorists with considerable experience were thwarted in their attempt to kill and maim officers. Their plan was to breach the perimeter of the station using a JCB digger, loaded with a primed three-hundred-pound bomb in the bucket, and in the aftermath shoot survivors. Due to TOPBRASS's infiltration of the cell, a specialist team of RUC officers lay in wait in the adjacent cemetery. After challenging the IRA unit, they concluded that all three had made threatening movements and were forced to open fire. None of the terrorist cell survived.

TOPBRASS was scheduled to take part in the attack and in order to ensure that he was not present, he agreed to undergo an arrest in the area the day before. His whereabouts were leaked to a low-level informant who in turn informed his British Army handler. TOPBRASS and another IRA member were apprehended at the home of the latter. Army and RUC colleagues were not informed of the ruse.

As a result of this, TOPBRASS was severely beaten both at the point of capture by the British Army and then subjected to intensive interrogation techniques at Castlereagh Holding Centre for almost a week. He was then released without charge, at a stage when I felt that suspicions would not be raised. TOPBRASS suffered a perforated eardrum, extensive bruising and tendon damage. I have advised him to claim legal compensation. The anticipated five-figure sum he should receive will only partly compensate him for the pain he has endured and barely thank him for the service he has given. May I recommend an immediate cash bonus of £10,000 in advance and in excess of any legal compensation he may receive?

Submitted to the chief constable: Detective Chief Inspector S. R. Fenton

Tucker read the news reports, though he didn't need to. He remembered the attack and the subsequent outcry. Allegations that the RUC had operated a shoot-to-kill policy, that there had been no meaningful attempt to arrest the men in balaclavas. The Irish republican PR machine had done a good job at making some hay from what at the time had been a crushing blow for the Belfast IRA. The failed attack had been renamed the 'Andytown Massacre' and memorials had been erected to the fallen. But it didn't change the fact that the IRA had lost a valued active service unit. Three were killed and, from what Tucker could now piece together, a guy called Patrick Glenholmes had been sent down for his part in the Ballycarrick bombing. Only TOPBRASS still walked the streets. If this information got out it would be damning for the republicans and the British alike. Tucker knew that nobody involved in the dirty war wanted the lid lifted on what had been done. Least of all TOPBRASS.

Another photograph of Tucker. This one was of Roddy and himself, on one of their fishing trips. Tucker looked plastered. Roddy looked chuffed with the fat trout he'd landed. No title, no words. Tucker squinted at the background. There was a sign on wooden stakes, the name of the river. He set the book down.

'Fuck's sake, Roddy.'

Ballycarrick Brook. Close to the spot where the bus bomb had exploded. Was it some kind of sick obsession? Did Roddy get a thrill from knowing the significance of the place as he compiled the book? Tucker shook his head. 'No idea,' he confirmed. But it was very weird. The sign was old even then, blotched red with rust. Tucker picked up the book again and quickly flicked back the pages until he found the cryptic crossword. His heart was beating. He'd cracked it.

'Rusty-looking locks'.

Three plus four.

Red hair.

# CHAPTER THIRTY-FIVE

The coffee kicked in and Sheen made great progress. By the time he came up for air it was past midnight, but he was satisfied that he would be able to get through the guts of the rest of the documents before the end of the night and definitely by close of business tomorrow. Which would probably make Dr Shaun Maitland a happy man. The old guy had clearly been uncomfortable holed up in the SHOT offices at Grosvenor Road. Not his natural habitat.

The picture that was emerging of events that day in Cyprus, as Sheen had expected, did much to vindicate the claims made at the time that the killings of the three IRA members had almost certainly been unlawful, while probably exonerating the British authorities from allegations of an outright shoot-to-kill exercise or conspiratorial cover-up. There was other evidence that Sheen could turn to of course. He could insist on tracking down eyewitnesses from the locality and perhaps he would. There was a possibility that he might be able to speak to the SAS soldiers, if they were still alive, and under oath, but he knew that the red tape involved in such a task would be monumental and even then, those boys need only stick to their original testimonials: namely that all three IRA operatives had made threatening movements and were deemed to pose a threat to life. The chief had effectively steered him towards a version of events which suited the political needs of Northern Ireland today. And there seemed little that Sheen could do but recount it as such.

After the bomb disposal expert had concluded that Danny Caffery's white Renault posed an imminent threat, it was the job of the Cypriot Police to keep the IRA team under surveillance until matters were handed over to the SAS. The police, according to MI5 memos, managed to lose the team of three. Although Sheen thought this was possible, he deemed it improbable, especially as the car they had hired was judged to contain a bomb. It was this window that MI5 used to explain the under-informed approach by the SAS unit who closed in to arrest the IRA members a short time later. Sheen was able to read the back and forth between the sergeant commanding the SAS unit on the ground and MI5 officers in the Operation Severus command room which had been set up in a nearby village. IRA bomb technician PJ Wilson was spotted carrying an unidentified parcel wrapped in beach towels, with Caffery and Gleeson walking close behind him. The communication between the command room and the soldiers on the ground definitely became a little frantic and in the end the order was ambiguous. As though both sides were feeding their uncertain reading of the situation from one to the other, waiting for someone to take control and assume responsibility. Questions about whether there was a bomb were answered repeatedly with the response that 'TECHNICIAN' (the codename assigned to PJ Wilson) had an unidentified package. In the end the order from the command room was to 'Take them'.

SAS soldiers in plain clothes emerged to intercept the trio. Caffery split from Wilson and Gleeson and started running south. Two SAS soldiers approached Wilson, and Gleeson who were later claimed to have made threatening movements. The soldiers opened fire, hitting both multiple times, first Wilson and then Gleeson. An SAS soldier pursued Caffery, who was alleged to have turned around and reached for a gun. He too was shot multiple times. All three were later found to have been unarmed. Sheen also had a copy of eyewitness reports gathered at the time by a television company who broadcast a documentary, stating that the SAS soldier continued to fire multiple times into Caffery's body as he lay on the ground. As a copper, Sheen found such an approach hard to accept. However, brutal as that was, the SAS were trained, and arguably employed in this case, to eliminate the enemy when they believed that they posed a threat to life. There was poor communication, ambiguous orders and sloppy work in letting the suspects slip their surveillance in the first place. Sheen was personally unconvinced that the intention had not always been to execute all three, but there was simply no way of proving that based on the evidence at his disposal. According to the MI5 data, those in the Operation Severus command room 'fell into a stunned silence when told that all three had been killed' before the ensuing panic to evacuate the area of the supposed explosive device on PJ Wilson. Which on closer inspection was found to be bags of sugar.

Sheen stretched and checked the time. It had gone 1 a.m. And no Aoife. He took out his phone, which, of course, was still dead and then he finally plugged it in. He felt a flutter of unease. She said she would come back and help him work through these papers. And that was several hours ago. He glanced at his phone which was still coming to life and thought about calling her using the landline. She'd probably messaged him. Maybe Ava was unwell or wanted to come home from the sleepover. He'd wait and check his phone before waking them. Sheen returned to the trove of papers, started reading one of the few files he had yet to give his attention to and was suddenly engrossed again, though once more he felt his stamina begin to lag. A single sheaf among many others caught his attention. It was a typed letter sent from the head of MI5 to the RUC chief constable, dated three weeks after the Cyprus killings. Sheen scanned the page.

It was a thank-you note.

*There is no doubt that without the last-minute and invaluable intelligence from your Special Branch asset [REDACTED] [REDACTED] the IRA unit would not have been detected as they entered Cyprus and could not have been stopped as they were. It is evident that your man from Ballymurphy helped to save countless lives, while risking his own. We all owe him an enormous debt of gratitude for his bravery and continued good work.*

A thump of excitement coursed through him. This was it. This was what he'd been searching for. He had concrete evidence that a Special Branch informer was involved in the killing of the Cyprus Three. An agent from the Irish republican heartland of Ballymurphy, the same estate where the patsy Red Giuseppe Morelli was murdered. And no more than a mile from where the Cyprus Three had lived. The time had come for Sheen to call on Chief Stevens for help. The same man, according to what Geordie had unearthed, who years before had quite possibly suppressed the investigation into Dennis Lamont's murder. It felt like a long shot, despite the chief's enthusiasm for answers in the Cyprus Three case. But right now he was Sheen's best hope. He needed the original unredacted version of this letter, because in it, if he was correct and if he was lucky, he'd find the name that Tucker Rodgers had told him to seek out. The agent with the dirty red hair, who was both ally and enemy, depending on the day. The killer and the protector of British soldiers. TOPBRASS.

# CHAPTER THIRTY-SIX

Aoife opened her eyes. But the darkness did not abate. Only the pain, throbbing in thick, nauseating waves from the bottom of her neck, across her skull and down her face confirmed that she was alive.

Or in hell.

She tried to swallow but her throat was dry. All she managed was an arid cough, the effort turning the agony in her head up a notch to a pitch she had not known existed. It was worse than when she'd been shot, and she had taken a bullet in the gut. She forced herself to take stock, demanded that her brain focus beyond the epicentre of pain and talk to her body, still sheathed in total darkness.

She was seated. Her arms were by her sides. Aoife tried to raise her right arm and found she could not. She was tied to something. Both wrists tightly clasped with what felt like plastic zip ties. She felt the faint sensation of dampness on her hands which were otherwise almost numb. If her head didn't hurt so cataclysmically, her wrists would surely be screaming with pain. Legs next. She tried to raise her foot, aware for the first time that someone had removed her shoes and socks. Nothing, same as her wrists, the unyielding bite of zip ties around her bare ankles. Wherever she was it smelt dank, like a cellar. She blinked in another fruitless effort to adjust her eyes to the thick and all-consuming darkness, but it did nothing more than sent a backwash of pain from her temple to her neck and add to the awfulness.

She uttered an involuntary moan. It sounded alien and not of her body. It sounded like a wounded animal. There were other sounds in response. A door being opened and steps. What could have been the turning of a handle and then, there was light. Harsh and bright and suddenly filling her world, hammering her as though it were a physical thing. She squeezed her eyes shut, the pressure of doing so marginally preferable to the spears of light that had stabbed into her brain a moment before. She heard a chair being scraped across a hard surface and then nothing. The white-hot pressure of the light on her closed eyes faded and turned more muted. She relaxed her lids and then slowly, very slowly, eased her eyes open.

Poured concrete floor. The feet of a plastic chair. A pair of legs seated, clad in black. She raised her eyes, squinting in pain, but forced herself to look. A big man, he towered over her even while seated, his arms were folded. The base of a dark-haired beard was visible beneath the bottom of the black balaclava he wore. Another figure entered the room. Similar attire. And also, a man. He was smaller than the other one, but squat and nearly as wide as the doorway where he now stood. Like a whiskey vat on legs. Beyond him there was what looked like a hallway of some kind which was quickly masked from view as the squat man closed the door behind him. They stared at her, their eyes and presence heavy in what she could now see was the confines of a small cell. To her right was a blank wall, constructed of the same smooth, poured concrete that formed the floor. To the left was a pair of rudimentary bunks, formed of the hard, moulded plastic on which the large man in front of her sat, and she could only assume, which she did too. They may have left her barefoot, but she was clothed at least. Her mind finally started to compute, using the data which had just been inputted and accessing the last saved memory she had.

She'd gone to Glenholmes' address. Been taken by surprise. Had been so bloody stupid. Aoife felt her mental ground give way under her, the beginnings of an irrevocable slide into self-condemnation, self-pity and despair. She couldn't. It would not help; it would make it worse, if such a thing were possible.

So, focus.

This place, it felt secure, and customised and official. They might be dressed for the occasion but the men in front of her were therefore unlikely to be the IRA. Another throb of sickening pain from her neck. Whatever these men had used to incapacitate her, had come close to doing lasting damage. Close, but just shy of it. Whether it was a cosh, the hard edge of a hand or a taser, they had been measured in their application. Whoever had hit her could have killed her. But they had not. She was alive and this gave her hope. Now she had to make sure that didn't change. It was all that mattered. The large man who was seated produced a bottle of water from his jacket and opened it. Her wizened tongue flexed in her mouth and her eyes watched it greedily. How long had she been out?

'You need to drink.' Not Irish. Hard to place. Maybe lowland Scottish, maybe the borders. 'I'll give it to you, but slowly,' he warned.

Aoife nodded pleadingly, tried to ignore the pain that moving her head generated. He uncapped the bottle and slowly decanted a trickle into her waiting mouth while the other man watched. At first she gagged. He stopped, let her recover and then repeated the process. Better this time, she swallowed and felt her mouth rehydrate, her tongue become supple. The bottle was removed, even as her open lips pleaded for more.

'That's enough,' said the tall man as he returned the bottle to his jacket. The smaller guy stepped aside, and the big guy left the room. The vat of whiskey remained and stood with his arms folded. She glanced up to his masked face.

'Don't fucking look at me!' he barked. Belfast, or thereabouts. He stepped towards her as the other man re-entered. She shrunk in the seat, kept her eyes down. She heard something being unwrapped. The bigger man was down on one knee, an open energy bar of some kind held between them. A marriage proposal organised by Satan. The thought turned her mind to Sheen. Which opened the door to Ava. She felt tears prickle her eyes.

'Eat,' he stated. Neither aggressive nor sympathetic. Neutral.

She took a small bite, though she did not want it. Peanut butter, oats and chocolate chips. Gaggingly sweet. She finished half and shook her head when more was offered.

'There won't be more. For a while,' he said.

'Water,' she said, her mouth once again dry, and now sticky with the confectionary he had demanded she eat.

'It speaks,' commented the other man. The whiskey vat. He lowered himself so his masked face was close to her own. She caught a whiff of his odour. Onions and spearmint. Like he'd necked a burger and then had chewing gum. She did not raise her eyes to meet his, which she felt boring into her nonetheless. The water bottle was offered, and she took a large gulp before it was withdrawn. The tall man stepped back, taking the food and water with him. Her head still ached, but with her immediate needs satisfied for the time being, her mind turned to her hands and feet, so tightly fastened that she could not really feel the former and had pins and needles in the latter. Her buttocks were cold and dead. The whiskey vat was speaking.

'I say we make her speak for us,' he said, turning to look at his partner. The tall man said nothing. Aoife's bladder was suddenly straining. Perhaps it was the ominous intent behind the smaller man's words. Or maybe it was because her body had finally woken up. And if her hands and feet were anything to go by, she may have been seated here for some time already.

'I'm going to need to use a toilet,' she said quietly, looking up at the tall man. If she could manage to achieve that it would be a victory. A chance to get her circulation moving, and a psychological point scored too. The good guy/bad guy split was the oldest ruse in the world, and thus far these two fitted the template perfectly. But there was nothing to be lost in trying. A strong hand grabbed her throat and squeezed, radiating twisted waves of agony from the back of her head. It felt like a whiplash, only worse. Whiskey vat was in her face. She could feel his hot spittle spray her cheeks and he hissed his words through clenched teeth.

'You'll pish and shit where you sit,' he snarled. He kept hold of her neck and she could feel the pressure building, her airways closing. Now she did look at him, glared into his eyes with a hate to double his own, a look that said she would kill him when she got free. His brown eyes widened. 'Oh yes, you have a mouth on you all right. I can hear what you're saying, even when it's shut,' he said.

The tall man tugged him away from Aoife by his shoulder. She gasped and choked and drew in a breath, slumped forward on the seat. The whiskey vat said again that he wanted to question her. Aoife tried to make herself even smaller in the chair, regretting that she had let her emotions show. She had riled him, and she was pretty sure that asking her questions would only be part of this thug's intentions. The taller of the two paused, considering his partner's suggestion, and then produced a phone from one pocket and raised his hand to the other man.

The tall man stepped out of the room. Aoife listened. He was making a call. In her banging heart she knew that her fate most likely depended on its outcome. She could feel the nasty energy, full of violent intent, that pulsed towards her from the man who still stood beside her in the room, close enough to smell the ghost of a smoked cigarette off him, mixed with the onions and gum she'd caught from his breath. She fixed her eyes on the floor and listened.

A short exchange. The tall man on the other side of the door did most of the listening. Most of it was too muffled to hear, until the whiskey vat, perhaps getting impatient to begin what he'd planned for her, nudged the door ajar. That was when she heard it.

'Understood, sir. We will return to Ardtullagh and await orders.'

Ardtullagh. It sounded like it was Gaelic, but Aoife didn't recognise it. She repeated it internally again and again, not allowing it to be forgotten in the stress of the moment. So far that word was the only thing that these men had inadvertently revealed to her. Nothing about their location, their roles or their ranks if they had them. If she had to choose Aoife would have said they were specialist military, but the use of the Irish word again made her doubt it. Either way, none of this was good news. She held her breath, waiting for the tall man to explain what the outcome of his call meant for her.

'Well?' asked whiskey vat.

The tall guy gave a firm shake of his head. Aoife exhaled slowly. The request that she be interrogated had been declined.

'She's to remain alert. He wants her alive. Nothing else.'

The whiskey vat cursed and turned to where Aoife waited, helpless and tied to the chair. She gave an involuntary cry and braced herself for the blow she was sure would follow. The tall man had also been taken by surprise. He lunged after his stocky counterpart and gripped him by the shoulder. The smaller man gave him a sharp glance and then shrugged off the bigger man's hand. He relaxed and turned his eyes to Aoife.

'For now,' he said. 'But before long you'll be mine. I have a use for that mouth. When I start on you, you'll beg to speak,' he said. He held her gaze as he retreated out the door.

It was then that Aoife felt rage fill her. It was his sordid threat that did it. She tried to resist the pull of the anger, but it was too late. All pretence of self-control was gone. She snarled at him and struggled pointlessly against the plastic that bit into her flesh. The fire in her was fuelled and intensified when she saw that he was now chuckling.

'You fucking bastard! Fuck you!'

The tall man followed without comment. Without looking back at her he closed the door behind him. The fury still had her in its hands, and she couldn't resist it and she didn't want to, though it was stupid and dangerous.

'Fuck you! Fuck you, you little man. You! Little! Fucking! Man!'

Silence.

She waited and listened. For a murmur of conversation. For a scrape of furniture on the ground. For a door handle turned or a light switch pressed. For a tap running.

Silence.

The tears she had contained now arrived. Hot and plentiful and coursing down her face in streams that could not be wiped away. First tears of anger, then of fear and then of pain. She screamed for help. But the walls of the cell absorbed her cry and kept it for her ears only, she was certain of it.

The light turned off without warning.

Silence was joined by its sister, darkness.

Aoife screamed until her voice was hoarse, and she felt her mouth and throat turn dry. She had no water. And she had no idea where she was, and neither could anyone else. She tried not to, but she wept, wept until she had run dry.

Ava's was the first face that drifted from the blackness, and started to speak, but she was not the last. Trapped in a place where time had lost its bearings, Aoife was not sure how long had passed before she started to question how she'd come to be in this place. As waking and sleeping morphed, reality and dreams became a revolving door, until Aoife McCusker was sure of nothing, not even who she was. But when she came close to the edge of that precipice, she repeated the same word again and again. The word the tall man had let slip, her sole little victory in this dark and despairing hole. And a word that she would use to find them when she escaped from this mess.

Ardtullagh.

# CHAPTER THIRTY-SEVEN

Sheen jolted awake, and almost fell off the chair on which he had fallen asleep in the SHOT office. He blinked away the last vestige of whatever troubled dream he'd been having and recognised the mundane interior of his workplace. His arse was numb as a rock and he had a crick in his neck. Despite the fact that the office was kept at a comfortable room temperature, he also felt cold. He checked his watch. It had gone 5 a.m. He'd managed to do an all-nighter after all, but not exactly in the way he had planned. He stood up and stretched, swallowed a mouthful of cold, bitter coffee with a grimace and ignored the rustling need for a smoke. It would pass. Mornings were by far the worst when it came to cravings.

Sleep or no sleep, he'd put a significant dent in the Cyprus documents. And it had been well worth it. The diamond among the coal was the letter of thanks from one boss to the other. It energised him and despite the poor quality rest he wanted to get back to it. Starting with a straight conversation with Chief Stevens. He needed the unredacted version of the MI5 document that Shaun Maitland had provided. It could be enough to crack the mystery of TOPBRASS and if Jackson managed to locate the missing Special Branch files, they would have even more to go on. He picked up his phone and removed the charger.

Three missed calls. One from Aoife. Timed at 10 p.m. the previous evening. Then two further missed calls, but not identified. The first at 1 a.m. and the last was just fifteen minutes ago. Something must have happened. To her or her kid. And he'd been out of reach. She'd reminded him to plug his phone in and he'd bloody well forgotten. As he took this in, another call, again not identified, flashed up. In that instant, still partly befuddled and dazed, he did not stop to consider why Aoife would appear on his caller ID once but not thereafter. And he didn't think why she would not have simply called the SHOT landline the previous evening after Sheen's phone went straight to voicemail. The call was answered.

'Aoife, darling. I'm so sorry. Are you OK?'

A dry and rasping chuckle. A man's voice. Sheen felt the office slip out of focus for an instant and his stomach fall.

'Very touching. But maybe you should work on answering your phone?' the softly spoken man said. Hard to place his accent beyond it being Northern Irish. He was pitching his voice at little over a whisper.

'Who are you?' said Sheen, his shock now overtaken by a protective anger.

'Never you mind. I have her. She's safe. For now.'

Sheen was fully awake now, and his brain processed what the voice on the line had just told him. Someone had taken Aoife. She'd been kidnapped.

He forced himself to think, tried to push the rising anger aside. Three missed calls, the first from Aoife's phone at 10 p.m. and then two more unidentified. If all three came from whoever had taken Aoife, he still had a sliver of hope.

'Let her go, you bastard.' Words that sounded as weak and ineffectual as they surely were.

Sheen thought about the matt grey hatchback. The stocky man who had broken into his apartment. Never in his life had he wished to have killed another person as much as he did right now. One clear shot. But he'd bottled it. And now they had her.

'Shut up. Drop the TOPBRASS line. Now. Finish up your work for Chief Stevens and forget about Tucker Rodgers. When we're done this end, she walks.'

'I don't know what you're talking about, mate,' attempted Sheen.

Staccato tuts from the other end, cutting off his words.

'We have your notepad. We know,' he replied. Of course they did.

Sheen closed his eyes, desperately fighting the flaring anger that wanted to be released, trying to see an angle here that he could use, anything he could offer to get her back. But he could not. He'd ballsed it up. And not for the first time. Aoife McCusker was in peril because of his ineptitude and selfish single-mindedness.

The voice on the line asked if he had Sheen's attention.

'Yeah.'

'We see you sniffing where you have no business, she dies. If one of your little band of misfits pokes his nose into this any further, she dies. If Chief Stevens becomes unusually interested in pursuing this further, she dies.'

'I want proof of life.'

'You don't get to give the orders any more. We don't want a dead peeler on our hands. But if you force us, her blood will be on your head.'

The line went dead, but Sheen remained with the phone to his ear listening to the silence, demanding that his stunned brain kick in and get up to speed with the perforated reality he had just been dealt. Finally, he set his phone down.

The man who had attacked him and done over his apartment could have ended Sheen's life when he had the upper hand. And Sheen had no doubt whatsoever that he would have taken a professional pride in doing so. What the kidnapper on the phone had just told him, therefore, could hold some weight. Murdering an old loner like Roddy Grant and passing it off as suicide was one thing. But kidnapping and killing a police officer was another matter entirely. It was heat that would simply never really go away. Which meant there was a chance. That she was alive, and that he could get her back safely. But he also believed that the abductor was serious about him dropping TOPBRASS and about what would happen if he, or his team, continued to work the case and try to save Tucker Rodgers' life. What would be revealed in the process was evidently devastating enough to those involved to up the ante to the highest level.

Sheen sat down and put his head in his hands. The allure of total despair was strong, like the gravitational pull from a supermassive black hole that wanted to consume everything. A place from which nothing, not even light, could escape. But didn't someone once say that it takes just a single candle to defy and define the darkness? The thought of a candle, burning like a solitary hope gave him a modicum of it. And it made Sheen think of someone who might be able to help. There was a way. It would be dangerous to attempt it and almost certain to yield nothing. But it was all he had and that meant it was all that stood between Aoife and the moral chasm of the man who had kidnapped her. He checked his watch. Half five. Early for some, but not for the woman he needed.

'Hayley?' She'd answered after just one ring.

'Sheen? Is everything all right?' From her tone Sheen could already tell that she knew it was not.

Forty minutes later Sheen was in the sacristy of Clonard Monastery in West Belfast having entered from the church satisfied that he had not been seen. Hayley, ordinarily assisting as a lay person at dawn Mass, was by his side as the priest gave out Communion in the church adjacent. Sheen had attended a grisly crime scene here not so very long ago and the memory of what he'd encountered was still fresh. But this morning, he had a new horror to cope with. He finished giving Hayley an update when there was a rap on the door that led out to the car park. Dermot Fahey, Sheen's investigative journalist mate, entered.

'Hayley, good to see you again', he said and closed the door behind him. Sheen had called Fahey this morning immediately after he had got off the phone with Hayley. Fahey had been post-launch party groggy and not massively pleased to have been woken up. At first, he thought that Sheen was calling to apologise for missing his book launch. Sheen had not had time to give Fahey more than a superficial overview of what was going down, but by the end of their conversation Dermot was awake, alert and intrigued. He looked over to Sheen as he took a seat. 'Was it absolutely necessary that I attend dawn Mass? Last time I did I was about eleven and serving as an altar boy.'

'Do you no harm, Dermot,' commented Hayley.

'Yeah, sorry about that,' said Sheen. 'I have to assume I was followed. And I can't afford to be seen with you. You're fairly well known as a journalist,' he explained.

'Aoife,' said Dermot, grim-faced.

Sheen nodded and went over what he had just explained to Hayley, including the fact that he had driven up to Glenholmes' address in Gransha and found Aoife's old Micra parked up outside, locked.

'I could tell you both more, about why this has happened, but it will take time and frankly I'm not entirely convinced I should. Sometimes knowledge is a very dangerous thing.'

'Especially here,' replied Hayley, and sighed. She was also sombre, but beneath it, Sheen could see the glow of anger. Someone had taken Aoife, her friend. And Hayley was a woman Sheen would think twice before crossing, regardless of her capacity for compassion and dedicated spirituality.

'But I want you to know that when I can, I will. Especially you, Dermot. There's a story here that the public needs to hear,' he said, but kept the last thought under wraps. Namely, if they all managed to get through this thing alive. Hayley asked him how he thought they could help.

'In different ways.'

Sheen explained to Fahey that he thought Special Branch and maybe Military Intelligence were involved in Aoife's kidnap.

'On the books?' He meant whether what was happening had official sanction.

Sheen shook his head.

'Doubt it. Which leads me to believe that they are unlikely to have taken Aoife anywhere on the radar. An army barracks or even a secure government building with restricted access. Too risky.'

Fahey was nodding.

'I'm with you on that. Even a safehouse could cause them difficulties. Unless Aoife is sedated, or something else, they might have a hard time keeping a lid on it,' he said.

Sheen's mind was assaulted by a horde of unwanted images. Aoife in a coma like Dave Rodgers. Aoife gagged and choking, unable to breathe. Aoife sedated with something government-made that would shut her up but rot her brain. But there was also the image of what she would say if someone tried to hold her against her will. And how she would communicate it.

'Which is why I need you, Dermot.' Fahey was well connected, had written articles with anonymous sources who had worked as former Special Branch officers and spies for both the British and Irish.

'I have my limits. I don't know many of the real names of the Branch men I've spoken to, and definitely not the identities of their informants and assets. The information I get tends to be specific to the stories I'm writing,' he said.

'I didn't expect you to give me names, Dermot. I just thought there might be something, anything you can recall that could give us some leverage here,' said Sheen, that sinking feeling once again upon him, like trying to jog through quicksand.

Dermot Fahey had gone quiet, his chin on his chest.

'There might be something. But it's rumour, nothing concrete.' Sheen asked him to continue. 'Have you ever heard about priest holes?'

'From the Penal times, when Catholicism was outlawed in Ireland,' said Hayley.

'Indeed. Priests would say Masses in hedges and isolated spots and people would have hideaways constructed across the region. Dugouts and shelters that a priest on the run could use to avoid detection,' Fahey explained.

'How's this related?' asked Sheen.

'I was drinking one time in the Stormont Hotel with this old Special Branch guy. Ages ago it was. I wasn't even after anything. It was just that journalists and Branch men used to drink in the same spots. Anyway, he told me that in the late 1980s the government commissioned the construction of a number of underground bunkers, priest holes they called them. Do you recall the case of the two undercover British soldiers who were murdered at that IRA funeral?'

'Yes,' said Sheen. The world's media were there and had filmed the men being surrounded and dragged from their car. They were severely beaten and shot dead by the IRA on waste ground soon after. An army helicopter hovered above, but no one came to the soldiers' assistance.

'The thinking on the part of British was that it must never happen again. They could not always risk entering dangerous areas to rescue their spies and agents, but they could offer them a safe place to hide.'

'Where?'

'West and North Belfast. Apparently,' Fahey emphasised.

'The priest holes were hidden in plain view, constructed in secret and usually inside or in the grounds of derelict houses and abandoned buildings.'

'Ten-a-penny back in the day,' said Sheen.

Fahey agreed.

'But less so now,' he added.

'Meaning that what once was ubiquitous could now stand out, and be more obvious, easier to find?'

'Maybe. But I'm telling ye, this is high rumour, the stuff of end-of-night conspiracy whispers between journalists and drunken cops,' he cautioned. Sheen had seen enough conspiracy theory proven as fact in the last year not to be entirely dissuaded. 'And if, and I mean if, this turns out to be true, you then need to work out a way of gaining access. You won't break in using a sledgehammer or a crowbar.'

Sheen turned to Hayley.

'Aoife said you were able to help with the piece of ripped fabric we found,' said Sheen.

'Hardly. I gave her some general pointers, things that I picked up,' she replied. All of which had been bang on the money as far as Sheen could tell.

'What if I wanted you to go further? Could you sense where someone is, especially someone you are already connected with emotionally like Aoife?'

Hayley was shaking her head, her eyes apologetic.

'I don't know where she is, Sheen. I'm not a GPS.'

The quicksand was back just when he thought he'd struggled free.

'If she were here, in Clonard, and she was upset, terribly upset, would you sense it?'

'Probably. Yes, I could. But I'd need to have something of

336

hers. To act like a sort of divining rod or an antenna,' she said.

Sheen reached inside his jacket and took out the saffron pashmina scarf that Aoife had left on the coat stand at the SHOT offices.

'Like this?' Hayley tentatively reached over and took it from him. She closed her eyes, and Sheen and Fahey waited, said nothing.

Finally, Sheen could not hold off.

'Do you . . . see her?' he asked, unsure of how to phrase what he meant.

Hayley opened her eyes and shook her head.

'No. But I can tell that she's in love with you,' she said.

The words cut him, and he felt a lump form in his throat that he forced away. Hayley rested a big hand on Sheen's arm, and he cleared his throat.

'We will try. And if I have anything to do with this, we will find her. Right, Dermot?'

'Damn right.'

Sheen nodded and thanked them both.

'I've asked for triangulation data on the last call made from Aoife's phone last night. I had a missed call from her last night at 10 p.m. and if we're lucky it was made by the kidnapper. It'll give us a place to start. As soon as I know it, I'll pass it your way. And for God's sake be careful,' he said, and told them to be alert to being followed, especially by a grey hatchback.

Hayley called his name as he was about to depart.

'You be careful too,' she said.

# CHAPTER THIRTY-EIGHT

Traffic was patchy on the Dublin Road in South Belfast at ten minutes to eight in the morning, and pedestrians were few and far between. He stood alone outside the double fronted shop. One was a mobile phone shack and the other a vaping shop. Both were shuttered and closed. Looked like a makeshift partition but it had clearly been here a while. Though not always. The last time he paid this address a visit, it had been an ice-cream parlour.

He scanned the exterior for evidence of a CCTV camera and saw none. There was a police camera pointed in this direction that stood on the end of a high, black pole but it was about a quarter of a mile or more down the road and was primarily used for traffic enforcement. Besides, if it picked him up it would have little to tell. His face was obscured with a cap and scarf as befitted this brisk March morning and his clothing, which would be later disposed of before he returned to his parked motorbike a few built-up residential streets away, was dark and nondescript. He scanned the upper floors of the building and saw the curtains were drawn on the first floor. A small side entrance appeared to service the upper floors. He pressed his gloved finger on the first-floor buzzer for five seconds and waited. He might get lucky. He had every reason to believe he would. The luck of the Irish and the luck of the devil combined were a tough combination to beat. And he held both cards.

A voice, bleary and slow with the word.

'Yeah?'

'Belfast City Council. Planning department,' he replied.

A long pause at this. He thought he was going to have to buzz again and then he heard the squeak of wood as one of the upstairs windows above his head opened. He stepped back from the doorway but did not turn his face directly up at the man who now appeared. He was wearing a dirty-looking grey T-shirt, and his hair was standing in tufts and spikes. His eyes looked full of sleep.

'The shop doesn't open till twelve. What's this about?' he said, and then coughed, raspy and full of phlegm.

'Our records say this shop should be one unit. There's been no planning permission given for this,' he said, and gestured at the divided shopfront. He had a lanyard round his neck with a staff identification card that he'd used for the previous year's West Belfast Festival, or Féile as it was called. It obviously would not stand up to scrutiny, but if his life had taught him one lesson above all others, it was that people could be easily misled by appearances. And most would look no deeper than the mask you wear.

'That's bollocks,' he retorted, but he didn't sound like a man who had been accused in the wrong. The allegation he had just made was a flip of a coin. Either there was permission given, or there was not. Both should be enough to get him what he wanted.

'That's what I am here to determine. There's been a complaint you see. Probably best if I come up.'

'Fuck's sake. Was it that peeler?' he asked.

He did not reply to this, simply shrugged. The man's head disappeared and a moment later the door buzzed, as he was granted entry. He took a furtive glance both ways and saw that he was unobserved, and then he entered. The narrow stairs creaked under his weight and the place smelt of dust and old carpet. He tucked his bogus identification inside his jacket. The overweight man in the grey T-shirt appeared from a door on the first-floor landing wearing a pair of blue shorts and sliders with no socks. They were face-to-face and he raised his chin, let the lump of lard have a look good look at him.

'You Alexander Lamont?'

'Yes,' he replied, and confirmed that he owned the property. Lamont stared at him, not in an accusing way, but definitely for a couple of seconds longer than he would have liked.

'You said the peelers were here. Did you have trouble?'

Lamont invited him inside and asked that he excuse the mess. He closed the door behind him.

'Yeah, but no big problem. It was about ancient history,' he said. 'Is that who made a complaint?' he said, his voice tentative now.

In reply he said, 'Am I right thinking this place used to be an ice-cream parlour?'

Lamont looked away, mumbled that it was but a long time ago. It was a vaping store now. He looked back up, a frown growing on his face.

'What did you say your name was?'

'I don't believe I did,' he said, returning Lamont's furrow with a warm grin.

'Do you have any ID, mate?'

'Of course,' he said, and reached into his jacket pocket. Where his Féile staff card was tucked away. And where the old Ruger Speed-Six also waited. He made a show of fumbling and not locating.

'You look familiar. Have we met before? Or have you been on the TV?'

Lamont was staring at him intently now, and the frown on his face was joined by caution.

'I get that a lot, funny enough. I'm a bit of a changeling, Alex, you know?'

His smile faded. Lamont took a small step backwards, alarm flooding his features like cold seawater gushing into the hull of a torpedoed ship.

'This vape malarkey. You can get all sorts of flavours, am I right?' He slid the gun free from his pocket and cocked it. The sound was enormous in the sudden silence that had filled the space between them. No response. 'Tell me, do you have mint choc chip?'

Alex Lamont's eyes widened, suddenly understanding, finally seeing him, but too late to change his fate. He grabbed a cushion off the chair and shoved it into Lamont's face, then pressed the muzzle of the gun into the muffler he had just created.

Two shots. Still loud enough to ring in his ears but

partially silenced to the world beyond. The back of Alex Lamont's head exploded outwards, and he collapsed in a heap on the filthy carpet. He tossed the cushion, which was emitting a lazy trail of white smoke, and stepped forward to confirm what the gunshot had told him. Lamont's eyes were open, but blank and lifeless as two lumps of coal.

# CHAPTER THIRTY-NINE

Sheen sat in the car park of Ladas Drive PSNI station with a cup of tea in a styrofoam cup and a sausage roll, neither of which he wanted but both of which he forced himself to consume. It was a little after 9 a.m. and Aoife had been gone for over twelve hours. The longer he sat on this, the greater the chance that the worst could happen. What he was doing was reckless, breaking every basic protocol of the job. He met his own eyes in the rear-view mirror. If this backfired and Aoife ended up dead, he would be responsible. But just as he'd called Aoife's mate Marie, claimed they were swimming in work, and asked that she have Ava for one more evening, so too must he conceal this from the chief. For now. For although coming clean would set the full force of the organisation in motion, Sheen simply didn't trust that such an operation would retain the necessary stealth and discretion. What he did trust without hesitation, however, was that the man who had called him this morning had meant what he had said. That Aoife would die should he get a whiff that Sheen was still pursuing TOPBRASS, or if the police made a move to find her. So, this was it, his final throw of the dice. He was taking a risk even coming here and seeing the chief, but the caller had also told him to wrap up his work at this end. To do so, he'd need to meet his boss. A call from Geordie came through on the dash. He answered it using his phone, unwilling to risk using the speakers of the car, should he somehow be overheard.

'Sheen, you heard the news?'

Sudden panic flushed through him at Geordie's words. He shut his eyes.

'What's happened?'

'Massive explosion, off the Falls Road,' said Geordie.

Sheen's mind swerved to keep up.

'Terror attack?'

'Gas. Apparently,' said Geordie.

'What's it got to do with us?'

'It was on Fallswater Street. One person confirmed dead.'

The street name switched on an alert in Sheen's tired and overworked brain. It took him a few seconds to recognise the significance.

'Bernadette Bell's home?'

'Yes.'

'Christ almighty,' said Sheen.

'Looks as though someone is tying up loose ends,' suggested Geordie.

Sheen thought about the dates that he had jotted in his notepad. One of which had corresponded to Bernadette Bell's murder in 1981. It was vital information that, if he had managed to retain, her father, Liam Bell, may still be alive.

'Geordie, Alex Lamont,' said Sheen.

'Shit. I'm on it. I'll drop by right now, tell him to be on guard,' said Geordie.

'How'd you and Aoife get on last night?'

Sheen closed his eyes. He needed to decide. Keeping it away from the chief, for the time being, was one thing, but hiding this from Geordie could do more harm than good should he charge ahead with the case despite the warning to back off. And besides, they were a team, partners. Sheen put a hand over his mouth as a guard against being lip-read and started to speak. He kept it brief and ended by asking Geordie to keep it quiet.

'Jesus, Sheen. I don't know.'

'I'll take responsibility.'

'Aye, but you won't wipe my conscience clean if this goes wrong.'

Sheen understood. He waited.

'OK. For now. But not indefinitely,' said Geordie. Then he asked about the court order for the search of Shandon Park Golf Club.

'Ice it. For now,' he said after a pause. Sheen assumed he was being watched, and although he suspected that his opponent didn't have indefinite resources or manpower, he could not afford to risk Geordie's administrative task being interpreted as defiance of the order to step away. And it would be hard to conceal a formal application for a search.

'Jackson?'

'Geordie, I like him, but I don't want him told. It's not personal.'

Geordie waited, but there was nothing more to add. Sheen felt bad, but the more people who knew, the bigger the odds that news of Aoife's kidnap would leak. And too many people knew already. Plus, Jackson was Chief Stevens' nephew. So far, that had not figured as an issue when it came to the day-to-day operations of SHOT, but Sheen was not prepared to run that risk and in doing so put Aoife's life on the line. Though God knows his job, and Geordie's too should their concealment be discovered, was pretty much against a wall wearing a blindfold.

'What can he get on with?' He meant Jackson.

'Ask him to keep searching for the Branch documents. But tell him to go very cautiously. That he needs to assume we are being monitored.' A risk, but best to keep Jackson occupied. And Sheen was pretty sure that surveillance and tracking by their enemies could not extend to the dark recesses of old storage units where forgotten police files had been dumped, and that's where Jackson's work would take him.

Geordie signed off as Sheen received an update on the last location of Aoife's phone the night before. It wasn't much to go on, but it was a start. West Belfast, somewhere between the Glen Road where she had gone to visit Glenholmes and the upper Falls Road a few miles south. Of course the other calls, including the one he had answered from Aoife's kidnapper, were untraceable. Probably made from a burner phone. He forwarded the details to both Hayley and Fahey as he got out of the car and headed for the station. Sheen pulled his collar up against the drizzle that settled over Belfast after the downpour of the previous evening.

The chief, as expected, was busy. His personal assistant said he was booked into meetings all morning with the policing representatives of each of the main political parties and later with the newly elected Northern Irish policing minister. Clearly greasing the tracks in preparation for the relaunch of the devolved assembly in the coming weeks.

'Tomorrow?'

The young officer shook his head after moving his fingers over a tablet device.

'He's up in Stormont all day. Meeting the First and Deputy First Ministers elect,' he said. Which confirmed Sheen's original assessment. Many cogs and wheels turning in unison. And he was supposed to be one of them, busily preparing conclusions about the Cyprus Three case that could further lubricate the political machinery. The assistant asked him if he wanted to try to book a meeting for the coming days, but Sheen thanked him and declined. Sheen returned to the corridor and rested the back of his head against the wall. The chief was a busy man. But he was still only a man.

Forty minutes later, he spotted him, approaching the toilets outside which Sheen stood. He nipped around the corner and let his boss go and make his peace. When he exited, Sheen was waiting.

'Sheen,' said the chief. Surprise, suspicion and mild irritation mixed into one word. The guy certainly had a way.

'Sir, I need to have a word,' he said.

The chief's eyes remained on Sheen for a long moment before he spoke.

'Walk with me,' he replied, starting slowly back along the corridor. 'How's Cyprus going?'

'Fine, sir. Headline is it looks like they were likely unlawful deaths. No smoking gun to suggest Whitehall set out to action a shoot-to-kill policy, but it was a shambles. The Cyprus Police have a lot to answer for.'

'Very good, Sheen, very good,' he replied warmly. Like Sheen had solved the riddle of the chief's own design. But Sheen's pause told him there was more. His brows narrowed.

'Sir, I believe that Cyprus was the result of home-grown intelligence, a Special Branch agent here in Northern Ireland.'

Now the chief's face darkened to match the grey Belfast sky that brooded above Ladas Drive.

'So not such a chance encounter after all. What in hell is it about you and Special Branch, eh? You're like two opposite ends of a magnet, nothing in common, but nothing will keep you from being drawn together, from ramming into each other,' he said.

'It's significant, sir. It's how the authorities were alerted to Caffery and his team in the first place.'

'It's a detail of history,' spat the chief. 'Irrelevant. What counts is the way the overall operation was mismanaged by the security services.'

'There's an MI5 memo,' persisted Sheen. 'It gives a name, but it's been redacted. I want you to request the original. It holds the key, sir,' said Sheen. He'd raised his voice, unintentionally. But if he could get the chief on board, get that document in hand, this might end now. He'd know the truth about TOPBRASS and do it in a way that would almost certainly not draw fire from those who were pitted against him. It might not lead him to Aoife, but if nothing else it would be the ultimate bargaining chip to help secure her safe return.

The chief looked at him, his eyes widening with realisation.

'I see. This is about that man, the missing police officer Thomas Rodgers. And this TOPBRASS thing. Your hobby horse.'

'It's linked, sir. It's all linked.'

'This is not going to be about Special Branch,' snapped the chief. They were almost nose to nose now. Sheen felt his pulse beat in his neck. 'Drop it, Sheen,' he said. Like Sheen was a dog that had found a bone the big man wanted to stay buried. That was when the anger boiled over. Maybe it was the fatigue, but mostly it was the stress of knowing Aoife was in danger and that he was helpless to turn this around.

'Like you dropped Dennis Lamont?'

'What did you just say?'

'You heard me. July 1984. A cop killed in cold blood by a police-issue gun. Your investigation. And you let it go,' said Sheen. His finger was pointed close to his superior's chest.

The chief inhaled and Sheen could see it in his eyes. Ordinarily composed, right now he wanted to smash Sheen in the face.

'You have a week. I want Cyprus wrapped up and smelling of roses. And then I want your resignation. Or I'll destroy you.'

Sheen nodded. Given his insubordination, and what he'd just accused the chief of, it was to be expected. But his wrath was a tempest, on which his free will struggled to remain afloat.

'Special Branch tell you to back off, did they?'

And Sheen was not alone on the sea. The chief grabbed

him by his jacket and pushed him against the wall. Sheen stayed still. The instance of physical contact seemed to defuse the circuit of his rage. He looked Chief Stevens in the eye and read the layers of the man, and the distance now between them. Resignation aside, they could never again work together. The chief let go of Sheen, turned and walked away without another word.

Sheen sat for a long while in his car, listening to the rain. The chief would never call on MI5 to identify the informer who had set up the Cyprus Three. If Jackson found documents buried in storage, he'd also doubtless block access. Another dead end.

His phone. Geordie.

'Sheen?' Geordie sounded tense and, in the background, Sheen could hear the commotion of other voices.

'Where are you?'

'Dublin Road, Alex Lamont's shop. Sheen, he's dead. Shot in the face.'

Sheen watched a drop of rain trickle down his windscreen, indifferent to the calamity of the world of men.

'Why the fuck did they kill him? He was just a kid back then. He couldn't remember a thing.' Geordie's voice was cracking with emotion.

'I'm sorry, Geordie,' said Sheen. It didn't seem right, or seem enough, but it was all he had. 'Get on to Patrick Glenholmes, find out where he is and tell him he's in danger.'

Glenholmes was the last link that remained from the IRA cell who carried out the Ballycarrick bombing. Chronologically, it was next in line in Tucker's list of dates. Sheen told Geordie to be careful and ended the call. And after Ballycarrick was Cyprus. Sheen's chances of finding TOPBRASS were dwindling fast. Those with any connection were being systematically erased. It was hopeless.

But maybe not entirely. There was one other person that Sheen could call on. Someone outside the field of play who would not arouse suspicion if Sheen did. A man from Sheen's forgotten Belfast childhood who had given him information to die for once before.

# CHAPTER FORTY

Sheen spent nearly half an hour he knew he didn't have driving in repeated grids around the streets of Belfast city centre until he was mostly satisfied that he was not being followed. Only then had he taken the road north out of the city and then drove well over the speed limit up the A6 and then the A26 towards Antrim and Ballymena before joining the M2 after Broughshane. From there he drove deeper into the Glens of Antrim then headed north-east for the coast and the little village of Waterfoot. He was headed to see Billy Murphy, a man who had come to Sheen's assistance last summer when he had first returned to Belfast. Billy had first used his fists to get Sheen out of a jam and then gave him information about who he believed was responsible for Sheen's brother's death. Billy had known Sheen as a child in Belfast long ago and had come from the same ladder of Sailortown streets that he had once called home. Billy had worked on and off collecting debts for a loan shark back in the day, in a place where hard men were not in short supply. If there was anyone who might be able to help him, and who Sheen knew he could trust, it was Billy.

Sheen pulled to a stop after following the winding road to the sea that descended from the glacier-scoured glens. Waterfoot was a beautiful spot. No more than a cluster of whitewashed cottages, a pub plus a few shops perched on the lip of a sweeping, stony stretch of coast. Billy Murphy's land was on the far side of the bluff. Sheen inhaled the fresh air, tasted the sea and saw an expanse of sky had started to open up as the rain finally started to clear away here. He could see why Billy wanted to be here. It was clean, and quiet, but it tasted like the Sailortown home he had left behind. As Sheen took a left turn off the coast road, he spotted the man he wanted. Billy was seated outside his little whitewashed cottage on a deckchair. Same brown tweed cap that Sheen remembered on his head. Same thick glasses on his nose, magnifying his watchful eyes to absurd proportions. As he got out, Billy Murphy called his name.

'Owen Sheen. Don't remember leaving you a forwarding address.' He hadn't. Sheen had looked him up. The last time they had spoken had been in Muldoon's pub, on a stagnant wharf on the derelict edge of Sailortown. Muldoon's, like Billy's Housing Executive home where he'd lived a lifetime, was just a memory. Sheen knew how Billy could afford to buy this little homestead on the Irish coast, but he also knew that neither of them would ever mention it again.

'Nosy peeler, Billy,' he said, approaching the cottage up the steep little incline.

Billy stood up. It didn't add much height, but Sheen

knew that it counted for very little. If the bastard who had broken into his apartment and got the better of Sheen had faced a younger Billy Murphy, he would have had the shock of his life. Billy offered his hand.

'*Céad míle fáilte*,' he said. Gaelic. *A hundred thousand welcomes*.

'Cheers,' said Sheen.

Billy invited him in, spent a long time showing him framed photographs of his son and daughter-in-law. Sheen now recalled that his son was based in Cambridge.

'The wife's out and about, otherwise you'd be fed. I can offer you a dram,' said Billy, pointing up at a shelf well-stocked with much amber.

'Not this time. Cup of tea would be great though,' replied Sheen.

'So, it's business I see,' said Billy.

Ten minutes later Sheen was on a deckchair beside Billy, enjoying the view and the silence. He asked Billy if it was a crop of potatoes he'd seen in the field above his cottage.

'Aye, it is. I always wanted my own wee crop. But you never came here to talk about the spuds.'

'I've got trouble, Billy.'

'Course you do. Go ahead,' he said.

Sheen wasn't sure what to say, or where to begin, so he started with Dave Rodgers' walk-in and ended with his altercation with Chief Stevens.

Billy drained the last of his tea.

'You may as well have stuck the head on him. You're out of a job after this anyway by the sounds of it,' suggested Billy.

'I think he came close,' said Sheen. 'But ending up in a cell was not on my agenda today. And losing my job's the least of my concerns right now.'

'TOPBRASS, wha? They love their James Bond antics, don't they? Why not just stick with ginger nut?'

'Ever heard tell of it?'

'No. Not that name. So well done, you've found something I never heard of.'

'Not really why I drove up here, Billy.'

'Were you hoping that I'd tell you who he is?'

'I don't know what I was hoping for. A miracle?'

'No can do, Owen Sheen. But I'll tell you something about Cyprus you clearly don't know.'

'What?'

'There was one that got away.'

Sheen turned in his chair. Not what he'd come for, and not what he was expecting. But it was new information.

'Impossible. There's nothing to indicate that. Not in all the MI5 records I trawled through. Not from any of the family members we spoke to. Not in any news reports.'

Billy pushed his glasses up his nose and shrugged.

'Maybe not, but I know that's true. And I'm sure some others you've been speaking to are well aware of it,' said Billy.

Sheen thought about Peadar Caffery's blank refusal to budge on any questions about the Cyprus operation in which his brother had died. And the way he had momentarily lost his composure after they had mentioned TOPBRASS.

'Why would they stay quiet?'

'Lots of reasons. First and foremost being it's supposed

to be a secret. And there's always an agenda,' said Billy.

Sheen thought about the chief's preferred version of events, and how they dovetailed in the main with men like Peadar Caffery.

'So, this is him? This is our man, TOPBRASS?'

'Never said that. But the same guy did get a label as a tout.'

'You know him? His name?'

'Not personally. His name is Brian Maguire. Comes from Andytown. I know for a fact that he got away with his life from Cyprus. I also know that people who never dared say it to his face called him a tout behind his back. But that's it. I like to work with facts. Suppose he might be your man, but I doubt it.'

'Why?'

'He's alive.'

Sheen pondered this. It made sense. Anyone suspected as an informer of that magnitude would never have survived.

'And?'

'He's not a redhead. Least not back then.'

'So, this geezer Maguire, he was used to distract attention from the real tout? A guy who survived against all odds and ended up falling under suspicion?'

Billy got up and collected their mugs.

'So say you. But you just stepped away from the facts again.'

Billy walked him the short distance to his car. Sheen thanked him.

'You been asking these sorts of questions about Cyprus in Belfast?'

'Yeah.'

'Then Brian Maguire may know you're after the tout who sold out the Cyprus Three. And if he does, there's a fair chance he's out hunting for him too. Whoever this boy is, he set up Maguire's mates to get killed and left him holding the tab. If I were him, I'd be looking for the bastard.'

# CHAPTER FORTY-ONE

Maguire had given up trying to follow Owen Sheen, for now. Two days before he had almost clocked Maguire near Danny Caffery's place in Beechmount, but this morning it was even harder to go undetected. It was like the guy was on red alert. Sheen had been driving in circles, impossible to keep on his tail. Maguire had no choice but to let him go, had watched as Sheen headed north out of the city. There was absolutely no point in Maguire visiting Peadar Caffery. The guy hated him, and he had no doubt that Danny's brother had been responsible for darkening Maguire's name over the years. If he went to his house, it would end badly. Maybe for Maguire and definitely for Peadar Caffery. So he opted for a different approach and had come here, to the staunchly Irish republican enclave of the New Lodge in North Belfast. After an hour of waiting and being checked over by his bodyguards, Maguire had finally gained access to the top-floor flat of the man he had come to see.

The apartment was warm and smelt of candle wax and menthol. He passed a small kitchen to his left and a closed door to his right and entered a spacious living room with a wide panoramic view that looked south-east across what had been Sailortown and the docks. Maguire took a couple of seconds to drink in the vista, which was a sight, despite the dreary weather. He could see the twin yellow cranes in Harland and Wolff, the Arena complex, the Titanic Studios, and in the distance, the Stormont building which was soon to house the devolved executive.

'Never gets old. Unlike us.' The voice came from an armchair in the corner with its back to Maguire. He walked over to the window, and Cahill McKee turned in his seat and faced him. Thin as a bird, but with a thick head of white hair, combed off his face in the same style he'd worn it since the 1950s. McKee was ninety-seven years old. He'd been an old hand when Maguire had first met him in the 1970s. He wore a thick woollen jumper that could fit two of him and had a set of rosary beads in his liver-spotted hands. Beside him was a painted statue of the Virgin Mary. Maguire had never seen anything like it outside a church. It must have been five foot tall. He looked down on McKee where he sat.

'Cahill,' he said, and nodded.

'Sorry about the wait. You know how it is,' he said, and gestured to the small table beside him where Maguire could see his keys, wallet and phone which had been confiscated by McKee's security.

Maguire said he understood and took back his belongings, then sat down on a small stool that stood next to McKee's chair. The Mother of God stared down at him, brimming with sorrowful knowing. Cahill McKee was old enough to be a great grandfather, but he was also the aged patriarch of Dissident republican violence in Belfast. The old warhorse had refused to compromise when the Peace Process was floated. He'd returned to the political wilderness from which he had emerged when the Troubles kicked off in the late 1960s and word was that he was the galvanising influence behind the recent unification and strengthening of Dissident groups under one banner. And his time was once again at hand. They'd scored points, taken scalps and put the peelers and mainstream republicans on the back heel. Brexit and stalemate at Stormont had left the future as murky and untrusted as the Belfast weather, and in times of darkness, men like McKee would reap a bitter harvest.

'Do you know why I'm here?' asked Maguire.

'I'm hoping that you've finally seen sense. That you'll throw your lot in with my boys,' replied McKee.

'Afraid not. I just want to talk,' he said. McKee scoffed. Maguire paused. 'It's about Cyprus.'

'Ah, I see. You came knocking once and now you're back.'

McKee had been in his late sixties in 1987. Too old for active service but indefatigable, he had refused to retire. And he was trusted. The Army Council had assigned him a role that reflected his standing and status. He was the safe man. McKee operated a series of residences in Dublin which were safe houses, to be used only in the event of volunteers returning from operations abroad which had been compromised. McKee would liaise with the leader of the cell and agree a number of places which would be reserved. He would prepare for all contingencies. The shipping of volunteers to the United States, homes in Ireland that could accommodate men on the run in rotation, protection and preservation. If the volunteers could follow their escape plan and reach McKee, they were home and dry. So it had been for Maguire, when he finally reached Dublin a month after his team were killed in Cyprus. Penniless, emaciated and spent.

'I want answers. There was a tout. TOPBRASS.'

'And you think it was me?' McKee hooked him with a hawkish stare that dared Maguire to call it.

'Absolutely not,' he replied. 'But I know it wasn't me.'

McKee nodded, his eyes far away and his fingers threading the prayer beads.

'You knew Sands, didn't you?' Bobby Sands, the first IRA hunger striker to die in the H-Blocks during the 1981 prison protests.

'Aye.'

'And if he'd called on you, at the time, to join him on the fast. Would you have done so?'

'Yes.'

'Yes, I know you would have,' said McKee, and looked at Maguire. 'I never said you were a tout. But Belfast was rotten. They were a cancer that ate away the revolution from within. Me and you, we were maybe the last two who didn't get turned. Of course there was a tout. More than one.'

'Do you remember when I arrived in Dublin that night?'

'Yes. Like a tramp you were.'

'You opened the door. And you looked at me. All those years, I've never been able to place what was behind it, but I have been thinking about it a lot, for the first time in years, actually. You were surprised. Why? Did you not know I'd survived?' Maguire knew that the deaths in Cyprus were international news. McKee like everyone else in Ireland knew three had been killed. And though the safe man never knew the identities of those whom he was tasked to protect until they came to him for help, he did know the numbers.

'You don't know, do you?'

'Know what, Cahill?'

'Danny Caffery told me to have room for five.'

'What?' Maguire was suddenly overcome by vertigo. He gripped the base of the stool as the world swooned from his high perch over Belfast city. The Virgin seemed to warp and loll towards him. They were supposed to have been a cell. Four. Tight. No one else.

'I was surprised all right. I expected there to be two of you. Three dead, two on the run,' confirmed McKee.

'Who?' But Maguire already knew the answer. McKee had been on a need-to-know. He'd not known Maguire was part of it until he turned up for help.

'Someone that your gaffer must have trusted enough to bring on board. Someone well placed, high up.' *TOPBRASS*, thought Maguire. 'My lads found a big pistol in the boot of your car when they went for a look.' Maguire turned and looked at McKee accusingly. 'Don't fret. It's still there. You sure that all you're interested in is talking?'

Maguire stood up, waited to make sure that he was steady on his feet.

'I have to find out who that was.'

'I'm sorry, I can't help you, Brian. But I know this: it was someone that Danny Caffery trusted. And it cost him his life.'

'Thanks, Cahill. I'm going to go now.'

'*Ard mór*. You said that you'd have laid down your life for Ireland. Whoever it was that sold you out might have

362

killed for their own cause, but they'd never give their life. That's the kind of bastard you're after.'

Maguire returned the way he had come, descending the steps like a man entering the Underworld. He walked slowly through the housing estate, his brain crackling with what Cahill McKee had just said. He looked up, expecting to see his parked car but then realised that he had taken a wrong turn. A dead end. There, in front of him was a gable wall, and on it, the famous portrait of a man he had known well.

Danny Caffery.

Maguire's heart skipped a beat, and his mouth went dry.

He knew where that image had come from. A photograph, one that had been given pride of place in Danny's Beechmount home. But it wasn't just Danny Caffery in that photo. And just like that, Maguire knew who had betrayed the Cyprus Three. As though in front of him, he could again see the smiling face of a man with dark red hair who had posed with Danny in that old photograph, a man that Danny had trusted, enough to invite him into the fold of his elite unit. A man that Maguire knew was as cold as a fish on the slab. A ruthless killer who had pulled the trigger many times for the cause but whom Maguire had always doubted would have the courage to die for it.

Maguire knew his name. And knew exactly where he where he could find him.

# PART FIVE

TOPBRASS

# CHAPTER FORTY-TWO

Fenton brought the flame of the match to his Dunhill and inhaled. He was in his dressing gown and slippers and still had not had his morning cup of tea, but he'd emptied his bag. And he still had a smile on his face after ending the call with Owen Sheen. Some men liked skirt, others loved the booze, but for Fenton no thrill had ever bested the buzz of checkmating an opponent. And Sheen was no pushover. But he'd trapped his queen and now the king had nowhere to go.

He'd call his boys when the time was right. Tell them to dump her somewhere a good bit away from wherever they had kept her. He didn't know the details and he didn't want to know. He had survived a lifetime in the intelligence game by primarily ensuring he remained ignorant of those things that could come around again and explode in his lap. He started to read the local news feed on his phone as he drew on his smoke. The smile slowly dropped from his face.

Gas explosion in a street off the Falls Road. One man killed. The father of an IRA volunteer who had been murdered as an informer by the same organisation. He scrolled down to the next story.

A man had been shot dead in his Dublin Road apartment in South Belfast. The burning cigarette fell limp in Fenton's lips. Alexander Lamont. He scanned the story, his heart galloping unpleasantly. In a bizarre twist he was murdered on the same premises in which his father, an off-duty member of the RUC, was also gunned down in 1984. Police assume the motive may have been a robbery gone wrong. As Fenton slammed his smartphone down, burner phone number four rang. No number, but there could be only one caller.

'*A chara*,' said the voice in greeting, before Fenton had the chance to say a word. 'I told you to keep me informed.'

'Don't friend me, I just read the news. Didn't I tell you I had this in hand?'

'And I told you I'm in charge,' he growled.

'Two bodies. That's a trail. They will investigate. It won't just go away.'

'Cue you, Fenton. You're the master of making problems disappear.'

Fenton had a home in Spain. Under a different name. He could go there today. Arrange to have it sold up and move on. South America.

'Wake up, man! Do you think this is the old days? There are rules now. You should know that better than me, given your position.' Nothing from the other end.

Fenton thought about the dates. There was another.

'What about 1986, the other date that was in Sheen's notebook?'

'My old mucker Glenholmes? I'm not concerned. He did a long stretch and kept his beak closed. And he's living the life of Riley. He won't talk. And if I think he's likely to become a problem, he won't talk.' A long chuckle ensued at this from the line. Fenton did not participate. The laughing stopped. 'But what is a problem, is our friend Tucker. He's got shit on me. And you were meant to find him.'

'I will. In time. He's obviously no immediate threat and he might even be dead for all—'

'Tell your boys to get in touch with me. I want to know where this peeler McCusker is being held.'

'Why?'

'If she knows where Tucker Rodgers is then, after I finish the day job here, I want to speak to her.'

Fenton gulped. He understood what this meant. He needed Aoife McCusker alive. Damage limitation. But if this man got to her she'd be better off dead and would likely end up that way. But if he objected?

'Do you hear me?'

'Yes, yes, I can hear. I will get in touch with my team. Explain it,' he said quietly, his stomach turning and his forehead starting to blister with sweat.

'Sheen. Update.'

'Not a lot to tell. The plan is working well,' he said. *Until now*, he thought. He explained that Sheen had gone to dawn Mass at Clonard, and later had driven up to the Glens of Antrim and back again. Had tea with an old boy, maybe a relative. No one they needed to be concerned about.

'Sheen a Fenian?' He meant Catholic.

'No idea. He's from London. I spoke to him today. He's under manners.' Behaving himself.

'Dead on. Let's hope he stays that way. Don't forget to get one of your girls to give me a call. Burner five next.' The call ended.

Fenton lit another smoke as he dismantled burner four, set a flame to the SIM card and dropped it into the ashtray.

He had to find this bastard Tucker Rodgers. If he didn't, a cop was going to die. And die badly. It would start a fire that would never be put out, even if they Disappeared her body. His mind danced between the facts, the nicotine sparking his synapses and making connections.

He thought about Roddy Grant. A man who had bled information from them like a fat leech.

He thought about Tucker Rodgers, the man Roddy had trusted, a guy that he had given all the secrets to.

He thought about Owen Sheen and what had been said about his religion. He must be Catholic. Why else would he seek refuge in a church, with a priest?

Tucker Rodgers, chatting with Roddy Grant at the golf club.

A priest.

Two unrelated ideas, but they fused together in Fenton's mind and he finally realised what he was missing. Grant must have known more than he had admitted to Fenton's boys before they had finally strung him up. And he'd clearly passed it on to Tucker Rodgers. No wonder nobody had been able to find him. It was the very reason why they had made the priest holes in the first place. A man could disappear, and stay alive, hidden in plain view.

But which one had Roddy told Tucker about? There were a number, mostly in West Belfast. Fenton closed his eyes, forcing himself to see long-destroyed documents, decades old, that Grant could have seen. He struggled to recall when he had made reference to a priest hole and which one it was.

'Got it!' he said. Right in the heart of West Belfast. It had to be the one. If Tucker had managed to hitch a ride from his home, he could easily have found it. Fenton stood up. He killed his smoke and snatched his car keys and gun off the table. No time to get dressed; he'd have to do.

He knew where Tucker Rodgers was hiding.

# CHAPTER FORTY-THREE

When Sheen arrived at the SHOT offices the next morning, he felt like he wasn't really connected to the world. Jackson and Geordie were at their desks. Geordie gave him a look, and Sheen returned it with a small shake of his head. He saw Geordie's expression deflate.

'Bad news about Aoife, sir,' said Jackson.

Sheen glanced first at Geordie who remained impassive and then looked at Jackson.

'Stomach bug. Nasty. You're not looking too hot yourself, sir.' Good for Geordie. He'd towed the line.

Sheen caught a glimpse of his reflection in the glass of his office window. Jackson had a point. He'd barely slept, and though he knew he should not, he had bought a bottle of heavy-duty red at the store where he'd picked up a ready-meal lasagne for his dinner the night before. The food remained untouched, but he'd done the wine. And then spent most of the night staring out his skylight window, thoughts of Aoife puncturing his drunkenness until he sobered and was left with the agony of what she must be experiencing.

Earlier in the evening after returning from his visit with Billy Murphy in Waterfoot, he had driven to Brian Maguire's address in Andersonstown. Same street as PJ Wilson, the place where Sheen had sensed he was being watched. No doubt Maguire had taken a keen interest in his investigation, just as Billy Murphy had said. The security grille that fortified the front door of his home was locked and the place was empty when Sheen had approached it. Maybe Maguire was having more luck sniffing out TOPBRASS than he was.

Hayley had called him soon after. Nothing. She and Fahey had driven the length and breadth of West Belfast for hours with Hayley holding Aoife's scarf and Fahey asking her for directions, but she said she'd not picked up the scent. Too much interference. Fahey had taken the initiative and searched out derelict-looking properties and parked up outside a few. Again, it proved fruitless. Hayley called Sheen again on his way to work this morning. She said that they would give it another go but Sheen could hear the defeat in her voice and she also asked him when he was going to report Aoife's kidnap as a crime. He'd told her that midday was their cut-off. And he hoped that he'd not so badly misjudged this that high noon would not be too late to make this official.

'Rough night, Jackson,' Sheen said. 'Any joy on those Special Branch files?' he asked, but more by way of making conversation and keeping up appearances. He'd all but abandoned Cyprus. He didn't give a damn any more. Not about the report, or TOPBRASS, or even Tucker Rodgers when it came down to it. All that mattered was Aoife.

'Not a thing, sir,' said Jackson. The kid looked disconsolate. 'It's as though those files have just vanished.' Which was exactly what had been engineered, he was sure. Perhaps years ago, after Castlereagh was closed and demolished. Only Roddy Grant and now Tucker Rodgers had copies of that information in hand.

'Managed to catch up with your man Glenholmes, the one from Gransha,' said Geordie. 'He's in Turkey, on holiday. I gave him the heads up and told him to mind himself. He didn't seem to be unduly worried.'

'Who says crime doesn't pay, eh?' asked Sheen.

Jackson spoke.

'Oh, I forgot. Someone called, a Graham Saunders.' His old Highbury school friend/enemy. He'd forgotten about his request for help.

Sheen thanked Jackson and went into his office. He had three hours before he called in Aoife's abduction, and effectively called time on his career with SHOT and most likely his career full stop.

He sat down and opened his laptop. He might not be able to save the day this time, but before time ran out, Sheen might be able to do one good thing and help Graham Saunders. He found Graham's message and read it again from the top. His eyes focused on the year. And then the month.

Sheen sat up in his chair and found the letter, the one that Tucker Rodgers had sent, the one with the original list of dates.

'The eighteenth of March 1987,' said Sheen.

He got up and fetched *The Bradley Index* book from the shelf and found the date, then ran his finger down the list of names. The Cyprus Three. The INLA murders caused by the internal feud. There were more. Sheen slowly turned the page, his heart hammering. There it was. The details of Benny Saunders' murder. The same day.

*Private. 4th Battalion, Royal Green Jackets. Age: 17. Killed when a remote-controlled bomb was detonated in a derelict shop on the Whiterock Road in which he had sought cover. Police and army lured to the spot on the pretence of an armed robbery at an adjacent business.*

He walked into the main office where Jackson had displayed the map of Belfast. He moved his finger over the west of the city and stopped when he found the address on the Whiterock Road. Sheen's finger was at the epicentre of the small cluster of pins that they had positioned to mark the territorial boundaries of the crimes investigated. It was no more than a mile from where Bernadette Bell had been lured to her death by the IRA man with dirty red hair. Less than that to where the bomber Patrick Glenholmes had resided at the time he was convicted of the Ballycarrick attack. The same attack where a man dressed as an RUC officer had diverted the coach, a man with red hair. The same man, Sheen was absolutely convinced, who had scoped out the RUC checkpoint in Castle Street before it was attacked and who later murdered Dennis Lamont with a police-issue gun. And finally, just a stone's throw away from where the patsy, Red Giuseppe Morelli, was shot dead in his home in Ballymurphy, a man whose daughter had always claimed was set up to die and was the victim of collusion.

Who was it that said Cyprus was on Tucker's list? That had been Sheen's call, his ultimately futile attempt to toe the line and respect the chief's orders. All Tucker had given them was the date. And the date matched Saunders' murder as much as it did Cyprus. And it also fitted what they knew about the geography of the crimes. Fitted it perfectly. Sheen turned to Jackson, listed the details of the crime and told him to get everything he could find on the murder of Benny Saunders. He returned to his office and paced the floor. If the files were buried or had been destroyed, it was all over.

Half an hour later Jackson called him.

'Anything?'

'Nothing that links to Special Branch.' Sheen's heart sank. 'But there was this,' he said. 'An arrest sheet. Standard issue.'

Geordie had joined Jackson.

'They lifted someone in connection with the murder,' noted Geordie. Sheen waited as Geordie scanned the document. 'Charges later dropped,' he continued.

Sheen could hear a tremor of excitement in his voice and asked Geordie if he recognised the suspect.

'Don't you?'

Sheen walked over and looked at the photograph on the screen. It took him a few seconds, but then he did. He'd seen this man's face before, pictured beside a young Danny Caffery. In the faded photograph that was still framed in Danny Caffery's home. Geordie said a name. And suddenly it all made sense. This guy was not just a player from the distant past. Sheen recognised his eyes, even though the man Geordie had named was now bald and clean-shaven. Sheen had seen him more than once in news reports about the reinstatement of the Northern Irish parliament in Stormont. Sheen asked Geordie if he was sure it was the same man.

'Yup, that's him. Ballymurphy born and raised,' said Geordie, his eyes wide and transfixed on the old arrest sheet. Sheen scrolled down until he found confirmation. Geordie pointed at the list of physical attributes. Hair colour.

'Red,' said Sheen.

'We got him,' said Geordie, slapping Jackson on the back.

It fitted. Tucker's final date was Benny Saunders' murder. And TOPBRASS was as guilty of it as he had been of the murder of Bernadette Bell, Dennis Lamont and the eight squaddies blown to bits at Ballycarrick. Without seeing the name on the redacted MI5 document Sheen could not be certain that TOPBRASS had also set up the Cyprus Three. But given that he had clearly been close friends with Danny Caffery back in the day, it made sense. But no matter. Right now, he had his name and that was enough.

His phone vibrated. An incoming call with the number withheld. He retreated into his office and closed the door.

'Sheen,' he answered.

'My friend, I wanted to see how you're doing.' It was the same voice, the man who had called to tell him that they had Aoife and to warn him to keep away.

'Tell me she's OK.'

'She's having a great time. Won't want to come home,' he chuckled.

Sheen gripped his mobile and held his tongue.

'And you're doing very well. You were right to go to

Clonard and say a prayer. This will be over soon,' he said.

*Sooner than you fucking think*, thought Sheen, as the mocking tones abruptly cut off as his tormentor ended the call.

*I know who he is. And I'm coming for him.*

Sheen was coming for them all.

# CHAPTER FORTY-FOUR

Tucker set down Roddy's booklet and shook his head in disgust.

That soldier Benny Saunders had been just seventeen when he was blown away in 1987. A boy. The army should never have sent him into a theatre of combat like Belfast, not when he was that age. And of course, he didn't deserve to be slaughtered the way he had. TOPBRASS was up to his neck in it, yet again. He'd actually been arrested after the event, and this was rich enough to choke on, after a member of the public had called the confidential telephone line and informed against him. But, of course, Fenton had managed to pull the strings, claim that his man was not directly responsible, and the case was mothballed.

Tucker saw another crossword waiting beneath one of the news articles about Saunders. He was about to get stuck in when something caught his eye. A page number on the top right corner had been circled.

6

Tucker flicked through the pages until he found another one.

2

Tucker made a mental note, he had no means of writing them down, and then looked for more. He soon found them. Two zeros, followed by another two, and then finally, number one. Tucker recited the numbers in order.

'Six-two-zero-zero-two-one,' he said. Tucker jumped off his seat. He walked to the sealed front door and looked at the keypad, speaking the numbers he now held in his mind out loud.

He didn't need to rehearse it any further. He already knew the configuration. It was the phone number of the Shandon Park Golf Club. And it was the entrance code that he had used to get into this bunker.

Tucker stumbled back to the plastic table and chair where Roddy's booklet awaited. If Roddy had hidden the entrance code inside his book, then it stood to reason he might also have concealed the exit one too. Tucker flicked frantically through the pages, looking for other circled numbers and finding none. All he saw was the crosswords, most mentally complete now, but one still to do. Why had blank spaces been left in the first place? Roddy had been a wizard at these things.

They were clues that Roddy had clearly left to be discovered. Tucker spoke out the solutions he had found.

'Ballet, six letters.' He found the second clue. 'Murphys, seven letters.'

And it was then that it fell into place for Tucker. He could finally see. Not at all unlike the way it felt when he finally nailed the cryptic crossword clue. Only this was bigger. This was going to reveal the whole picture and break a larger puzzle.

'Ballymurphy! Six and seven.' He found the next riddle. 'Leaning, seven letters,' he said, but nothing unlocked this time. Then came the cryptic clue, the one that had really stumped him. 'Red hair, three plus four,' he said. 'Red hair from Ballymurphy.' The final clue. It was a quick crossword. He could do this.

'Irish monk and missionary, five letters.' He immediately thought of Saint Brendan, known as the Navigator, and patron saint of boatmen and mariners, though he already knew it was wrong. He closed his eyes and flushed his mind, refused to allow that wrong response to recur and colour his thinking. Tucker had been raised a Methodist; he knew little about monks and less about Catholicism. He allowed the solutions to guide him, repeated them over and over, asking that a picture form in his mind. They were linked and one would help reveal the others.

'Red-haired from Ballymurphy. Redhead leaning on Ballymurphy. Lean redhead from Ballymurphy.' Tucker's closed lids snapped open. He could see.

'Aidan,' he said. Five letters. A fit. And Tucker didn't need to phone a friend to check if he was correct. 'Aidan Lean,' he whispered. 'Fuck me, Roddy, no wonder they wanted us dead,' he said, his hands trembling. He got up and walked back over to the door, still limping slightly because of his bruised knee. He was holding Roddy's booklet, his old personal protection in the pocket of his wretched dressing gown. Just as he had arrived. He raised a finger to the keypad.

'Ballet, six.' As he called out each number, Tucker inputted it on the pad.

'Murphys, seven. Leaning, seven. Red hair, three and four. Aidan, five.'

He waited, and then he heard the low mechanical drill of the bolt unlocking. The door popped open. Tucker cried out, jammed his fingers into the gap that had been created and pulled the door open wide. He was panting, and tears coursed down his thickly stubbled cheeks. He looked back at the cell, then turned and struggled up the steps, emerging from the coal bunker.

Daylight.

Tucker rolled out and onto the overgrown grass and lay on his back, whooping at the top of his lungs and not caring who could hear him.

He was free. He stood up. He was a new man, different from the one who had crawled into a hole to hide. He wasn't afraid any more. And he knew the truth. Tucker gripped Roddy's booklet in one fist and trudged through the garden. Once he'd been a cop, maybe he could be one again. He needed to find his son and make sure he was safe. And then he was going to find the bastards who had murdered his friend.

# CHAPTER FORTY-FIVE

Hayley was waiting at the front of Clonard Monastery having already helped serve at dawn Mass when Fahey picked her up. She was holding Aoife's saffron scarf and dressed in her gym gear; soft cotton grey Adidas tracksuit, latest line, her Asics running shoes and a sweat band to hold her hair off her face. Yesterday had felt wrong. Like there were too many layers to sift through to try to reach Aoife. Hayley's own perfume, the feel of her skirt, distracting her attention as it kept riding up her thighs in the back of Fahey's little car. The noise and confusion of a Belfast afternoon in all its honking and hollering glory. In her gym gear she could zone out, feel at ease. And this time of day, things would be a bit more sedate. Plus, she had another plan too. She opened the door of Fahey's car and got in the passenger seat this time.

'Morning, Dermot.'

'Morning, Hayley. My wife thinks I'm bonkers doing this,' he started.

'All you're doing is driving. You leave the bonkers shite to me,' she said, and patted him on the hand. She explained that she had spoken to Sheen, and that they had a few hours, no more, before things were out of their hands.

'Quite frankly, I want it out of our hands.' Hayley said nothing. 'But mostly I want to find her. I know she's your mate.'

'God loves a tryer, Dermot,' she said, and started to wrap Aoife's scarf around the top of her face, obscuring her eyes.

'Are you serious?'

'You drive, I'll try to give you directions.'

'Do you know what this is going to look like? People will think we've fucking lost it.'

'This is West Belfast, Dermot. I doubt you'll get a second glance,' she said. 'Now shut up and drive. If I say nothing, you decide.'

Hayley could no longer see Dermot Fahey's expression, though she could easily imagine it. But as soon as the scarf blotted out the morning light and filled her nose with Aoife's distinctive fresh apple scent, she felt herself begin to drift off, almost as though she were floating just above the car which had started to move. This felt better. Already the vibration of the car's movement felt distant, as though a memory or a dream. What was real, and now, was in her mind, and a world above it. She knew that Dermot was driving away from Clonard and towards the Falls Road, but the layout of the streets and roads no longer mattered. The car was far, far below her now. It was as though Fahey had pulled to a stop at the crest of a wide cliff and there was only silence and stillness and the expanse of an ocean beyond. Hayley took another breath. In another universe, a voice spoke, it sounded dreamy and half asleep.

'Turn right.'

She was standing on the cliff now. When she looked around, Fahey and the car were nowhere to be seen. A breeze had picked up and she could taste the last of Aoife's perfume on her tongue. Above, the sky had darkened, a deep and foreboding blackness that broiled and emanated from what looked like a hole in the atmosphere. On the wind, a different scent, this one less pleasant, it made her want to cover her nose. It was dank and damp and overlaid with the thickness of dried urine. It smelt of despair. Hayley could hear the crash of waves from below her, and they were getting louder. She backed away from the edge. From the sky, a long roll of thunder, and on its tail, fat drops of rain. She heard the hiss as it fell, felt her face dampen and her hair flatten against her head. And then a voice on the wind, ephemeral and full of sadness.

It said, 'Right.'

Hayley touched her cheek and then lifted her damp finger to her mouth and tasted.

It was salty.

The rain that fell was a deluge of tears.

It was full dark now, and it invaded her, filled her with a panic and fear as black as the hole in the sky. She reached out, wanted to find its parameters and realised that she could not. Her hands were fastened, her fingers numb and her wrists were on fire. Hayley gasped now, tasting only the foul air and a panic that is reserved for those on the threshold of drowning. She tried to run but her feet would not budge. They were imprisoned just like her wrists and she was seated once more, but not in Fahey's car. This was a bad place. So dark that no hope could penetrate. Her throat was raw and dry, but she took a breath, filled her lungs and got ready to scream.

'Stop!'

Hayley felt the car skid to a halt and heard the crunch of Fahey applying the handbrake.

'Hayley, talk to me. Are you OK?'

She could feel the soft fabric of Aoife's scarf on her face. Smell the apple scent once more and feel the lumpy upholstery of Fahey's front seat under her. She was back. Hayley slipped off the scarf and squinted at the bright Belfast sunshine. She touched her face. Wet. She had been crying.

'Where are we?'

'Near the top of the Whiterock Road,' he replied.

She nodded, and quickly adjusted to her surroundings. To their right was the Ballymurphy housing estate and a bit further along was a college, once a secondary school that was in the advanced stages of being demolished. On their left was the black basalt wall that marked the boundary of Belfast City Cemetery, with an entrance just a little further along. The area was densely populated, but this stretch of the highway was typically quiet, and at this time of day both the road and the cemetery were desolate. Hayley pointed to the open gates of the cemetery.

'Here,' she said.

Fahey found a place to park in a nearby street and they both entered the cemetery on foot. And then stopped.

'Good spot to hide someone. This place has nearly a quarter of a million graves,' said Fahey.

Hayley raised a hand and he quietened.

'She's close,' she said, and turned right.

Fahey followed her as she walked along a grave-lined pathway that ran parallel to, but was entirely obscured from, the road beyond. The graves in the main looked well-tended. People had taken pride and care in maintaining this place.

'Can you feel something?' he asked.

In response Hayley stopped at a small archway which led to a bricked-off section of the cemetery. Above it she could see an inscription, not in English.

'That's Hebrew,' confirmed Fahey. The Jewish plot.

Beyond the arch Hayley could see it was overgrown and unkempt. She knew little about Belfast's Jewish population but was fairly confident that, just like in most cities, they would be a small minority. And this part of West Belfast had been a virtual no-go area for many outsiders during the Troubles. They entered the plot. Hayley was immediately aware of how enclosed and sheltered the little space felt in comparison to the wide expanse of the cemetery beyond. And she could sense Aoife, like a third person in their midst. She was close, very close, and she was alive. But where to begin?

'Shit! Someone's coming,' said Fahey. He tugged her by the arm and they both crouched behind a big overgrown bramble.

A man appeared in the entrance arch. He had wild white hair and was wearing a dressing gown. His eyes searched the space. Hayley and Fahey stayed still. The big man took a step inside, his eyes still alert. Hayley noted he was wearing slippers. She also noted the grip of what looked like a gun peeking out from one of his pockets. She pointed. Fahey looked and then nodded. When the man turned his back to them and continued, Fahey spoke in a whisper.

'I can see what you mean about West Belfast,' he said.

Hayley motioned for them to follow him. Very slowly, very carefully, they did. The man stopped at an overgrown corner adjacent to the dark stone wall of the plot. Hayley and Fahey stopped too and watched as he bent over and shifted what looked like an embedded gravestone out of place with a grunt. He took a step back and then, improbably, the man disappeared, descending into the clay. Hayley searched the ground and found a rock. She and Fahey inched closer, keeping low, until they were at the edge of the hole the man had gone into. Hayley peeked over the edge.

There were steps. The man was at the bottom, standing beside a metal door. There was what looked like a keypad, and he was pushing the buttons. Hayley waited, her face set. She recognised the smell: damp and dank. She heard what sounded like a mechanical drill and then, the door opened inwardly. The man pushed it wider with one palm, and as he did, a light sparked to life from within. And then, a voice, hoarse and ragged, but one she knew.

'Help me! Please! Help!'

Aoife.

Hayley moved and as she did the man turned and saw her framed above him. The shock that her presence clearly elicited, however, replaced the surprise that was already etched on his features after he had heard Aoife's wail. Whoever he expected to find down there, it definitely didn't look like it was Aoife McCusker. And then his face darkened into a grimace of fury. He reached for the weapon in his pocket, but Hayley's arm was faster. As a kid in West Belfast she'd learnt how to throw a stone. The rock she released hit the old guy square on the temple with a sharp crack. His eyes rolled and his jaw went slack. He crumpled to the floor before Hayley had to see the blood begin to flow.

'Aoife! Aoife!' she called and bowled down the steps. She leapt over the man and into the bunker, Fahey behind her.

'Hayley?' She could hear the disbelief, and the relief. A small hallway, two doors. She kicked open one and a light burst on. There was a sink, a cupboard. Empty. She turned and opened the other. Another light. Aoife. She was tied to a chair. Her eyes found Hayley and her face melted in a medley of emotions. Amazement, joy, incredulity and trauma. She went to her and embraced her friend who, for the time being, could not hug her back.

'I've got you. I've got you. I've got you,' she repeated.

# CHAPTER FORTY-SIX

'Hayley,' said Sheen. Her call had come through the car's speakers. He was weaving between lanes along the Sydenham By-Pass in East Belfast, hurtling at speed towards the Parliament Buildings at Stormont.

'Sheen, we found her!'

His heart leapt. He stifled a cry and thanked her.

'Where?'

'Fahey was right about the priest hole,' she said. Hayley gave him a quick run-down.

Sheen struggled to believe it, but he was happy to. Aoife was safe, she'd been found.

'Who the hell was the old guy?'

'No idea. He didn't have ID. But he wasn't a friend; he was going to shoot me,' said Hayley, and Sheen could hear the emotion in her voice.

'Where is he?'

'Tied up in that bloody bunker. I hope someone knows

the code to get back in because we don't. Dermot used his belt and shoelaces to secure him. I was impressed with the knots.'

Fahey's Dublin accent from the background. 'Catholic Boy Scouts of Ireland,' he said.

Sheen allowed himself a smile and then it fell away.

'How is she?'

A pause from Hayley, and Sheen held his breath.

'She's very shaken. And she won't speak. We're on our way to the Royal,' said Hayley.

Sheen was no fool. He could decipher what Hayley meant. Aoife was traumatised. She was alive but there was no telling what the bastards had put her through.

'OK. Give her my—no, you tell her I love her, Hayley. You tell her that.'

'I will,' said Hayley. She was crying now, and Sheen was close to his destination.

'I'm going to have to go, but I'll call Geordie and tell him to meet you at the hospital. He'll be armed. He won't let her out of his sight,' said Sheen.

Sheen turned into the entrance of Stormont and skidded to a stop at the mouth of the mile-long driveway that led to the Parliament Buildings. The pillared facade, constructed in classical Greek style and made of English Portland stone, would be the home of the reconvened Northern Irish Assembly. It also housed the political offices of the main parties as well as the headquarters of the Deputy and First Ministers.

Sheen was going right to the top. Just as Peadar Caffery had told him to do a couple of days ago. But not in the way the man would have hoped.

The office of the First Minister elect, the veteran IRA man Brendan Kielty. It was there that he knew he would find the man he had been hunting. Aidan Lean. Long-time second-in-command to Kielty and now special advisor in waiting to his role of First Minister. The man who once had red hair and who had been arrested and released without charge on suspicion of the murder of Benny Saunders in 1987. The same man who had been permitted to kill and had others die in his place.

TOPBRASS.

Sheen showed his ID to the uniformed officer on guard and was allowed to drive through the security barrier. He parked up, then climbed the wide entrance steps that led into the main foyer where he picked up a map of the large complex. He showed his warrant card to the WPC on duty and entered the building. Lots of white marble, wide staircases and chandeliers. It spoke of the industrial wealth of Northern Ireland as a freshly minted state in the early twentieth century, but it also screamed of bombast and colonial insecurity. He navigated the corridors until he found the room he was looking for. There was a sign on the door written in Gaelic that Sheen did not understand. Hopefully it wasn't 'Please keep out' because Sheen turned the handle and walked straight in.

Three men waited in the high ceilinged room. All eyes turned to Sheen. Two were seated behind a dark, wooden desk. Chief Stevens, dressed in casual attire, his Polo top pressed to perfection with sharp creases down each sleeve, and beside him, the First Minister elect, Brendan Kielty. Kielty wore his trademark tweed jacket. The black hair and beard of his youth were all but white. Kielty observed him with those same inscrutable, obsidian eyes that Sheen had noted in numerous television reports and interviews. The man Sheen wanted was standing opposite, holding a dry wipe marker, apparently in the middle of listing bullet points on a whiteboard in some kind of shared brainstorm that Sheen planned to put on permanent hold. Aidan Lean. He stared at Sheen, and then his eyes narrowed and his forehead creased with anger.

The chief spoke, his voice full of fury.

'DI Sheen, what the hell are playing at?'

Sheen pointed to Lean, ignoring his boss.

'I'm here for TOPBRASS,' he said.

The chief stood up. Lean dropped the marker and stared open-mouthed at Sheen, who was suddenly unsure of exactly what he was going to do next. He could accuse, but to walk out of this room with Lean in cuffs would require a sustainable reason for arrest. But all he had was Lean's alleged involvement in Benny Saunders' murder, and that case was as cold as the stares that he could feel coming from Kielty and the chief.

An alarm sounded, cacophonous and filling the room.

'That's an intruder warning.' said the chief, and now Kielty also stood up and moved along the desk. He'd made it to the edge closest to Sheen when the door burst open and a burly man bundled in and came to a stop to Sheen's right. He wore a loose-fitting army surplus coat and had a massive revolver in one hand. He was sweating and panting hard as he swung the gun around the room, taking stock of those present. Sheen saw his eyes widen when he clocked Lean, and he raised his piece and trained it on him. Sheen recognised him. He'd looked up his photograph after returning from his trip to see Billy Murphy in Waterfoot. Brian Maguire. And he recognised his jacket. It had been Maguire who was tailing him in Beechmount, the guy who had been behind the wheel of the airport taxi.

'Maguire, take it easy,' he said, trying to have his voice heard above the din.

To his left, the chief had produced his gun which he now levelled at Maguire, who seemed not to notice or care.

'I've come for you, you fucker,' he said.

Lean had his hands up and had started to edge to his right. No doubt with a view to dive behind the desk as soon as he got close enough.

'Not another inch,' said Maguire.

Lean stopped dead and nodded his agreement.

'I have no beef with you, Brian. None at all,' he said.

'Fucking big of you. You killed my friends and you tried to kill me. You watched as I lived under the cloud of being called a tout. TOPBRASS! Not so top any more.'

Lean's face creased with what looked to be honest confusion.

'You mean Cyprus?' Lean said, and shook his head. 'You're wrong, I had no hand in that, Brian. For fuck's sake I was lifted for that wee Brit that was blown up in Whiterock the same day.'

'You're lying! I know that Danny Caffery trusted you enough to bring you in on Cyprus. And you used it to have him murdered!' screamed Maguire. He glanced Sheen's way. Sweat was now trickling down his face from his bald head. Sheen could see a seed of doubt in Maguire's eyes. But he kept his gun on Lean, who was still as a marble pillar.

394

Kielty was moving again, slowly, and then he stopped. He was almost right beside Sheen now.

'Brian, I can see you don't want to kill this man,' Sheen argued. 'If you do, it makes you no better than him.'

'Don't be so fucking sure, cop,' answered Maguire. 'This is all he deserves.'

Lean now looked at Sheen.

'Get him to back off,' said Lean. 'I'll come in. I'll talk. I'll admit killing that Brit, in Whiterock. Plus the rest.'

'Drop the weapon!' shouted the chief, better late than never.

Maguire glanced again at Sheen. This was Sheen's chance. He could see that Maguire was trying to take the measure of him. What he said next would be crucial, life or death.

'I give you my word. He'll pay and I don't give a damn what this snake says, he will be named for Cyprus too,' assured Sheen.

'Like fucking hell I will, cop,' retorted Lean. 'You think you're so clever but you've no idea what you're talking about. Cyprus? Have a word with my old commanding officer here. I think you'll find that he'll have more to tell you about that than me. And if I go down, we all go down,' he said with a sneer. But he was looking at Brendan Kielty as he made his threat and Sheen did too.

Kielty, who had now produced a gun and had it pointed at Aidan Lean.

Lean's snarl dropped and his eyes widened. In the slow-motion seconds that passed before Kielty pulled the trigger, all the pieces slotted into place for Sheen. And they all fitted perfectly.

Kielty was also side by side in that old photograph with Danny Caffery, not just Aidan Lean. He, too, was Caffery's old pal, from the very beginning. A man Caffery likely trusted as he did his closed cell of handpicked volunteers. And in the world of spies and double agents, it's friends not enemies that need to be treated with suspicion. Friends like Kielty, who had spent his life in the IRA but never did serious time. Kielty who was also a lifelong Ballymurphy resident. Just like the agent who had betrayed the Cyprus Three and had been praised for it in the letter from MI5 to the chief constable that Sheen had found. Lean was telling the truth, perhaps for the first time in his life. If Sheen could read the unredacted version of that letter, he knew the name that would be revealed. Brendan Kielty.

The explosion from Kielty's gun filled the room and momentarily drowned out the sound of the alarm. Sheen had time to see the back of Lean's head explode across the whiteboard, a brainstorm to shame all others, and then Sheen fell to his knees, hands on his head. The first gunshot was almost immediately followed by another. Sheen felt the bullet from the chief's gun displace the air in a gust in front of his face and then Maguire's head was punched to the side and back, as though he had been delivered a blow by an invisible heavyweight. His body slumped lifelessly to the floor less than a second after Aidan Lean had collapsed in a heap.

Sheen fumbled for his gun, ears ringing, and watched as Kielty calmly walked to where Brian Maguire now lay. Kielty placed the gun he had used in the dead man's hand and stood to one side before pulling the trigger, using Maguire's finger under his own. Very controlled and done very quickly. Sheen flinched at the sound. A large chunk of plaster was blown out of the far wall behind where Lean's lifeless body lay. Kielty now picked up Brian Maguire's big pistol that had fallen to the floor. At last Sheen reacted. He withdrew his gun and stood in the middle of the room with it pointed at Kielty.

'Drop the gun!'

Kielty glanced at him, still completely composed, and then looked over Sheen's shoulder and stared at the chief. He sidestepped Sheen and walked back to his desk where the chief waited. Sheen watched as his boss tossed his own gun to the floor.

'Jesus Christ, sir, what are you doing?' shouted Sheen. He kept his gun trained on Kielty and watched as he opened his desk drawer and dropped Maguire's gun inside, then locked it. Sheen screamed another warning. But his own voice sounded distant, ineffectual, and reality had taken on the sickening proportions of melting plastic. He turned his attention once again to the chief.

'Sir, we need to arrest him,' he said.

The chief had gone very pale, and Sheen could see that his hands were trembling. He did not look Sheen in the eye. The spineless bastard was going to try to let Kielty get away with it. Once again, the exigencies of political stability were being put above all else. The chief raised his voice over the din of the alarm.

'Sheen! Drop your gun, man! You're going to get shot dead!' he roared.

The tactical response team would surely come through the door any second. Sheen knew that if he had a gun pointed at the First Minister elect and two dead men on the floor then they would ask questions later. The alarm blared, counting precious seconds. Sheen watched as Kielty made his way coolly to the middle of the room and waited with his hands behind his head. Sheen turned to the chief and forced him to look him in the eye. For a long second Stevens did and then he looked away, staring intently at the far wall, his hands raised high over his head.

Sheen let his gun drop to the ground and raised his hands in the air too in what felt like a terrible act of surrender. In the same instant the door was kicked open and a flood of black-clad saviours arrived. He was bundled to the ground, a knee on his back and a gun to his head, face-to-face with Brian Maguire, whose eyes were vacant as the abyss.

# EPILOGUE

## One week later

Pearse Maguire responded to a rap on his front door in Andersonstown after several minutes of deliberation. He opened the inside door very slowly, saw that nobody was there and then he spotted the holdall beside the bin. Pearce unlocked the security gate, and after a few furtive glances on both sides of the door, he went and took a look inside the bag. There he found forty-five thousand pounds in unmarked sterling. As Pearse phoned his boyfriend to tell him the news, Geordie Brown walked into the SHOT offices across town.

'Look who's come to say hello,' said Geordie.

Sheen got off his seat to meet Tucker Rodgers and his son, Dave, who followed Geordie in. Dave wore a neck brace and had lost a lot of weight, but he was alive. Tucker looked like a new man, compared to the dishevelled creature who had turned up at Grosvenor Road a week before.

'I'm taking this lad home. Gonna stop with him for a few days too,' he added.

Sheen shook their hands and wished them well. As he let Jackson do the same Geordie spoke to Sheen.

'Any word from Aoife?'

Sheen shook his head. Geordie meant her Sergeants' Exam which was scheduled for this morning, but of course Sheen also knew that he meant her general well-being. As good as it was to see Tucker and his son, Sheen had hoped that Geordie would bring Aoife with him when he had arrived. She'd been signed off since the ordeal and though Sheen had seen her daily, it was like visiting a different person. She shied from his touch and he knew she was not sleeping. He had not mentioned the subject of them moving in again, but he would not give up on it. Or give up on her. He had no idea if she had actually sat the exam and he would not judge her for one second if she had decided to shelve it.

'What about the booklet?' asked Tucker, taking a seat across the desk from Sheen. He meant Roddy Grant's booklet TOPBRASS: A SECRET HISTORY. Sheen had it locked in the SHOT's safe.

'Hell of a read,' he said. 'But TOPBRASS is dead and my days here are numbered.'

Roddy's evidence was compelling but ultimately it was largely circumstantial. There was no doubt that the agent had existed, and that there had been collusion. But Aidan Lean's death had been painted as an old grudge, held by Brian Maguire, a disillusioned volunteer with links to Dissidents like Cahill McKee. The forensics confirmed that Maguire had fired the gun that killed Lean, and Chief Stevens was being sung as a hero for risking his life to help save the now First Minister Brendan Kielty. If it came to it, Sheen had privately resolved to leak Roddy's booklet to Dermot Fahey and let him print it all and be damned rather than have this chapter in the history of the dirty war buried for ever.

'Sure about that?' asked Tucker.

'I'm packing up my desk,' confirmed Sheen.

The sound of the office door. Sheen looked up.

'Doing a runner, are you, Sheen? Just like every other bloke in my life – a chancer.'

Aoife McCusker closed the door behind her and accepted the greetings from those present. Sheen went to her last.

'How are you? I wasn't sure we would see you.'

She nodded, her jaw tight, and Sheen could see her eyes had filled. He embraced her, held her for longer than the rest. When she spoke her voice was strong, stronger than the fragile look she had allowed him to share, and stronger than she had sounded over the last week when he visited her.

'Oh, you won't be getting rid of me that easy. Had my Sergeants' Exam, not that anyone asked.' On cue everyone then did, and this time Aoife laughed, a snapshot of her former self that told Sheen that maybe, with time, she was going to be all right.

'I had a convent education, lads. We don't fail exams. Getting kidnapped is one thing but messing up your exams and having to tell the nuns, that's in a different league.'

Aoife nodded to Sheen's half-packed box of belongings, and he told her that his time in charge of SHOT was up.

'Even if Stevens wanted me, I could never work under him. No offence, Jackson,' he added.

'So, you really don't know? Your mate Chief Stevens has walked the plank,' confirmed Aoife.

'Bullshit.'

'It was on the news when I drove over here. Do I always have to keep you informed, Sheen?' she asked. 'Looks like some English fella will be his replacement. Might be a man who speaks your language?'

'Maybe,' said Sheen, still trying to absorb what Aoife had just said. Stevens was gone. Maybe shooting dead a former IRA man in Parliament Buildings was a step too far, whatever the circumstances. Or maybe Stevens had been deemed to have failed. He'd been tasked to grease the tracks and ensure the PSNI played their part in re-establishing political harmony. The Northern Irish Parliament had resumed. But thanks to Sheen, the legislature had returned with as much controversy as it had previously collapsed under. Perhaps the incoming chief constable would spare Sheen, maybe even let the TOPBRASS case see the light of day or permit Cyprus to be fully investigated. Including that MI5 letter.

But Sheen didn't like the odds.

'Any sign of Fenton?' asked Aoife.

'No.'

Samuel Royce Fenton was gone and the bunker wide open when they returned to the priest hole in the City Cemetery. No doubt freed by the goons who had imprisoned Aoife there. His name had indeed appeared in the list of Shandon Park Golf Club members which Geordie had finally managed to get through on a search warrant. And, of course, it was all over Roddy's files. They'd gone to Fenton's house, but he was long gone. So far, he'd managed to stay that way. His testimony could verify everything about TOPBRASS in Roddy's documents. And, more importantly for Sheen, he could be brought to justice for what he'd done to Aoife.

Tucker Rodgers and his son said their goodbyes and

made to go. Sheen asked Tucker to keep in touch, and told him he might be needed, assuming the case might still have some life left in it.

'That boy Fenton, he can't run for ever. The truth catches up with you eventually,' said Tucker.

*That's for sure*, thought Sheen.

'Still off the drink?'

Tucker looked over at his son.

'Doing the steps. No more wasted years,' he replied.

When they had gone, Aoife called Sheen over to her computer.

'Fenton may not have disappeared as efficiently as he thinks,' she said.

Aoife had all but cracked the TOPBRASS case. She'd discovered Roddy was an archivist at Castlereagh, had found the place where he had likely stashed his copied documents and, most importantly, she had demanded that Sheen give Dave Rodgers their time in the first place. The fact that she was returning from a traumatic incident with a fresh lead hardly surprised him.

'When those guys had me in the bunker, they let something slip. Looking back one of them, the taller one, must have been speaking with Fenton. I think they wanted to know if they could interrogate me, or torture me maybe,' she said with a small shudder.

'What did you hear?' asked Sheen.

'They were given an order. To return to Ardtullagh,' she said. Sheen shook his head.

'Sounds Gaelic. Did you recognise it?' he asked.

'No, not initially, but that's exactly what I thought too. I did a bit of digging between revision sessions,' she continued. Aoife's fingers moved over the keyboard and she pointed to the screen.

'Ardtullagh was the site of a palatial house that was the home of the Bishop of Down and Connor,' read Sheen. It was one of the main Catholic dioceses in Northern Ireland.

'Until it was bought by the UK War Office in 1886,' said Aoife.

Sheen felt a little tingle of excitement. The guys who had attacked him and kidnapped Aoife had been a tight unit, very professional, very dangerous.

'A military base?' asked Sheen.

'Not just any military base. The site of Ardtullagh is now occupied by Palace Barracks in Holywood County Down,' she said. Aoife went quiet, and Sheen knew she was letting the impact of her words sink in. Sheen had heard of Palace Barracks, and he knew it housed British Army troops in rotation. But that was not what interested him.

'That's MI5 headquarters in Northern Ireland,' he confirmed.

'Fenton had moved down the road,' she said. It was a local term used by law enforcement and others referring to the fact that MI5 had headhunted former RUC Special Branch officers when the police service was reformed in Northern Ireland.

'God knows it may not even be MI5. Fenton could have been running his own little rogue squad,' suggested Sheen.

'Only one way to find out. Now that you probably don't need to pack up your desk, I was wondering if you'd like to join me. Thought we could go and knock on the door of Palace Barracks, see if we can ask a few questions,' she said.

'Yeah, I'd like that very much. That's what detectives do, after all,' he said.

'Regardless of the odds that are stacked against us,' said Aoife.

Sheen asked Aoife to give him a few minutes before they set off on another mission. He sat at his desk and found Graham Saunders' email. He was about to finally type a reply when, instead, after checking that he had included an address, Sheen smoothed a clean sheet of paper and picked up a pen. Under the circumstances, given the letters that had been written and received, it seemed only right.

*Dear Graham,*

*I'm sorry this reply has taken so long, and that I don't have the news that I'd like to be able to give you.*

*The man who murdered your brother was called Aidan Lean. He's dead. I was there when he was shot, but I was not responsible. I wanted to take him in and bring him to justice. I tried to. But you could say that his past finally caught up with him before I had the chance. What I've told you is not official. What you do with it is up to you.*

*I hope this information brings you closure and not more pain. Knowing things from the past is not always what it's cracked up to be. Whoever came up with that saying about not peering through a keyhole had a point. They really did.*

*Take care Graham.*

*Yours,*

*Owen Sheen.*

*(Belfast Child)*

# AUTHOR'S NOTE

*Never Ask the Dead* is a work of fiction. Any resemblance to real persons living or dead is purely coincidental, and any reference to real events is done so through the lens of fictional storytelling. Of course, Belfast is real, as is the surrounding countryside mentioned in parts of the book. However, I have taken the liberty of changing and inventing things, when and where it suited my story.

# ACRONYMS AND ABBREVIATIONS

INLA: Irish National Liberation Army. Illegal Irish republican paramilitary splinter group with communist ideology. Aimed to take Northern Ireland out of the United Kingdom and create a United Irish communist republic.

IRA: Irish Republican Army. Sometimes also referred to as PIRA or Provisional Irish Republican Army in reference to a split that occurred in an earlier incarnation of the group. Illegal and the largest Irish republican paramilitary organisation which was active throughout the modern Troubles. Aimed to take Northern Ireland out of the United Kingdom and create a United Irish republic.

The Met: The Metropolitan Police Service. The police service responsible for the Metropolitan Police District of London which consists of all police boroughs apart from the 'square mile' of the City of London.

MI5: Military Intelligence Section 5. Also known as The Security Service, MI5 is the United Kingdom's domestic intelligence and security agency. Since 2007 MI5 has led security intelligence work related to Northern Ireland (previously PSNI).

PSNI: Police Service of Northern Ireland. The police force of Northern Ireland from 2001 to date.

RUC: Royal Ulster Constabulary. The police force of Northern Ireland from 1922 until it was replaced by the PSNI in 2001.

Special Branch: RUC Special Branch. Undercover police unit tasked with combating the IRA and other paramilitary groups by recruiting informers and working closely with MI5. Later replaced by C3 Intelligence Branch of PSNI, though still referred to as Special Branch.

UDA: Ulster Defence Association. Illegal loyalist paramilitary organisation dedicated to keeping Northern Ireland a part of the United Kingdom.

UFF: Ulster Freedom Fighters. A cover name used by the UDA when launching paramilitary attacks, especially prior to August 1992 when the UDA was outlawed and proscribed as a terrorist group by the British government.

# ACKNOWLEDGEMENTS

Thank you as always to my wife, Sacha, and my children, Leila and Jack, who loan me out to Owen Sheen and his parallel Belfast reality during my weekends and our shared school holidays. When I return, blinking into the sunlight and sometimes lamenting what Sheen has (again) got me entangled in, you are there to set me straight and remind me that I have found my way through before and can do it again. As the first draft of this novel took shape at breakneck speed over a hot summer, Sacha was there to offer perceptive and honest feedback as a first reader, so double thanks for that.

Without the expertise and effort of my agent, Lisa Moylett at CMM Literary Agency, the DI Sheen series would likely be in cold storage in my hard drive, not commanding a space on the shelves. As well as making this happen, both she and Zoe Apostolides gave invaluable feedback at the crucial early stages of this book, and for all of this I want to thank you.

Thank you to the amazing team at Allison & Busby who took Owen Sheen in and gave him a home, believed in the series and have nurtured and made it grow in strength and number. From start to finish, you are a class act. The editorial input from Lesley Crooks and Kelly Smith was indispensable and helped me see the novel with fresh eyes again and again. For Christina Griffiths' great work on the brooding, signature noir cover designs and for the hard work of Susie Dunlop, Daniel Scott and Christina Storey behind the scenes in rights, sales and distribution, I offer my praise and thanks to you all.

Finally, dear reader, I want to thank you. Whether *Never Ask the Dead* is your first Sheen novel or your third instalment after enjoying *Blood Will Be Born* and *Killing in Your Name*, it's you who make the stories come to life and who make all the hard work worth it, every time. Reviewers, star raters, book bloggers and bedtime readers, your buzz is my buzz, my thanks to you all.

GARY DONNELLY is a writer and teacher who was born and raised in West Belfast. After attending a state comprehensive school, he read History at Corpus Christi College, Cambridge and has lived and worked in London since the late 1990s. *Never Ask the Dead* is the third novel in the DI Owen Sheen series and follows on from Gary's debut, *Blood Will Be Born*, and the sequel, *Killing in Your Name*.

donnellywriter.com    @DonnellyWriter